The Misguided Thief

Robert T. Hunting

Wordwooze Publishing
wordwooze.com

© 2017 by Robert T. Hunting
All rights reserved

Without limiting the rights under the copyright reserved above, no part of this book may be reproduced, stored in or introduced into a retrieval system, or transmitted in any form or by any means—electronic, mechanical, photocopying, recording, or otherwise—without written permission from the author or publisher. The scanning, uploading, and distribution of this book via the Internet or any other means without permission is punishable by law. Your support of the author's rights is appreciated.

ISBN: 9798684227462

Cover by Margaret Loftin-Whiting
Learn more about the artist at
https://www.zazzle.com/store/artdivination

This is a work of fiction. All characters spring from my fertile imagination.

I don't like the word 'strong', because a strong character is never an interesting character. A character is made interesting by their vulnerabilities and weaknesses.
   — Actor Helen Mirren

Chapter 1

Stellan Nieves vanished into a Chicago night with several cases of hard cash worth 2.1 million dollars belonging to mobster Dusan Kovačević. From that moment on, both Stellan and Dusan's life changed in ways neither could have imagined.

Stellan called Chicago, the nation's third-largest city, his home. He and everyone who lived there knew it as multiethnic. Among others, the Irish, Latinos, Jews, Chinese, Poles, Russians, and Germans called Chicago their home, too.

So did 500,000 Serbs, few more loathsome than mobster Dusan "Squeezebox" Kovačević. The compact, bad-tempered criminal earned the nickname "Squeezebox" because of his concertina. Similar to many second-generation children of immigrants, he overidealized his roots and loved all things Serbian, including its mournful folk music.

In his teens Squeezebox took it upon himself to sing and play the accordion. As much as he tried, his stubby fingers could not accommodate the cumbersome instrument. In frustration he switched to the concertina.

Few dared to criticize what passed for talent in Squeezebox. Fewer yet grew bold enough to call him by his nickname.

Donning his suit jacket, scarf, and winter coat, Stellan walked to the stairs of *Stringent Accounting, Small Business Specialists*.

"Night, Deana, Grady, Frank," he called out over his shoulder to the bookkeeper and two of his colleagues. "See you Monday."

He didn't wait for an answer, shut the door, and hurried out the three-story office building. Outside he burrowed into his coat and hurried along to a bus stop. The bus would take him to the "El," a short block from Union Station. Inside he'd line up with other commuters for the daily ride to his Lake in the Hills home.

The city's frigid, biting winds arrived earlier than expected. Stellan tucked into his coat and mumbled, "Too soon for this. Why couldn't it wait at least another month?" Festive lights on streets and in stores cheered him a bit. Stellan toyed with the idea of picking up something small for Nina and the kids. Couldn't hurt, and might lessen the never-ending tension between him and her. The more he played with the idea, the more he liked it. He'd get Nina some perfume and the twins a few accessories for their doll collection.

He set off in search of his gifts.

An attractive Asian sales clerk in the department store considered the lean customer with his triangular face and bits of gray at his temple. Would he have salt-and-pepper hair in another five years? Hard to say. She made him out to be in his mid-to-late twenties. Handsome, although the bags under his sorrowful eyes suggested he needed more sleep. His face presented him with a stern look, though the creases at the sides of his mouth faded when he smiled.

She handed him his credit card receipt. "Here you are, Mr. Nieves." She followed with a full smile and handed him the perfume. "Early Christmas shopping?"

Her cleavage caught Stellan's attention. Aware she might see him staring, he forced himself to meet her gaze.

"No, not yet."

The sales clerk draped her hair forward and smiled again. "Well, I hope she'll like it."

Insight came to Stellan. *Damn. She's flirting. And I'm enjoying it.* He wanted to stay and revel in the dalliance. His physical height registered at five foot eleven, but at the moment he felt ten feet tall, flattered and aroused.

Down, boy, an inner voice warned. *Flirting can mean something or nothing. How do you know she doesn't flirt with every male customer?*

He pulled himself out of his reverie. "Me, too. Anyway, I better get going. I know it's early yet, but Season's Greetings."

"Thank you, and the same to you."

Stellan worked his way into the cavernous Union Station, weaving through crowds to get to the Metro train lineup. It snaked forward to the accessible platform.

Seated on the train, he indulged himself in a fantasy about the sales clerk. If she had invited him for a drink or something, would he have gone? Of course. Be a fool not to. In the last six months he'd basically undergone forced celibacy, not of his choosing.

Forty-five minutes later Stellan unlocked the front door of his house. He heard competing noise from the TV in the living room and Nina on the kitchen phone. The twins would be watching one of their favorite programs. Nina, as usual, was involving herself in some drama with her mother or a sister. She came from a large Polish family. A day didn't pass when she didn't have the phone to her ear over an approaching or current crisis. Stellan once joked the phone was attached to Nina's ear.

Nina didn't share his joke.

Coat hung up, Stellan again experienced his usual bout of disappointment when no one came to greet him. *I could be invisible for all anyone cares.* He stepped into the kitchen. Nina, at the table, wiggled her fingers in recognition, accepted a quick kiss on her cheek, and all but dismissed him. "Could she have been any ruder?" she said into the phone.

Stellan handed Nina her gift. She continued to cradle the phone between her head and shoulders, slid her hand into the plastic bag and extracted the fancy container. She examined it, peeled off the cellophane, lifted the lid of the cardboard box, and pulled out the perfume bottle. She lifted the top, held it to her nose, gave it a perfunctory sniff, and offered Stellan a cold smile before she returned her attention to the phone conversation.

Stellan pushed down his irritation and moved off to the living room. "Hi, Daddy," Mia said, waved, and returned her attention to the flat screen. Joanna gave him an inattentive half wave.

Stellan long ago thought his daughters were mini-Ninas in appearance and temperament. *Man, if those two got twenty-three chromosomes from Nina and the other twenty-three from me, my side sure got the short shrift. Not a single thing about them says Nieves. Everything says Dabrowski.*

Both girls had their mother's light skin tone, full lips, and large blue eyes with long, dark lashes. Both inherited her mousy brown hair. Stellan knew he shouldn't but allowed himself a small delight at their imperfection. Little beauties with mousy hair. He chased away the thought. *Nina's hair didn't much bother you when she first slipped off her panties.*

No, he admitted, but she had a killer body and a nice ponytail. What guy doesn't go gaga over a girl with her ponytail in a scrunchie?

He forced himself to return his attention to the girls. "Look what Daddy's got for you." He held the packages of doll clothing. Both girls jumped to their feet, hurried over, snatched the packages, and rushed off to their bedrooms.

"You're welcome," Stellan shouted after them.

The family sat down for supper. Of late, Stellan found family meals bothersome. The twins fidgeted, often interrupted his conversations with Nina, whined, threw temper tantrums at the smallest provocation, and skirted the edge of rudeness, especially to him. Stellan made numerous attempts to rein them in. Nina always defended the girls, said they were kids, they'd grow out of their ways, and he "shouldn't be so uptight."

Bedtimes proved equally difficult. It took many tries, threats of punishment, and arguments with Nina before the girls fell asleep.

With the twins down, Stellan and Nina watched TV in silence, both withdrawing into their quiet, emotional corners.

Nina at last rose and left to do her nightly rosary. On her knees, she'd make the sign of the cross and do the Order of Prayers—The Apostles' Creed, one Our Father, three Hail Marys, another Glory be, more Our Fathers, Hail Marys and finish with Hail, Holy Queen.

Stellan had tried his best to be tolerant of Nina's faith. Even attempted to pray with her. In time, however, he moved in the opposite direction. He endured Sunday one-hour masses and used the time to solve work-related problems. He thought Catholic rituals were claptrap but kept his opinion to himself. Offering it up would rain a world of trouble down on him.

Half an hour later, bored with TV, he at last followed Nina to the bedroom. He held out an olive branch.

"C'mon, Nina, do we have to go through this every night?" He kept his voice low, worried the kids might hear. "I've been unhappy for a long time. You have, too. I'm starting to agree with the counselor—there's not much holding us together."

His wife's gaze held his. Her eyes narrowed. Chin out, a scowl in her tone, she said, "I'm not the one who blew $40,000 at the casino."

Snow at the top of the mountain dislodged.

Stellan exhaled through his mouth and took another breath of air.

"And here it is again. I thought we were maybe making some progress. I guess not."

He looked down at the carpet and up at Nina. "You're never going to let me forget this, are you, never going to forgive? We've gone to counseling; I go to my GA meetings. I've apologized I can't tell you how many times. I messed up. Everyone knows what I did, especially you and your family. You have a right to be mad at me and all those other things, but I've got to tell you, at some point you have to let it go."

"*You* spent forty thousand dollars that belonged to this family."

The words arrived hard, cold, and carried their usual malice.

The avalanche cascaded down the mountain. Stellan felt the muscles in his face tighten. Through gritted teeth he said, "When you're perfect, get back to me." He slowly shook his head. "Yep, forty thousand. You're never going to be done emasculating me about this. For the record, forty thousand *I* earned. Me, not you."

She glared at him.

Stellan exhaled. "Aside from what I did, Nina, there's a meanness to you, a meanness no amount of saying your rosary on your knees changes."

He twisted his mouth to one side. "You do remember the counselor telling you I used the casino to relieve stress? You didn't care then, and you don't now. What matters is you won't forgive. You hoard my wrongdoings like a miser counting her coins. Gotta say I'm not sure how much longer I can live with this deep freeze."

Nina crossed her arms high. "I'm not giving you the deep freeze."

"Yeah, you are. And you know what else? You've poisoned the well with the kids. How do you think it makes me feel when they talk badly to me, their father?"

"Oh, now you're dragging them into this? Nice. Well, it's not true."

"Oh, get off it. It's been true since we brought them home from the hospital. The moment they arrived, it was the end of the line for me. And then there's your little us-against-Daddy plots." He lowered his head, raised it, and said, "Damned if I know why we don't divorce."

"I'm Catholic. We don't divorce."

Stellan shook his head in dismissal.

"No, no divorce for my sanctimonious wife. Shakespeare had it right. Hell is empty. All the devils are here. I'm married to one."

He closed and opened his eyes.

"They don't make bigger fools than me. I was heading off to college and you, afraid you'd never see me again, played me with your phony pregnancy, remember? Like a sap I believed the lie and the one that followed—the supposed miscarriage. We rushed to get married. You were really after a good address and kids. And you saw me giving you both."

Nina's body stiffened. "Finished?"

"In ways you can't imagine."

"Meaning?"

"Nothing."

Nina wheeled about, marched to her side of the bed, yanked back the blanket with intensity, and met his gaze.

"I'm married to a thief is what I am. You brought this all onto yourself. You, not me."

"Back to this, are we?" Stellan gave a dismissive wave of his hand. "I stole, but I'll say it again—it was my money. Doesn't absolve or acquit me, but if I'm a thief, you're a fraudster. I didn't enter this marriage under false pretenses. You can't say the same, can you?"

His lips set in a grim line, Stellan continued. "So, we know what my shortcomings are, but I guess it's the God you pray to who'll decide which one of us is worse."

Nina climbed into bed, switched off her lamp, and gave him her back.

Stellan lay awake for hours seething with anger and resentment at his bitch of a wife. Why hadn't he seen it from the start and looked closer? All the Dabrowski women had the bitch gene. Too late now.

He rolled over, flipped and pounded his pillow, and grieved for a different life. He hated his job and hated his wife and family but saw no way out. How had it all come to this? If only he could change it. In the dark he watched the LED digital displaying the time. Bit by bit he arrived at a decision. He'd leave Nina Dabrowski and her children. The idea brought a small measure of relief.

Chapter 2

The deafening shrill of the alarm woke them.

Stellan hustled into the bathroom, showered, toweled off, and stepped aside for Nina. She avoided eye contact and refused to acknowledge him. Not that he cared anymore. His decision to leave had liberated him.

His mind turned to the twins while he shaved. He wouldn't miss them and doubted they'd miss him. If mothers gave their children unconditional love, what about fathers? In most cases the conditions were tied to behavior. At least for him. He held to the firm belief they would have been different, better, if Nina had been different. Or if he'd married someone else.

He snorted at the thought. If he'd married someone else, they wouldn't be his children.

Stellan slapped on aftershave and thought about how Nina would react when he left. Knowing her, she'd fret about the stigma of a failed marriage. Tough. Maybe she'd toss her sweats, wear some decent clothes, and go find a job. Or not. It wouldn't be his problem.

He made his way to the kitchen and drank a glass of juice. Nina entered.

"I've got an early appointment," he said, and set the glass in the dishwasher. Nina busied herself and didn't acknowledge his remark. "Mia, Joanna, leave the TV and come eat."

The twins ignored her. Their defiance annoyed him, but he refused to say anything. *My new mantra is "No longer my problem."* He stepped into the hallway. "See you tonight," he called out from habit. No one responded or came to see him off.

He walked to the train station with a newfound sense of freedom and repeated his mantra. Yes, he'd hang onto it until he no longer lived in the house.

He recalled reading how the weight of a man's problems affected the way he walked, talked, and thought. A reflection in a window confirmed it. The rounded shoulders—when did he start slouching?

His father had always preached about good posture.

On the commute Stellan tried to guess how much money he'd have after a divorce lawyer cleaned him out. He scoffed at the image. A whole lot of nothing. He'd manage, but just. Being free from that bitch would be worth it. To make ends meet, maybe he could teach an evening course at the community college. Or do taxes.

And what about a place to stay? He'd ask around the office and scour the want ads. With luck he might land something in his price range.

A new thought arrived—the car? Let Nina have it. He'd manage without it somehow.

Later that night, Nina's words came in a hiss.

"What do you mean you're leaving?"

Stellan opened his mouth to answer, but she cut him off. "You picked a great time to drop this on me. Christmas is only two and a half weeks away." Her gaze turned to the bedroom door.

Stellan let loose a rush of air.

"Christmas has nothing to do with this. I've found a furnished place in Lincoln Square—the upper part of a house. It's not the greatest, but it'll have to do. For now."

"You can't leave," she insisted. "We're Catholic. It's a sin to divorce. You'll be excommunicated. And for sure I won't give you an annulment."

A half-chuckle left Stellan's throat. He stared into the unkind face of the woman he once professed to love.

"This isn't negotiable. I'm leaving. End of story. And as for the Catholic thing, I became one to please you. Being excommunicated isn't something that's going to cause me a lack of sleep. Now I'll just be one of those lapsed Catholics who still prays to St. Anthony whenever he's lost something."

She glowered at him. "Is that supposed to be funny?"

He couldn't hide his self-satisfied smile. "I think so."

She folded her arms across her chest. "You'll never see the kids again."

He'd anticipated this ploy. The easy and honest answer might have been to say he didn't care. He held back, aware that if he said it, Nina would all but needlepoint his reply, frame and mount it on the kitchen wall.

He forced himself to hold her gaze.

"Do what you have to. Wrap yourself in the famous Dabrowski bitterness and show the kids how it's done. Or help the rest understand why we split. Your call."

Nina's cold eyes narrowed and penetrated him.

"Get out of this bedroom. Go sleep somewhere else. Tomorrow morning leave, and never step inside this house again."

———⇒∘⇐———

Stringent Accounting closed at noon on Christmas Eve.

Stellan, his secret Santa gifts in one hand, briefcase in the other, waited in the commuter bus line for his half-hour ride to Lincoln Square. He'd now been on his own for eight rough, stressful days.

No surprise, he'd received several letters from Nina's lawyer. In addition, a letter arrived from the Archdiocese of Chicago with a questionnaire. Nina had applied for an annulment.

"That didn't take long," Stellan said out loud.

Nina's brother and sister, Frank and Gabby, had shown up at Stellan's flat a few days earlier to talk to Stellan about returning to his family.

"Think of the kids," Frank said. "The girls need a father. All marriages go through rough patches."

Gabby nodded in agreement. "He's right, you know. I thought about leaving Barry a few times, but I didn't."

Stellan forced himself to hide a smirk. *No, Gabby, you may not have left Barry*, he silently said to himself, *but Barry quit on you long ago. He's been playing let's hide the salami with a cute bottle blonde on nights you think he's bowling.*

Stellan determined the easiest course would be to hear them out.

He made no effort to argue, aware their intention came from a good place. He'd offer ambiguous nods and let them read into it whatever they wanted.

Frank shuffled in his chair.

"Gabby n' me, we don't understand, but we have to respect your position, Stellan."

His two guests had run out of things to say. Stellan remained quiet and let the social awkwardness work for him. Frank at last climbed to his feet, Gabby with him. They shook Stellan's hand and wished him a happy Christmas, left, and promised they'd remain neutral and in touch.

Stellan had his doubts about the second thing: he and Nina's siblings never cared much about each other.

Father Kiesel arrived next. Stellan failed to discover who sent him. He made coffee. The two men suffered through a difficult half hour while they sipped their hot beverage. As with Frank and Gabby, Stellan worked to make the silence his ally.

Kiesel let his gaze scan the flat. "A nice place you have here, Stellan."

Stellan tossed a shoulder in response. "I guess. It's in a good neighborhood. Lots of pubs, restaurants, shops, none of which I can afford, mind you. Anyway, this will do. For now."

"And your family, you don't miss them?"

"Ouch. Not very subtle, Father. Okay, let's get this over with. I'm not going back, if that's why you're here. My life, my decision. I ask you to respect that."

The rail-thin priest shuffled his feet. "Think about it, Stellan. You're not the only one in this equation."

Stellan answered by retreating back into a silence and pulled the priest with him. He held the priest's gaze and thought, *You're what, maybe five or six years younger than me? What wisdom have you acquired to talk to me about life?*

The absence of sound filled the living room and made Kiesel

fidget for a moment before he changed the subject.

They made small, useless talk until at last the priest took his leave. He gave Stellan a blessing and hurried out.

Stellan spent Christmas alone. He'd braced himself for this day, unsure how he'd manage. Would he feel depressed? He didn't hear from Nina, didn't expect he would, and certainly didn't hear from the girls. No doubt not getting Christmas presents from him hurried their decision along.

The day passed without too much distress. Stellan read a novel and surfed the Internet. Excited squeals and shouts came from the Beckers downstairs. He guessed it had to be their adult children and grandchildren.

In the evening Stellan bundled up, ready for a walk, when his cell phone rang. He froze and stared at the number. His mother. He let it go to voice mail and again readied to step outside.

Once more the phone rang. His sister. He ignored the call and stepped outside.

Much like his father, Stellan leaned toward being a loner. He liked socializing but in small doses. His parents had split up in his junior year of high school. His father, Joe, a buyer for a large retail chain, came home one afternoon to find his wife in bed with his best friend, Vincze. Outraged, Joe Nieves rushed across the bedroom floor and pummeled a naked Vincze. The dentist did his best to ward off the blows while he tried to scurry into his shorts.

Evie, Joe's wife, screamed and begged Joe to stop. His nose bleeding, Vincze tumbled down the stairs, his trousers in his hand and Joe behind him. Evie hurried into a sweatshirt and jeans and followed.

The drama spilled out onto the Nieves' front lawn and fast enough brought gawking neighbors.

"You're a slut, Evie," Joe shouted at his wife while Vincze raced to his car. "A slut, and you're never stepping into this house again." He turned his rage back on Vincze, eager to back out of the driveway.

"I ever see you again, you son of a bitch," he shouted through the closed window, "I'll put you into the hospital."

Vincze stopped long enough to let Evie jump into the car. He sped off.

Two days later Joe filed for separation. A temporary court order allowed Evie to return and collect her personal belongings.

The neighborhood buzzed with gossip for weeks.

Evie moved in with Vincze. She asked Stellan, then sixteen, and his sister, Ashlynn, fifteen, to join her. Both declined.

Within a year, as Joe Nieves drove through an intersection, a distracted woman ran a red light and T-boned his car.

Illinois, being an "at fault" car insurance state, allowed Stellan and Ashlynn's lawyer to sue. They accepted a $600,000 settlement, plus the cost of college tuition for both.

Stellan applied to Northwestern for the following year. Ashlynn lacked his ambition and gave herself over to causes. Stellan compared her to a feminine Don Quixote, always ready to tilt at the next windmill.

In Stellan's sophomore year Ashlynn took a lover, and soon afterwards she made her grand announcement. "I'm coming out. I'm a lesbian." By year's end she'd acquired tattoos on her arms and dyed her hair purple.

Stellan often wondered if his and Ashlynn's lives might have turned out differently had tragedy not struck. He did so again this night while he walked through the downtown business section.

Ashlynn becomes a lesbian, I marry a crazy Catholic, and neither of us has much to do with each other. Man, we'd make a textbook study for somebody.

The whole nature versus nurture debate played itself out in his mind. Would he have been more outgoing if his mother hadn't been such a damn man-chaser and his father was home more? Maybe he'd have done a better job at mate selection, and Ashlynn would not have turned into a way-out-there lez. He'd never know. Besides, what was the saying about playing the hand you're dealt?

Chapter 3

Stellan returned to his flat and phoned his mother and sister. Both wished him a merry Christmas and asked how he was holding up since his split with Nina. He met their inquisitiveness with short and polite answers. Nothing much left to say, he wished each one well and hung up.

In the afternoon he made a trek to his father's grave, returned home, and busied himself cooking two Cornish hens with roasted vegetables. His culinary success perched on a wobbly TV tray, he ate and watched a lackluster basketball game.

The next morning a deep Midwest freeze arrived when Stellan took the commute to The Loop, Chicago's commercial district. A homeless man, a dog by his side, sat on the sidewalk. "Spare any change, sir?"

Stellan's hand slid into his coat pocket. He always carried change for such encounters and made it a point to establish eye contact.

"Thanks, buddy," the man said. "God bless."

"Welcome," Stellan murmured.

Having reached his office, he put his lunch in the fridge and hung up his overcoat and jacket. He turned on the computer to check his day's schedule. A brief email from his boss, Hal Paley, read:

> *I've had Cheryl book you an 11 am meeting with a Dusan Kovacevic of Fiery Dragon Enterprise. He has an import-export business. Ditched his old accounting firm and is looking for help with inventory valuation.*

Stellan read the email twice. Nothing he couldn't handle. Inventory valuation. It might be anything from freight costs, inventory handling, storage, delivery, or whatever. He'd have to look at their books and do an on-site inspection. The latter would take time but contribute to a fair number of billable hours. Paley loved billable hours.

Eleven o'clock came. Fiona at reception buzzed Stellan.

"A Mr. Kovacevic is here to see you."

Stellan winced. He had no idea how to pronounce the man's name but felt certain Fiona had massacred it. Terrific eye candy, Fiona, but no staggering intellect. Everyone knew Paley hadn't hired her for her brains. She liked to smile in seductive ways and wore lots of V-necks. No one complained, at least, not the men.

Stellan rose, donned his suit jacket, and took the elevator to the first floor. He allowed himself a quick look at Fiona's low-cut angora sweater. An hour with her...Man.

Fiona made a head jerk in the direction of the waiting area. Stellan nodded. With a fixed smile, he approached the sole client in the waiting area, perhaps a year or two older than he. His gaze took in the client's soft leather jacket over a denim shirt. The shirt matched the jeans, which covered a pair of expensive cowboy boots. A thin gold bracelet hung from his wrist. Appearance-wise, the new customer didn't fit the profile of most of Stringent's clients. Most, but not all.

Stellan approached and held out his hand.

"Hello. I'm Stellan Nieves. You'll forgive me, I hope, if I don't say your name correctly. How do you pronounce it?"

The short, squat man with thick, shaggy hair chucked the magazine on a table, raised his head, and stared at Stellan with a pair of slate gray eyes. He shot Stellan a half-smile, rose, and yanked up on the belt under the beginnings of a pot belly. He accepted the proffered hand.

"Kovačević. Koh-VAH-cheh-vich." He took care to linger over each syllable. "Dusan Kovačević. A Serbian name, but I'm red, white, and blue born American. And you say my first name like doo-SHAN."

Stellan sounded out both. "Got it...Mr. Kovačević." He released the man's hand and said, "Now, if you'll accompany me to my office."

They walked to the elevator, Stellan careful to slow his pace to match that of the shorter man. Both continued to offer each other polite smiles while the elevator carried them to the top floor.

Something about his client's over-slicked hair and linked bracelet annoyed Stellan. A bracelet? What kind of guy wears a bracelet? Worse, his breath did nothing to endear the man to him.

Stellan ordered himself to relax. *So, he's got gaudy jewelry and bad breath. It's not like I have to hang out with him.*

They entered Stellan's office. He invited Kovačević to sit opposite his desk with its large monitor. He seated himself. "Now, what can we help you with?" he said, grateful for the physical distance.

His new client picked up a six-sided desk toy Stellan kept for fidgety clients. He pressed non-functioning buttons and said, "I got this import-export business, and I need to be more on top of things. You get what I'm sayin'?"

"I'm not sure. You'll have to tell me more."

"So, like, we have three floors in my warehouse with stuff from China, Indonesia, Pakistan, Mexico. Cheap stuff, like. It gets here, and we sell it to outlets like those dollar stores. Here's the thing—the bean blowers I hired, they were no good, so I got rid of 'em."

"Bean blowers?"

"Yeah. Like you."

Stellan forced himself to smile. "Ah. Accountants. Never heard that expression before. Right. Got you."

"I need help with all that—what's coming in, going out, tracking it better, you know. Your boss said you could do the job."

"Well, we can start by looking at your setup and inventory control costs. From there, we can help you establish a better, more reliable system." He raised his chin. "I'll have to visit your warehouse, take a look at your books, and then make any recommendations."

"Sounds good. When can you come?"

Stellan tapped a finger on his keyboard and gave his attention to the monitor. "Let's have a look."

Squeezebox opened his car door and settled in behind the wheel. He thought about the accountant. Bit of a candy-ass, but who cared?

He dismissed the man. Should he go home or see Stephanie? Stephanie. Time for assault with a friendly weapon. He buckled his seat belt, pushed the ignition button, and drove off.

A Serbian expression came to him: *he who sings, thinks no evil*. He clicked his tongue. Whoever coined the phrase didn't have him in mind. True, he might sin without repenting—a lot—but he wasn't totally wicked. He did go to church and donated to Orthodox charities. So, some of his peers called him psycho, a cutthroat, and crazy. Just jealous, is all.

A grade school dropout, Squeezebox worked the streets, stole off trucks, and broke into bodegas. By fifth grade a school board psychologist diagnosed him with learning difficulties along with poor impulse control, inability to concentrate, and hyperactivity.

Where Squeezebox failed in the classroom, he succeeded elsewhere. A combination of fists and peasant cunning earned him a street reputation and two terms in reformatory. By the age of nineteen he'd become a career criminal and the undisputed leader of a small gang. Squeezebox elbowed his way into a share of the local numbers racket, human trafficking, and prostitution. Always able to sniff out new opportunities, he moved into blackmail, computer fraud, arson, hijacking, extortion, kidnapping, and loan-sharking.

He also learned to ingratiate himself with powerful Italian mobsters. His ethnic lineage prevented him from ascending higher than associate in their organization. On occasion he'd be called on to do certain favors, to see to it so-and-so met with an unfortunate death. In return, Squeezebox enjoyed an occasional "taste" of larger criminal windfalls.

Life was good. Crime did pay, and well.

Crime also attracted closer scrutiny from law enforcement.

Worried he wouldn't be able to explain cash surpluses, Squeezebox bought several businesses and "whitened" his profits. By his mid-thirties he had acquired two pawn shops, a strip club, a check-cashing store, an electrical contracting business, three party stores, and his flagship import-export company, Fiery Dragon Enterprise. When excessive profits couldn't show up on accounting books, Squeezebox sent the monies to an offshore account in the Cayman Islands.

Squeezebox kept a furnished flat over his electrical contracting shop near Rogers Park.

"I need a place to think," he told his wife of thirteen years, Anka. "Somewhere to unwind, where I can be alone with my thoughts and not have people hassling me alla time. I'll buy some furniture, nothing fancy, but I'll make it homey-like. You understand, don'tcha?"

Anka wasn't fooled. She ran lacquered nails through her dark bowl-cut hair. *Why lie to me, Dusan?* she thought. *I know what you're doing in your "place to think."*

She knew about the furniture he bought for the flat: the king-size bed, a dinette set, a state-of-the-art stereo system, and the 77-inch flat screen. She heard about the satin sheets and the thin, long-legged 19-year-old who took up residence in the flat.

Dusan's mistress didn't overly trouble Anka. As long as he remembered where he lived and didn't turn his back on his family, she could look the other way. Sex had never been great with him, anyway. He'd quickly revealed himself for what he was—a grunter, selfish, and always quick to finish.

After the boys had arrived, sex dwindled to once a month, then every few months. Now neither bothered much with each other.

Anka loved Dusan and recognized he loved her. In his own way. No point in causing scenes. It wouldn't change anything. Men cheat. *All* men cheat.

She nodded at his claim. "I get it. If you think this will help, I guess you should do it."

Fiery Dragon Enterprise sat on a small side street in Chicago's old Warehouse District north of The Loop. Over the last decade the area had transformed itself. Artists in search of cheaper accommodations arrived first and repurposed some of the smaller warehouses. Yuppies and investors followed and nudged out the artists. Descendants of the original industrial heavyweights sold off numerous warehouses and converted these into shops and must-have lofts for the well-heeled. Some warehouses resisted the creeping gentrification.

Stellan signed out one of three company vehicles to visit Fiery Dragon. A ten-foot chain link fence surrounded the four-story, old brick building. Dirt, sun, debris, rain, and snow had all beaten up on it. In places mortar surrendered its hold and toppled to the parking lot. Grimy windows, their frames infected with various stages of dry rot, hadn't received cleaning in decades.

Stellan searched for a spot on the street but couldn't find one. Frustrated, he drove up to the main gate. A security guard stepped out of his hut and approached. Stellan rolled down his window and looked up at the older man. "I have a 10:30 appointment with Mr. Kovačević. I can't find anywhere to park around here."

The guard pointed opposite the two loading dock doors.

"Pull in and park with the other cars by the fence. You can get to the office by the back door beside the loading dock. Follow the sign in the hallway."

Inside the warehouse, Stellan made his way along an uneven floor of dirty, dry, and stained floorboards. In a few places they creaked under his weight. Heat from radiators intensified a musty, stale smell. Dust, cobwebs, and mildew had long ago found a permanent home.

Forklift trucks raced down wide corridors with pallets taken off wooden rivet shelving. Other trucks raced to and from the loading dock. Stellan allowed himself a short, quiet laugh. *The entire third world produces useless materials we don't need, and we keep buying it.*

The office took up the southwest corner and had the feel of an afterthought. Stellan doubted it had been part of the original design.

He knocked on a glass-paned wooden door, likely there since the beginning, and entered. Two battered desks took up room behind a counter. Farther back Stellan saw a separate, smaller office. A green, vintage, freestanding safe kept vigil next to it. Stellan gaped at it. The safe had to be at least five feet high and maybe fifty inches deep. Where it came from he had no idea. It was certainly not part of the original warehouse.

A double-chinned, middle-aged woman rose from her desk and approached the counter.

"Mr. Nieves?" She followed the question with a warm smile.

Stellan bobbed his head and answered with his own smile. "Yes."

"Welcome. We've been expecting you." She moved to undo the latch on a waist-high gate in the counter and gestured for him to enter. "I'm Helen Lukin." She pointed behind her to a small, smoky-gray-haired woman. "That's Senka Beader."

Stellan and the woman exchanged quick waves while Lukin continued.

"I'm the bookkeeper and secretary here. Senka is our part-time assistant. Mr. Kovačević won't be here. An emergency came up. He sends his apologies. It might be a few days before he returns." She took a breath. "I understand you'll be with us for a spell."

"Likely, yes."

"Well, why don't you use Mr. Kovačević's office in the back? I'm sure he won't mind. If there's anything you need, we'll be happy to help you."

Stellan responded with a nod, turned, and entered Kovačević's cubbyhole of an office. Strange. Kovačević hires him and then disappears for a few days.

He set down his briefcase on the scratched steel desk, removed his coat, and gave the office a once-over. The overall affect depressed him. By comparison, the outer office felt cheerful. Spartan would have been a generous adjective for this poor pigeonhole with its pressboard walls painted white. No hint of any personal human touch—no knickknacks, pens, papers, artwork, or even a plastic plant. A beat-up chair, a table, and a telephone. That was it.

His mind returned to the safe in the outer office. A hefty thing. How did it get here? It looked out of place. He guessed it had once belonged to an insurance company or maybe a bank.

Stellan opened his briefcase as Helen entered. "Is there anything we can help you with?"

Stellan raised his eyes.

"A good place for me to start is to see where the previous accounting firm left off. I need to look at your books to make sure everything is up-to-date before I head into the warehouse to get a better sense of things."

"All right, then. I'll leave you to it."

Stellan visited the warehouse the next day. He found the two women pleasant and ready to answer all his questions. Senka, the shyer of the two, only spoke when he initiated conversation. Yet he liked her warmth and dignified manner.

Helen shared many of the same qualities but confessed to being "a bit of a chatterbox." She'd make coffee and talk about her boss.

"He has a nickname, you know," she confessed in a low, conspiratorial voice. They call him Squeezebox." She giggled. "Not to his face, though."

Stellan lowered his own voice. "I'm not sure you should be telling me all this." Helen waved away the objection. "Something tells me the secret is safe with you. You look trustworthy."

Several times Helen hinted but never quite voiced what Stellan sensed—Dusan Kovačević might be unscrupulous. The new information fed Stellan's general impression. He wanted to ask how two nice women could work for someone like Kovačević but thought better of it.

On Stellan's fourth day two men wheeled in a pair of black, leather-bound, oversized, document cases on folding file carts, the kind Stellan saw lawyers take into court buildings.

Both men could have auditioned for a Hollywood mob movie.

The larger of the two wore a soft leather bomber jacket. Dark sunglasses, even on this dim, gray Chicago day, hid his eyes. Everything about him said muscle.

His partner favored a suede jacket and a flat cap worn backwards.

The men removed the safety cords from the carts, set the heavy cases on the floor, and folded the carts' telescopic handles. Stellan tried not to stare as Helen stepped up to the safe.

The taller of the two men glanced in Stellan's direction. He quickly put his head down.

"Want us to wait?" Stellan heard Muscle ask Helen in a hoarse-sounding voice.

Helen twirled the dial of the lock. "If you like."

"Probably better if we stay."

"Yes. Why not? Better safe than sorry, huh?" She looked at Muscle. "I think I just made a joke."

He didn't respond.

She pulled on the heavy door. The men looked on while she pushed it wider and placed the document cases into the safe. She forced the door back and twirled the knob.

The little drama intrigued Stellan. Helen did nothing to dampen his curiosity when she walked to his doorway, arms crossed, and said, "Um, I'm sure what you saw looked odd, but it's best you don't say anything to anyone about it."

Stellan played the innocent. "I tend to tune out when I'm working on projects."

Helen uncrossed her arms, gave him a fast smile, and spun about. He followed her with his gaze.

Stellan had many questions but no one to ask. *Odd? No. More than odd. Way more.*

———⋅◊⋅———

In the afternoon Helen minded the office while Stellan returned to the aisles. He realized he'd brought his clipboard and paper but no pen. He hurried to the office. He was ready to put a hand on the doorknob when a sight stopped him, Helen by the far wall. She cast a glance his way.

On instinct Stellan pulled back, hoping she hadn't seen him. A quick glance to his left and right assured him no one else hovered nearby.

He dared another look into the office to find Helen, her back to him, struggling with one of the cases. A desk blocked Stellan's full view.

A moment later Helen straightened and picked up another case from the open safe.

A crease deepened between Stellan's eyebrows. What was she doing—moving the cases out of the safe? He pulled back from the glass door, waited, and allowed 90 seconds to pass before he tried the doorknob again. He found Helen pushing the ponderous door of the safe closed.

"Forgot my pen," he said by way of explanation. "I'd lose my head if it wasn't attached."

Chapter 4

Stellan knew what he saw had nothing to do with him but couldn't refrain from thinking about it. Something unusual had happened, something probably felonious. He wanted to understand what he'd stumbled onto.

He couldn't recall ever seeing anything so suspicious in such a blatant manner: four document cases transferred from a safe, a safe so secure it would take a couple of days to crack with a blowtorch. Now they likely disappeared elsewhere. Stellan didn't quite know where. The desk obscured Stellan's view. And what could be in them—drugs?

The whole thing didn't make sense.

"Quitting time, Mr. Nieves," Helen called from the outer office, and struggled into her coat. "It's dark and cold out. Time to be tucked into your nice, cozy home."

He didn't want to leave until he had solved this Gordian knot.

"Agreed, but you know, I think I'll stay a bit longer. If you don't mind. About an hour should do it. I can set the alarm if you trust me."

Helen considered the request.

"I guess that would be all right. I'll give you the number. Don't write it down."

"No, I won't. I have a good memory." He followed with a fast smile.

She gave him the number. "When you're ready to leave, Gus, the night watchman, will open the parking lot gate for you."

She left.

Stellan returned to his desk but didn't sit. He waited until he felt certain no one remained in the building.

Pipes banged, and the warehouse gave off inexplicable noises, sounds one might expect from an old building. Satisfied he had the building to himself, Stellan approached the spot where he saw Helen stoop.

Careful to stay clear of the front window, Stellan studied the area. Nothing. She certainly couldn't have hidden the cases in the small drawers of her desk. Where else? His gaze moved to the dry, unpainted floorboards. He crouched and examined them. They looked snug, yet...

His hand shot out and opened the top drawer of Helen's desk. Inside he found a sturdy letter opener, He slid it between two floorboards, pushed at the end, and jimmied one of the boards. It came up without dispute. So did the next three. Bingo!

Stellan stared down into a deep, wide box lined with black felt. On hands and knees his hand moved down and made contact with an expanse of cloth. Nothing other than the cases. He grabbed for the handle of one of the cases and pulled. Back-breaking. He had to brace himself to lift it. *You must have good upper body strength*, he murmured to Helen.

The case out of the box, Stellan flipped open its business locks, his heart beating fast. They gave. His hands shook, and his breath caught when he gaped at the interior of the cotton-lined case. Straps of hundred-dollar bills, each with Ben Franklin's picture, filled the case.

His eyes wide, Stellan picked up one of the straps. "My God," he whispered. "so much money." He'd never been this close to such a sizable amount of hard cash. Where would it have come from, and what did Kovačević intend to do with it?

He struggled to retrieve the second case. Again, he flipped the locks; again, he gaped at the money. More crisp Ben Franklins.

A fast guesstimate told Stellan each case held around a quarter of a million dollars. All this money. The two hoods handed it over to Helen without any real concern. What would they think if they knew she'd squirreled the loot under the floorboards?

He shut the case and pulled out the other two, identical to the first. Unbelievable!

On his commute home Stellan fantasized about what he could do if he had 2.1 million tax-free dollars at his disposal. *I'd no longer be an economic slave. Wouldn't I have some choices open to me? What would I do? I could start all over. Anywhere.*

He dreamed about the money that night.

His alarm went off, but he remained under the blankets and reveled in the minutia of the dream.

Stellan arrived at the warehouse before 9:00 to find a small army of law enforcement officials. Police vehicles sat beside the curb on the narrow street and off at all angles.

Stellan felt certain the police would find the money. He parked a block and a half from the warehouse. In the parking lot he spotted several uniformed and plainclothes officers who surrounded Kovačević. He approached the small group. His eyes found Kovačević. The Serb jerked his head. *Go away. Get lost.*

Stellan answered with an imperceptible nod, turned, and headed for the gate. A raucous voice called out, "Hey, you. Wait."

He pretended he hadn't heard the man. "Stop him," the voice called out, louder this time.

Two uniformed cops blocked Stellan's way. One pointed to a slender man with an open winter coat racing toward him. Stellan turned, faced the opposite way, and took in the oval face, high forehead, and tortoise shell eyeglasses.

"Who are you, and what are you doing here?" the man demanded.

The question triggered an agitation in Stellan. He took a deep breath and in the calmest tone he could manage, said, "I'm Stellan Nieves, an accountant for Stringent Accounting. And you are…?"

The other man paused for a moment. "Kevin Uxley, ADA with the Department of Justice. We have a subpoena to search these premises."

Stellan held the official's gaze.

"Good for you, I guess. I don't know what you're looking for, but whatever it is you need, I can't help you. My firm was hired to do Mr. Kovačević's accounts."

"Why did you turn away?"

The question caught Stellan unawares. "Huh?"

"You left suddenly when Kovačević gave you a look."

Stellan shrugged away the comment.

"I figured it made no sense for me to stand around in the cold."

Uxley studied him for a few seconds.

"So, as his accountant you'd know about irregularities—criminal irregularities—like when he might have fudged books?"

Oh, boy, he's pulling me into something I want no part of.

"I know nothing of the sort. I've only been here a few days. If you're looking for more, I haven't got it to give you. All I can say is, call my superior at Stringent Accounting, Hal Paley. Or our lawyers. Now, if you'll excuse me, I have to go."

Uxley looked away for a moment before he returned his gaze to Stellan. He moved his hand into his coat pocket and came out with a small notebook and a pen.

"Name, address, and phone numbers. We may summon you to appear in front of a grand jury."

"Fine." Stellan supplied him with the information.

The DOJ lawyer wrote, stared at him for a long second, and at last said, "You can go."

Stellan threw another glance at Kovačević followed with a fast shrug, turned, and headed for his car.

Back at the office Stellan asked to meet with Paley. He detailed his morning adventure.

"My guess is they're on some kind of fishing expedition," his large-headed boss said, fussing with his silk tie. Stuck in the '80s, Paley still favored suspenders, French cuff shirts, and slicked-back hair with a perfumed cream. Stellan couldn't help but think, *If they ever make another Wall Street movie, Hal would be convincing in the role of a shyster stockbroker.*

"Yeah, I guess. Spooked me. But there's more to this than meets the eye. Are we getting sucked into some kind of criminal quagmire?"

Paley tossed a hand in the air.

"Let's not get ahead of ourselves. It sounds like they executed a search warrant. How about we wait and see what plays out. And for you being shook-up by the ADA, ah, what he did could have been nothing more than braggadocio. He may not summon you at all. In the meantime, I'll call our lawyers to give them a heads-up. This is a decent-sized account. Let's wait a bit before we rush into any decision. If things get uneasy for you, we'll talk some more."

"I'm uneasy now."

"How so?"

Stellan fought the impulse to tell Paley what he discovered. At a minimum it would cause him humiliation to admit he'd snooped. Worse, it could lead to suspension, a firing, or an investigation.

"I got a bad vibe about this guy. It wouldn't surprise me to hear he's in tight with the mob."

Paley's manicured fingers flicked at a speck on his designer tie.

"Hmm. Here's what we'll do. My guess is Kovačević's going to be real busy hunkering down with his lawyers for the next little while. The feds have probably sealed his building. For now, call him or leave a message and say you're prepared to pick up again when things settle down. And then we'll wait and see. If you're still uneasy later, we'll talk some more about saying bye-byes." He slapped his leg to indicate the end of the discussion.

Nothing to add, Stellan stood up.

"Fine. I'll wait for further instruction."

True to form, Nina sent Stellan numerous, spiteful emails, followed by threatening letters from her lawyer. Next, she used social media to condemn him. He checked her Facebook page. She'd eviscerated him to her 146 friends and who knew how many others. Not content with that, she also ran up one of his credit cards.

He dialed her number.

"Hello."

Stellan wasted no time with social pleasantries. "There is such a thing as libel, Nina. I could sue you."

"What are you talking about?"

He snorted. "What am I talking about? The nasty stuff you post about me."

"You don't like it, don't read it."

"Keep it up, Nina, and see what happens. You're doing a good job of making my life a living hell. What next—circulate a rumor I abused the kids? C'mon. You have everything—the house, the car, most of my salary. I almost have to literally count my pennies." He stopped, exhaled, and waited for her response.

Nina said, "Too bad. Things are only going to get worse for you, buster. You made a commitment when you married me. You don't get to walk away like nothing happened."

The muscles in his neck tightened.

"I left. Deal with it. Clearly you can't. A big mistake, dialing your number and expecting an adult at the other end."

He disconnected. His hands trembled, yet he took a small measure of satisfaction in standing up to her. She'd call back.

The phone rang. He ignored it. On the fourth ring his voice mail kicked in. Nina. He turned off the volume. When she'd exhausted her rant, she'd hang up.

A drink. He needed a drink. He poured a shot of bourbon and sat on the threadbare couch. *Wrong wife, wrong life.*

Ten days later Kovačević called him at work. Stellan heard, "My lawyers got my business up and running again. I'm gonna sue those bastards for loss of revenue."

And hello to you, too, Mr. Kovačević, Stellan silently said. *An excellent conversational opener.* He cleared his throat. "Glad to hear it, sir. Does this mean we carry on where we left off?"

"It's exactly what it means. I want you over here to finish whatever needs finishing. Then we got to get ready for tax filing.

Sure as rain falls, those fuckers at the IRS will audit me until I hurt. They do it every year. It's only gonna get worse for me."

Stellan consulted his day planner. He said he'd come over on the following Tuesday.

On his arrival at the warehouse, he hadn't known what to expect. Nothing looked amiss. Helen and Mrs. Beader greeted him, but Stellan sensed something amiss. It came to him. Both women had retreated into strict formality. He guessed it had to do with the aftershock of the raid.

Kovačević almost startled Stellan when he stepped out of his office, Muscle, one of the two men Stellan saw with the cases, behind him. The thug looked at Stellan and gave him a dismissive sneer.

"You're here," Kovačević said. "Good. I'll clear outta the office. Later you need to go into the warehouse with me to discuss inventory?"

Stellan said he did, but could it wait until after lunch?

"Yeah. No worries. We'll do it then. I gotta take care of some other things."

Stellan and Kovačević wandered the aisles, impervious to lift trucks racing to and from shelves. A young worker traveling too fast and carrying a wider load, attempted a tight turn into an aisle. He failed to negotiate it. His heavy payload struck a shelf post and caused the payload of his truck to topple.

The din got everyone's attention. Workers raced over to help and offer words of commiseration to the shaken driver.

Kovačević hurried over.

"Listen up," he shouted, "we'll clear this up. Get back to work, alla youse." He pointed to the driver. "You, you stay here. I wanna talk to you about this."

When the aisle emptied, Kovačević approached the nervous driver, grabbed him by his neck, and delivered a powerful kidney punch. The man doubled up, and the Serb drove a knee into his face.

Stellan heard bone or cartilage crack.

The driver dropped to the floor and moaned. Kovačević kicked him several times.

"You shit. Look what you've done. You cost me. Any damage comes outta your wages. Got it?"

The bleary-eyed driver struggled to his feet, blood oozing out of his nose. He nodded.

"Get the fuck outta here," Kovačević ordered, "and clean up your blood stains."

The man stumbled away.

Breathing hard, Kovačević met Stellan's gaze.

"Good thing we don't have a union here."

The drama produced fear and indignation in Stellan. He'd had enough of this deranged man. He'd ask Paley to take him off the account.

Chapter 5

Head down, Stellan sat at Kovačević's beaten-up desk, his client next to him, and pored over sheets of inventory data. He hated being in the constricted space with the Serb and his bad breath. Worse, the Serb's nervousness drove him to near-distraction.

Stellan ordered himself to focus on the numbers and block out everything else. If he didn't, he might give in to the impulse to strangle the man.

Late evenings were the worst. Kovačević tended to grow antsier by the hour. His leg wouldn't keep still, bouncing up and down. Calls to his cell phone interested him more than the work at hand.

One evening Kovačević supplied another excuse to leave.

"Got an emergency to go to. You'll be fine here by yourself. Helen showed you how to set the alarm?" Without much interest in the answer, Kovačević abandoned his accountant.

Paley insisted Stellan remain on the account.

"I thought you said you had my back on this, Hal," a disappointed Stellan said, and stared down at his boss behind his desk. "Didn't you hear what I said about the lift truck operator?"

Paley threw a hand in the air. "I understand. Take a seat."

"No, sorry, but you don't understand," Stellan shot back, and plunked himself into a chair. "You didn't see the beating."

Paley straightened his mouse pad and returned his gaze to Stellan.

"Look, I get it you're upset. I told you before, this account is a moneymaker. Finish up the valuation. Maybe a week or more. If there's still work to be done after that, I'll reassign the account."

Stellan groaned. "A couple more weeks. I don't know if I can last a couple more days."

"Come on. Finish it. There'll be a nice bonus at the end."

The word "bonus" perked Stellan up.

"Really? All right, but for this miscreant and his account, I want the bonus now. I'm broke. My ex is bleeding me dry."

"So, you'll do it? Good. Let's talk about how much."

"I gotta meet with some associates," Kovačević said at 6:30 PM, then rose and moved to the other side of the desk. "You're probably done soon anyway, right?"

Stellan worked to keep his smirk hidden. *Associates?* he thought. *You mean ones with rap sheets?* "Sure. You go. I'll finish here."

Back and neck muscles aching from sitting too long in a fixed position, Stellan stretched. He thought about the cases under the floorboards. Were they still there? He approached the spot and removed the floorboards. To his delight, all four cases remained in their hiding place, along with a note. Stellan took the note. *No later than March 11th.* Cryptic, but excellent penmanship. A woman's? Helen's? And did it mean the cases had to be gone by March 11th?

Stellan pulled up one of the cases and opened it to reassure himself. Yep, the money was still where he last saw it. He returned the case and checked the others. Damn. He'd never much thought about the weight of money. Heavy.

He replaced the floorboards. After a moment of consideration, he arrived at a decision. He'd steal the money, all of it.

"You were right, Nina," he said to his unseen wife. "I guess I really am a thief."

The thought disappeared, replaced by a new one: he wouldn't be stealing from a normal person; he'd be stealing from a mobster who'd move heaven and earth to get him. He'd better make damn sure Kovačević never succeeded. To make that come about he'd have to vanish from the face of the earth.

Could he do it? Sure. Why not? The few people he might miss, well, he'd get over them, and they him, soon enough. Life went on. His father's graveside—he'd miss those visits. They comforted him, but he trusted his father's spirit would understand.

The idea of the theft brought on a rush. Stellan understood how criminals might enjoy the excitement of their enterprises.

He walked back to his desk. Only a while back he thought his life couldn't get any worse, and now... He had a great deal to do in order to make the snatch. Pen and paper at hand, he jotted down his tasks. He'd have to strike before the money vanished and hope everything went according to plan.

A memory came to him. A professor at college had lectured about tax evasion and focused on something called moral turpitude.

"In general," the professor had said, "our courts view moral turpitude as 'one shocking the public conscience.'" He went on to detail obvious examples: armed robbery, murder, assault.

Heads down, Stellan and the others had taken notes while the elderly man remarked that moral turpitude became harder to define in white-collar crimes.

Here in the warehouse Stellan asked himself if stealing from a crook qualified as moral turpitude. It sure wouldn't get him nominated for any Man of the Year award. This was theft and couldn't be anything but theft. Did it matter whether you stole from a saint or a sinner?

He pondered the matter further. Ripping off Kovačević would also be ripping off the Serb's victims. Kovačević took it from them, and he, Stellan, would take it from the Serb. Nobody would thank him for being some latter-day Robin Hood and for sure not Kovačević. He didn't care. He had a goal, a purpose, and would put his energies into relieving Kovačević of the money in order to start his new life. The hell with everything else.

He arrived home and made a late supper while he listened to his voice mail messages, including another screechy, threatening one from Nina who insisted hell awaited him in the next life. She finished with a Bible quote, "Where the worm does not die and the fire is never quenched."

Stellan smirked. "Good to know what you think is in store for me, Nina," he said to the machine. "Makes what I'm about to do all the easier. Until I finally get to hell, I'm going to have a lot of fun."

In a different message, someone with a noticeable East Indian accent offered him a deal on replacement windows.

His sister left a message to tell him about a protest march against patriarchy next Saturday.

"You should go, Stellan. There'll be other men there."

He scoffed. Other men? The only men who'd likely be there would be ones who've been castrated. Matriarchy, the new frontier for women like Ash, who wanted to keep their feet on the necks of men.

"Can't, Ash," he said to the machine. "I'll be a little preoccupied. You'll have to change the world without me."

He erased all messages.

Halfway through his evening meal his doorbell rang. Stellan's head tilted to one side. The lines in his forehead furrowed. Who could it be at this hour of the day? Had Kovačević somehow divined his wicked plot and come for him?

With anxiety he opened the door to the cold night air to find two men, both dressed in parkas, their vehicle still running. Were these Squeezebox's men?

The one on the right spoke.

"Mr. Nieves, Stellan Nieves?"

"Yes," a nervous Stellan replied.

"FBI," the man said and reached into his parka. He handed a folded document to Stellan. "This is a subpoena for you to appear in person and testify in front of a grand jury."

Relief flooded Stellan. The FBI, not a couple of strong-arms. He released a rush of air. Had they noticed? Did he look suspicious? If they found anything unusual in his reaction, they didn't show it. "About what? I don't know what I'm getting a subpoena for."

"It's in there, sir. You've been served."

Nothing else to add, the agent turned and headed for the heated car, his partner beside him.

Stellan shut the door and walked upstairs. He sat at the kitchen table and read. *United States v Dusan Adam Kovačević.*

The subpoena commanded him to report to the federal building in six days.

He thought the document wordy, arcane, and little more than a fishing expedition. He didn't have anything to help the DA with his case. No matter. He'd turn it over to Paley.

Kovačević knew about the subpoena.

"It's not like you got somethin' to tell those cocksuckers, right? They're trying to nail me for racketeering. Me. They been watching too many of them Mafia movies. I'm a legitimate businessman who's being harassed by the government, is all."

Stellan caught the false bravado in Kovačević's tone. *The guy's sweating bullets.*

"Exactly. They've summoned me, but I haven't got anything they want. I've only known you for the smallest of time. What can I...? What am I supposed to know?"

"Nothin'. I hate rats. They don't live long."

Kovačević couldn't have done anything worse than issue his veiled threat. This subtle menace fortified Stellan's resolve to run with the money. He swallowed and said, "You have nothing to worry about me."

Kovačević peered at Stellan for a few seconds, then slapped his back.

"It's good. Forget about what I said. Blowing smoke outta my ass, is all. You're good people."

Stellan wanted to laugh and say, *Good people? You won't think I'm good people when I pull off this heist.*

Chapter 6

Stellan's slide into larceny began in earnest.

He started with spending considerable time at the main branch of the library reading everything pertaining to vanishing—how to bring it about, how to change his appearance, where to go, what to take, and how to confuse any possible pursuer. Prevailing wisdom advised against walking away without first covering his tracks.

Armed with fresh knowledge, Stellan quit his email account and social media favorites. For sure the Serb would come after him. When the usual methods failed, he'd no doubt track him down via social footprints. Why make life easy for him?

Stellan's extensive research reading led to eye strain and a sore back but resulted in a gold mine of information.

Through back copies of newspapers on microfiche and websites, he found obituaries of six local male babies born the same year as he. He searched for certificates of death on all of them. Phone calls and website information from the Division of Vital Records and The Circuit Court revealed two babies weren't formally registered as deceased. He guessed their parents couldn't afford the death certificate.

Stellan underlined two names and drummed his pen. Which one? Which name would he try for? Eenie, meenie, minie, moe.

He settled on Peter Middleton Harris from the village of Bellwood.

"Peter Harris," he said under his breath. It had a nice ring to it. Would he go by Peter or Pete? The latter felt closer to his social temperament, but he wouldn't be rigid. He'd answer to either.

Here goes, baby Pete, he silently said to the dead child when he entered County Clerk's office. *I'm sorry for taking over your name. Hope you understand. If you don't, there's nothing I can do about it.*

He discovered birth and death certificates were granted online, but doing so came with risk. The biggest? Leaving a social footprint.

Presenting himself at the County Clerk's Office also had risk.

He weighed both options and chose a personal visit. Human contact might give him more wiggle room should he need it.

His decision made, Stellan debated on when to visit. He chose noontime. Most of the staff would be on lunch. The skeleton crew faced a long line of customers eager to get their tasks done and return to work.

Stellan arrived and filled out the requisite form. He chose the longest line and hoped he'd find a frazzled employee eager to process people and get to lunch.

He waited with apprehension. What if this went wrong? What if the clerk saw through his BS?

His mouth dry, he shifted from foot to foot. *Calm down*, he ordered himself. *Keep it together.* He remembered a punchline his father liked to use—more nervous than a rattlesnake at a hoedown. That would be him. The memory brought on a smile. He exhaled.

His line inched forward. The woman in front of him stepped up to the wicket. "Next."

Stellan stepped up to the gate, flattened his tie with the palm of his hand, and stared through the grille at a late-middle-aged woman. He saw the familiar bored look he'd witnessed so often on civil servants over the years.

Application and money ready, he slid both over to her and gave her his best smile.

She studied the application for a moment. "See some ID, Mr. Harris?"

Okay, here we go. Stellan leaned forward on the counter, lowered his voice, and dove into his gambit.

"I got mugged." He followed the statement with a right shoulder shrug. "I lost my wallet, credit cards, the whole shebang. It drives me crazy, crime. Shit! Pardon my French. Anyway, I can't do a thing without ID, and to get it I gotta have my birth certificate. Can you see my problem?"

She peered across at him. He held his breath and willed her to commiserate with him. A second later she said, "We hear these kinds of things all the time." She leaned forward and let the weight of her words sink in.

"We've got serious rules about handing out birth certificates." She tapped the application with her forefinger. "This ain't 'nuff. Far, far from 'nuff. You're a stranger, and you walk in with no proof of who you are and want a birth certificate. You seein' the problem here?"

Stellan's heart sank. Ready to turn away, he couldn't believe what he heard next.

"I shouldn't do this, but you remind me of someone. All right, lemme ax you some questions. Where and when were you born? Who're your folks? I need answers."

Relief flooded through Stellan. Grateful he'd done his homework, he answered and amplified where he thought the narrative required it.

The woman listened and said, "If you wait, we'll get you a new print-on-demand certificate. Go sit in the waiting area, and we'll call you."

Stellan silently exhaled.

"Oh, thank you. Thank you so much. You're an angel." He turned his head and allowed himself a small smile of victory.

His first deceit accomplished, Stellan ran into a wall at the DMV. A new license required him to be fingerprinted in accordance with federal compliance.

He gritted his teeth. *Goddamn those terrorists, and goddamn Homeland Security to boot.* He took a few minutes to regain his composure. No point stewing about it. An important piece of ID, the license, but he'd figure something out. Maybe the black market. But not here, not now in Illinois. In the meantime, nothing for it but to use his own identification to rent a car.

The same day he visited a car rental and selected the most unobtrusive vehicle, a subcompact. It wouldn't entice most thieves.

He presented his own credit card. It didn't matter. In another day, he'd tear it up for good.

He consulted a map of his escape route while a rental agent typed his information into the computer. The first stretch would take him to Fort Wayne, 140 east. From there he'd find alternate transportation and disappear.

"You'll be dropping this off at our Fort Wayne office on Dixon?" the young man behind the counter asked.

"Right."

The agent answered with a nod.

"If you need more time, call the Fort Wayne office. All set to go, Mr. Nieves." He handed Stellan the keys.

Back in his flat, Stellan looked at Pete Harris' birth certificate. So far, so good, but he had more to do before he could make his escape. Now, if everything went according to plan...

The next day Stellan visited a dollar store and bought a pair of eyeglasses with thick, black, plastic frames. Spectacles on his face, his necktie gone, he walked into the Social Security office to get an official verification number.

Anxiety again got the better of him. He ordered himself to breathe—deep, slow breaths.

The lines at the counter were long and busy. Stellan took his time to inspect each of the clerks. The young one with the kind face and oversized glasses—he'd try her. He'd filled out most of the SS-5, unsure of some of the questions, so he left them blank. When she got to them, he'd plead ignorance.

His turn came. He approached the counter. She met him with a practiced, professional smile.

"Hi. My name's Peter Harris. I'm applying for my first ever Social Security card." *Don't give her more than she needs*, he ordered himself. *Let her ask the questions.*

She didn't disappoint.

"Your first Social Security card? Hard to believe. Are you telling me you've never had one...ever?"

Stellan rolled out his lie. Careful to avoid eye contact, in his softest voice he said, "I... I'm embarrassed to say this, but I've been in and out of psychiatric hospitals most of my life. My social worker, Mrs. Wolsey, is helping me get more independent. I got my ID here. See?"

"Uh-huh."

Stellan made a show of looking around the cavernous room. "Mrs. Wolsey's around here somewhere." He turned his gaze back to the counter and gave the clerk his best wide-eyed, sheepish look. "I gotta be more independent."

The woman studied his birth certificate and chewed on her lower lip. "In hospitals, huh?"

She wants to believe me. Seal the deal, but don't push.

"Yes. And group homes. I wasn't, you know, woo-woo crazy. I've got this thing they call stress response syndrome. I'm taking all my meds, am a lot better, and will soon have my own apartment."

He waited, grateful for having boned up on mental health disorders.

A nod gave him his answer. Her gaze left him and moved down to the form. She tapped it. "You need to finish this."

She's buying what I'm selling, Stellan thought and swallowed. He allowed himself to relax while the clerk took more information and helped him complete the form.

"A card will be mailed to you in about ten to twelve days."

"Um, right, but I'll be moving upstate before then. I don't know my new address yet."

"I see. Well, Peter," she said with the patience of a mother coaching a child, "what I'll do is print out your number on our letterhead. When you have your new address, phone us, go online, or come back here. We can help you get your new card."

He wanted to smile but forced his face to remain expressionless.

"So, I'm finished here?"

"Yes, you are, and I wish you well with everything."

"Thank you, Miss..." He made a show of studying her name tag, "...Prendergast."

An emotionally drained Stellan left the Social Security building. Two deceptive maneuvers done. How did consummate liars manage it? He couldn't remember who said it, something about all liars needing good memories. Honest people didn't have to remember what they said. This lying thing demanded a lot, but he knew it would be a constant companion from here on in.

He needed a coffee or something stronger to settle his nerves.

Chapter 7

Kovačević peered at Stellan.

"'Cha get lucky?"

"Pardon?"

"Get lucky, score some pussy? You got some kind of shit-eating grin on you. Never seen that before. Figured you got some, and not from the wife." He followed with an obscene wink.

Stellan pretended to enjoy the loutish comment.

"I did, yeah. If things go my way, I'll get lucky again."

"Good to hear it. Always thought you accountants were wrapped too tight. Gotta chill. Gettin' some's a good start."

Stellan forced a grin and changed the subject.

"So, Mr. Kovačević, we're almost done with this part. I can finish up here if you like." He waited and hoped the Serb would agree.

"Nah, let's get this done. I don't wanna look at it again for some time."

The answer foiled Stellan. He'd hoped for a different response. He needed Kovačević gone. *Please, please, please, don't let this backfire,* he prayed to some unknown god.

He tried again.

"I know most people think accounting is boring. Nothing like what you do." He used the end of his pen to point to the spreadsheets. "We'll tough our way through the last of these together. Might be a longer night."

The Serb took the bait. He let loose a soft moan.

Stellan repressed an inner chuckle. Man, if he could wind this cretin up, it had to be a cakewalk for the guy's wife. "Once we come up for air, we'll be done. This will be my last late night, and I'll sleep in tomorrow. I don't mind if you've got to be somewhere."

Kovačević rose. "Seein' you put it like that, okay. I'll call your office tomorrow when you're in. And I'll put in a good word with your boss."

Stellan would have loved to do a fist bump. "Kind of you. I'll probably get back before noon?"

"Okay. I'll talk to you again then. Don't stay too late."

"I'll try not to, and have a good evening."

Stellan shook with excitement in anticipation and waited until the last worker left the warehouse. He reviewed everything. All he needed sat in his garment bag and small suitcase in the car's trunk. His laptop and cell phone remained in his flat, both damaged beyond repair.

Convinced he had the building to himself, Stellan said, "It's going to happen. It's going to happen." He allowed himself a long, leisurely exhalation. "Time to get on with it. Let's hope the money's still there. If it isn't, all for nothing."

Seconds later he pried a floorboard, thrilled at what he saw. The floorboard back in place, Stellan stepped out to the parking lot.

Gus, the night watchman, sat in his heated hut and looked up from a crossword when Stellan approached. He kept his hands in his pocket, worried they might betray him. "Hi, Gus. Kind of cozy in there," he said and pointed to the electric heater.

Gus' brows narrowed in a scowl.

"It's not, but better than being out in this cold. What can I do for you?"

Stellan pointed to the warehouse. "I'm pulling my car up to the back door and loading old documents, heavy ones. Then I'm done. The place'll be yours."

"You sure you're not stealing stuff from the warehouse?"

The comment caused Stellan's stomach to drop. His face must have betrayed him, because the guard said, "Relax. Kidding. Nothing but junk in there anyway."

Stellan forced himself to laugh and hoped it sounded convincing. "I know what you mean. Keeps the dollar stores in business. I better get back. Have a good night."

"Yeah, you, too."

Stellan's butterflies flew in every direction while he backed the rental car to the door. He didn't know what was worse, his adrenaline or his anxiety. Satisfied his car blocked Gus' view, he hauled each case to the car. A quick look in Gus' direction told him the guard's interest remained on his crossword puzzle.

He placed three of the cases in the trunk and the third on the backseat floorboard, slammed the door shut, returned to the warehouse, and set the alarm. "Least I can do," he said to himself.

An idiom came to him: locking the stable door after the horses have bolted. Life was rich with irony.

Relieved he'd succeeded with his theft, Stellan slid behind the wheel and drove up to the electric gate. He honked. The gate slid open, and Gus waved him off. Stellan returned the wave. His car disappeared into the night.

The corners of his eyes crinkled as his smile widened. When was the last time he'd allowed himself such a spontaneous smile?
He thought about what they'd find in the office: spreadsheets on a cluttered desk but nothing else amiss. Until they looked under the floorboards. There they'd find an empty space and a typed note which read, *Cui bono?* For whose benefit?

"Pete Harris, Pete Harris, Pete Harris," the newly installed millionaire repeated past the Skyway Toll on I-90. "My name is Pete Harris. If anyone ever, ever shouts out 'Stellan,' I won't turn and look. From now on I'm going to think and act like Pete Harris."

He checked his speedometer. Good. No speed violation, no improper lane change, nothing. Best to be safe and invisible. "I'm on my way to a new life," he said out loud.

His mind wandered back to when he'd surfed the Internet for places to live. He'd ruled out the entire Midwest. Too conservative. The Deep South? No. Too fundie. Who'd want a steady stream of right-wing religious wackadoos knocking on your door and asking, "Can we talk to you about our Savior, Jesus?" Besides, his Chicaaaago accent would make him stand out.

Pete narrowed his preferences to the far West and the Northeast. In the end he chose Martine Maines, Vermont. How could you not be attracted to a town with such an interesting name?

He liked what he saw on the Internet. A picturesque little town in the Green Mountains, the town boasted a population of 9.600 or so, and had a small, accredited liberal arts college, *Montesquieu*, nicknamed *Monty* by the locals. If he craved a taste of big city life, New York and Boston were within striking distance.

Stellan had lived in Chicago all of his life but had no affinity for it. Or any other large city. Martine Maines might be an excellent fit. A thousand miles from Chicago and fourteen hours by car. He'd be safe there. Well, in truth, there'd be no safe harbor anywhere. Ever. Martine Maines would do fine as long as he didn't do anything to draw unnecessary attention.

The adventure ahead excited Pete. He'd settle into the town, get a place to live, and let his hair grow longer. He'd grow a beard and wear different clothes. Not accountant clothes. He might even apply for admission to the college and take whatever interested him.

He'd planned out his escape route to Martine Maines and found two ways to reach the town. The shorter one brought him through Canada. They'd ask him if he had anything to declare.

No, nothing.

Pop the trunk, please, sir. What's in these cases?

Those? Oh, nothing to be concerned about.

No, he'd stay in the U S of A.

The glare of headlights blinded Pete. He flicked the rearview to nighttime driving. Better. The vehicle behind him caught up and raced past. A sleek sports car.

Pete checked his mental list of everything he needed in his new identity. His birth certificate sat in his breast pocket. The Stellan Nieves ID stayed in his wallet. So, too, did his credit cards. He'd need new ones. Without them, so many things became difficult. He knew the fastest way to get one without a credit history would be as a student.

He knew credit screenings for students were "soft," meaning companies barely did any checks. The downside of the cards was that they came with high interest rates. He didn't have to worry. Once he had a card and paid his balance, he'd have the beginnings of a credit history. That would allow him to apply for other cards.

Two miles ahead Pete saw flashing reds and yellows. His heart jumped. He checked his speed. Not him. His vehicle drew closer to the police cruiser. A state trooper had pulled someone over—the sports car.

Pete pulled off at the Fort Wayne exit. His stomach growled. Back at the warehouse, he'd had no interest in food. Adrenaline saw to that. Now he could relax and eat.

He took his time and searched for a motel to his liking. He found a high-end one with plenty of CCTVs around the building. Good. They'd deter criminals. Like him? No. He smiled at the thought.

At the reception desk he asked for a room on the ground floor. "Somewhere I can see my car," he said to the young clerk. "It's a rental. I'm a little worried about it getting dented. I should have got the extra coverage, you know."

"Of course," the young, perky woman said. "I understand. We do have closed circuit monitoring."

"I know. Just being extra cautious."

She gave Pete an outside room. He paid with his Nieves card and assured himself he'd never use it again.

The motel had a restaurant still open. Pete inspected the menu. Tex-Mex. Decent enough by the looks of it. He'd park the car by the front door. Only somebody with brass balls would try to steal it from there.

He ate with pleasure, paid his bill, and drove to his room. He backed the car to the doorway of his room. A quick check convinced him no nosey neighbor showed any interest in him. Satisfied, he brought the cases into his room. Curtains drawn tight, his garment bag and suitcase came next.

He double-locked his door and set the small chain onto the security track.

A rough, fitful night of sleep followed. Pete put it down to nervousness and worry. All this money. He plotted out his next steps. Tomorrow he'd check used car lots and classified website ads for cars. There'd be no paper trail if he could score a car under his new name and pay cash. People weren't inclined to declare private cash transactions.

He wished he had a laptop with him. He could check for cars now. The motel lobby had free computers. Pete wouldn't use them but stopped and looked at them with temptation. No, best not. Security cameras would monitor him, and any skip tracer might discover his searches.

Morning arrived. Pete changed into a sports jacket and jeans, checked the pockets of his suit and hung it. Good suit, but let somebody else have it. If and when he needed a new one, he'd go for bolder colors and slimmer cuts.

At 10:00 he drove downtown, the cases in his car. He parked on the busy main street, Madison, and made sure his overcoat covered the sole case on the rear floorboard.

By chance, Pete passed an electronics store. He stopped. A cell phone. Sooner or later one would come in handy. Fifteen minutes later he left the store with a disposable one with $100 of prepaid minutes.

An idea came to him. Should he risk it? It might be worth his while. He wavered on the decision for a few minutes before he made up his mind.

Pete drove around and located the less desirable parts of town. If a neighborhood grew too challenging, too unsafe, he drove out.

He found something on a street with a single sidewalk and post-WWII bungalows, most with door and window grilles.

Pete parked a block from Baudeans Garage and walked back to

the company. He hoped his car would be safe.

The auto repair shop had both of its wooden bay doors down, each struggling with the ravages of time. Pete entered what passed for an office. His senses took in the familiar scent of gasoline, welding fumes, oil, solvents, two cars up on hoists—all things he associated with Joe Nieves, who loved cars. He'd often visit his friend's garage and bring his boy along.

Pete's gaze took in two men busy working on cars, while two others involved themselves in some discussion. None paid the slightest attention to the honky-tonk music blaring from a tinny radio.

Of the two, the taller, solid one with olive skin at last broke free and approached Pete. He guessed the guy probably played linebacker in high school. Much of the muscle had now gone to fat.

The man wiped his hands on an oil rag and placed it in the back pocket of his long-sleeved, greasy coveralls, his beer belly noticeable.

"Help ya?"

Pete drew in a breath of air.

"Um, yeah. I don't know how to start this, so I'll come out and say it. I'm looking for a new ride. I'll pay cash. Don't need a receipt, but the car's got to have good papers."

He stopped and waited for the older man to reply.

It took only a second.

"Get the fuck outta here. This is a legit business, not some chop shop. I should report you to the cops." The mechanic's eyes narrowed, and the lines between his brows bunched.

Pete swallowed. "Sorry. Big mistake. I apologize."

He spun, hurried away, and cursed himself. He heard the door behind him open again. A surge of adrenalin raced through him. His chest tightened. He gulped air.

The man's voice called out. "Hang on a sec."

Pete stopped and turned, unsure why, afraid of the worst.

The mechanic gestured with his head to come back inside.

No real plan to retrieve himself from this situation, Pete obeyed and followed him back into the garage. In the office, the mechanic said, "Thought about it, and I don't think you're a cop. You wouldn't be white as a ghost if you were."

"No, not a cop."

"But to be on the safe side, you won't mind if I frisk you?"

"No." Pete raised his arms shoulder high.

The mechanic ran open palms over his chest and back, his arms, waist, and legs. Finished, he faced Pete.

"Show me some ID."

"I don't have much," Pete said and produced his Stellan Nieves license. "That's part of my problem and why I came asking about a car."

The other man's attention moved from the license to Pete.

"How'd you find me?"

"Spur of the moment thing. Like I said, I need a set of wheels no one can trace to me. I searched the web, but didn't see much. This idea came to me."

The other man's eyes stayed on Pete. He dropped his own gaze. Once more he questioned the wisdom of coming to the shop.

The mechanic cleared his throat. "What're you looking for?"

"You have lots of choice?"

The mechanic swept his arm over the garage.

"It look like I got lots of choice? Cars and trucks don't stay in one piece long. I got a couple of things, but only one could be your ticket. You like pickups?"

"Uh, never thought about it. Tell me a little about it."

"Tell you about it? Hmm. Okay, it's one of those Detroit pint-sized pickups. It'll be cut up before day's done if you're not interested. The parts will go to Malaysia. If you like what I'm selling, you'll save me work. You win, I win."

Unsure of what else to do in the moment, Pete nodded.

"A pickup. I'm trying to imagine myself in a pickup. Is it big?"

"Nah. Like I said, pint-sized. Two-door. Shiny, candy apple red. Not a scratch. Polished. Probably belonged to a guy with a small pecker to impress women. It's got one of those hard thermoplastic deadbolt bed covers. Keeps everything safe."

Pete stuffed his hands into his pockets. A truck? Why not? He could make it part of his new persona.

"So, where is it?"

"Not here, but I'll show you a picture. Wait."

A moment later the mechanic returned. He handed Pete a photograph.

"Came up from Arkansas. Got all the toys. We checked it. No tracking device on it. We'll put a new VIN on the dashboard and torch the one on the engine. You get a new bogus number. Won't be able to tell. You can check for yourself before you buy. If you want the truck, we'll give you a receipt with a dealer name. I'll register it at the DMV and sign the ownership when you pay up. No hassle."

Pete made up his mind.

"How much?"

"Twenty grand, cash, but if you get it today, you drive away for fifteen. I can't have it sitting around long. Too risky."

Pete studied the photo and then looked up at the mechanic.

"I like it, but..." He rubbed his hands together. "We don't know each other. What's to say one or both of us doesn't stiff the other?"

The mechanic considered the question.

"Point. So neither of us comes up on the short end of the stick, leave me a goodwill deposit of four grand. In three days be at the DMV office on Euclid at 10:00. You know where it is?"

"No, but I'll find it. There's only one, I'm guessing."

"Right. So, come at ten with the rest of the dough. There'll be lots of folks around. We do the transaction in the parking lot. You then step into the office, get new plates, register the truck, insure it, and we're done."

The words convinced Pete.

"Deal." He caught his breath. "There's another matter you might be able to help me with."

"What?"

"I need a new license. I've gotta lose the one I have. You wouldn't happen to know anyone who can get me a passable one?"

"I do. It'll cost."

"You can do it? Incredible. How much?"

"Depends on how fast you want it and the quality. The new 'compliant' ones with a gold star cost more."

"Makes sense. Will it be scannable?"

"Damn right. You want it for what state?"

"Vermont. Can you do it?"

"Not overnight. It'll take a couple of days. I can deliver the truck and license the same time."

"And the cost…?"

"You get what you pay for," the mechanic said. "Good quality and not the Chinese shit the kids use to get into bars. Takes time 'cause we gotta monkey with the state's DMV database. Once you get the license, you've got no more worries."

Impressed, Pete considered the information. Chop shop? Yeah, he could see this guy doing that, but fake licenses? What a world. Still, he might not find anything like this elsewhere.

"I'm interested, but after you do it and we finish with each other, you have no record of me, right? I'm going on good faith here, blind faith."

"Both of us," the man said. "There is honor among thieves. Not much, but some. The trick is to pick the thief. When we're done, we say adios. Don't know each other. Never seen each other."

Pete liked what he heard. "So, again, for this quality license, how much?"

"Fifteen hundred. You come back here tonight after 6:00 with the money for the license and the four grand for the truck. We'll take your picture and use our kit for your fingerprints. In three days you get both license and truck."

"So, tonight with the deposit?"

"Yep. After 6:00."

Pete lost a good night's sleep, worried he might have committed himself to a dangerous folly. He called the front desk and asked for housekeeping not to clean his room until he checked out.

He only left his room to eat. The rest of the time he watched pay-per-view movies and fretted. Would he be betrayed, would the mechanic hold up his end of the bargain, and would he leave Fort Wayne in anything but handcuffs?

The next few days dragged on. Pete swore he'd lost at least five pounds worrying.

He skipped breakfast on the morning of his meeting, too nervous to eat, and ordered coffee from a drive-through donut chain. It took him a while to find the DMV. He spotted the red pickup in the parking lot at once. The mechanic tossed him a fast wave from behind the wheel.

Pete climbed into the passenger side and clutched a gym bag.

"Morning," he said. "The red's an eye-catcher."

The mechanic nodded. "You noticed, huh?"

Neither man spoke for a few seconds.

"It's all here," Pete said and handed the gym bag to the other man.

The mechanic looked around. Satisfied no one showed any interest, he opened the bag and whistled.

"Bettin' there's a hell of a story how you got your mitts on this. Never mind. I don't wanna know." He took his time, counted the money, and selected several bills for closer inspection by holding them up to the windshield.

"These are the real deal." The bills back in the bag, the mechanic looked at Pete. "Mind if I keep this?"

"Help yourself. I can get another one."

"Great." The mechanic slid a hand into his coveralls and pulled out a plastic, credit card sized driver's license, ownership of the truck, and bill of sale.

"Here you go...Mr. Harris. Everything you need. Slap insurance on the truck, get the ownership changed, and you're off."

Pete studied the license.

"Nice. I look like a terrorist."

"You ever hear anybody say they take a good picture?" the other man said. He pointed to the license. "It'll fool the cops and everybody else. And your Pete Harris prints are in the computer now. A word of warning—you ever decide to get or renew your passport, do it in the name of Pete Harris. Anything else and you'll set off all kinds of alarms at Homeland Security."

"Got it. Good advice." Pete had never applied for a passport as Stellan Nieves.

"Let's get this done," the other man said. He started the engine. "I'll take you to a place now where you can get insurance. Then we come back here and finish up getting this registered in your name."

The mechanic drove Pete to an insurance broker. It took half an hour to get full coverage. Back in the DMV parking lot the mechanic looked at Pete. "Bye, and see you around. No, wait. Not yet. Want some advice before I go?"

"Sure."

"First chance, repaint this truck. Red—bright red—draws attention like you wouldn't believe, especially from the law. Don't ask me why, but cops get boners every time they see a red car whipping by. Attention is something you do not want."

"Okay. I'll do that right away."

"Oh, one more thing." He handed Pete a screwdriver. "On the house."

Pete took it.

"Nice doing business with you. When I think about it, this whole thing could have blown up in my face."

"Could have, but didn't," the other man said. Without another word he opened his door and walked away. Pete, too excited, didn't bother to see where he went. He took the keys, stepped into the DMV office, and filled out the requisite forms. His palms wet, he half-expected alarms to go off and the police to rush in, but nothing happened.

He allowed himself several deep breaths while he put on his new plates.

The seat adjusted to his liking, Pete pulled the truck beside his car. He scanned the area. No one showed any interest in him. With care Pete transferred everything into the back of the pickup. A final sweep of the area. Nothing to cause him concern. Nothing left to do but drive away.

What about the car rental? Should he do the right thing and return it to the dealer? He snorted. He'd already committed any number of felonies, misdemeanors, and who knew what else. Abandoning a car rental wouldn't exactly cause an Amber Alert.

He placed the keys in the ashtray and locked the car. Pete dialed the local car rental dealer. A female voice answered.

"This is Stellan Nieves," Pete said. "The car I rented is sitting in the parking lot of the DMV on Euclid. I left the keys and cash payment in the ashtray."

He hung up.

His stomach growled. Pete drove to a donut shop drive-through and ordered a breakfast sandwich and coffee. He pulled into a vacant spot, turned off the engine, ate, and studied every piece of Stellan Nieves' identification. A last swallow of coffee and he destroyed his old ID. He scooped up the remains, left the truck, and tossed them into a garbage bin.

Ten minutes later Pete turned onto the interstate. So many things could have gone wrong, yet they hadn't. He'd pulled off the heist but not without a large measure of luck. All the same, he swore he'd lost a year of his life, old and new, from the stress of these last few days.

If his father could see him now. He might not smile at what his son had become, but then again…

He spoke out loud to his father. "Well, Dad, your son is driving a candy apple red pickup. Me, the former Stellan Nieves, who always drove sensible cars. Even you joked about me being a bit too stuffy for my own good. I'm in this Arkansas pickup and listening to *Adagio for Strings* on a kick-ass stereo. In the back I've got over two mil. Can my life get any weirder?"

A two-seater sports car passed Pete. The brunette in the passenger seat caught his eye. She gave him a Madison Avenue toothpaste smile and a thumb-and-forefinger approval sign for the truck.

He grinned and tossed a fast wave. He'd definitely get the truck repainted, maybe somewhere around Cleveland. What color would he like? He considered his choices and settled on some kind of forest green.

A new thought arrived. Wouldn't he like to know what was happening back in Chicago?

Chapter 8

A lot happened, much of it frantic.

Squeezebox arrived at Stringent expecting to meet with his accountant, Stellan. He waited for three quarters of an hour before he rose and approached Fiona.

"Hell's goin' on? I been sittin' on my ass here for the better part of an hour, and Nieves still not comin' down. What gives?"

Fiona called Paley and explained the situation. He, in turn, phoned the warehouse. Maybe Stellan had gone there. A woman answered. No, she told Paley, Mr. Nieves hadn't arrived, and he left spreadsheets on his desk. She found it odd. He'd always been so neat and tidy.

Paley relayed the information to Squeezebox. "Something's wrong here."

His client held the same opinion as evidenced by his rigid body language and tightness in the face.

"No shit, Sherlock. You better do some s'plainin'. I thought you was supposed to run a tight ship. Don't look like it to me. My time's as good as yours. I got better things to do than waste it lookin' at month-old business mags."

"I'll call his home," a nervous Paley said by way of conciliation. He searched for the number on his rotary desktop card index and dialed. The call went to voice mail. Frustrated, Paley sent Kevin Mosley, the office manager, to Stellan's house.

After some persuasion, Helmut Becker let Mosley into the flat. He found a disabled laptop, a damaged cell phone, and a guidebook to Pebble Creek, a suburb of Tampa. Maps for Tennessee, Georgia, and Florida lay on a laminated coffee table. Everything suggested Nieves had packed and left in a hurry.

"What do you think happened to your tenant?" Mosley asked the landlord. "All this doesn't make sense. Looks like he left, and in a hurry."

The retired landlord agreed.

"Ja. Somezink. I am zhinkink vhe should call ze pol-leeze."

Mosley shook his head in reply.

"I'm not sure what the police can do. It looks like Stellan buggered off to Florida." He pointed to the laptop. "Can't figure out why he'd leave that, but let me take this back to my work. It might help us locate him down there. I'll itemize everything and give you a receipt."

It took some convincing, but at last Becker agreed.

A mortified Paley couldn't offer a logical explanation for his employee leaving without any explanation. "We're as stumped as you, Mr. Kovačević. From what we can tell, he's disappeared."

"Disappeared?" an agitated Squeezebox repeated. "What the fuck you mean he disappeared?"

"Like he left, suddenly." Paley's mouth opened and closed like a fish gasping for air. "I'll do my best to get to the bottom of this."

Panic seized Squeezebox. In his fatalistic heart he knew: Nieves had skipped town with his money. "Not fuckin' enough," he snarled. "I'm paying good money, and for what? The guy who does my books vanishes? Gimme his address. I wanna talk to him."

"As I said, he's not there, and you'll understand we can't give out personal information, sir."

"I wanna talk to him and ain't askin' again. Gimme…his…address."

The tone and matching anger caused Paley to feel heat spread across his face. Why was this guy so angry? Stellan's computer files would have all of the information. Another accountant could finish up the work.

Paley couldn't understand the reaction, but he hated confrontation. He caved, again consulted his desktop card index, and wrote Stellan's address on a pad. His hand shook as he handed the paper to the Serb.

"He's renting a flat. The upper part of a house."

Squeezebox seized the slip of paper and without a word made

for the door.

"I'll be sure to have someone call you when we find out what's going on, Mr. Kovačević," Paley said to his back. "Let's hope Stellan didn't get into some kind of accident."

"Yeah, let's."

For the second time that day, Helmut Becker allowed someone into the flat. He considered calling the police when the wild-eyed man arrived and demanded to see his tenant's flat. Instead, something told him to comply. He followed the man around the flat, sensing the tension and listening to the visitor's labored breathing.

"He say where he was goin'?" the visitor asked.

Becker shook his head slowly. "Nein. Vhe are not knowing anyzhink."

The man left without a goodbye.

Becker locked the front door. If anyone else came and asked for Stellan Nieves, Becker wouldn't answer, but instead call the police.

His nerves taut, Squeezebox fought the urge to race to the office and tear up the loose floorboards. He couldn't, not with the women around. They'd see the empty space under the floorboards and his humiliation. Too horrible to bear. He'd have to wait.

At the height of the evening rush hour, Squeezebox climbed into his German luxury car and drove to the warehouse. He gave a soft honk at the parking lot gate. Gus let him through.

Squeezebox rushed into the warehouse and unlocked the office door. Inside, he shed his overcoat, knelt, removed the floorboards, and gaped at what he so dreaded—the empty space.

Squeezebox's eyes blinked rapidly. His heart raced and his fingers tingled. He couldn't catch his breath. The room spun. Sweat poured down his temple. His neck grew clammy. Air. He needed air. He couldn't get enough into his lungs. To compensate, he sucked air through his mouth hard and fast.

He flopped onto his back. *Fuck, I'm dying. I gotta be having some kind of heart attack. Should I call 9-1-1? What if the ambulance don't get here in time?*

He didn't phone but remained on his back and suffered. His waves of panic lessened, and his heart returned to a near-normal rate. At last he forced himself to sit up and stare into the hiding place. He saw something. A note. Where had it come from? He bent, reached for it, and brought it closer. Two words: *Cui bono?* What did that mean? No idea. Cui bono. It smacked of education. Probably Nieves. The prick intended to mock him. But how did Nieves get wind of the money and know where to look?

Squeezebox couldn't answer the question. No point wasting any more time. Right now he had to find Nieves. "We'll see, cocksucker," he said to the absent thief. "Laugh now. You won't be laughing when I get my hands on you."

Squeezebox's thoughts turned to how the cash came to be under the floorboards. That hadn't been the original plan. His snitch at the cop shop called and warned him of an upcoming raid. "If you don't want anything found, Dusan, hide it."

Squeezebox knew he had other, secure places to hide the money. "So, what do I do instead?" he said to the room. "I'll tell you what. Too lazy to stash the dough in another hidin' spot, I stick it under the floorboards. Dumbass!"

A few weeks earlier Squeezebox had approached a Colombian intermediary about buying coke.

"Look, Mateo, I got some spending cash. I can wash it, but it won't work sittin', doin' nothing. You're simpatico with the Sinaloa cartel, right?"

The hollow-cheeked Panamanian answered with a shake of his head.

"No, my friend. I know nothing about this."

Squeezebox answered with a disrespectful snort.

"Spare me, Mateo. Don't shit a shitter. I'll make it worth your while."

Mateo stared at him for a moment. "He who lives on illusions dies of disillusion."

"Enough with the Latino sayings, or whatever, Mateo. I got Serbian ones if you want. You make this happen or no?"

"My friend, even if I knew someone, this is a dangerous undertaking for you."

"Not if it comes out right. Me, I'll get a good return, and your friends, ah, you know how it goes? C'mon. Whatcha say?"

The Panamanian feigned ignorance but at last conceded. "I will put my ear to the ground, but I promise nothing."

"Yeah, yeah, whatever. So, listen, in theory, if you did know someone in Sinaloa, and if they did have coke and were willing to sell, how much does 2.1 mil get me?"

Mateo whistled.

"A lot of money. Well, in theory, I would guess you would have about 40 bricks, each weighing under two and a half pounds. And if they were available, it would have to be a fast cash-on-demand transaction."

Mateo had set up a meeting. An excited Squeezebox had delighted in the possibilities even as he fretted word might get back to the Russian Popovs or the Italian dagos, both big in drug trafficking. Now he knew he'd better contact Mateo. Fast. He'd have to do more than cancel the deal. The Colombians weren't nice guys. They'd need something to placate them, a goodwill gesture to say sorry for your troubles.

It came to him: he'd let them run a tab and give them access to his girls in the strip club. They could unload their product to the dagos, the Popovs, Hell's Angels, the Albanians, Puerto Ricans. The product never lacked for customers.

Squeezebox consoled himself that maybe he'd be all right. Still, it burned. Something like this had never happened. The fuck stole *his* money. He'd find him, but the hunt had to be done with utmost secrecy. If word of the snatch got out, his reputation would be in the toilet. Worse, if the boys at the Calabrian social club or the Russian baths heard what he'd intended to buy, his reputation might be the least of his problems.

Squeezebox got to his feet, still a bit light-headed. He set off in search of Mateo. He found him at his favorite coffee house and pulled him aside.

"I need you to call off the meeting with the Colombians."

The Panamanian tugged at his cuffs and rearranged his jacket from Squeezebox's rough handling.

"Why?"

Squeezebox threw up his hands. "All's I can say is I got blindsided by somethin'. I'll take care of it, but I need you to get ahold of these guys." He explained what he intended to offer by way of an apology.

"They won't be pleased, you wasting their time," Mateo said, "but your offer should help. We will see. Pray I catch them in a good mood. If not..." He finished with a what-can-you-do shrug. "You may have to do more."

"Whatever it takes."

"Oh, and one more thing. Never expect to do business with these men again. Ever."

"I hear you," a grateful Squeezebox said. "Sorry I burned my own damn bridge. Maybe best I keep clear of the whole narco thing. I'll see you get a little cash offering...you know, for your troubles."

"I appreciate the consideration," Mateo said. "Give me your number, and I'll call you back. It'll probably go fine. It's not like you pulled a fast one."

At home, Squeezebox's stomach burned, and he suffered mild nausea. He chewed on a couple of antacid tablets. Thinking about the Colombians' response and word getting out of his botched-up deal fired up his emotions.

He refused Anka's offer of food.

"A nice plate of kebabs in flat bread, Dusan? You know how much you like it."

He knew she meant well, but he still snapped at her.

"Hell's the matter with you? I'm not feeling well, and you're trying to shove food down me. Lemme alone."

He caught the hurt in her face but couldn't bring himself to apologize. Instead he stomped off into his lair and brooded. This brazen theft offended him on so many levels. Anka and the boys stayed clear of him the rest of the evening.

Squeezebox suffered in silence throughout the night. When he didn't wallow in self-pity, he indulged in the fantasy of how he would punish the snatcher.

In the morning, a fatigued Squeezebox ordered Boban and Marko to visit Stellan's flat and his ex-wife.

"I want info on this prick. Whatever you get. Everythin' useful. When you have it, come back to me."

A look Squeezebox didn't like passed between the men. He stormed across the room and pushed Marko in the chest. "You got a problem with somethin' I said?"

"No, boss."

"Then get the fuck out of here and do like I told ya."

The Panamanian phoned him with good news.

"Our friends have agreed to let the matter rest but expect to visit your club and enjoy all its amenities."

"Yeah, no problem," Squeezebox said, pleased at what he heard.

He visited Stringent. "You got pics, any pics of this Nieves guy?" he asked Paley.

Paley nodded. "Of course, of course. We have photos in our company album from last summer's picnic, and, of course, the Christmas party. I'll see what I can get you."

"I want a good one, head and shoulders."

"I'll get on it right away. If you'll wait..."

Stellan's disappearance raised considerable eyebrows elsewhere. Nina ranted, railed, and cursed his name. A sudden arrival of two men she swore were hoodlums did little to improve her disposition. They demanded to know everything about Stellan and where he might be.

Her voice shrill, she said, "Why? What's he done? Has he been gambling again? Is this why he disappeared? He's caused his family a lot of grief."

The shorter of the two stepped forward.

"For chrissake, get a grip, willya? Just answer our questions, and we'll be gone. Where's he gone? What can you tell us about finding him?"

She convinced them she didn't know anything. After they left she called her lawyer, her sisters, and spent hours on the phone, telling everyone "a couple of loan sharks came to break Stellan's legs or something." She offered various theories of where he might be hiding.

Kevin Uxley, too, wondered about Stellan's disappearance when the accountant failed to show for his grand jury date. When investigators couldn't find Nieves, Uxley filed a criminal contempt of court order. He sensed from the start Nieves knew something about Kovačević. The man's sudden disappearance only confirmed his suspicions.

Chapter 9

Pete Harris sat in the customer waiting room and looked out the large window to the garage. Two body shop painters removed the last of the masking tape and cleaned the windows of his truck. He liked the dark green color. Good choice. Definitely didn't scream, "Look at me."

He turned his mind back to creating his new persona. He'd rent a private mailbox for his Social Security card and anything he didn't want coming to his new address. Maybe he'd get one somewhere in Pennsylvania. It meant he'd have to travel to retrieve mail. An inconvenience but one worth the bother. Oh, and he'd better check to make sure the Social Security Administration would send mail to private mailboxes.

What else did he need to do? He'd read that you could disguise your appearance but never your fingerprints and rarely your walk. He'd work on changing how he walked. Clothes? Done. While they repainted his truck, he found a department store and traded in his old clothes for jeans, plaid shirts, sweatshirts, a black canvas winter coat, and a pair of leather waterproof boots. On the spur of the moment he treated himself to a baseball cap, convinced it went with owning a pickup.

He rubbed the beginning of his beard. Would he like it, get used to it? He guessed he would. He'd never had one but thought he'd keep it full but trimmed. What would Nina think of his new image?

The enormity of reinventing himself, deceiving, struck Pete again. Taking on and perfecting this new persona required considerable planning and even more lying than he imagined. For some, Pete knew lying required no effort. Not him, or not the man he used to be a long time ago. Bit by bit Stringent Accounting changed that. Deviating from the truth became a way of life at the firm. Clients lied on their tax filings. Accountants lied to keep their clients happy.

Hal never ordered the staff to help clients with tax fraud, but you didn't need to be a biblical Daniel to read the writing on the wall.

Every accountant succumbed to some audit frauds around bank deposits, cash expenditures, and offshore accounts. They all had the company's criminal tax attorneys on speed dial.

Payoffs for bending the rules came by bonuses at the end of each fiscal year.

In time, Pete accepted lies and bonuses as part of being a Stringent employee.

Welcome to Vermont, The Freedom and Unity State, the highway sign read.

Pete pulled off the interstate and into a pastoral countryside. He imagined its serenity during the summer, birds fluttering about and singing, the land abundant with tall grasses, the wind coursing through leafy trees.

A new sign drew his attention. *Warning. Do Not Pick Up Hitchhikers.* He caught his first glimpse of high, thick, granite walls guarded by four watchtowers. A prison. Two parallel, twelve-foot high chain link fences with coiled wire ran around its perimeter.

Convicts in thick, denim coats and warm caps cleared snow leading to the institution. Distinctive black and white, horizontal-striped cotton pants beneath the coats announced their status. A guard on horseback watched them.

Pete read a sign leading to the institution. *U.S. Department of Justice, Federal Bureau of Prisons. Franklin Stillwell Federal Correctional Facility.*

The place unnerved him. If he didn't know better, he'd have sworn this had to be an ominous sign. Here, he, Pete, drove past the prison with ill-gotten gains in his trunk. Could it mean something?

He scoffed at the notion. Yeah, it meant he got away with something and nothing more, a different voice argued. He'd boosted money. Without doubt the prison had been there long before he stole his money.

He ordered himself to think cause-and-effect and stop looking for cosmic signs.

Four miles past the prison, Pete arrived in Martine Maines. He allowed himself a leisurely drive around the town, pleased at what he saw. It had a nice feel to it. Picturesque, the kind of town they'd use in some romance movie. Nina ate up those kinds of flicks.

Pete vowed if they shot any movie around here, he'd make damn sure not to be around.

He parked the truck on Madison Avenue, put money in the meter, and walked a bit. He remembered his gait and tried to vary it. Half a block later he guessed he favored a splayed-foot style with his spine in an S-curve. Time to correct it, but it would require a lot of concentration and practice. He forced himself to keep his shoulders back and his stand less bent.

People smiled, nodded, and made eye contact when they passed. So different from Chicago. You could drop dead, and everyone would step over you to get to their destination.

He walked on, stopped at a newspaper box, and bought a copy of *The Martine Maines News-Standard*.

His stomach growled. The street had several fast food outlets, but he decided on a cozy little upscale café instead. Would it serve food he liked? Didn't matter. In his new incarnation, he'd pretty well have to change everything about his former self, including what he ate. His old self liked fried, fast foods and lots of carbs.

Pete stepped into the café with its blue, light-filtering curtain tier. A nice, comfy feel to it. Maple tables and chairs were scattered around the room laid out with checkerboard tablecloths.

Some customers looked up. Pete took a seat by the window. A middle-aged server with chemically damaged blonde hair with roots in serious need of attention approached.

"'Lo." She handed him a menu and smiled. "What would you like to drink?"

"Coffee to start."

"'Right, then. Be back in a jiff."

He studied the menu and made his selection—baked bean soup and a tomato, cheese, and alfalfa sandwich on whole wheat. Why not give it a try?

To his surprise, he liked both. He ate and pored over the apartments and condos listed in the newspaper. A fair choice for a college town. And the prices, he couldn't get over them. If you offered prices like these in Chicago, you'd have a bidding war in no time.

An ad caught his eye, a sublet in *Red Fox Run*. He shook his head. Who came up with these cutesy names? No matter. It sounded worth checking out. He read it again.

Furnished Tudor-style house in a nice neighborhood. Security system, stereo, flat screen TVs in bedroom and rec room, dishwasher. Dual garage with automatic door opener. Cleaning lady comes every second week. $1,120 a month. Deposit required. Call or visit Friedan Realty. Ask for Linzie Hayden.

Linzie? Another cutesy name. No matter. He'd find her and check out the place.

When his waitress returned with the bill, he asked how to get to Fifth Avenue.

"Whereabouts on Fifth, luv?"

He glanced at the address and told her.

"Not far," she said. "Three blocks over." She pointed. "You can walk it easily."

Linzie Hayden, maybe six or seven years older than he, turned out to be another dyed blonde but with a better hairdresser. She never got the memo about scent-free work environments. Pete didn't mind, inhaled deeply, and took in her bright red lipstick and long, manicured fingernails. A big rock on her finger put her off-limits.

He allowed himself another satisfying whiff of her expensive perfume. Man, what he wouldn't do to tear off her clothes. *She reminded him of a famous, iconic black-and-white photo of Marilyn Monroe in her rhinestone-encrusted dress, crooning "Happy*

Birthday, Mr. President," to JFK.

Nina, a size eight, once told Pete that Marilyn had been a size twelve. Nowadays women considered a size twelve fat. Maybe so, but from what Pete knew, Marilyn never lacked attention.

He returned his focus to the real estate agent and told her he'd come about the sublet on Red Fox Run.

Linzie studied Pete in his baseball cap, jeans, sweatshirt, and boots with a measure of suspicion. *She's got doubts about me.* He took in a lungful of air and said, "If I like the house, I'll be a good tenant. I'm quiet, neat, and am looking to buy my own place soon."

His answer did much to melt her reserve. She grew more animated and offered to show him the house now if he had the time.

"Sure. Should I follow you in my pickup?"

"Pickup?" She hesitated.

Pete read into her response. Careful to keep his voice modulated, he said, "Not all truck drivers are rednecks and deadbeats, if you're worried. Like I said, I need a place for now while I look around for something of my own. If this works out, I'll be glad to pay the first month and the deposit."

She shot him a self-conscious smile. "All right, then. My car's parked out front, the black SUV. I'll wait for you."

"Fine. I'll only be a couple of minutes."

He followed her large, upscale Detroit four-wheel drive vehicle. They pulled into the driveway of the house. To make conversation, Linzie asked general questions while she unlocked the front door. Pete spun his story as they stepped into the foyer. Years at Stringent taught him an important facet of manipulation. A fast way to get people on your side was to play to their sympathies.

"I've been hospitalized for a long time. It's hard to explain in a few sentences. Mood disorder. I'm not some Norman Bates slasher, if you're worried." He blinked several times and finished with a one-shoulder shrug.

Linzie stared at him for a long minute and then said, "I got you.

Say no more."

Encouraged, he carried on with his narrative.

"They had me on meds for quite a while, but now I'm off them for good. And I've been doing well with independent living. Even bought my own truck." He pointed outside. "As you saw. Anyway, last month I decided I wanted to live in a smaller town, so here I am. I inherited my mom's estate when she died. I'm thinking of going to college or maybe opening an art store. Probably college."

He stopped, looked at her, and held her gaze. Had he blabbed too much? No going back.

"You'll keep this information confidential, I hope. I don't want people thinking they have a lunatic in their midst."

He hoped his sad tale would dissuade her from asking for a credit check.

"Oh, don't give it another thought," she said. "My lips are sealed. You have to in this business. And we all struggle, don't we? I know someone who had a nervous breakdown."

She clapped her hands lightly. "Let's tour the house. If you like it, we can come back to the office and do the little bit of paperwork, and you'll be all set."

The house sat at the end of a cul-de-sac, hidden from its neighbors by a grove. The owners had avant-garde taste in painting and sculptures. Not what Pete liked, but he could live with it. He did, however, like the back deck facing a ravine.

Linzie told him the house had earlier been sublet to three graduate students, but they ran into personal difficulties. "I shouldn't say this, but it's been empty for five weeks. Professor Mullen and his wife will be returning in six months. They'd be really pleased to know someone responsible is in it and taking care of it."

Pete followed Linzie while she took him through the house.

"I like it," he said when they finished the tour. "When can I take it?"

"You want to take it? Um. Sure. Anytime. It is very nice. The street's quiet. Everyone works except Mrs. Kendell at the top of the street. Well, no, her, too...sort of. She's a volunteer at the hospital." She paused. "And you definitely want to rent this house?"

"Uh-huh."

"Well, then, all we need to do is a little paperwork, and you can move in. I need you to cover the rest of this month and lay down a one-month deposit. So, how do you want to pay?"

Ready for the question, Pete said, "Let me go to the bank and set up an account. I should be able to get back to your office, in, say, half an hour."

"All right. I'll meet you back in the office."

"Sounds good."

Cash in his pocket, Pete returned, pleased Linzie had accepted his reason for not having a credit card. Instead, she took copies of his DMV, birth certificate, and Social Security information.

"We do credit checks," she said in a soft, hushed tone, "but you know what? In your case, given what you've told me, I'll leave it. Please don't disappoint me."

"I won't, I promise. You'll find me to be a good tenant."

"Then we've nothing to worry about, right?"

"Exactly."

Three hours later Pete backed his pickup into the garage of his temporary home and wandered around the house. The owners liked the minimalist look, Scandinavian blond furniture with lots of bright, big, throw pillows. They also had an extensive music library of vinyl disks and CDs. Their taste ran largely to what Pete would call crossover jazz, but they had a selection of other kinds of music, too.

Their bookcase impressed him with the selections. "If I get snowed in," he muttered, "I won't have trouble keeping busy."

His detailed inspection of the upstairs finished, Pete went down into the basement to a rec room. A small, unfinished room ran off it. He opened the door to the musty room, entered, and found a light switch. A dim, naked bulb revealed a furnace and an adjoining pile of lumber and drywall pieces cast in a loose pile. Water stains marked the concrete blocks. Cobwebs told him few came into this room. Perfect. No one would show any interest here.

Pete retrieved everything from his truck. He took the cases to the basement, then arranged and rearranged the lumber and drywall over the cases until he believed they wouldn't cause suspicion.

"Have to do," he murmured. A final look and Pete turned off the light switch. His hiding place might not be any improvement over an old man hiding savings under a mattress. He'd need a safer home for his money. The sooner, the better.

Chapter 10

Squeezebox couldn't shake off the dark, nervous depression which arrived like an uninvited house guest that refused to leave. Worse yet, it brought along dreaded anxiety. Lately, he'd had difficulty catching his breath. Not always but often enough. He smoked, true, but medical tests gave no indication of respiratory failure.

His doctor, Phil Metzger, who didn't look old enough to drive, though he'd graduated three years ago from a prestigious medical school, said, "Dusan, are you familiar with the term psychosomatic illness?"

"'Course," Squeezebox conceded. 'Cause I didn't go to some fancy school don't mean I can't read and pay attention. It's one of them...whatchamacallit...mind-body things. You sayin' I'm gettin', what—wingy?"

Metzger allowed himself a quick look at the wall. He'd bought the practice from old Stanley Calloway. He liked most of his patients. Most, but not all, and definitely not Dusan Kovačević.

"Well, yes, a 'mind-body' connection but in this case one that doesn't have an organic base. Which is why we need to consider other options. You've also complained about tossing around at nights and bouts of chills."

"Yeah, and I get where my heart's runnin' a hundred miles an hour. Then it goes away, but I'm all wired up for another spell to jump me."

"You're making my point," Metzger said, "which is why I brought up the psychosomatic angle. You're having panic attacks. I can prescribe tranquilizers. For now. Pills won't solve what's troubling you. What you need is something more intense, specialized."

"Like what?"

"A referral to a psychiatrist."

Squeezebox swiped the air with his hand. "A head shrink? Nah, forget it. Gimme the tranquilizers."

Metzger studied his patient. "If you insist. I'll monitor your condition. If you're still suffering, let me know, and we'll talk about the other thing some more."

The tranquilizers helped but failed to give Squeezebox his old sense of control. He dreaded his life and longed for the Dusan of old when nothing much rattled him.

He returned to Metzger.

"Okay, maybe you're right. Make the appointment for the shrink." He blew out his cheeks. "Can't believe I'm asking for this."

Metzger ignored the last comment. "I'll have Colleen set up an appointment and call you."

Gordon Staggert took a moment to learn how to pronounce his patient's name. He stroked his thick salt-and-pepper beard and pushed a finger on the bridge of his eyeglasses.

"So, what's on your mind…Mr. Kovačević?"

Squeezebox sat in one of the two leather chairs opposite the psychiatrist. His nervous eyes moved from the parquet floor to Staggert.

"Somethin's gotta hold on me and ain't lettin' go. I feel like I'm comin' apart." He stopped, licked his dry lips, and said, "This is, like, confidential, right, what I tell you?'

"Yes, unless you're at serious risk to yourself or others."

"Me?" Squeezebox shook his head. "Nah, but lately I bin wonderin' if I'm losing it. My mind, I mean."

"All right, tell me about it."

"Where do you want me to start?"

"Do you know Lewis Carroll?"

"What's this Carol got to do with what I'm telling you?"

Staggert pushed the frames up to the bridge of his nose.

"Nothing, other than a quote from him. 'Begin at the beginning and go on until you come to the end, and then stop.' The same advice for you. Start at the beginning."

"Oh, okay."

Squeezebox took a deep breath and started his tale of woe. "Um, somebody stole money from me. A lot of it. I ain't goin' into details. I can't go to the cops, neither. Sooner or later I'm gonna get this guy, but it's eating me, what he done."

Staggert raised an eyebrow.

"I see. And it's important to you?"

Squeezebox's voice rose with impatience.

"You serious or not listenin'? Yeah, it's important. Whaddaya think? I'll say it slow. He...took...my...fuckin' money. Mine. Nobody's ever done somethin' like that before. Nobody. And this jerkoff is laughing his ass off, thinking he fucked me over." A half-shrug followed. "I got nobody to talk to about this, so you're it."

As Staggert's patient continued, a profile emerged. Staggert jotted onto his pad: *Patient suffers from ulcers. By his own admission he feels awkward in larger social situations. He copes with the use of drink and narcotics.*

Squeezebox carried on with his story. Staggert wrote *gelotophobia* on his notepad and placed a question mark beside it. *Patient expresses a pathological fear of being laughed at. Says he's the victim of theft. What worries him more is the thief mocking him.*

Staggert stopped writing and looked up at his patient.

"So, **Mr. Kovačević**, let's spend the rest of this session talking about the underlying meaning of the stolen money and your overriding desire to seek revenge."

"Yeah, fine."

"Is it safe to say you've personalized this whole matter too much?"

Squeezebox made a face.

"You fuckin' serious? They pay you to ask these kinds of shit questions? How'm I supposed to *not* 'personalize' this? You would—anyone would—if you found someone walked off with your money and laughed at you."

Staggert waited until Squeezebox finished.

"I'm not discounting your right to feel bad, but you cannot seem to let this go. There is, I think, a more important issue."

"And that is?"

"That you've somehow lost face."

Squeezebox mimicked the statement. "Somehow lost face? How's about speakin' English?"

Staggert allowed himself a long, labored breath over this irritating man. He rebuked himself for his unprofessionalism. *You're engaging in countertransference. Stop it. Control yourself and your voice.*

"Losing face, Mr. Kovačević, means you feel you've lost the respect of others, maybe somehow had your reputation damaged. We need to work on your fear of being laughed at. If you conquer it, all this won't matter so much."

The two men considered each other. Staggert pulled air into his lungs.

"And then we come to the matter of the police. You won't go to them. Filing a complaint with the police is a normal response to an act of criminality." He held Squeezebox's gaze for a moment, looked away, wrote on his pad, and raised his eyes.

"Setting aside your refusal to bring the police into this matter, is it safe to assume you reserve the right to mete out punishment when you catch this person? I'm presuming it is a man."

"Fuckin' A."

Staggert ignored the profanity.

"Can you understand, Mr. Kovačević, such an act is taking something personally to a whole different level. Unless you catch this person, there'll never be the opportunity to move on, to learn from the experience. You're feeling humiliated, and the greater you feel it, the greater the need for revenge. But what you may not realize is this thief has a hold on you, whether he knows it or not, whether he cares or not."

Squeezebox squinted at the psychiatrist. "You saying I should lay off and let him get away with it?"

Calm voice, Staggert reminded himself. *Keep your voice calm.*

"No. I'm saying you have other choices, choices not involving violence. We need to look at those. You're experiencing panic attacks. Those attacks are about your feelings of losing control. If you reframe all this, look at it differently, maybe use other strategies, you have a good chance of bringing the attacks under control."

He glanced at the wall clock. "Our time is up. Do you want to make another appointment?"

Squeezebox hesitated. "I don't know. No. I guess. Wait. Yeah, all right."

Staggert got to his feet. "My secretary will make another appointment for you. We'll continue next time."

Squeezebox offered a nod, opened the door of Staggert's office, and approached the psychiatrist's secretary. A new appointment made, he left Staggert's suite, stepped into the elevator, then exited through the lobby of the Medical Arts Building. Had his meeting been successful? Maybe. He didn't feel so bugged-out, but didn't like the shrink getting his number right away. Who wouldn't worry about being laughed at after being played and ripped off? Whenever Squeezebox dwelled on the theft, he became nearly incapacitated. All because of that shit, the accountant. He'd for sure find him and make his last few hours a holy hell.

He started the car and headed for *Azbuka Kafe* to spend some time with the boys. Coffee, laughs, and bullshit might help take his mind off his troubles. From there he'd call Stephanie, tell her to wear the pink baby doll, and get ready for a visit. He hadn't felt the itch between his legs in a while.

The promise of the day cheered him. On his way to Little Serbia, Squeezebox reviewed his progress in finding Nieves. Boban and Marko hadn't come up with anything beyond scaring the hell out of Nieves' wife. Muscle mass, those two. Muscles and empty heads. He should have gone with a pro right from the start.

"I've wasted too much fuckin' time with those two," he said out loud. All right, he'd put out feelers for a private dick and go from there.

Pigeon-chested Myles Colloros looked at the client opposite his desk. His old police suspicions kicked in. He knew of Kovačević and his reputation. He'd have to be careful around this thick-bodied man. Funny, both men on opposite sides of the law now found themselves with a potential business proposition.

He combed his thick hair with his fingers, looked at his notes and then over to his client. "So, you're interested in finding this Stellan Nieves?"

"You got it. The faster the better. It looks like he up and split for Florida, but it don't matter. He's gone. I need him ungone."

Why not just get rid of the guy? Colloros asked himself. He could just say, "Sorry, but too busy to give the case the time and attention it deserves." Maybe recommend someone else to him. Then again, they'd entered early winter, a slow time of year, and guessed Kovačević would probably pay well and in cash.

He made up his mind to take the work.

"Tell me what you've done so far in locating..." He looked down at his pad and across his desk at the man "...this Stellan Nieves."

"Everything," his client said. "Poof, the guy takes a powder. I checked his work, his home, you name it. I mean, how's he just vanish into thin air? Like one of them magician acts. All's I wanna do is find him and talk to the guy."

And what else? Colloros silently asked, but pushed the thought aside.

"Okay, so from what you're saying there are no leads. We'll have to start from scratch. Nobody disappears forever. We may have to hire a skip tracer. It'll cost you more."

"Yeah, fine, I guess, but what are those things you said?"

"Skip tracers? Investigators who find missing people but do it electronically. Everybody leaves some kind of footprint these days. So, we hire a skip tracer and scour the Internet, social media."

"If it's that easy, why'd I need you? I already had people doin' that."

Don't argue with him, Colloros told himself.

"I won't challenge that. But the kind of person I'd hire is a specialist and looks at things ordinary people might not notice. They're very detailed and in my experience very helpful."

He looked across his desk. Kovačević stared at him through narrowed eyes that hid his pupils. *Best not to do an eye lock*, Colloros thought. He looked away for a second and back at his potential client.

"I'm a foot slogger, Mr. Kovačević. In this kind of work you need a foot slogger like me to put pieces together. Some of the pieces may come from skip tracers who can pinpoint where to look. It doesn't guarantee anything, but it's a helpful tool." He stopped, drew in a breath of air, and said, "Do you want me to take your case?"

Kovačević's eyes widened, and he nodded. "Yeah, go ahead with it, and use a skip tracer if you gotta."

Colloros lightly slapped the desk with the palm of his hand. "Then let's do it. All right. I'll need a retainer, and then Stella outside will go through our itemized charges with you."

"Okay."

Colloros leaned forward.

"Now, before you leave, I want you to know there's the chance we may not find this Nieves in spite of doing our best. Success depends on how well he's put together his plans to stay hidden."

"I got no choice, I guess. Just do your damn best."

Colloros soon developed a grudging admiration for his prey. The man had vanished for the better part of three weeks.

In Colloros' experience most runners didn't last more than five weeks and left traces the first two. They made calls back home, to friends, or sent emails from libraries. The majority grew homesick, ran out of dough, or both. Not Nieves. He remained silent.

Colloros contacted Nieves' wife. She proved no help, went practically apoplectic at the mention of her husband's name, and wanted him dead.

Nieves' mother and sister refused to cooperate with Colloros. The accountant's former employer, Stringent, couldn't shed any light on Nieves' disappearance.

With little left to go on, Colloros hoped the Internet, Social Security, and Nieves' credit cards would lead him to his target.

Nieves' credit card use took Colloros to the car rental and, in turn, to Fort Wayne. Encouraged, Colloros arrived to find Nieves had dropped off the rental. The young woman recognized Nieves when the PI showed her a picture.

"He left the car for us. I don't have anything else I can tell you."

She shook her head when Colloros asked if she might know how Nieves left. "No, sorry. Can't help you."

The PI located Nieves' motel. A few dollars slipped into willing hands allowed him to review the CCTV video. He found grainy pictures of Nieves in the lobby, taking a moment to stare at the guest computer desk before he moved on. It gave Colloros a possible lead.

He itemized what he knew about Nieves' stay at the motel: the man arrived, ate, and slept, but nothing more.

The PI visited the three libraries and showed Nieves' picture around. Had anyone recognized or remembered this man near the computers?

No one had.

Bus and rail stations—needles in haystacks and busy all the time. Still, Colloros had a job to do, so he checked them out but came up empty. The airport—no point bothering. His skip tracer hadn't found the slightest evidence of Nieves stepping onto the property. Nowadays it was nearly impossible to hide one's self at an airport.

"You're damn sure not making this easy," Colloros muttered to his unseen prey. "No one remembers much of you or seeing you."

Two likely possibilities existed: Nieves hid out somewhere in Fort Wayne, or Nieves had fled for parts unknown. Colloros favored the first possibility. An old joke came to him: I spent a week one afternoon in Fort Wayne. Okay, so he'd cross the city off as a hiding place. That left blowing town, but how would Nieves get out? Not public transit. That much was certain. The law of probability suggested Nieves split in a car. If so, that meant new or used.

Colloros visited all car lots and flashed a phony police badge. No one matching Nieves' description or with his name bought a car in Fort Wayne.

The PI next spent a day and a half calling private ads and used car dealers, No luck. All right. Unless Nieves stole a vehicle, which was highly unlikely, how would he get wheels? Colloros hit on a theory: what if the man bought a car from a chop shop?

The following day Colloros visited police headquarters, flashed his PI badge, and asked to speak to anyone in the Auto Theft squad. Ten minutes later he met a craggy-faced detective with a buzz cut who stepped out into the lobby and presented himself as Sergeant Miles Duggan.

Colloros rose, smiled, stuck out his hand, introduced himself, and let it be known he'd retired from the CPD.

"All right," Duggan said. "Always good to meet another member of the Blue. C'mon back to my desk, and we'll talk a bit more." He waved to the clerk behind the Plexiglas. A metallic buzz sounded, and the two men entered the station.

They got on well. Colloros told him of his search and theory. "So, I'd be grateful if you could save some time and give me the usual subjects you suspect are chop shops."

"I can," Duggan said, "but we never had this conversation, right?"

"What conversation?"

"Exactly."

Colloros returned to the street an hour later, ready to visit every garage suspected of dismantling and selling car parts. He hoped his cop instinct would lead him to something.

His third visit brought him to Baudean Garage.

He walked through the doorway of the repair shop. A tall

mechanic looked up from under the hood of a car. He frowned, stepped around the car, and approached.

"Yeah?"

Colloros held out a picture of Nieves. "I'm looking for this man. You wouldn't happen to have seen him, would you?"

The mechanic didn't bother to look down. "No."

"You didn't even look," Colloros said.

"S'right, and if I did it would still be no. You a cop?"

"No. Private investigator."

"Then go investigate somewhere else. What do we look like, the lost and found? Unless this guy's a customer here, I wouldn't know him."

"I thought maybe he might have bought a used car here."

"You thought wrong. You see a sign outside that says *We Sell Cars*?"

"No. Sorry for wasting your time."

"Yeah, you did."

The guy was lying. Something about this guy set him on edge. Still, he had no power or influence. So he gave a curt nod, spun on his heel, and left the garage.

As he suspected, none of the body shops offered any help. All insisted they'd never met anyone named Stellan Nieves.

Colloros returned to Chicago empty-handed. He had nothing on Nieves and no further leads to follow. Whatever the man did to Kovačević, it had to be bad. Everything told the PI Nieves would never return.

"Hat's off to you, buddy," Colloros said to his invisible target. "You hid your tracks well." No matter. He'd submit his bill, glad to be done with the case.

Chapter 11

Pete opened an account at *Folsom-Agee Savings and Loan*. Over the next two days he deposited under $10,000 on each visit, aware the bank wasn't obligated to report him. While large deposits weren't illegal, they would most certainly come to the attention of the IRS and trigger a visit from the cops.

He continued to visit the bank over the next few weeks. He also bought a high-end laptop with a sophisticated firewall and spyware app. He paid for a top-of-the-line VPN server to hide his IP address whenever he needed to send out anything in the name of Pete Harris.

Secure in the knowledge his laptop wouldn't betray his location, Pete initiated the second stage of hiding his money. He searched the Internet and found what he wanted in Montpelier—a registered financial agent to help him set up an offshore shell corporation.

Two intensive days of emails, which included electronic payments, one with a legitimate lawyer and the other for a proxy director of a bogus board of directors, resulted in the creation of a fake corporation.

"Here goes," Pete said, and placed a gym bag with $50,000 onto the passenger seat of his truck. He drove to Montpelier to meet Angus Beardsley, the agent responsible for setting up the shell company.

Newcomb Investments occupied a suite on the second floor of a professional building. Pete parked his truck in a municipal lot. He scanned the lot for anything suggesting challenge or danger. A few minutes later he sat in the reception area and made small talk with a friendly receptionist.

Beardsley arrived and introduced himself. If the late middle-aged agent seemed surprised at Pete in jeans with a closely-trimmed beard and gym bag, he didn't let on. He himself wore an expensive suit with a silk tie, and soft, tasseled loafers.

"Nice to meet you, Mr. Harris," he said, a wide smile on his face.

Pete rose and accepted Beardsley's extended hand.

"Why don't we go to my office and look at your portfolio, Mr. Harris?"

They spent a minute on idle talk before Beardsley cleared his throat and in a smooth and diplomatic way steered the conversation to the purpose of their meeting. He began with how had Pete heard about Newcomb? Who recommended him? Did he work for or know anyone in either state or federal law enforcement, or the SEC?

The questions felt like a mild interrogation to Pete but ended with, "We have to be careful, Mr. Harris, you understand? And I must go on record to say this conversation cannot be recorded without my permission."

Pete answered, "I understand what you're getting at, believe me. I don't have any recording device on me."

"Good. It's necessary for me to ask. We have to be thorough in knowing our new clients."

"Makes sense. The door swings both ways."

"Precisely, and thank you."

It took the better part of ninety minutes for Beardsley to complete federal and state paperwork related to Pete's business. The investment broker looked across his desk. "So, Mr. Harris. Now, let's talk about what comes next."

"Yes, money. I have a lot of it, cash that I need to deposit."

If anything in Pete's statement raised concern with Beardsley, it failed to register on the man's face. His gaze held Pete's. "Very well, but before we get into the mechanics of it, I have to go over a few matters with you."

"Okay."

Beardsley set down his pen. "I'll begin by talking about our fees. Then I'll explain how we transfer your money to an offshore account in your corporation's name." He began his talk. A few minutes later he said, "Do you have any questions?"

"No, I'm good."

"Well, then, let's discuss your money." Beardsley swung his

monitor to face Pete. "I'll go through this with you and show you what happens when you hit 'send'." He craned his neck to look at the monitor and explained how funds "fan out" before arriving in Bermuda. He looked from the screen to Pete. "Are you with me, Mr. Harris?"

"Sure am."

"Okay, then. Now I'll show you how to log into your account once we've set it up, and how to deposit or withdraw funds."

"Good."

Beardsley answered with a fast nod. "So, let's go over it again, just in case, right?"

"Right."

The lesson finished, Beardsley shifted in his chair.

"Are you comfortable with everything so far?"

"I am."

"In that case, let's make your first deposit. I'm assuming you have the money with you." He pointed to the gym bag in Pete's lap.

Pete patted the bag. "I'm ready. Fifty thousand. Cash, of course."

"Certainly. I do need to verify it."

"No problem."

Beardsley counted the money and issued Pete a receipt. "So, now we send off your money." He typed in the amount in US funds and hit the send button. Both men watched.

Beardsley looked up from his keyboard.

"Your money is now on its way to Bermuda, where it will collect interest. I'll write down your passkey number. Like I said before, you can check anytime, either from your phone or computer, what's going on in your account. And if you lose or forget the number, here's how to retrieve it." He explained the procedure.

Pete listened and said, "One last question."

"Sure. Go ahead."

"Well, you saw I had a great deal of cash." Pete stopped, inhaled, and exhaled. "I'll be bringing more. It might be too great of a temptation for someone if they know I'm carrying it." He tossed a shrug. "I have to be careful."

Beardsley raised his chin.

"I get what you're saying, and no need to apologize. Let me put it this way. You're a customer. If you're worried about someone in our organization robbing you, please know that is the worst kind of publicity for us."

The assurance did much to settle Pete's concerns. His empty gym bag in hand, he left *Newcomb Investments*, pleased the first of his funds now sat in a tropical paradise. He couldn't believe he'd pulled this off.

"I'm a millionaire," he whispered. "I…am…a…millionaire. What would the Mullens think if they knew they had so much cash in their basement?"

Pete forced himself to think of the practicalities of his wealth. He'd have to make the money work harder, get a better rate of return. Bit by bit he'd bring it stateside without drawing attention. Long-term strategies of mixing real estate investments with safe-dividend blue chip stocks and other investments would give him an expanded portfolio and ensure he'd stay rich.

Linzie Hayden proved an unexpected and pleasant surprise. Pete hadn't imagined he'd see much of her, let alone anything. She surprised him and popped in from time to time. At first, he assumed she came around to check up on him, but little by little he realized she liked him.

"So," she said, one noon when he prepared a sandwich for himself, "are you liking your home and our community?"

Her perfume… In the small kitchen she stood close enough for her perfume to fill his nostrils. It had been so long since he'd last enjoyed the pleasures of a woman. His hand, holding the knife for the mayonnaise spread, shook. He turned his body away from her and concentrated on his sandwich.

"I am, yes, and nice of you to drop by again."

"No problem. Consider me your local, one-woman welcoming committee." She stepped closer.

The words came out before he realized it. "Are you...trying to seduce me?"

She stepped closer yet and pushed plump breasts against him. Tilting her head slightly, she aligned her lips with his and gave him a seductive smile. Her sweet, warm breath filled his nostrils.

"Is it working?"

Pete set down the knife and circled her waist. *Take your time, take your time.* In the bedroom her tongue probed his mouth while he undid her silk blouse. *Go slow.* He stared in a greedy manner at her charms encased in a pink, lacy bra.

Their passion at last spent, Linzie curled up against him.

Pete considered his seductress. When had she discovered the hold she had over men? Had to be at least in or before middle school. And for sure by high school all kinds of guys got into punch-outs over her.

Dancing fingers under the sheet took his mind off his rumination.

After their second bout of lovemaking, Linzie said, "You must think me awful, doing this."

Not at all. Pete couldn't believe his good luck and would forever be grateful. He kissed her. "Are you serious? I'm still in shock you gave yourself to me. If I had a poetic heart, I'd write a sonnet to you. If I could compose, I'd craft a symphony in your honor."

"Aw, how sweet. But I don't sleep around, you know."

He did not intend to challenge the claim. Whether she did or not, he didn't care. He nuzzled into her neck. She giggled and pushed him away.

"So, tell me more about yourself, Peter." She liked using his formal name.

Here we go, Pete thought. Weeks of rehearsing his story, examining possible holes in it, the time arrived to offer his fictional account.

"That's dreadful," Linzie said when he finished. "So, now you're alone in the world?"

"Yeah, after my mom died."

Linzie kissed him. "You might not think it much consolation, but at least you're not destitute or homeless. Thanks to your mother, you've got money to make life easier. I'm on the board of a women's shelter, and I see what poor people are up against every day. Especially women."

"You're right. I do count my blessings."

She fell silent. "So, can I ask you, how come you drive a pickup?"

"Not sure. The idea just appealed to me. Maybe I wanted to be some kind of macho guy."

She giggled.

"You, the man who talked about opening an art store...uh, no. You're manly, and you sure proved it this afternoon. Manly, but definitely not macho. Are you still going to open your store?"

"Uh, no. I thought about it some more and figured it's not the best fit for me. I've got an appointment with the Dean of Admissions Tuesday. I checked, and can apply as a mature student."

"Really? Good for you. You'll like Monty. I went there. What will you take?"

"Don't know yet. Something to challenge me."

Chapter 12

Squeezebox pushed away the remains of his *pljeskavica* (meat patty), took a pull from his beer, set it down, and let out a burp.

"Almost makes me think it's kinda racism, Anka. Against Serbs. I mean, what else explains the DA's hard-on for me? He's been after me from forever. Now he's gonna stick me fronta this grand jury for bein' 'a criminal organization and profiting from those activities.'"

He let loose a derisive snort. "Yeah, like *I'm* a criminal organization. Why'nt he go after the Wops, the Popovs, and the 'Ricans? There's your big criminal organizations, but nooo, he's gotta come for me."

Anka looked at her husband, afraid to speak her mind.

"What's Mr. Ludwigsburg's strategy?"

"Him? Says they got a good case against me, and he's gonna 'put up a vigorous defense.' He better. I pay him enough. Accordin' to him, the DA's lined up those two rat-finks who worked for me. Ludwigsburg's guessin' the DA's laid serious time in front of them and offered them cheese to squeal. Shoulda never trusted them. I treated *them* good, and…"

Squeezebox gave a slow shake of his head. "No honor anymore, Anka." He pressed his eyelids with thumb and forefinger. "I gotta bad feelin' about this. Like everything's 'bout to come crashing down. Lookin' at twenty years on each of them charges. An' the feds froze alla my businesses. If Ludwigsburg messes up, I go up river. The only way I'm gonna leave prison is feet first in a cheap box."

His wife stretched her arm and patted his hand.

"Don't give up hope yet. Have faith. I pray to St. Sava every day for you. For us. Besides, didn't you say Mr. Ludwigsburg thinks he can get a judge to release the party stores and the electrical contracting from, um…what do they call it…seizure? It has to count for something."

Squeezebox drew in a lungful of air and leaned across the table.

"Listen, Anka, I better go over how to get at the offshore money again."

She shook her head.

"No. I got it. The kids and I will be fine. The government hasn't won yet. You're not in jail, so don't give up. Now, I have a question."

"Yeah."

"The money. There's a lot of money, Dusan?"

"'Uh-huh. I'm what they call a 'prudent investor.' What're you gettin' at?"

"Nothing, other than I didn't know we had so much money."

"I told you. We ain't hurtin'. It's all you gotta know. If I'm gone and you got questions, go talk to this Barry Pressfield at *Thorn and Company*. He'll tell you what's what."

"Yes, but…"

"No yes-but. He'll help."

Anka peered into her husband's face. "All right. Try not to worry. Everything might come out fine."

"Thanks, Anka. You're a good wife. I don't deserve you."

Squeezebox's panic attacks returned in force. Being handcuffed in broad daylight, with his neighbors watching, and pushed into a police cruiser, heightened the attacks.

Staggert had to up Squeezebox's antidepressants.

Colloros hadn't improved Squeezebox's state of mind, either. The PI had invited him down to his office for an update and shared his findings.

"What the fuck you mean you can't find Nieves?" Squeezebox said, his face flushed. "I'm payin' you good money to find him."

"You are, Mr. Kovačević, but I warned you from the start we can't pull rabbits out of hats, can't do the impossible. We've done everything we can to find this Stellan Nieves. He rented a car, drove to Fort Wayne, and from there his trail went cold."

Squeezebox stared at the floor. "Fuck!"

Faint music from the outer office reached them. Both men remained silent until Colloros said, "Statistically, Nieves will surface somewhere. In time. For now, he's dropped off the grid." He followed with an apologetic shrug. "Sorry." The apology delivered, he said, "Do you want us to keep the file open?"

A resigned Squeezebox took in a few deep breaths. "Yeah. No. Okay, look, forget it. And sorry for gettin' worked up. Like you said, you can't do magic."

Shoulders hunched, Squeezebox trundled to his car. He felt like shit. Maybe he should visit Stephanie. He dismissed the idea as fast as it came, certain he didn't have the enthusiasm to bang her. So, what did he need? Comfort, solace—the emotional kind, not skinny thighs and big tits. Stephanie wouldn't have clue one how to listen and give support. Anka, now she could and did do both well. But wives were supposed to, weren't they? He didn't discount her help, but... But what? He couldn't open up to her. He'd never done it, so why start now?

All right, not Anka. Who then, his shrink? Uh-uh. Squeezebox didn't know if he really connected with the guy. The shrink sat like a bump on a log and wrote on his notepad or gave him advice he couldn't use. "Goddamn pill pusher is what he is," Squeezebox mumbled to himself when he pulled out of Colloros' parking lot. "Only diff between him and a drug pusher is a license."

Despite his scorn, Squeezebox kept his next appointment.

All right, Mr. Kovačević, what would you like to talk about today?"

Squeezebox's eyebrows pulled together.

"Fuckin' amazin'. You ask me the same question alla time. What'ya think I wanna talk about? My panic attacks is what. You know, doc, for a headshrink you ain't addin' nothin' to my day."

Staggert set down his pen. "What do you mean?"

"What do I mean? I'll tell you what I mean. How's 'bout beginnin' with my appointments? I'm supposed to get fifty minutes, but I never get 'em. Lucky if I get forty. Either the guy or broad before me is runnin' extra long, or you're hustlin' me outta my paid time. And in my sessions, you ain't listenin' half the time. I don't know where your head's at but for sure not in this room. You out on some boat on the lake dreamin'"bout bangin' some broad or somethin'?"

Staggert raised his eyebrows. "I've really annoyed you."

"Fuckin' A. I'm either thinkin' I'm borin' you, or when you do pay attention, all's you got is a goddamn sermon. If I wanted one, I'd go to church or make an appointment to see my priest. For free."

"You don't think these sessions have helped?"

Squeezebox offered a dismissive wave of his hand. "Some, but not much."

"You are definitely not happy with me."

"Duh. You think? I'll say it again. I ain't gettin' a whole lot outta these sessions. Sometimes you act like the people who come to see you don't count. You can be a douchebag. Just sayin'."

Staggert's eyes widened. He pulled air into his lungs and uncrossed his legs.

"Thank you for telling me, Mr. Kovačević. I apologize if I've offended you. I understand you believe you are deserving of more and better respect. I'll address those concerns at once. Now, what can I do to develop a better doctor-patient relationship, to no longer be 'a douchebag'?"

"I want you to pay attention, to listen like it means somethin', like I mean somethin'. And lay off the goddamn preachin'."

Squeezebox slid behind the wheel of his car, his mind agitated. He needed to feel better. What would it take? Azbuka Kafe. Yeah, he'd go shoot the shit with some of the boys.

He pulled into the busy traffic.

Several coffees and more slivovitz later, Squeezebox's mouth ran more than he intended. He didn't catch the looks between a few of the men.

"I better go," he said at last.

Someone asked if he shouldn't drive. He waved off the concern. "Nah. I'll be fine."

The following morning Squeezebox ate breakfast with Anka. She announced she had to leave for her morning coffee with her cousin, Rose.

"I know you've got lots of time on your hands, Dusan. You're welcome to come, but it's girl talk, and you'd be bored."

"Don't worry. I got things to do. See you at supper."

He kissed her and went off in search of his car keys.

He pulled onto the small street and thought he'd drive by the warehouse. *No*, a voice within cautioned. *Stay clear of there. You'll only get yourself more worked-up to see it locked.*

Okay, he'd keep away from the warehouse. Where, then? Stephanie. Why not? Skinny thighs and big tits appealed to him today. Afterwards, he'd take her out and talk to her about her future. He might beat his rap in court, but in his pessimistic heart, he doubted it. Stephanie, he'd leave her the equivalent of a year's salary. If she wanted, she could go back to stripping.

His thoughts turned to Nieves. He'd put so much hope in finding the accountant. The memory of the theft caused his pulse to race. Bad enough the theft, but the weasel laughing at him, mocking him brought on another panic attack.

Squeezebox drove into a strip mall, turned off the engine, popped a pill, and waited to calm down. He pulled his seat back and closed his eyes. His own damn fault thinking about Nieves. Staggert had warned him about this. When would he learn not to make things worse? Every time he recalled the theft, he'd get royally pissed off and head for another attack.

Ten minutes later, careful to stay clear of thoughts of Nieves, Squeezebox drove to Stephanie's.

The whispers started.

Squeezebox heard them on the street and in the remaining haunts he visited. Word had it that he, a man who'd earned respect and fear on the streets of Chicago, got played by a lousy pencil pusher. The amount taken varied from place to place, but the essence of the story didn't change much.

Squeezebox knew he couldn't stop the talk. If he tried, he'd only make things worse. People believed what they wanted to believe.

Who started these rumors? Stephanie? No. Squeezebox didn't do pillow talk with her. When they weren't fucking, they watched movies or played video games. Who else? Anka? Forget it. She'd take a bullet for him. Who, then? Staggert came to mind. Squeezebox ruled him out. He hadn't given him any details.

The truth revealed itself. Azbuka Kafe. Squeezebox thought back on his last visit, his need to unburden himself. He squeezed his eyes shut in horror. Him. It had been him all along. He berated himself for not keeping his big yap shut. Now look.

The gossip wouldn't die. Squeezebox knew it stood an excellent chance of following him into the joint. Jackals would come nipping at his territory. He'd no longer carry the image of the tough guy he'd projected.

Made numb by this insight, Squeezebox headed home. Nothing else to do and nowhere else to go. Mouth open, Squeezebox sat behind the wheel. Tears rolled down his cheeks. He did nothing to stop them, nor did he swipe at them. In a brief few hours, convinced he'd been among friends, he, Dusan Kovačević, had permanently damaged his own reputation. Too much slivovitz and too much careless talk.

His court date arrived.

Squeezebox couldn't get over the packed courtroom. He leaned toward Ludwigsburg and whispered, "Lookit all these people. What's up? I'm not John Gotti."

"No," Ludwigsburg said, "but the media's painted you as the leader of a criminal organization. And don't forget where we are—Chicago, birthplace of the Mafia."

Squeezebox looked down at his expensive suit, shirt, and tie. "Maybe I shoulda toned it down."

"Who knows?" Ludwigsburg said.

The DA did his best to vilify Squeezebox.

On instructions from his lawyer, Squeezebox didn't react. He sat in the most stoic manner and reminded himself the jury couldn't enter into his private feelings. At one point he whispered to Ludwigsburg, "This shit's pretty well got the jury believin' Capone, Manson, Bundy, and Jim Jones are all saints compared to me."

Martin Ludwigsburg delivered a robust defense, challenging the credibility of witnesses, producing his own, and calling into doubt much of the evidence. He had Squeezebox believing he might walk out a free man.

Three and a half weeks after a parade of witnesses, forensic accountants, and other incriminating evidence, the Assistant DA addressed the jury in summation of their case against "one of Chicago's most notorious mobsters."

When Ludwigsburg rose to address the jury, he mocked the deliberate mischaracterization of his client. He reminded the jury the State's case "against my client was and is nothing more than a house of cards, easily toppled."

"The ADA's theatricality aside," he told the jury, "this is nothing more than the railroading of an innocent man to jail. It damns the entire justice system if he does not leave this courtroom a free man."

He broke off to let his words sink in, thanked the jury for its service, and said he knew they'd do the right thing. "Thank you, ladies and gentlemen."

Squeezebox and Anka visited an Italian restaurant.

Anka looked up from her menu.

"He did well today, Dusan...Mr. Ludwigsburg."

"Yeah. I think so, too."

The waiter arrived and took their order and choice of drink. A minute later he returned, poured their wine, and left.

An emotional Squeezebox raised his glass and toasted his wife.

They set their wine glasses down.

"Anka, I gotta tell you a couple of things in case this goes south for me. You bin a good wife...no, a great wife...and an even better mom to the kids. I'm sorry, luv, I didn't get to be the kinda hubby I shoulda bin."

Anka reached across the table and stroked her husband's arm.

"Nobody's perfect, Dusan. Maybe you could have done different, been better, but I haven't been walking around deaf and dumb. I count my blessings, and you are among them."

Squeezebox shook his head.

"If I go down, luv, I ain't coming back."

Anka tried to say something, but Squeezebox cut her off.

"No, no. Wait. Hear me out. You're young, a good-lookin' woman. If I get time, don't wait for me. Go find a love you deserve. When you're ready, get the divorce papers, and I'll sign 'em. All's I ask is you tell a new guy you don't know nothin' 'bout what I done, or 'bout the money. And the only other thing...lemme stay in touch with the boys."

Anka sniffed. "Why are you talking like this, Dusan? Mr. Ludwigsburg's done a great job. You said so yourself."

Squeezebox took her hand. "I know, luv, but promise me you'll keep an open mind about what I told you. I won't stand in your way."

Her eyes filled. "We made our vows at the altar. You're my husband, Dusan. For life."

They retreated into their own thoughts.

Anka at last challenged the empty silence with, "What about Boban Rakitić and Marko Kolarac? What happens to them?"

Squeezebox showed his contempt by breathing noisily.

"Kolarac. He hurt me but not as much as Rakitić. You seen him in court. Singin' like a goddamn canary. I shoulda never hired them two."

Squeezebox ran a palm across his face.

"I figure Rakitić will try to take over my old business. I ain't sure he'll make it. Hope he don't. He's too stupid not to screw up. Word's out about him. In time people'll maybe forget about what he done."

Squeezebox shook his head in disapproval. "If the cops ever nail him for somethin' big, he better hope they don't send him wherever I'm goin'."

"Stay positive, Dusan. This will come out all right."

The jury deliberated for three days and reached a verdict: guilty on all counts. Squeezebox heard soft cheers behind him and Anka's yelp of despair. He turned to her behind the wooden rail and gave a shrug. She answered with an I-can't-believe-it slow shake of her head.

He thought back to the previous week when the ADA office offered him a lighter sentence in return for rolling over on other notable criminals. He'd refused. "Put my ass in the slammer. Nobody's going to say Dusan Kovačević turned rat to save his own hide. So, fuck you and your offer."

A bailiff escorted Squeezebox into the holding cells below the courtroom. A week later Squeezebox, cuffed, shackled, and dressed in an orange jumpsuit, stood in front of the Right Honorable Walter Glass.

Did the accused have anything to say before sentence was pronounced? Glass asked.

"Say? Yeah, I gotta lot to say, but it ain't gonna change the shitload of hurt you're 'bout to put on me, is it?"

An imperious Glass peered at Squeezebox over his bifocals. "The accused will conduct himself with a measure of decorum."

Squeezebox sneered.

"A measure of decorum? You're sendin' me to the slammer for the rest of my life, and you want me to talk hoity-toity? What is this...one of them garden parties?"

Ludwigsburg tugged on his arm to calm him down. Squeezebox pulled away and kept his gaze on the judge.

"What're you gonna do if I don't use 'a measure of decorum'?

Take away my desserts?"

The comment brought combined laughter and murmurs from the courtroom.

Glass banged his gavel and demanded silence. When calm returned, he studied something on his desk and looked up. He sentenced Squeezebox to three consecutive twenty-year terms.

Anka visited him at the county jail. She stared at her husband through thick, scratched Plexiglas and picked up the phone next to her.

"How are you doing, hon?"

Hair mussed, droopy eyelids, Squeezebox tried his best to appear nonchalant. "I'm good, Anka."

"Did Mr. Ludwigsburg tell you he intended to appeal?"

Squeezebox answered with an indifferent nod.

"Do you have any idea where they'll take you, Dusan?"

Squeezebox raised and lowered his shoulders in reply.

"Nah. Could be the one in Colorado, maybe Atlanta, or a supermax in Pennsylvania. Pretty sure not here in state. I don't know. Wherever it is, it ain't good."

Chapter 13

Linzie Hayden's lustful appetite matched Pete's own. She showed no restraint and eagerly initiated or participated in any new action.

"'A lady in public and a whore in the bedroom,'" she'd whispered into Pete's ear while he lay panting. "I think the quote comes from Queen Victoria."

He ran his palm along her naked hip. "I'm glad you share her views."

"So, you liked?" she asked.

"How could I not?"

"I'll accept the compliment. I enjoy my body and hope others do, too."

Pete pretended a hurtful face. "Others, as in people not already mentioned?"

She stared at him under long lashes. "You're not one of those jealous types, are you?"

Pete gave her a tight-lipped smile. "Well, I don't know. I've never been in this situation. But now you've got me curious about those others."

"Oh, stop it. I like sex, but I'm not a tramp. I didn't sleep with anyone before Griffith. He thinks women exist only to add variety to his diet." She lowered her voice and added, "And the variety occasionally runs to young men."

"No."

"Uh-huh." She bobbed her head to lend support to her claim.

"Like I said, he likes variety. He's been unfaithful from the start. We'd barely put away our wedding gifts when I found him in bed — *our bed* — with one of his secretaries. Can you believe it?" She delivered a dismissive shake of her head. "Men! You never like it when the goose repays in kind. Don't like it one bit."

"And you're okay with how things have settled out?"

A coolness came into her voice.

"'Okay'? In a way, I suppose. I've adapted. Griffith cheated and I followed suit. And found I liked that part of it. We have—what did they use to call it in the '70s?—an open marriage. And I make Griffith drive to Burlington every few months to get tested. We never have sex without protection now."

"So, it's understood you both can step outside the marriage?"

Linzie offered Pete a deadpan expression.

"We once saw a marriage therapist. She told us we'd entered into a collusion about our marriage. I suppose that's right. Anyway, Griffith insisted I should be faithful. Me, not him. I once found he'd hired a private detective to follow me. I threatened to leave if he ever did it again."

She flashed a mischievous smile. "Martine Maines is a small town. Like all small towns, people gossip. I have to be careful who I invite to my bed."

"I'm glad you invited me." Pete buried his lips in the cleft of her neck.

Linzie looked at her watch. "I better get back to work, sugar." She rose and slipped into her panties. "I still have a job to take care of."

Pete watched her reapply her makeup in the bathroom mirror. Each slow movement accentuated sensuousness. He found himself aroused again but forced the thought away.

"Do you mind if I ask you a question?"

"Sure. Why not?"

"Well, I don't really know much about you."

She looked at him through the mirror while she applied lip gloss.

"The same can be said for you, can't it? Anyway, local gal. Born and bred, went to school here and married Griffith."

Pete chuckled, admiring the rise and fall of her cleavage in her lacy bra.

"No. I mean your real estate job. Is it full-time or part-time? And what does your husband do?"

Linzie straightened and turned toward him.

"That's more than one question. I work part-time because it gets me out of the house and away from Griffith. This may be hard to believe, but I do love him, but am not blind to his faults."

She played with her hair. "When he's on, he's on. When he's not, look out. To keep my sanity I made up my mind to get out in the world. Deanna Friedan, my boss, gave me a job. I like it, and it keeps me grounded."

She watched Pete in the mirror. "I'm married to a Hayden. It's a big name in these parts. Has been for a long time. They like to think they came over on the Mayflower."

"But isn't Hayden a German name?"

"I thought so, too, but Griffith says it's not. It's English." She waved the matter away.

"In any case, try and find a town within a hundred miles of this place without a hospital wing, a library, or an arts center not named after the Haydens. Griffith and his brother sit on all sorts of boards, including the very liberal Montesquieu you're attending. Griffith's brother, Brice, even sits on the prison's early release board."

She made a there-you-have-it hand gesture. "They also own *Sperling Data*, which employs over three hundred people."

A quick spritz of perfume to the nape of her neck and Linzie turned to face Pete. "As I said, Griffith's not an easy walk in the park. Early in our marriage he hit me. He apologized later. I told him I'd get up one night, take one of his guns from the cabinet, put two bullets into his junk, and watch him bleed to death."

Impressed with the story, Pete said, "Wow. How did he react?"

"That got his attention. He listened when I said I'd hire a good lawyer and use a 'burning bed' defense."

"I bet that would get any abuser's attention. And you stayed."

"I do love him. And the money. We live in a nice house and have an enviable lifestyle." She lifted her shoulders in a half-shrug. "We all make concessions, don't we?"

She gave Pete no time to answer, kissed him, and said, "So, now you know...well, some of it."

Pete placed his hand on her waist and pulled her closer. "Grrr, your perfume...it drives me crazy. Wanna have one for the road?"

She grabbed her purse. "No. No more time. I've got to go."

Pete stood at the front window and watched her car disappear. So different from Nina. What would she think about his life now?

His mind returned to his conversation with Linzie. She had other lovers. Well, why not? Sexy as hell. It wouldn't take much to imagine a lineup of sexually aggressive men wanting to jump her bones. He should consider himself honored she invited him to her bed. And she didn't lie to him. More than he could say.

Pete missed the full semester deadline for enrollment, so he audited courses in environmental studies, political science, and English lit. He didn't have to take tests and exams.

In his past life college had been a pressure cooker. Monty gave him a different experience, starting with him taking courses of interest and challenge. He'd be a Renaissance man, pursue education for its own sake.

He read all the assigned chapters. Where his younger classmates looked bored during the lectures or tippy-tapped on their laptops, Pete listened hard and scribbled copious notes into a thick notebook. Perhaps his enthusiasm revealed itself to his professors. He noticed they'd train their gaze on him during lectures—in particular, those closer to his own age.

He caught a few funny looks from students. What would make them curious about him? His dress and manner didn't stick out. It came to him: they thought he might be a narc. Most of the students knew each other through dorm life, courses, and hung out on weekends. Pete stood out. Give it time, he told himself, and let them get to know you.

He liked reading the bulletin boards with their profusion of flyers. Something for everyone: upcoming events, housing, cat to a good home, for sale items, political action groups, Bible study groups, a science club, cinema club, chess club, drama, gay and lesbian groups, an eco-group, volunteerism notices.

One notice invited interested parties to their campus NRA club. Someone had written over it with a black felt pen: *Gun wackos love authoritarianism and fascism.*

Months passed. In small stages Pete adjusted to his new persona and life. He registered for full courses, developed a few easy school friendships, and seldom sat alone in the cafeteria.

Exams started. He studied and did well.

Linzie sent him updates of real estate listings. One caught his eye, an empty, two-story brick townhouse on Court Street, a few blocks from where he currently lived. The present owners, a couple of nature photographers, had moved out a few months ago. Painted a tasteful gray with a solid, bright red door, the house sat at the end of a row of townhouses.

He toured it with Linzie and liked that it had a deck facing the ravine. The sliding patio door didn't thrill him; they never had. He'd heard enough stories of burglars entering through them. The solution: a good monitored alarm system plus a security PIN and a solid blocking bar placed in the door sill track.

Linzie showed him the two bedrooms—both upstairs—two bathrooms—one up and one on the main floor—a study, living room, a well-designed kitchen and dining area, and a small basement. He'd have to share an inside wall with whoever moved in next door.

Pete liked what he saw. He could take out a mortgage and use his built-up investments for collateral. No loan officer would turn him down. Before he signed off, he'd insist on a pre-payment buyout clause. It would allow him to pay down the mortgage faster without raising eyebrows.

Linzie interrupted his thoughts.

"You haven't seen the garage yet. Come on, I'll show you."

They entered through the kitchen door. She hit the wall-mounted automatic door opener. "You do know I won't be able to come see you here. Court Street's quiet, but not everyone is off at work."

He pulled her to him and nibbled on her neck. "Then we'll have to find creative ways to do the nasty elsewhere. I've got new, exciting things to do to your body."

She pushed against his chest. "Peter, don't be so crude. You know, for someone who's led such a sheltered life, you wouldn't know it listening to you. Where do you get all this stuff?"

He chuckled.

"Making up for lost time. I guess my inner caveman has come to the fore. I've been too nice, too correct all my life. This is way more fun. Besides, all men are perverts, or haven't you noticed?"

He made a mock lunge at her. Linzie easily avoided his clutch. "All right," he said, again speaking about the house. "It's nice and looks well-built. I can get a bike and ride to the college from here. It's also empty, so my guess is the owners have either split up or may be carrying some kind of bridge financing with another house. Good chance they'll want to sell. They're asking three-oh-five. Put in a lowball offer of two-sixty five. If they won't budge, I will. And you get the commission. You can use some of the money to get us a fancy room at a four-star hotel in Montpelier."

She smiled at what she heard. "Are you sure?"

"I am. If they accept, I'll bring in a home inspector. If all goes well, I could move in within a couple of weeks. Oh, I almost forgot. What about the Mullens?"

"You mean giving notice? Well, if your timetable works, leave them an extra month's rent. I doubt they'll quibble. It won't be long before they return."

Pete didn't have to up his initial offer. The owners accepted it. And the bank approved his loan. He turned his attention to moving into his new digs. He contacted a painter to redo the interior. Much of it had favored what the salesman at the paint store despairingly called "smoke."

The master bedroom now became sky blue; the spare, taupe. Pete had the study done in bright red walls, the kitchen goldenrod, and the living room soothing green. When the paint dried, he had a home security system installed, bars on all basement and first floor windows, plus a security grate on the patio door. If a serious thief wanted to break in bad enough, he'd find a way, but these measures discouraged run-of-the-mill crooks.

Pete next set off in search of furniture. What would he like? Nothing to remind him of Nina and her love of black, cushiony leather sectionals, beige carpeting, and forgettable art.

Linzie offered to help him search for furniture, but he declined.

"Thanks, but good or bad, it'll be my decision. I have to live with what I choose."

He did his research and narrowed in on the kind of fine furniture he liked. Pricey and buying too much in one go might draw attention. The solution: he'd do it in increments.

He checked the Internet and found a few high-end furniture stores in Montpelier and Burlington. Three had sales. He bought a dining room table and chairs, a Shaker writing desk, an Amish bookcase, and a solid oak bed with an impressive headboard.

"You've got nice taste," Linzie said when she visited him and examined the furniture. "Nothing wrong with buying things a little at a time and when they go on sale."

"Exactly my thoughts. As you know, they left the fridge, stove, washer and dryer. I bought the big-ass TV. I'll eventually get everything I want. When I do, I'll look at some art reproductions."

On a Friday night Pete and Linzie untangled from the sheets in a Burlington hotel room. Both took a moment to catch their breath.

"Wow," Pete said. "You make my toes curl."

Linzie grinned. "And you really are a pervert."

He kissed her. "Yes, but did you like it?"

"I did. What's wrong with me? Where'd you learn that?"

Pete replied with a half-smile. "Watching porn on the Internet."

She moved closer. "Say, do you own a tux?"

"Uh, no, Guys who drive pickups don't own tuxedos."

"Well, can you buy one or rent one, a nice one? Nothing tacky. Go for the classic look."

"I guess, but why? Wouldn't it be a bit too provocative, me walking into the lion's den with Griffith there?"

She dismissed his concern with a wave of her hand.

"You'll be all right. Griffith's hosting a formal. It's a dual thing, both a fundraiser for the new library wing at Monty and a welcoming for the incoming president. Anyway, the high society, or what passes for high society in our little town, will be there. Would you like to go?"

"*Me*? I'm not the upper crust, the opposite—the hoi polloi."

"So, come anyway, Mr. man-of-the-people. You might enjoy yourself."

Pete wanted to refuse the invitation but pushed the impulse down. "Sure, I guess. I'm not big on social gatherings. I haven't been to many, as you can imagine." He changed the subject. "Will some of your other lovers be there?"

"You'll never know. And besides, I thought you weren't the jealous type."

"I'm not. I'm only having fun. But back to Griffith. You said he's always wrestling with the green-eyed monster. Risky, don't you think, you with your lovers in the same room as Griffith?"

"Let me worry about that. Do you want to go or not?"

"Yeah, I guess. How will you introduce me?"

"A client. A single client new to town. I made a good commission on the house, and I'm showing my gratitude. So, come with a good attitude."

Pete took no delight in imagining an evening of tedious small talk with strangers, including facing Linzie's husband. He preferred deeper conversations with a few intimates, not idle cocktail chatter. He'd done enough of that with Stringent.

Don't overthink it, he warned himself. Linzie had extended

herself, shown a generosity of spirit. The least he could do is accept the invitation with a measure of grace. He fixed her with a smile. "You're right. Happy to come."

"Good, and stop with this hoi polloi stuff. You're as good as anyone and better than many."

He kissed her. If only she knew.

Chapter 14

The Haydens lived in Matlock Farms, a gated community on the edge of town. Pete's green pickup pulled up and stopped at the entrance gate. A security guard stepped out of a kiosk.

Pete powered down his window and gave his name to the security guard. "I'm attending a party at the Haydens. 149 Green Ash."

The guard let his gaze take in the pickup, a hint of disapproval in the slight curl of his lip. He inspected Pete in his tuxedo. Pete, in turn, couldn't hide his amusement and wanted to say, *Don't get many pickups here, I bet. They'd clash with the Beemers and Mercedes.*

He kept the thought to himself.

The guard consulted a clipboard and said, "149 Green Ash. Go straight. Second left."

"Got it."

The safety rail rose. Pete drove on. He imagined this whole subdivision had once been farmland. A bumper sticker came to mind: *Suburbs: where they rip out trees and then name streets after them.* Still, he couldn't help but be impressed by the large, opulent houses. Many would have cost more — much more — than what he stole from Kovačević.

He pulled onto Green Ash and searched for a spot to park. He found one half a block from the Hayden house. His truck parked, Pete walked back and studied Linzie's house. He had no expertise in architectural design but knew what he liked. Not 149 Green Ash or its immediate neighbors. Because something had a high monetary value didn't make it tasteful.

The house boasted gray stone siding. A blue Spanish tile slate roof, probably with one of those exotic names like Mediterranean, shielded the roof against the elements. Pete thought everything lacked proportion and found it odd to see front windows of different sizes. The entire effect gave the house — Pete struggled to find the word for a moment — an irregular-shaped look.

A solid, dark oak wooden door with a brass door knocker stood sentinel. Pete knocked. A reedy man with a white pencil mustache clad in a tuxedo opened the door and smiled. He gave a small bow and extended his arm toward the guests milling about in a spacious wood paneled room. "Welcome, sir. Please come in."

His guide directed him in.

Pete swore he'd stepped into a 1940s movie set. He stared at an expansive foyer with a spiral staircase. A large oil painting of poppies in a field hung over a blood red leather couch. A manned bar stood near a bay window.

Pete's gaze took in the two or three dozen guests, all in formal wear, huddled in various groupings. He searched for Linzie and found her. The room had black cocktail dresses aplenty, many featuring plunging necklines. Some revealed more cleavage than others.

Linzie spied him and broke away from a couple with whom she'd been chatting. She approached with a dazzling smile. Her cocktail dress clung to her. Pete tried to imagine her in flat shoes or sneakers and couldn't. Did she even own a pair? He forced himself to keep his eyes on her face and returned her smile.

"You made it, Peter. Good, and you look really nice. The tux fits you well."

"Thanks. I didn't really know if the tailor would come through with his last-minute alterations. He did. Here I am. You should have seen the look on the guy at the gate when I stopped my truck. He didn't know what to make of me."

A slightly fat but solid-looking man with a dramatic widow's peak, an inch or so taller than Pete, approached.

Linzie's eyes moved from Pete to the other man. "Griffith, I want to introduce you to Peter Harris." She turned to Pete. "This is my husband, Griffith."

Pete stuck out his hand and showed his best warm smile.

"Nice to meet you, sir."

His host ignored the proffered hand and looked Pete up and down.

Pete felt himself redden. He recognized a sizing-up ritual when he saw it, especially from what he guessed to be an alpha male, who turned to her and in a truculent voice said, "So, this is the guy you were talking about? Doesn't look like much."

The hostile tone, the compressed lips, the tense body behavior reminded Pete of his unpleasant encounter with the forceful ADA back in Chicago. He hated drama and avoided it wherever possible. If pushed he could push back but preferred flight over fight.

In seconds Pete felt his heart race, his palms sweat, and his neck grow hot. His mind worked to understand this bad-mannered reception, particularly in their home. Had Griffith suspected him of dicking Linzie? No matter, he didn't want any part of this. He turned his body, ready to make an excuse and leave when Linzie seized his arm.

"Please, Peter, wait."

Unsure of what to do, Pete stayed put.

Linzie released his arm, scanned the area, and turned to her husband.

"What in God's name is the matter with you, Griffith?" she hissed. 'This guy' is our guest, my client, who's been good enough to let me sell him a house. I invited him here, and you, what do you do—make a fool of yourself."

Pete had never seen a combative personality like Griffith taken down so fast by a woman. Head down, crestfallen, he looked like a child eager to free himself of a scolding. He almost felt sorry for Griffith.

Linzie showed her displeasure with her arms tight and rigid against her body while she drilled her eyes into Griffith. She kept her voice low.

"I've had more than enough of your acting-out."

Griffith wouldn't meet her gaze and stared at the floor.

Linzie wasn't done. "Now, tell our guest you're sorry for your unprovoked hostility. If you don't, I swear you'll pay in ways you can't imagine."

Griffith's eyes moved to Pete. He exhaled with might and stuck out his hand. "Sorry."

Pete didn't want to shake, but propriety offered him no choice. He accepted the limp hand and wished he could crush the bones.

"It's okay. Forget it." He turned to Linzie. "I should just go. This really isn't my thing."

Linzie pleaded. "No, please, put this behind you and enjoy the evening. You'll be glad you did." She held up a finger. "Give us a minute to talk." She turned to Griffith. "Meet me in the study. Go now."

Griffith nodded and walked past the clutter of guests.

Linzie returned her attention to Pete.

"I'm sorry about this. I'd like to say I don't know what gets into him sometimes, but I can't. The same thing every time—jealousy and the double standard. It's my fault. I should have known."

Pete had no idea what to do with her confession.

She spoke again.

"Anyway, please stay. There are nice people here. Mingle and give yourself a chance to meet them. I have to go."

Without another word, Linzie spun about and slipped through her guests.

Pete glanced around the room. What should he do? He hadn't wanted to come in the first place. Besides, the unpleasant encounter with Griffith unsettled him. Out of courtesy for Linzie, he'd stay a little longer. In the meantime, he'd get a drink to steady himself. He navigated his way through the guests to the bar.

"What can I get you?" the server behind the bar asked.

"Huh. Oh, wait. I know you."

The server acknowledged the claim with a nod and fast smile.

"Yeah, you're right. I think I know you, too. You're in my poly-sci class. So, what would you like?"

Pete had to think for a second. Okay, order something Stellan wouldn't.

"Whisky sour. Can you make me one of those?"

"You bet. Coming right up."

The drink helped take off the edge. Pete ordered a second and felt warm and cozy. Time for food. He loaded a plate with canapés. Still no sight of Linzie or Griffith. Some tough guy. Man, she must really be reaming him out. The image made him want to laugh.

Linzie and Griffith at last reappeared and dove back in among their guests. No telltale signs of their brief scrap showed itself.

Pete moved around the room. Were any of Linzie's other lovers here? Hard to guess.

He had a pleasant conversation with the coltish interim head of the Psychology Department, Roger Fowler. Pete thought the man quick-witted with an engaging smile, someone who refused to take himself seriously.

The sentiment didn't extend to Fowler's conceited companion, a fetching, auburn-haired woman with a boyish figure and small breasts, what Nina called "bee stings." The woman had attitude written all over her. What nature denied her she made up for in haughtiness. From the time Fowler introduced her, she treated Pete as someone inconsequential. Her empty hand remained in constant motion, often flicking her shoulder-length hair. She let her gaze flit around the room, perhaps in search of better kinds of people.

He had enough of her.

"I better go mingle some more," he said to Fowler. "Nice to meet you in a different context, Roger. If I see you in the halls, I'll be sure to stop and say hello."

"Yes, do. Enjoy the rest of your evening."

Pete spun about and moved away. No point saying goodbye to Roger's bitch girlfriend.

A distinctive tapping of a spoon on a wine glass grabbed

everyone's attention. Griffith stepped into the center of the room and made a brief speech welcoming the incoming president, Dr. Myles Kendrick. Polite applause followed. Griffith cleared his throat and reminded the room, "We're also starting our pledge drive for our new library wing tonight and ask all of you to consider contributing generously towards its financial support."

Linzie's husband proved himself a good speaker with a certain magnetism. Pete found it difficult to reconcile this Griffith with the one who had earlier made such an embarrassing scene. He glanced at his watch. How much longer should he stay? Ah, give it another half hour.

Griffith's speech done, the guests returned to enjoying the ambiance. Pete moved to the large picture window and stared out at the backyard with its kidney-shaped swimming pool. Griffith approached. This time he flashed capped, pearly-white teeth. *Capped*, Pete told himself. *Had to be*. He'd seen his share while working at Stringent.

"So, I understand you're new to our town, Peter, and attending Monty."

Pete played along and matched Griffith's insincere smile with his own.

"Right. Yep, settling in."

"Well, I won't hit you up for any donations...this time. "So, in school now? What have you been doing with your life so far?"

Pete had no idea what Linzie shared with Griffith. It couldn't be much. Something about the question, but more so about the man, unsettled him. With a wariness he said, "Nothing much, really. Getting on with my life, you know?" He offered Griffith another smile.

Griffith looked away at his other guests. "Good for you, then. Enjoy the party."

Linzie came by. "I saw you had a tête-à-tête with Griffith."

Pete smiled in amusement. "If you can call it that. I'm trying not to speak ill of him."

"But...?"

"I could see wheels turning. He really doesn't like me, does he?"

Linzie dropped her gaze and ran a finger around the rim of her drink for a moment. She looked up.

"You know, I owe you an apology. I don't think this was the wisest thing for me to have done. I didn't think it through. I'm certain he knows I'm sleeping with you."

"You think?"

"I do, and sarcasm doesn't become you."

"Fair enough. So, what convinced you he knows?"

Linzie shifted her weight from foot to foot. "It's more than just here." She stopped and peered into Pete's face. "Again, I'm sorry."

"You're forgiven. Back to my question…"

"Little things he's dropped. You live long enough with someone, you get good at taking their inventory."

"True," Pete agreed. He recalled coming home to Nina and within a minute knew what he could expect.

"Okay, so he knows, but why me? You did say I wasn't the only stud in your, um, stable."

Linzie offered up one of her patent smiles. "Clever, but don't be vulgar." She scanned the room and found Griffith, his back to them, schmoozing with a small group. "And maybe you are my favorite. Ever think of that? A lady has to keep some secrets. Just watch yourself."

"Don't worry. I will. I'm leaving soon."

"I understand." She started to turn. Pete stopped her. "One more thing before you scoot off. What's the deal with Roger Fowler's girlfriend?"

"Who's Roger Fowler?"

Pete searched the room and found Roger and his bony companion by the bar, in conversation with two other couples. "There," he said and pointed. "The woman with the reddish-brown hair. By the bar."

Linzie followed his gaze.

"Oh, Mackenzie Bowers. She married into money, and her husband, Steve, lost it. She and Griffith had a thing for a while after Steve left town. She tried to pry him from me. He's a lot of things but dumb isn't one of them. He takes what he needs and moves on. They still talk. I smile at Mackenzie when we meet, but she always gets nervous. I wonder why?"

Pete's head swiveled from the Bowers woman to Linzie. "She thought he'd take her over *you*? Talk about delusional."

"Now, aren't you the sweetest thing? Anyhow, Mackenzie's never got over losing her wealth and status. She behaves like one of those snooty waiters in upscale restaurants who put on airs even while they're serving you. It's about all she's got in her quiver these days."

"Quite a story."

"Isn't it? A lot of rumors flitted around about how Steve lost the family fortune. In any case, their marriage didn't survive. I sold their house. Steve's somewhere in Florida, and Mackenzie works at Darling Intimates selling ladies' unmentionables. Don't mind her."

"Thanks for inviting me."

"You are welcome, and for the final time, I apologize. I hope you at least had something of a good time."

"I did."

She nodded. "And I like you in the tuxedo." She paused. "Be careful. Of what, I'm not sure."

Chapter 15

Squeezebox discovered where they'd send him—Stillwell. Word had it the prison earned its hellhole reputation equal to that of Marion, Terre Haute, or Lewisburg.

Anka put a good spin on his new location. She pressed the palm of her hand against the Plexiglas and spoke into the phone.

"There is a silver lining, Dusan. I looked Stillwell up. It's just under a thousand miles. The boys and I can visit. And it allows conjugal visits. You and I can still be together even for a little while."

Squeezebox pushed down his impending anxiety. He wouldn't show Anka how scared he felt but knew a world of misery awaited him.

"Hadn't thought of it like that, babe. Good point, I guess. Yeah."

Well before the jail population at Metropolitan Correctional Center stirred, guards came for Squeezebox and seven other convicts. They placed handcuffs, ankle cuffs, and belly chains on the prisoners and watched as they shuffled along in single file to a metallic jingle-jangle cadence.

Squeezebox and the other cons arrived at a grate. A guard unlocked it. Cuffs and chains removed, the men stepped into a sparse room. Trustees followed and handed out burritos in cardboard boxes and fruit juice, one to each man. The men ate and waited. Trustees returned with bins holding prisoners' cleaned and pressed clothing.

"Get back into your civvies," a guard called out to the men. "Leave your jail garb on the benches. No talking."

Like we got anything we wanna say right now, Squeezebox thought.

Twenty minutes later the cons were ordered to form a straight line. Without speaking, they obeyed. A guard and two trustees approached. Each prisoner was fitted with a broad leather waist chain to which his hands were cuffed. The restraint restricted up-and-down movement of their hands.

Leg cuffs came next.

"Go make a line by the far wall," the guard ordered.

Each man shuffled forward. With the last prisoner in restraints, the guard said, "Okay, out the front door. Follow me."

Squeezebox and the others scuffled out to an inner yard where a mini bus awaited in the morning darkness. Two uniformed men with *Action Security* patches on the shoulders of their charcoal uniforms guided each prisoner into the side of the mini bus. Their prisoners seated, they chained their legs to D-rings on the floor.

Squeezebox found himself between two other cons. He allowed himself a fast look at his keepers, one middle-aged with chicken pox scars and a stomach resting over his belt; the other, in his late twenties, wore a perpetual frown and gripped the butt of his pistol.

None of the prisoners talked or made eye contact with each other. Each man stared off into space, studied the floor, or looked out the front window.

Squeezebox shut his eyes as if to block out the entire experience. A pig in a paddock could expect more dignity. A rueful sigh escaped him. He opened his eyes and studied the interior of the van. Vinyl and plastic. A thick thermoplastic shield with holes separated the guards from the prisoners. The bus had no side windows.

The heavier guard slid behind the wheel. His partner took the passenger seat in front of a mounted shotgun. The driver honked the horn. Seconds later the jail's wide gates opened, and the bus pulled out.

Squeezebox kept his eyes on the road ahead.

'*Bye 312* he silently said, a reference to the area code around the Loop. *Won't see you anytime soon or at all, truth be told. You bin good to me. Take care of my Anka and the kids.*

They drove for several hours.

"Hey man," one of the prisoners called through the Plexiglas speak hole, "how's about stopping soon? I gotta take a piss."

The passenger guard turned and studied him. "Hold it."

"I can't. That's what I'm sayin'. C'mon. Don't be like that. I gotta go."

The guard returned his attention to the road ahead. The suffering prisoner silently moaned and rolled his head.

Sometime later another prisoner complained. "We gots to piss, man. This gotta be unconstitutional or somefin, right? Y'all cain't be keeping us chained like this when we's in pain. We got rights, ya know?"

Once more the guard looked behind him.

"Rights? You've got no rights. None of you. You gave them up the moment you decided to become criminals. Here's a tip—that's why you're all shackled and sitting back there. Now shut the fuck up, and don't let me hear you again."

The warning had the opposite effect. One by one the complaints grew louder and more forceful.

We havta go.

You gotta pull over, man.

Where the fuck it says you get to treat us like dogs?

The guards refused to listen. In response, the prisoners hollered, pounded the Plexiglas, and stomped their feet.

"Break it up," the guard in the passenger seat shouted through the cut holes, "or I'll come back there and lay a beating on your heads."

"Then let us get out for a piss," a prisoner shouted back. "How's 'bout a little humanity? Animals be treated better than us."

The guard scoffed.

"Humanity? Gimme a break! You're losers, the bunch of you. You got nothing coming but slammer time. Where you belong."

The comment got to Squeezebox. He'd try to keep out of the fray, but the comment proved too much.

"Ah, fuck you, dickhead."

The guard's eyes found Squeezebox.

"What'd you say to me?"

"You deaf as well as stupid?' a defiant Squeezebox shot back.

In response, the guard looked at the driver.

"Pull over."

"No. Leave it alone."

"I said pull over."

A brief argument broke out between the guards. The bus swerved in its lane for a moment but at last slowed, aimed for the gravel, and came to a stop. The front passenger door flew open, a riled guard rushed out, flicked open his collapsible baton, and unlocked the side door. He leaned over the prisoner closer to the door, grabbed a handful of Squeezebox's lapel, and said, "You ever mouth off again, asshole, it'll be your sorriest day."

Squeezebox looked up at his tormentor and sneered.

"Big man, huh? He held up his wrists. "Take these cuffs off, and we'll see who has a sorry day."

The remark won Squeezebox a blow from the fat end of the baton. His head snapped back. A welt began to appear. He tasted blood, ran his tongue over his lower lip, and looked at the guard's name tag.

"Jed Applegate from Action Security. Damn sure I'll remember that name. I'm behind bars, Jeb, but it don't mean I got no reach. You catch my drift…Jeb? My memory's good, real good."

Something changed on Applegate's face. Squeezebox saw the eyes widen, the nostrils flare, and blood drain from the man's face. Good. Let him worry. The guard retreated from the van, locked the side door, and returned to his seat.

"Let's take a break," the driver said. A quick nod gave him his answer.

The mini bus made several stops before it reached its destination. At their previous stop, a national donut chain, the prisoners had their last restroom break. Back in the bus they received sandwiches, coffee, and candy bars before the guards went for their own break.

The prisoners talked.

"Way to go, man," a young, pimply prisoner in his late teens said to Squeezebox.

"S'right," another agreed. "You got some big cojones. Fucker looked like he was ready to shit his pants after what you said."

The other prisoners chimed in.

"Yeah," an older prisoner added. "In all my years, I never seen nothing like what you done. You mean it, what you told him?"

Squeezebox knew enough to keep his own counsel. He'd been in the company of criminals most of his life. Experience told him not to show his hand. He'd pay back Applegate and then some.

"Don't matter. Only thing matters is if he believes it."

Close to 9:00 p.m. the bus pulled up to the main gate at Stillwell.

Gonna be a helluva trip, Squeezebox thought as they drove past the inner barbed wire fence. *Helluva long trip for Anka to come see me.*

The bus passed through the main gate, beeped twice, and entered a specialty yard. Squeezebox watched a retracting metal gate close behind them and a reinforced steel door open into the interior of the prison itself.

Four COs (correctional officers) followed by eight trustees, stepped out of a building.

The side door of the bus flew open. A CO stepped in and unlocked the D-rings one at a time. The prisoners were helped off the bus, herded into a corridor and down to a bare room with a reception counter and showers.

His restraints removed, Squeezebox rubbed his wrists while a CO ordered everyone to strip.

"Leave your clothes on the bench, take a towel, and step into the showers. Come back when you're finished." He pointed to Squeezebox. "Nice threads. Had to set you back a bundle. No matter. On the bench with everyone else's."

Toweled, the prisoners returned to the room naked.

A new order arrived. "Raise your hands while a trustee sprays your groin and armpits against lice."

The procedure finished, the men lined up in front of the counter with their bundle. Each prisoner had his personal belongings catalogued, signed for them, and exchanged his civilian clothes for a prison-issue jumpsuit with horizontal stripes, lined jean jackets, and shoes. Each man also received bedding and toiletries.

"Come on, ladies," a ramrod-straight sergeant bellowed. "We haven't got all night. Get dressed."

Once more the prisoners formed a line.

A CO in the lead, Squeezebox and the others entered the prison's barber shop and received a close-to-the-scalp haircut.

Barbering done, they formed another line and headed for a different room. Weighed, fingerprinted, they waited for their mugshots. Once done, the sergeant said, "You're going to the Reception Processing Center in the morning. For now it's beddy-bye time. Okay, let's move it."

The newcomers marched through two steel grates and into a cellblock, empty of convicts.

"Find a cell," the sergeant told his charges. "Anything."

Squeezebox stepped into a cell. A few moments later the door locked behind him. He examined his new home. A tiny window with two-inch steel bars offered a glimpse of a large, bare, concrete yard. Cinder blocks painted a sickly green held a small ledge for personal belongings. Sink and toilet sat next to it.

His eyes took in the metal bedstead with threadbare linen and a gray, flimsy pillow. He folded and tucked his sheet into the thin mattress, spread the blanket, and thought of Anka and their king-sized oak platform bed with its imported sheets and matching pillow cases. Nothing like that now.

Finished, Squeezebox climbed into bed. In his six-by-eight cell, an emotional toll crashed in on him. He teared up and seized his pillow to stifle the sound of weeping. It wouldn't do for other cons to hear him. He knew some of the fish, new prisoners, cried aloud their first night in the big house. Word got out fast. The prison's chicken hawks, predators, would find them in the yard.

No, Squeezebox reminded himself, he had to look and be tough, carry his street cred into GP, general population.

The next two weeks Squeezebox joined a procession of new arrivals held out of GP.

In Reception, each man received a battery of tests, underwent psychological testing, and was scored on his level of security risk. A committee of five assigned Squeezebox to a category four level. He would never be a trustee or assigned to a dormitory. The committee assigned him to work in the prison's furniture shop.

With his bedding and toiletries in his hands, Squeezebox followed a CO who led him to the prison's central rotunda. They stopped at a grate.

"Key up," the CO shouted. A moment later a different CO opened the grate.

"All yours," the first guard said, spun about, and left. The second man locked the gate and demanded Squeezebox's pass. The Serb handed it to him. The guard gave it a fast glance and said, "Third tier, L-14. When you get there, wait for the CO to come to the grate."

Four minutes later Squeezebox dumped his meager belongings on a bed, astonished the accompanying bed sat empty. Had they given him a cell to himself? No. He knew the prison suffered from overcrowding. It didn't make sense to have the cell to himself. Still, no point in being ungrateful.

He chose an upper bunk, made it, stepped out of the cell, and walked to the dayroom at the end of the tier.

Word about Squeezebox's encounter with the private security guard preceded him.

So did how he'd been played for over two mil. He received curious looks from some cons in the cafeteria. How long, he asked himself, before some con would try to muscle him?

At Stillwell, the average sentence for theft or robbery came in at around four years. Most scores netted wrongdoers under $1,600. Benefits divided by incarceration time worked out to less than a buck and a quarter per day. Thus, a fish with a wad of money attracted attention. Even in prison money mattered.

On his third night in GP three cons paid Squeezebox a visit in his cell. Two stepped inside, while a third stood outside and kept watch.

Squeezebox looked at the intruders and rose from the cell's small table.

The larger of the two prisoners, a heavily tattooed man, stepped forward and demanded money.

"We know you got dough. I'm gonna give you a name and address, and you make sure a hundred grand gets there. You don't, your life here's gonna be hell, sweetums."

Squeezebox climbed to his feet. He did his best imitation of a man struck by fear. He looked at the floor and let his hands tremble. With luck these guys'd relax and stop being careful and attentive to his response.

The guile worked. Overconfident by the timidity of the fish and caught up with his own words, the bully stepped closer. His accomplice busied himself rifling through Squeezebox's few belongings.

Squeezebox pointed to Loudmouth's shoes. His tormentor looked down and never saw the sucker punch to his midsection. He doubled up and crashed to the floor but not before his face met Squeezebox's knee.

Squeezebox stepped out of the way and rushed at the other man. Smaller yet heavier, he accepted the first blow, stepped closer, and delivered a flurry of short, powerful punches. The con left his feet. Squeezebox delivered a volley of kicks to his face, neck, and midsection. Chest heaving with exhaustion, fists bunched in rage, Squeezebox glared down at the third man. He spit out calmly, "You…want some, too…c'mon in."

The con held his hands up in surrender and slipped away.

Noise from the fight brought two COs.

A fast investigation followed, and all three men were hauled in front of the shift supervisor, a no-nonsense lieutenant who'd worked his way up through the ranks. He demanded to know who and what started the fight.

None of the three offered anything approaching an adequate explanation.

The lieutenant concluded the two invading cons, who had no business in Squeezebox's cell, were at fault and sentenced both to six days in the hole. Squeezebox received four days for his part in the altercation.

Hands manacled, four COs including a short and solid female, escorted the convicts to the basement. Guards and cons entered a bleak room with a table, a bench, eight impenetrable steel doors, and a naked overhead light bulb.

"Face the cells," a male CO ordered.

All three obeyed.

"Strip."

Once more the convicts complied.

"Turn and face me."

All three abided by the command and placed their palms over their genitals.

"Cavity searches, ladies. Open your mouths and say ahh."

The female guard slid on a pair of blue latex gloves and approached Tattoo. Satisfied with her inspection, she moved to his partner and onto Squeezebox. He wouldn't meet her gaze and focused on her short salt-and-pepper hair.

She stepped away and reached for a tube of lubricant while another command arrived. "Time for the other cavity. Bend over and spread your cheeks."

Squeezebox waited his turn while the guard inspected the other two. Done with her inspection, she stepped up to Squeezebox. He reddened in embarrassment, aware of the snickers.

"Relax," she said to the amusement of her coworkers. "You're too tense."

He felt a cold digital finger probe him and winced. *Enjoy yourself, bitch. I ever get the chance to return the favor, I'll do it and more.*

A moment later he heard her say, "You're good."

Squeeze straightened.

The female guard moved away and peeled off her gloves.

A different guard stepped forward and handed each man a heavy, pale, sleeveless gown. The gown barely covered Squeezebox's groin area. He understood its main purpose: crush a prisoner psychologically and take away any true sense of being a man.

A comment from one of the guards backed up his suspicion.

"Aw, don't they look adorable in their baby dolls?"

All but the convicts laughed.

A CO opened a heavy door and gestured for Squeezebox to enter. Light from the outer room showed a cement floor with a hole in the middle. A roll of toilet paper sat alongside one wall.

Squeezebox entered. The steel door shut behind him. He heard a heavy key lock the door.

Darkness enveloped him. His arm out, he found the far wall and slid down against it. The muscles in Squeezebox's chin trembled. He couldn't hold back the tears. He dropped his head and sobbed into his chest, the man gone and the boy reappearing. Vulnerable, with no one to help him, he silently called out for his mother, long dead. "Help me, Mom. Please help me."

The last tear shed, Squeezebox crawled along the hard, cold, cement floor in search of toilet paper. His hand found it. He unwrapped a length, blew his nose, and exhaled.

"Pricks."

The man in him returned.

Squeezebox endured four of the toughest days in his life. The garment failed to keep him warm. He shivered the entire time. He pulled his knees up and under the dressing gown, preserving body heat. If he had to do his business, he felt for the opening and emptied himself.

Nothing to do and an inability to tell night from day, time lost all sense of meaning. His meals, brought and eaten in the dark, at first helped to gauge time but soon proved unreliable.

He heard other voices call out. One howled.

Squeezebox thought he'd go mad but held on. At first, he replayed the beating he gave the two cons. He drew some comfort from the memory and knew it would solidify his prison reputation. No one would mess with him again.

His mind took him to movie and TV scenes of men duking it out. All bullshit. No one ever fought like that. In Squeezebox's experience most fights lasted less than thirty seconds. If you couldn't do your damage then, you'd run out of steam. If you fought like in the movies, a heart attack would kill you, not the other guy.

He tired of thinking about the fight. What else? Sex? No. Not down here. What about the sonofabitch Nieves? If he ever caught him, he'd lay some serious, slow, and painful hurt on him. If.

On a deeper level, Squeezebox did hold a grudging admiration at Nieves' ripping him off. He didn't like it, but the theft had a certain...style...to it. He, if anybody, should appreciate what went down.

Bit by bit, Squeezebox's mind turned to thinking about his life in general. Never one for introspection, in the hold he found himself drawn to it. He examined his childhood, his life choices, and where he veered from the straight and narrow. He'd always felt his path had been laid out for him. He supposed that the way things played out for him, he had no choice but to form into the man who sat in the hole.

He thought about Anka, his kids, his mother and her fiery, drunken lout of a husband. He recalled the kindly priest at Holy Ascension, Father Loncar, who worked hard to instill proper and honest behavior in him. He'd let the priest down, let them all down.

How much time did he have left with his life? he asked himself. However long, that life would be here in the joint. Still, why not make changes? He didn't have to be a Boy Scout, would never be one, but he could try to do and be better.

His cell door opened wide.

"Out," a male voice said, and mispronounced his name. "Hope you learned your lesson. Shower, shave, and put on a fresh jumpsuit. Then it's back to your cellblock."

Squeezebox stepped out of the hole, squinting at the bright light. He'd survived the ordeal.

A surprise awaited him at his cell. He had a new cellmate, a slight, potbellied man in his late fifties who looked terrified when Squeezebox stepped in. At the sight of Squeezebox his eyes widened in dread.

"First time?" Squeezebox asked, and dropped his belongings on the upper bunk. He knew the answer.

His cellmate's head bobbed up and down in answer. He pointed to the lower bunk. "Is this bunk taken? It's yours if you want it."

"Nah, I'm good where I am, an' stop worryin'. I don't want nothin' from you and ain't gonna hurt you. My name's Dusan Kovačević. Doo-SHAN. It's Serb. I'm new, like you. A lifer."

His cellmate introduced himself. "Gates Tally, Dusan. How do you do?"

"Good. You got two last names?"

"I'm afraid so. My father's idea of a bad joke."

Squeezebox worked to make his bunk while Tally engaged him in light conversation.

"I'll be here for a while," Tally said. "Probably die in this place."

Squeezebox was familiar with prison etiquette. Rule number one: never ask what landed someone behind bars. If they wanted to tell you, fine, but their choice.

Tally shared without any prompting. "They sentenced me on a murder-for-hire rap."

"Heavy. We gotta lotta time to get to know each other. You gonna appeal?"

Tally shook his head. "Nothing to appeal. They have me blabbing in an undercover sting."

Tally, from Sioux City, Iowa, proved himself an excellent cellmate. Squeezebox discovered this former cultural anthropologist at Great Plains State University had put a contract out on his wife.

"If ever a woman could take a man's self-worth, Dora could," he said. "I'm deeply sorry to lose my freedom, but you know, at least in here I'm free of her. Nonetheless, you see in front of you a cautionary tale of never confusing education with intelligence, how I could have been so stupid in planning this."

The processing center assigned Tally to the front office.

Squeezebox grew used to his cellmate's use of ten-dollar words and asked what many of them meant.

The former academic taught him to play chess, euchre, and introduced him to a world of new ideas. Because of Tally, Squeezebox joined a club on public speaking, took evening courses to further his education, and participated in a self-help group.

Squeezebox began something new—reading. He managed in spite of his learning disorder and general restlessness.

He commented on it to Gates.

"I'm not a psychologist," Gates said, "but you're no longer that kid in class you described. From the little I know, my guess is you might have some kind of reading disability."

Squeezebox tilted his head and studied Gates. "You think?"

"Just a guess. But you know, some adults do grow out of it. And you've got to keep in mind your chaotic childhood. Is it okay for me to say that?"

"Yeah. Relax. We're just talking, is all."

"Right. My point is that in spite of our environment,"—he waved an arm to indicate the prison—"there might be one advantage here for you."

"What's that?"

"You're in a very structured environment. You can't run around and do anything you want, be distracted like before. Perhaps it will force you to slow down and focus more."

"Hmm. Never thought of it. Maybe you got something there."

One Saturday while Squeezebox and Gates played chess in the dayroom while most of the cons watched a game between the Rockets and Cavaliers, Gates said, "So, are you liking working in the library?"

"For sure, and thanks for gettin' me reassigned. How'd you pull it off? You ain't been here much longer than me, and you got no real juice, right?"

He waited and studied his cellmate. "Right?"

Gates gave him a half smile. "You got it. No juice."

"Then how'd you score it?"

"Ask me no questions..."

"Fine, an' thanks, man." Squeezebox leaned forward. "I wanna ask you somethin'. You talk good, and you got a lotta education. Can you teach me better?"

"Teach you what?"

"Talk good and, you know, think better."

"But you're taking courses. Give it time."

"Maybe, but I wanna practice with you. If I say things wrong, if I don't make sense, will you tell me?"

"Sure, if you want, but you won't get mad if I do?"

"Nah. I'm askin,' ain't I?"

"Very well. So, this will be like some sort of incarcerated Pygmalion."

"Pig what? What is it, the thing you said?

"Did you ever see *My Fair Lady*?"

"Me? C'mon." Squeezebox held back a beat. "Would I like it?"

"You never know. No matter. We'll go ahead with the experiment."

Squeezebox settled into life behind bars. Months passed. One day while in the dayroom he asked, "You think I have bad breath?"

Gates looked up from his newspaper.

"Pardon?"

"Bad breath. Do you think I have it?"

"Where's this coming from?"

"Herrero, the 'Rican I do weights with. He's not shy about saying what comes to mind. He told me. Well, do you?"

Gates considered the question.

"Stop stalling," Squeezebox said. "I know you. You're trying to be diplomatic. Do I, or don't I?"

"Well…"

"Why didn't you say something to me?"

"It's not the kind of thing you bring up in conversation, Dusan. Especially in this place."

"Damn. Why didn't I know it when I was out in the world? Even my wife never said nothin'. Wonder what I can do about it in here?"

"We do have dental care, but I use that word advisedly. It doesn't compare to anything outside, but make an appointment. And we also have volunteer dentists who come in."

"Yeah, good idea."

Weeks later a volunteer dentist scraped Squeezebox's teeth and instructed him in better brushing techniques. Afterwards Squeezebox purchased mouthwash from the commissary.

"I guess it's a good thing Herrero said something to me," he told Gates. "Talk about, um — what's the term? — better dental hygiene."

Squeezebox's street reputation plus the incident in his cell, elevated his status in the prison. A few Chicago old-time mobsters, their "soldiers" ever-present, invited him to join their inner ranks.

In turn, the Crips, Bloods, and Aryan Brotherhood left him and, by association, Gates, alone.

At first, Squeezebox worried his earlier rogue attempts to buy coke from the Sinaloa cartel would result in serious trouble. The Italians' only reaction was to laugh and mock his efforts and loss of cash. A few of the OGs, original gangsters, hung a new nickname on him — Danny Balls Up.

Squeezebox took a lot of ribbing about being made a chump by an accountant. Some of the remarks were flat-out caustic and irked him, but he held his tongue. Better to be mocked than shivved.

In time the remarks faded away. Squeezebox liked the camaraderie with the mobsters. They'd meet and swap war stories of life on the street.

He hadn't forgotten about the incident with Action Security.

One day he strolled in the yard with Tommy "Fat Fingers" Morello.

"Ask you something, Tommy?"

"What?"

"You know anybody reliable on the street who could do a job? I don't have any good contacts left."

"Depends on the job," the craggy-faced mobster said, his hands deep in his coat pockets.

Squeezebox didn't take long with his answer.

"Payback." He told Morello about the transportation incident. "I want someone to hurt this guy. Make sure he knows why."

The mobster stared at the cement ground while they walked.

"Yeah, okay, Danny Balls Up, go lay on Dominic what you know about this guy."

Encouraged by the comment, the Serb said, "Not much. Only his name and the company."

"It's a start. We'll find him. You're right. Beating a man in shackles ain't cool. We may be jail birds, but it don't mean we got no dignity." He broke off. "Normally it would cost you, you know?"

Squeezebox did and acknowledged with a nod. "'ppreciate it, Tommy."

Three weeks later Jed Applegate drove into the underground garage of his apartment building. He'd stayed late at the sports bar with his buddies but remembered to stop at a bodega and pick up some groceries for his nearly-empty fridge.

Applegate pulled into his parking spot, stepped out of his car, and leaned into the back seat to retrieve his bag of groceries.

The first punch to his kidney felled him. Air left Applegate. He struck his mouth on the edge of the floorboard. Rough hands seized him and pulled him to the ground. Boots and fists pummeled him before darkness released him from his horror.

He woke mid-morning, unsure of his surroundings. It took him a moment to realize where he found himself — in a hospital bed. He moved and winced, pain throughout his body but especially to his left arm, now in a cast.

A detective visited him to take a statement. Applegate couldn't be of much help. He hadn't seen his assailants but thought there were two. He passed out shortly after the attack began.

The detective thought the attack was personal.

"Whoever did this to you didn't take your wallet, your watch, nothing. I've got to ask. Does someone have it in for you? A husband, a boyfriend of someone you went out with? That kind of thing."

Applegate shook his head. No, he couldn't think of anything.

The cop left and said they'd keep digging. Half an hour later a memory returned to Applegate: the prisoner who'd threatened him. Hadn't he said something about a long reach? But he was behind bars, so how...?

Applegate reached two decisions by the time a nurse wheeled him to the front door of the hospital: he'd change his address and find a new line of work.

Chapter 16

A couple with a toddler moved in next door a month after Pete took ownership of his home. He caught a first glimpse of them and guessed they were a year or two younger than he. The man and child both had light blond hair; the woman, a medium brown. They drove a shiny, new, high-end German sedan. What would they make of his pickup?

One evening as Pete carried his garbage bin to the curb, he and his new neighbor met. He had almost reached the curb when he heard the other man say, "Excuse me."

Pete looked over his shoulder. His neighbor approached and shot him an obligatory smile.

"Hi. I'm Malcolm...Matt. My wife's Colleen."

Pete faced him. "Welcome to the neighborhood. I'm Pete Harris. New myself."

"Oh. Listen, I wanted to tell you a man came by asking about you."

"Me?" At once Pete's intrinsic suspicions rose. Why would someone, anyone, be interested in him?

"Yes," his new neighbor said. "Since we didn't know the guy and don't know you, we sent him off empty-handed. Anyway, I thought you should know."

"Thanks. Appreciate it."

"Sure. Good night."

Pete closed his garage door and looked through a window to see Matt return to his house. Satisfied, Pete entered his kitchen and double-checked the lock. Somebody had been snooping around about him. Kovačević? Could it be him? Had Pete slipped up somewhere? Then again, maybe it had something to do with Griffith.

Worry cost him a good night's sleep. He tossed and turned, the image of foreboding on his mind. Should have asked Matt about this guy — what he looked like, what he drove.

In the morning he checked the street. Nothing out of the

ordinary. The urge to talk to Matt lessened as the day wore on. He'd let it be.

Patches of snow remained here and there, but winter had begun to relax its hold.

On a balmy day Pete ventured into the neighborhood's semi-wild park. He inhaled the rich, early scent of spring and spied his first robin. Dogwood buds would soon open. Near a swampy area he saw his first pussy willows. He took pleasure in the walk and considered getting a dog.

Invigorated by the walk, he headed home and spotted a black mid-sized sedan on the street with a man behind the wheel. Pete already knew every house and every car. He took in the details of the vehicle as he approached from behind. Could this be the guy who'd asked Malcolm questions?

Pete bent and stared into the car. A jowly, bald man in a gray suit turned his head and acknowledged him with a head bob. Pete looked away. Maybe it's nothing, he told himself. The guy could simply be some estranged husband waiting at the curb for his kids.

Pete didn't believe his self-talk. By the looks of him, the driver looked too old to be waiting for kids.

Two days later Pete unlocked his bike at the college and placed his messenger bag in the rear rack. He walked the bike to the street, ready to swing his leg over when something caught his eye: the same car, the same driver, this time with his window down.

An intense anger coursed through Pete. Someone held an undue interest in him. Should he use his cell phone and call the police? No. It would invite attention, something he neither wanted nor needed.

His emotions got the better of him. He leaned his bike against a lamppost and moved with purpose across the street. To his amazement the man's attention focused on something in his lap.

Pete's arm shot into the open window of the car, grabbed a handful of tie, and yanked. With no choice, his victim's upper body followed. His head struck the window frame. Pete heard a thump and a heavy *oomph*. He pulled the man's head closer.

"Who the fuck are you, and why are you following me?"

"Let go," his shadower urged in a rasping voice. He did his best to open the door. Pete blocked it with his body and tightened his hold. "Get out of the car and your next stop's the emergency room."

"All right, all right," the stranger wheezed. "Let loose. I'm…having trouble…breathing."

"First you tell me who you are and why you're tailing me."

The driver's face had turned red. Pete relaxed his hold. The man coughed, gulped air, and worked to loosen the knot around his neck. He took a moment to pull air into his lungs.

"I'm a private investigator."

"Who hired you to follow and harass me?"

"Sorry, I can't and won't say."

"Then you better give me something. Local or far away?"

"Local."

"Okay. You tell whoever hired you that you got what you could, and you think I made you. And if I ever see you again…"

The threat hung there. Pete spun about and headed to his bike.

"You know, you could be charged for assault," the investigator said to his back.

Pete turned around and looked up and down the narrow street.

"Knock yourself out. Your word against mine." He guided his bike to the street. No sooner had he pedaled away than recrimination took over. What a stupid thing to do. Any number of people could have stopped and witnessed this street drama. Had someone called the cops, or a cruiser happened by, big trouble.

No point dwelling on it, he told himself. Nobody witnessed it.

He thought about what the investigator said about someone local. Griffith. He had to be behind this. Well, Linzie did warn him, sort of.

The lovers rendezvoused in Burlington two days later, pleased they'd have the weekend to themselves.

On the highway Pete checked his rearview mirror several times. No sign of anyone following him. He pulled into the underground parking lot of the small, superior, family-owned hotel, reputed to have accommodated several A-list actors during the latest movie shoot.

He'd changed into a single-breasted navy blazer over a lighter-toned Oxford button-down shirt and dusky brown chinos before he left town. "We don't have to go the Ginger-Rogers-and-Fred-Astaire-elegance route," Linzie had said earlier, "but I want you to step up the style a bit."

Pete retrieved his soft-sided leather carry-on from the truck, pushed the elevator button for the first floor, and approached the reception desk. No, the receptionist said, Linzie hadn't checked in yet. Pete paid for the room.

She knocked on the door a quarter of an hour later and entered with her leather overnight bag. Pete shut the door behind her. His gaze took in her flared purple and red skirt with a clinging black sweater. She smiled and clutched him before she pulled away.

"You look nice."

"And you look like you need to get out of those clothes." He pulled her to him and kissed her neck. "Smell great, too."

Linzie giggled. "Hold on. We're going out to eat first, remember?" Her palms pressed against her thighs and slid downwards. "After a nice dinner, and if you've been a good boy, I'll show you my new sexy underwear." She again tittered. "I bought it at *Darling Intimates*."

Pete growled like an animal and pulled her close. "How about showing me now?"

She slipped away, allowing her skirt to fall. "No. I've made reservations at *Chez Inès*, so we better leave. You go first. It's under your name. I've ordered the same private table. You remember the way?"

They enjoyed a romantic meal and knocked off a fine California

Cabernet Sauvignon. Both returned to their room the same way they left—separately. Later, sated from their lovemaking and draped in plush bathrobes, Pete poured them *Martell* cognacs from the minibar. He returned to the bed and handed Linzie hers.

Propped up against the headboard, she took it while he settled himself beside her. "Cheers."

They clinked glasses and sipped.

"So," Pete asked, "how's Griffith?"

"He's gotten really strange lately. He's been following me around like a lost puppy. He can't say he doesn't know what I'm up to, or he doesn't have girlfriends wherever, but, um, I don't know…"

"Do you think he's getting worse?"

"I honestly do. I wouldn't put it past him to install a GPS on my car. I drove here in a rental and paid cash. I also checked my rearview mirror all the way."

"Me, too. The mirror, I mean. So, now the pieces fit."

Linzie tipped her head sideways. "What are you talking about?"

Pete told her about the incident with the PI and finished with, "I knew I'd see you here, so I held off telling you." He saw the muscles in her jaw tense.

"It makes me angry," she said. "I'm going to talk to him."

"But why now?" he asked. "It's not like your affair with me is something new."

"Because it's *you*," she said. "Why, I don't know. For some reason he must feel extra threatened by you."

"Hard to make sense of this?"

"Yes. It also explains about the information."

"What information?"

She blinked twice and licked her lips. "Why there's no record of you in any public or private mental institution."

"No 'record'?"

She shook her head.

"No. Griffith let the cat out of the bag, without any prying by me, that they'd checked and couldn't find any evidence of you ever having been in an institution."

Pete found himself growing defensive. His voice rose.

"First, how would Griffith have known I've been hospitalized? It's not something I put out there. I shared it with you in confidence, remember, Miss 'my lips are sealed'? I guess they weren't. Second, do you...does Griffith...even know how many institutions there are in the Midwest alone? And last, did Griffith get my school marks, my DMV record, as well, huh? Am I a known pedophile, a drunk, a drug dealer? Something tells me this went beyond 'he let the cat out of the bag.' You and Griffith must have had a lot to talk about."

Pete climbed off the bed, shed his bathrobe, grabbed his clothes, and headed for the restroom. She hurried and followed him.

"You're angry," she said. "Where are you going?"

"Home."

She grabbed his wrist.

"Peter, please. I'm sorry. Stay. Come on. Don't go. I tried to defend you, and it must have slipped out. And he doesn't have anything useful on you. Let me make it up to you."

Peter shoved his things into his bag, zipped it, and opened the door. Without looking at her he said, "Stay if you want. I've settled with the front desk." He tossed a brief glance at a pained Linzie and shut the door.

By the time he reached the outskirts of town, Pete had cooled down. He'd overreacted. What in particular had bothered him about Linzie's confession? Betrayal? He thought about the word and its implications. No. She hadn't really betrayed him. He'd arrived in town with a persona built on lies. Griffith tried to dig up dirt on him. In some kind of argument, Linzie had defended Pete but let it slip about the hospitalization. It wasn't the end of the world.

"Nice going, idiot," he said out loud. "You managed to make things worse for yourself. Good chance Linzie might now believe whatever Griffith's feeding her." Should he go back? No. He couldn't face her. What would he say? What *could* he say—sorry for being such a dick?

A tightening, sickening feeling settled in Pete's chest. He pounded the steering wheel and screamed, "What is the matter with me? Why couldn't I just keep it together? After all, I'm supposed to be a new man."

Pete arrived home weary from his self-recrimination and ashamed of his conduct. The damage was done; whether he could repair it, he couldn't say. He didn't want to lose Linzie yet sensed he might have. Maybe, maybe he could come up with something plausible, and she'd forgive him.

Damn, he told himself, *it's exhausting, this double life. Wish I'd known then what I know now.*

Chapter 17

Past Cleveland's I-90 morning rush hour, a Bavarian sedan carrying Anka Kovačević and the two boys sped eastward. A light drizzle mixed with grime and oil made the road slick.

Tucked into the right lane, cruise control on, the three sang along to a pop song. The rain increased just as Anka saw the overhanging flashing yellow lights warning of an approaching sharp turn nicknamed Dead Man's Curve.

She braked but too hard. The action caused her car to hydroplane. Her car lifted off the pavement and sailed into the adjoining lane, where it struck a five-ton truck. It careened off the truck and back into the lane. There it spun clockwise, rolled four times, and flipped onto its roof.

Upside down, the car's fuel spilled onto the pavement. Moments later a *whoosh* followed. The flames sucked in all the nearby air. Witnesses later claimed they heard high-pitched screams.

The truck driver raced to the inferno along with other motorists. None got close.

Traffic backed up along the interstate. By the time fire trucks and ambulances arrived, the fire had burned itself out, leaving a nauseating smell of burnt gas and charred flesh.

Squeezebox was placing books from a cart trolley onto a shelf when a sergeant arrived.

"You're wanted," the CO said. A hard-ass reputation, the humorless and authoritative Daryl Cassidy's delivery didn't hold its normal gruff manner this time.

Squeezebox peered at him. Wanted? By whom and why? Nothing on Cassidy's face gave any hints. He stepped away from the trolley and followed Cassidy to the grate. A guard unlocked the grate to the range. Cassidy and the prisoner stepped out to a corridor.

Squeezebox reviewed all past actions capable of landing him in trouble. Minor things, they might get him a write-up but not a visit to the lieutenant. He felt himself tense up.

They stopped in front of the shift lieutenant's office. *Uh-oh, not good*, Squeezebox told himself. Whenever a con was called to the lieutenant's office, it always meant bad news.

Cassidy opened the door and pointed inward. "Stand in front of Lieutenant Goslaw's desk."

Squeezebox obeyed. He kept his eyes on the seated double-chinned man who did his best to study an open file. He took his time before he looked up. He cleared his throat several times and spoke.

"Uh, Kovačević," he said, and butchered Squeezebox's name. A lifetime of carrying an unpronounceable name allowed Squeezebox to become hardened to people mangling it. No point in correcting Goslaw. He waited to hear what came next.

"I have some bad news, Kovačević. Bad news, I'm afraid. Your wife and two children died this morning in a car accident on I-90. It appears they were on their way to see you. I'm sorry for your loss."

Squeezebox heard the words but couldn't make sense of them. *His* wife, *his* kids, killed in an accident? Dead. Could such a thing be possible? He blinked furiously, unable to hear Goslaw prattle on.

"…of your loss, we cannot chance you attending their funeral. At the present, you're too much of a flight risk. However, given this sudden and unexpected tragedy, we'll allow you to make all necessary funeral arrangements from this facility, monitored, of course."

Squeezebox could only stare at him.

Goslaw looked at the file and back at Squeezebox.

"I've contacted the prison chaplain, Pastor Dorothy Lister. We'll take you to her office. She'll supervise you while you make all necessary calls."

Later Squeezebox marveled at how he had managed to get through the day. He phoned Anka's parents, who'd always despised him. Her father, Philip Misita, told him in a brusque voice they'd already been contacted by the State Police. He couldn't get off the line fast enough.

Squeezebox hung up and shook his head. He'd get no cooperation from her family. He next called a funeral home, Shaded Oak Cemetery, and his lawyer.

Dorothy Lister, a young, warm, and nurturing Lutheran pastor, proved to be of great comfort to Squeezebox. She stayed out of his way while he made his calls and didn't offer any clichés about God's plan or life's purpose.

When Squeezebox completed his calls, Lister adjusted her eyeglasses and said, "They're going to put you on suicide watch for the next couple of days, Dusan. They won't let you return to shop until after that. Try not to take it personally. It's protocol. They're obligated to do so."

"Yeah, I guess."

"You must have a lot of questions, thoughts."

"I don't know. I'm still trying to—what's the word? —process what happened. Right now I'd like more info on the accident, how they died."

"I'll see what I can do to get you the information." Lister stopped "But no grisly details. You don't want those. They're not going to help you get through this."

Once again, Squeezebox fought to absorb and understand words directed at him. He blinked hard several times and nodded.

Lister allowed herself a deep breath.

"There is no prescribed formula for what happens now. One size does not fit all. But what I can tell you is if you're like most people, you'll get, in stages, sad, weepy, and angry. You'll shut down. You'll blame yourself. You'll blame life, maybe even God. It's all part of recovery, your healing. It's different for everyone."

She fell silent for a moment. "What I do want you to know is I'm here if you require my involvement. What you go through will be difficult, very difficult. I don't have answers, but I'll do my best to help...if you'll let me."

"Okay," a still numb Squeezebox said, and rose.

His anguish proved worse than he could have imagined. The strong impulse to take his life never left him during the early agonizing days. He suffered through intense psychological pain over everything left undone and unsaid. Shock, guilt, anger—these changed from moment to moment and often overlapped with helplessness, hopelessness, and despair.

Lister did help. He met with her on a regular basis, grateful for her presence and comforting words. Yet Squeezebox could not bring himself to open up to her. His friends offered what she couldn't. They rallied around him with comforting words and damned society as well as the prison system for not allowing him to be at the funeral.

They worked to pull him out of his low spirits and distracted him whenever they saw his thousand-yard stare. Ribald jokes, bitching about other inmates, bringing him contraband and pruno, the notorious bootleg prison wine, all helped.

Squeezebox and Gates had many talks about death, its meaning and cultural significance. Through Gates, Squeezebox discovered how different societies viewed and approached the topic of death.

"Do you think there's nothing, you know, after you're gone?" he asked Gates one day when they walked around the yard.

Gates tugged at a shirt sleeve and said, "I haven't found any evidence to lead me there. We...I mean scientists, not me...do suspect there are possibly hidden dimensions we've yet to understand. And they're pretty sure multiple universes exist. Put it all together, something might exist. Just conjecture and interesting, but at this stage not much more. For me, life comes down to being a good person, something I haven't managed. If I had, I wouldn't be in this dump. After that, phew, damned if I know."

The person Squeezebox credited most for saving himself from himself was a 48-year-old Cherokee with long braids, Daniel Son of the West Wind Takatoka. Sentenced to fifteen years for victimless crimes, Son of the West Wind bore his conviction with the stoic manner of his people.

A repeated and blatant offender of gambling, drunk driving, and causing disturbances on his reservation in North Carolina, Son of the West Wind might have continued on in his ways if the law hadn't stepped in.

His band council did its best to tame him but failed. With reluctance it turned to the District Attorney's Office which brought him up on numerous violations as well as careless disregard for the law.

Acute liver failure made the former orderly of the prison's fourteen-bed infirmary a permanent patient.

Squeezebox had met tall, lanky Son of the West Wind three months earlier. He liked him and introduced him to his cellmate. The three would walk the prison yard, an odd grouping—a gangster, an academic, and a Native American—yet they found much to talk about.

Gates often shared information about cultures, foundational knowledge, and the need to always ask questions. He pointed out how even in prison convicts created their own society with its distinctive rules. Son of the West Wind spoke with pride about his heritage, his love of the land, his spirituality, and the warrior spirit.

Squeezebox thought of Son of the West Wind the way someone might think of a library—a font of knowledge. It astonished him that a man with little more than a grade six education could know so much. His friend quoted Arabic poets, knew the difference between the Xia and Shanghai Dynasties, and spoke with eloquence about gravitational effects. And he did it all without conceit or taking himself too seriously.

"Man," Squeezebox once said, "you are, without a doubt, the smartest guy I ever laid eyes on. Well, you and Gates."

His friend lifted his hands.

"High praise, Dusan, but any man who dares to wonder will find the gift of knowledge available to him." He scratched his nose. "It's a saying among my people."

"I guess I've got a lot more wondering to do," Squeezebox said.

"But I see wisdom sprouting in you. Me, a higher IQ hasn't protected me against stupidity. I landed here and destroyed my liver. Not the earmarks of a wise man. I'm still drinking joint hooch and am surprised I haven't gone blind yet. Ah, tomato wine, aged one day to perfection." He chuckled.

For his part, Squeezebox regaled the other two with stories of life in the underworld. Both stared wide-eyed or shook their heads in amazement. He often suspected Gates and Son of the West Wind kept him talking only to keep his mind off his suffering.

Squeezebox visited Son of the West Wind in the infirmary whenever a CO bothered to take him. The last few visits convinced him Son of the West Wind wouldn't be long for this world. His breathing had grown more laborious, his skin had taken on a yellowish tone, and he spoke with a thick tongue.

Perhaps because of his own issues with loss, Squeezebox found himself at the edge of tears whenever he left Son of the West Wind.

"How're you doing, man?" he asked and sat next to his friend's bed.

"I've had better days. I'm ready to paddle down the river to my end place."

Squeezebox shook his head. "Don't talk like that."

"Unbearable truths can't be changed no matter how much we want them to. I will soon be gone. If a man is known by the tracks he leaves, I only wish mine had been more recognizable. No matter. I do not feel sorry for myself, and you should not feel sad at my leaving. I am glad we had many good hours of talks together. You have stepped onto a spiritual path yourself, my friend. Anyone can see it, but you must rid yourself of the weight you carry. Are your visits with Lister not helping?"

"I guess, but there are some things I can't talk to her about. I don't know how. It's not her, it's me. I wake up in the night and think about

Anka and the boys. Anka especially."

Squeezebox tapped the armrest of his chair with the palm of his hand.

"Don't know if I'll ever get rid of my shame. Maybe I don't deserve to. How could I have been so selfish, so careless? I could have been a better husband, loved her better, stayed at home, but no, I'm out doing my thing, and look what my thing brought."

His friend coughed for a few moments and took a sip of water.

"You're a broken man, Dusan. In time this may change. You must fight to stop your heart from becoming hard. Don't be like most of the cons in here."

Another coughing spell, another sip of water. Son of the West Wind returned his gaze to Squeezebox. "No choirboys in prison, that's for sure." He followed with a shake of his head.

"Like you didn't know. Most of the returning cons arrive the same way they leave, angry and concerned only with themselves. It does not matter whether they're here or out on the street. They're never going to change. You, on the other hand, make it different for yourself. The spirit of your wife... What was her name again?"

"Anka."

Son of the West Wind sounded it out. "Anka. So pretty. Her spirit will see the change in you. She knows you're sorry, knows you're trying to be and do better. She's pleased for both. Here's the question, then: would your changes have come about if you were still out on the street?"

"No, but..."

Squeezebox's friend lifted his hand.

"Don't give me any buts. The Greek philosopher, Heraclitus, said no man ever steps into the same river twice. You're not in that same river anymore. If you want to keep the memory of your wife alive, if you want to honor her, recognize the change, hang onto the good parts and strive to be better each day. Never give up on growth."

Squeezebox nodded his understanding.

A CO called his name and ordered him to return to his unit.

Squeezebox stood up. "I'll try to come tomorrow." He lightly slapped his friend's hand.

Son of the West Wind nodded. "Good of you, but I may not be here."

"Well, I'm saying you will be, so I'll see you then."

The next day word of his friend's death spread throughout the yard.

Squeezebox found himself close to the edge of tears. He swallowed several times, blinked hard, and said to Gates, "Sonofabitch! West Wind warned me this could happen, but I waved it off." He exhaled and said, "His time, I guess, but I didn't want him to go."

"Would you rather have seen him suffer?"

"Stupid question, Gates. 'Course not. Damn, I'm going to miss him."

"Me, too. We had great talks, but he's done telling his tales in this life."

"I wonder who'll come to claim the body?" Squeezebox asked.

After lights out, Squeezebox lay on his bed and felt tears roll down the sides of his face. He silently wept for Anka, his kids, Son of the West Wind, and himself. He swiped at his face with the palms of his hands and let out a laborious sigh.

Moments later a new thought arrived: his money. He still had a lot of it. It couldn't help him in the joint, so what would he do with it? Who would inherit it? Anka's family? No. Nothing he could ever do would bring him into their good graces. Why bother? But there had to be somebody.

Nothing came to him. He fell asleep.

Chapter 18

Pete closed Montesquieu's course catalog. Fall classes would begin in a few weeks. He couldn't wait. He'd selected courses intended to stimulate: two English, a political science, and a philosophy.

On his second day of the term he saw a bulletin board notice in the English Department. Stillwell Correctional Facility was looking for volunteers.

Intrigued, Pete read the notice. Volunteers were wanted to teach everything from remedial English to helping prisoners prepare for their SATs. Those interested would be trained by the English Department.

Pete mulled it over. The prison—it had to be the one he passed on his way to town. He didn't know why, but he thought volunteering there could be interesting, and he had spare time.

He made up his mind to find out more. He approached the Department secretary. A cheery young woman looked up from her monitor.

"Hi. Can I help you?"

"Yes. I'm interested in volunteering for the literacy program."

She gave him a full smile.

"Terrific. You wouldn't by any chance be good at arithmetic and math? We really need those subjects."

A thought flashed through Pete's mind. *Good at arithmetic and math? The world is ripe with irony.* He held back on sharing the opinion. "Yeah, I'm pretty good with both, but they don't fall under English."

"You're right, she agreed. "We should change the notice." She followed with a quick smile and shrug. "Still interested?"

"I am, uh-huh."

"Excellent." She gestured to some chairs across from her desk. "Can you spare me a few minutes? I have some forms for you to fill out. Government. It's necessary. After that, we'll call you when we have enough trainee sessions. You can then decide if the program's right for you."

He completed the forms and returned them. She looked down at them.

"Very good. We'll contact you for our next orientation date and time."

A moment later Pete stood by the elevator. He imagined himself teaching in the prison. A distant memory came to him. Hadn't Linzie said something about Hayden sitting on the prison's release board? Her husband sat on the board, and he, Pete, would volunteer in the institution. Maybe there was something to this six degrees of separation thing.

The thought of Linzie caused him to flinch and recall his behavior in the hotel room. He'd hoped she'd phone him. He'd apologize and vow to make amends. She hadn't called. He phoned her work and always got her receptionist.

"May I tell her who's calling?"

Pete identified himself.

Each time the woman returned to the line and said, "Mrs. Hayden is occupied at the moment."

Pete got the message. He texted her two short messages: "How are you doing?" and "I'm sorry and miss you."

No response.

Her silence said everything.

On two separate occasions he saw her SUV on Madison.

On Labor Day they'd bumped into each other at Gallagher's, the town's independent bookstore. Crowded with students and townspeople, Pete had turned down the C aisle of the fiction section only to see Linzie in profile. Dressed in a tiered indigo skirt with a button-down shirt and a row of bangles on her arm, she stood in the middle of the aisle absorbed in a book.

His eyebrows arched and his heart raced. Should he turn around, scurry out of the aisle and store?

She raised her head and saw him. Too late to make his exit. No viable alternative, he approached and smiled. "Hi, Linzie."

"Peter," she replied, her voice flat, her expression fixed.

"How're you doing?"

"Fine, thank you."

Fine, code for not wanting to talk about anything.

"I've missed you."

She received the comment in stony silence.

He tried again.

"You probably won't believe this, but I am sorry, so sorry about what happened. You know, sometimes I don't know what comes over me. You deserved better."

She kept her gaze on him. At last she spoke.

"You're right, I did deserve better. It's a pity you didn't figure it out, but never mind." She lowered her voice. "I'd hoped for such a wonderful weekend only to find you being horrible. And for what?"

"So, what do we do now?" he asked.

"We? There is no 'we,' and there is no now." She turned her head and stared at books on a shelf. A few seconds later she looked at Pete and said, "I have enough stress with Griffith. I thought I saw something in you I liked."

Pete had enough sense to clam up.

A woman entered the aisle from behind Linzie and stood back a respectful distance. Pete didn't know her, but her body language and refusal to move on told him she knew Linzie.

"Someone behind you," he'd said and pointed.

Linzie looked over her shoulder at the other woman. "Marlene. Hi," she said with a forced lilt and gave a fast half-wave. She returned her attention to Pete and in a louder voice said, "Nice talking to you again. Take care."

She changed direction and approached the other woman. No further interest in anything in the store, Pete hurried out and back to the street.

Classes and the fall season energized Pete. The cafeteria, the bookstore, the hallways—everything held an aura of anticipation. Everything felt new, seemed new.

He enjoyed watching the faces of first-year students, excited and a bit overwhelmed. He recognized and greeted a few familiar faces and had lunch with two students from last semester.

A letter arrived at his house. He'd passed the background check. Pete hadn't expected any difficulty, but he still felt a sense of relief.

Eleven other volunteers showed up for the orientation in a small lecture hall. Spread out around the room, they sat and waited for someone to go to the front.

Pete considered the other volunteers. He doubted no more than eight years separated him from them, yet he'd have sworn it had to be a small lifetime. As he studied them, he realized one examining him—a young, long-haired woman with high, defined cheekbones. She pushed a fringe of hair from her eye.

He held her gaze for a moment and then looked away. He'd taken in her details: a straight nose separating a pair of watery-blue eyes, a small jaw, and a pale, Celtic complexion. Peek-a-boo auburn hair framed her pale face.

Two people entered and headed to the front of the room, a lanky, middle-aged man and a younger female. They introduced themselves as Drs. Steven Foley and Adel Jonas.

The slope-shouldered Foley, with thinning hair, dressed the part of a professorial cliché—frayed corduroy sports jacket, faded jeans, and a denim shirt with a narrow tie. A fleshy nose separated close-set, kind eyes.

His colleague chose a different sartorial approach. A white blouse tucked into a conservative blue skirt at her small waist gave her a librarian look. Pete glanced at her shoes. Yep, sensible.

Foley led off in his sonorous voice. He welcomed everyone. "Well, now you know who we are, why don't we start by going around the room and introducing ourselves?"

One by one the volunteers spoke.

Pete took interest in the woman who'd earlier sized him up. Bexley Stryker. He liked the sound of her voice.

When the last student introduced herself, Jonas clapped her hands together and said, "Let me tell you about the history of this program, its intent, and the satisfaction we hope you'll receive in helping inmates improve their lives."

She talked of the prison, its educational needs, and what the program expected of its volunteers.

"Literacy," she said, "is part of a larger program whose aim is to make inmates ready to return to society with skills. The more polished these skills are, the greater the chance of inmates succeeding in the outside world."

Finished, she turned to Foley.

He told the class, "Upwards of 68 percent of prison inmates are either illiterate or functionally illiterate. With this disadvantage, they'll never be able to successfully compete for jobs once outside of prison walls. We intend to change these odds."

Literacy training covered a two-week span.

A prison sergeant lectured on inmate culture. He spoke of common themes in prisoners' lives: abandonment, poverty, bullying, abuse, addiction, custody issues, illiteracy, homicide, and suicide.

Something about the guy's delivery, although Pete couldn't pin it down, sounded so well-rehearsed, fake, mechanical. Pete didn't doubt his words but doubted the sincerity. It came to him—soulless. The guy probably didn't care about all this, just spewed it and collected his paycheck. Maybe too many years of working with the underbelly of life had killed his real enthusiasm.

The sergeant moved onto a long list of dos and don'ts while working with inmates. The don't list included not making physical contact; never accepting anything; never doing personal favors, giving out personal information, or asking an inmate about his crime. Volunteers were warned about the hazards and consequences of smuggling in drugs, weapons, or any contraband.

The do list covered wearing proper clothing: no short skirts, see-through fabric, or visible cleavage for women; no jeans, ripped or shredded clothing for anyone. Volunteers were encouraged to be vigilant about manipulation and to behave naturally and respectfully.

Dr. Ian Duggan, a criminologist from Rutland, came and spoke about the mixed bag of issues inmates carried with them. She hit on many of the same themes as the sergeant but did it with more believability.

Pete liked Duggan's delivery. She showed passion and sensitivity and didn't deliver a memorized speech. She spoke with a natural ease, connected with her audience, and left time for questions.

"It's not only vital," she said in response to a question, "to understand the mind space inmates inhabit but how that affects everything they think, say, and do. Learning for inmates is a challenge, an uphill climb most of us have never or will never encounter."

Pete enjoyed the teaching/mentoring part. He paid strict attention to learning styles, cultural backgrounds, and how to effect positive change. Foley and Jonas stressed the importance of bringing particular teaching problems back to the campus during regular, weekly updates.

Their last session took them to the institution itself. Pete sat in the back of one of the three minivans, next to Bexley Stryker. They offered each other quick smiles.

The small column slowed and drove through two twelve-foot chain link fences, stopped again at an electronic gate, and at last entered the prison itself.

At the reception area, Pete and the others surrendered their personal property. Keys, wallets, and cell phones found their way into manila files with names written on top. He received a red plastic

ID card on a lanyard. Done, he waited his turn to pass through an electronic scanning booth.

A senior lieutenant led the tour.

Inside the institution Pete caught a curious smell, one he would remember for the rest of his life—a combination of cleaning solvents, body odor, the hint of feces, cigarette smoke, and whatever might have come from the kitchen.

He wrinkled his nose.

Heavy clanging doors opened, closed, and allowed the escorted party deeper into the prison.

The lieutenant talked and answered questions. He took his charges down a long corridor, stopped at a grate, and waited until a CO unlocked it and waved them through.

"These are the classrooms," he said, pointing to a group of rooms, "where you'll be doing your...whatever. The classrooms look much like any grade school or high school class might. We run all kinds of courses, from English to yoga to parenting skills to who knows what."

He broke off, perhaps to let his words sink in on his audience.

"When you're here in a class, there will always be one correctional officer with you and one patrolling the corridor."

Pete's mind wandered. He could not believe he'd committed himself to volunteering in a prison. *Me, the guy who stole so much money, in here. Can my life get any weirder?*

Chapter 19

Pete's first evening class at Stillwell dispelled any idealistic notion about teaching in a prison. He knew from the orientation and the tour that teaching wouldn't be easy. Yet the group of men who trooped into his corner of a large, divided room unnerved him. They ranged in age from late teens to late fifties and stared at him with hard faces, many with tattoos.

They waited for him to begin. Dressed in chino pants and a checkered shirt, Pete said, "Hello, everyone. My name is Peter Harris. Mr. Harris, but if Pete works for you, that's fine. Now, before we start, maybe you can all introduce yourselves and help me find out what your learning needs are."

Pete soon realized he'd walked into an educator's nightmare. A few surly cons gave every indication they had no interest in anything Pete had to offer. Some had serious learning disabilities; others didn't get past the fifth grade; while different ones had a year or two years of middle school. One inmate got through half a year of junior college.

He rubbed his hands together. "Gentlemen." He drew in breath to say more when a con with tattoos over his cheeks and forehead interrupted in a loud voice.

"Fuck's he thinks he is, callin' us gentlemen? What next, callin' us for tea?"

A muscular con, his sleeves rolled high to reveal his biceps, answered.

"Shut it, Perez. Some of us want to learn. You, you already got kicked out of shops. Go ahead, get tossed the first day of class here, and head back to the hole where you belong."

He looked over his shoulder at the slowly pacing guard at the back of the classroom who did his best to ignore him.

Perez responded with a defiant stare, folded his arms high, and studied his desk.

Pete remembered the talk about encountering students who

arrived with attitude. If they won't participate, don't waste your time on them, the instructors had said. They'll usually drop out or get written up.

These men sure weren't anything like students he'd taught in his night classes at junior college. On the other hand, they were here, so maybe they were eager to learn.

He discovered his most vexing problem came from loud voices on the other side of the divider. He did his best to block them out and stay focused on his tasks.

Pete resumed where he left off. "Okay, you've all signed up for this course or been assigned to it," he told his class. The thing I'm discovering is we're all over the map, so to speak, on math. Some of you are interested in getting your GED, and others need to work on fundamentals like division, multiplication, and so on. The only thing I can think of is to break the class into two, one for arithmetic and the other for math. It might take a while for me to get it all sorted out, but I'll get there."

The class got underway, and before Pete knew it the CO called, "Time. Wrap it up in five minutes. Five."

The cons closed their workbooks and rose. Institutional training kicked in. They formed straight lines on both sides of the divider and waited for the CO's instructions. He opened the door to the hallway and peered out. Satisfied with what he saw, he motioned with his fingers to Pete's group.

They moved out into the hallway and against the right wall. The CO gestured at the other line to follow.

Pete and Nigel Thorpe, who taught English composition, came out and watched a guard count and recount noses, then shout, "Count's accurate."

A different guard on the other side of a grate opened it and let the men march through.

Ten minutes later Pete and five other students waited in the foyer for the van. While the others spoke with great animation about their first experience, Pete cast his mind back to the last three hours. He found the whole experience frustrating but exhilarating.

For some time Pete had a nagging suspicion he needed eyeglasses.

An eye exam at the optometrist confirmed his hunch. After searching through the store's inventory, he selected round, silver, frameless Trotsky eyeglasses with plastic lenses. He thought they suited his face and gave him a studious look.

The optometrist agreed.

"These will take a little getting used to," he warned while he fussed with the hinges on the earpieces, "especially since you've never had glasses. Don't take them off. In about a week your brain will make the adjustment." He finished his adjustments, placed the spectacles back on Pete's face, and studied him. "So, welcome to your new look."

School demands, plus preparing for his next class at Stillwell, took up much of Pete's time and concentration. Thoughts of Linzie receded.

With more new materials and the lesson plan in his head, Pete stepped into the van and sat next to Adam Coolen, a junior.

Bexley Stryker sat on Coolen's other side.

Pete gave both a nod, a smile, and reviewed his lesson plan. He hoped it would go well. If not, it would be a long three hours. Still deep in thought, Pete didn't hear the female voice.

Coolen nudged him. Pete gave him a questioning look.

Coolen pointed to Stryker. She leaned forward and smiled.

"Pete, right?"

"Right, but sorry, I can't remember your name."

"Bexley. Bexley Stryker. I wanted to say I like your new glasses. At least I think they are. They're good on you. Give you a kind of professorial look."

Coolen cut in.

"You going after the look?" He made sure to follow the statement with his own smile.

Pete understood the good-humored playfulness. "It's exactly what I'm after." He winked.

The three made small talk. Pete discovered Adam had entered his third year of business administration. Bexley, also in her third year, had a double major in anthropology and sociology.

"What's the long-term plan?" Pete asked her.

"Law school."

The van pulled onto the prison road. Conversation stopped. All watched the electronic gate swing open. The van drove through. Inside at the reception area the volunteers again surrendered their personal items and received plastic ID cards.

Nigel turned on the overhead lights in the large classroom he and Pete shared. Curly-headed, the freshman could have passed for a high school student instead of someone in college.

"See you later, Pete," he said and moved to his side of the divider. "It's strange hearing you but not seeing you."

"I know what you mean. It does feel a bit strange."

Pete moved to his side and set his materials on the desk. He liked the diminutive Thorpe. Could he have done what Thorpe did at his age? Would he have? No. Pete doubted he'd have had his confidence, enthusiasm, or willingness. *Here's a kid from Missouri, which has got to be what, around thirteen hundred miles away. He gets here, doesn't know a soul, and right away he's teaching cons. Talk about impressive. In spades.*

He heard a heavy key inserted into the hallway grate and the sound of shuffling feet.

"Showtime," Nigel called over to him.

Pete's students trooped in first and took their seats. All but two brought their workbooks. The class chatted among themselves while Pete handed out class material.

Within a short time, Pete's more advanced students busied themselves reading and answering questions on their assignment, while Pete gave his attention to the other students.

"Let's start with basic facts in arithmetic. To get to and solve number problems, you need to..."

An hour later, Pete had those students working on simple assignments. He moved back to the math students.

Ten minutes into his talk voices on the other side of the divider rose in anger. "What the fuck is your problem, douchebag? You see me talking to you?"

"Who the fuck you calling douchebag, asshole?"

The sound of chairs scraping reached Pete. So, too, did the higher-pitched, interventional voice of Thorpe.

"Okay, settle down," Andy Costineau, the CO called out from the back.

Work in Pete's class ceased. The cons looked at one another and at him.

Costineau hurried to the other side of the divider. "Sit the fuck down, or you're on report."

The words failed to calm the situation. Costineau rushed out into the hallway while Perez and Jarvis stood up. Pete called them back to their seats. Both ignored him and disappeared to the other side of the divider.

Seconds later the sound of chairs scraping, men grunting, and what might have been thrown fists, reached Pete's ears.

An ear-piercing mechanical alarm howl followed seconds later. It spread through the prison and competed with the prison's public address system. "Lockdown, lockdown."

A dozen black-clad members of PERT, the Prison Emergency Response Team, with gridiron face masks and full, black, protective body equipment arrived and rushed into the study area. Truncheons swinging, they made for the altercations, followed by other guards with pepper ball-spraying shotguns.

Throughout the prison, the alarm and PA system energized the population. Inmates banged cups on tables, cell doors, and grates, and shouted their general dissatisfaction about life behind bars.

Inmates and the PERT team fought each other. The former group used fists, chairs, and whatever came to hand, but they never had a chance. Clubbed and doused with pepper spray, they soon surrendered and obeyed the command to place themselves face down on the floor, arms out in front.

A keyed-up Pete pulled Nigel against a wall.

"Stay close to me. We don't want our skulls bashed in by the riot squad or the cons. First chance we get, let's make for the hallway. Keep to the walls."

"Okay," a frightened Nigel croaked.

Mouth dry, his heart racing, Pete gulped for air and inched his way along toward the door, Nigel beside him. Two guards spotted them and pulled them into the hallway.

Inside the classroom, a shift captain ordered the general alarm shut off and the volunteers escorted into the foyer.

With muscular PERT team members on either side, the white-faced, shaken volunteers made their way out of the prison. They waited in stunned silence for their ride back to town. No one chose to talk, all likely reflecting on what they saw and experienced.

News of the violent disturbance spread beyond the confines of the prison. Few, if any, in the institution might have called the disturbance a riot.

The news media and the public had a different take. Stories spread about a prison riot, hostage-taking, and prisoners shot. Media cars and vans pulled up to the main gate. Prison administration would not let them closer. "A news release will be forthcoming," a captain shouted to reporters and TV crews.

The volunteers hurried into the vans, which inched their way through the media scrum.

The last time Pete recalled his heart beating this fast was when he stole the Serb's money. Here, reporters, photographers, TV cameras—the very thing he didn't want. He made a point of sitting in the middle of a bench seat, head down, between Adam Coolen and Paul Simpkins.

The small convoy reached the gate to the main road. Pete kept his head down while members of the news media pressed up against the minivan and shouted questions.

Simpkins powered down his window and in response to something shouted, "What?"

Bright lights invaded the interior of the van, and someone said, "Were you afraid they might kill you?"

Simpkins answered while Pete tapped the driver's shoulder. "C'mon. Can't you get us out of here any faster?"

The van reached the road. All the way back into town a distressed Pete worried he'd been caught on tape. Worse, film footage of the vans was carried on news outlets.

The next day Pete's classmates said they saw him on television.

A thousand miles away Nina Dabrowski (she refused to call herself Nieves anymore) stood in the doorway of her kitchen, the phone stuck to her ear. With her back to the large flat screen television in the living room, the mute on, she involved herself in an animated conversation with her mother, Julita.

"I'm not taking it back to the store for a refund, Mom. It's fine the way it is. You worry too much."

She listened and filed a nail while her mother spoke. By chance Nina turned and looked up at the television screen. She saw state troopers outside a prison with a "prison riot" banner beneath the lead story on the five o'clock news.

Nina reached for the remote to unmute the sound. A female talking head appeared against the distant backdrop of the prison and talked about the riot.

"We don't know all the details yet, Carmen," she told the news anchor, "but behind me, you can see civilians coming out of the prison. We're told prison guards heroically saved them from their captors."

The camera panned several minivans making their way past a throng of reporters and TV crews. One of the volunteers rolled down his window and said something. Beside him, a man with a beard and wire rim glasses turned his head from the camera.

The reporter kept talking.

Nina pushed playback. Was it? Could it be? No.

"Nina, you there?" the tinny voice at the other end of the land line asked.

Nina didn't answer and hung up. She replayed the film footage and gaped at the screen. Yeah, it sure looked like Stellan, but she couldn't be sure. This man had a beard, longer hair, and John Lennon glasses. Stellan fussed about his appearance. He wouldn't look like a hippy. Still...

The phone rang.

"Mom, telephone," Joanna shouted from upstairs. "Mom."

"Get it and take a message." Stellan. The mere thought of him and this lookalike, or whatever, brought a surge of anger to Nina. "Bastard," she whispered under her breath. "Rotten bastard."

The image of this Stellan double stayed with Nina even when she readied for bed. It stuck with her, but much of her anger's earlier ferocity was lost. Why get upset anymore? She hadn't loved Stellan since forever, it seemed, and now she had a new love, Borys. She'd managed to keep the house, and if she reels Borys in, all the better. Electricians make good money, she knew.

A last thought before she fell asleep: the guy did kind of look like Stellan.

The story caught the attention of someone else in Chicago, Boban Rakitić. He'd been sucking back a beer at *Fodor's Tavern* when the 45-inch screen showed the news. The lead story opened with a riot at a prison, Stillwell Federal Correctional Facility.

Rakitić ran his tongue along the inside of his cheek. Stillwell. Didn't they ship Dusan off to Stillwell?

The story gripped Rakitić's attention. He straightened. The guy on the screen, take away the beard, the glasses, and the longer hair, looked like Nieves.

After Dusan went up river, Helen told Rakitić about the disappearing cases. They'd never been found. You didn't have to be an Einstein to figure out what happened and why Dusan went nuts trying to Nieves.

Dusan gone, Rakitić tried to reclaim his boss' old territory. He talked Marko Kolarac into joining him.

They couldn't manage it. Tougher, meaner predators had moved in. Rakitić accepted he and Marko would now be bottom-feeders. But hey, it beat working for a living. But the idea of getting two mil—better than a lottery windfall, way better. Probably just a coincidence, but if this guy he saw was Nieves, he, Rakitić, could score the money himself and never fork out a dime for taxes.

He cast his mind back to the hunt for Nieves. Had he kept the picture Dusan gave him? He didn't know. He could check when he got home. In the meantime, he'd pay closer attention to the story. They'd run it again in the next half hour.

Chapter 20

News of the prison riot flooded the town and campus the following days. Identified, the volunteers became local heroes. Montesquieu's newspaper, *The Sacagawean,* did its best to track down each one and run a small piece alongside a photograph.

"How'd you find me?" an incensed Pete demanded of a student reporter with a wispy beard who blocked his progress in the hallway.

"Relax, man. Mostly luck. Who cares? I'd like to hear your take on what happened and get a pic." He raised his camera up to eye level.

Pete held a hand in front of the lens. "Not interested."

"Don't you want to be famous?"

"No, again. I've already used up my fifteen minutes of fame." He moved.

Undaunted, the student rushed in front of him and again aimed his camera.

Anger welled up in Pete, still unsettled by the news cameras at the prison. He snarled at the student, "Get your camera out of my face, or I'll break it."

"Fine, okay. Your loss," the student said to his back.

In his house, a red light on the answering machine flickered. Someone called, but no message.

Pete went to the kitchen and prepared his supper of lemon cod with avocado and tomato salad. His cell phone rang. He answered.

"Hello?"

"Hi, Peter," a familiar female voice said. "Am I bothering you?"

Pete's heart jumped at the sound of her voice.

"Linzie. Oh, hi. No, not at all." He allowed himself a quick inhalation and exhalation, and then said, "What's up?" The words were no sooner out than he regretted them. *What's up? Dumb. How about starting with, I'm sorry about what happened in Burlington?*

"I saw you on TV the other night. At the prison. At least it looked like you. Was it?"

"Yeah. I'm doing volunteer work."

"Oh, and you've got glasses now."

"I do, yeah."

"They look nice. Anyway, I just called to see if you were okay."

"Yeah, I am, thanks." Did she still have an interest in him, in the relationship? He didn't know how to approach the subject. Maybe an opening would come up.

"Volunteering at the prison. Good for you. What are you doing there?"

"Teaching literacy. Well, math."

But for her faint breathing, the phone remained silent for a moment.

"Hmm. No offense intended, but I wouldn't have guessed you were the volunteering type, whatever that is."

He answered with a nervous laugh.

"Know what you mean about me volunteering. I saw an ad on a bulletin board. I had spare time and..."

"Are you liking it?"

"It's too early to tell. I wasn't at it long enough, and then this riot thing; well, more like inmates letting off steam. Anyway, the administration's suspending all volunteer work for a couple of weeks to let things settle down again."

"And you're not scared about returning?"

"A good question. I probably should be, if I had any sense, but no, I don't see a repeat."

He wouldn't admit he had more than a bit of trepidation about returning and toyed with dropping out. He'd wrestled with the idea and reasoned quitting might draw unnecessary attention, so he'd stay.

Linzie's voice intruded into his thoughts. "Well, I'm glad you're safe."

Pete saw his opening.

"Thanks. Um, listen, I know I shouldn't start on this again, but I still feel bad about Burlington. Whether you believe this or not, I didn't intend to ruin our weekend. Will you accept my apology, and is there a chance we can start again?"

He heard a hint of sadness in her voice.

"I want to believe you. I also want you to know nobody is watching you. Nobody will, now or ever. I had a talk with Griffith."

The line went quiet for a moment.

Linzie spoke again.

"What happened made me a little afraid. There's a lot to like in you, Peter, but I think there are some mysterious, maybe dark places you keep hidden. They may surface when you least expect them and whether you want them to or not."

He heard her breathe and then say, "I could be wrong. Like I told you, I have enough on my plate with Griffith. I looked forward to a little fun and something—I don't know—joyful. What I got instead was a pan of cold water."

"So, for sure we're done?"

"In the way we relate to each other, yes."

A regretful sigh left him.

"All right. I accept your decision but will miss you and our time together."

"Thanks. Okay, you take care. Bye."

The line went dead.

Pete lost his appetite. He put plastic wrap around his food, placed it in the fridge, poured himself a glass of wine, and moved to the sofa. He'd miss Linzie. But what about her did he regret losing? Well, her body, the sex, her self-confidence, kindness, sparkling wit, and insight. How had she guessed he kept things hidden?

In a silent salute he raised his glass to Linzie's other lovers. *Hope you treat her better than I did.*

Three weeks later, Drs. Foley and Jonas scheduled a meeting with the volunteers. Jonas led with, "Stillwell would once again welcome back volunteers but has made extra security precautions.

You'll have more prison officers with you and patrolling the hallway. We've been told the ringleaders of this, uh, event, have been punished, and the others are eager to get back to their studies."

She turned to Foley, who said, "What we need to do with the rest of this time is talk about what you can expect your first day back and what to say to the media if they approach." He lifted his hands. "Though, it's old news now, and I doubt they will."

Pete's next teaching rotation went better than he could have imagined. A new and beefier CO kept vigil at the back of the room. Without Perez and Jarvis the other inmates focused on learning. He remembered his two-week training and how to encourage motivation.

He opened with a talk to the advanced students and handed out an exercise. While they busied themselves with it, he focused his attention on helping the others with remedial arithmetic. The evening lesson explained, worksheets out, Pete patrolled the two aisles and offered assistance to anyone needing it. He recalled Duggan's advice about looking past the tattoos, false swagger, and tough guy image and seeing the lonely, unsure, and rejected boys who dwelt within. He took his time and helped all those who struggled.

The effort paid off. He sensed less inner agitation in the men as they gave themselves over to problem-solving.

"Time," the CO called out.

Pete's class put down their pencils and closed their workbooks. All rose and waited for the CO's instructions. They filed out behind Nigel Thorpe's class.

"How'd it go, everyone?" Paul Simpkins asked when he climbed into the minivan along with Bexley Stryker. Pete sat behind them and studied the back of her head.

The question received positive response. All agreed the previous dust-up settled everyone down.

"Now we reap the benefit of those wanting to learn," Nigel said.

Pete nodded. "Good way of putting it."

Bexley smiled at him. "And you're liking it? Teaching, I mean?"

"I am. Say what you want, but these guys want to learn. You can tell."

Coolen agreed. "You can. They're grateful we're back. Well, most of them."

The van stopped in front of the student center. Bexley still on his mind, Pete unlocked his bike. He liked her but resolved to admire her from afar like some smitten knight of old. The Bexleys of the world needed safe, reliable partners who'd offer good marriages, nice houses with maybe proverbial white, picket fences, and Norman Rockwell-esque Thanksgiving gatherings. They didn't need his kind — outsiders and loners.

She did cause Pete to think of Linzie, and that in turn led him to thinking about an itch needing a scratch.

The following afternoon Pete sat in his room at the refurbished Adison-Loxley hotel, half a block from campus. He paced and looked at his watch. She should call any minute.

He recalled his initial conversation with a pleasant woman who answered the phone. With pure honeyed sexiness in her voice, she explained their service and answered all his questions, including payment.

"Your 'date' will go over it with you in more detail, sir. Payment is by cash or the mobile wallet app on your cell phone."

A dry smile reached Pete. What a world. You can pay high class hookers with a debit or credit card. To assure himself of the app's safety, he asked, "So, paying through the app, there's no adverse effect, you know, like you keeping records of your customers?"

"None at all, sir. We are a legitimate business. You swipe your card, and the transaction is done entirely with the credit card company. We don't keep a record of anything. With regard to your date, at the end, if you so wish to leave her any gratuity, it's entirely at your discretion."

His room phone rang. He picked it up and listened.

"Yes, okay. Eleventh floor. Room 1142. Good. See you then."

The soft knock came a few minutes later. Pete opened his door and smiled at the woman whose picture he studied on the escort service's website. Bouncy shoulder-length, leaf brown hair framed a diamond-shaped face. Large, bottle-green eyes looked out from under soft eyelashes and defined eyebrows. Her pouting lips would make any model envious.

He guessed she'd be six to seven years younger than him. Different, her elfin, limp-thin body, he told himself, so different from Linzie's robust curves.

"Hi, Pete."

"And hello to you, Fay. You look exactly like your picture." He closed the door.

Fay turned to face him in her yellow, one-button skirt suit with a gray blouse underneath, and spaghetti strap high heels. Classy yet sexy. "Were you expecting something different?"

He gave her a sheepish grin. "I hoped not, but you know…the Internet? What you see may not be what you get."

"Ah. Then I'm glad I didn't disappoint."

"Far from it." He stepped closer, unsure of what might come next.

"Okay, Pete, before we do anything else, I have to ask: are you a policeman? If you are, you'll break my heart. I'm only an escort, and you found me on our date-escort service, one for which we charge stated fees."

"I'm not a cop."

"Good. Anyway, like it says on our website, the service is $450 an hour."

"And, um, anything extra?"

"That depends on what's wanted."

"Then let's get this part out of the way."

Fay removed the credit card reader from her oversized purse and handed it to Pete. "Confirm the amount, and tap it with your card when you're ready."

Pete reached for his credit card. Seconds later, the electronic transaction completed, Fay set her purse on a four-drawer credenza and stepped closer. She placed her arms around Pete and nibbled on his ear.

"Are you interested in any extra?"

"Yes, I think I am."

"Whisper what you want in my ear."

He did.

She pulled back. "My, you have a lustful appetite. I can satisfy that. Here's what I charge." She brought her lips close to his ear and massaged his groin. "Do you still want to go ahead?"

"Yeah," Pete said in a shaky voice.

"You won't be disappointed. Do you have the cash?"

Maddened with lust, Pete nodded.

Fay pulled away. "Okay, lover, put the money on the table while I undress and get into bed." With a practiced, seductive fluidity she slid between the sheets.

Pete counted out the amount, set it next to Fay's purse, and climbed in with her. "So, what do you do?" she asked and stroked him.

"Student. Enough talk. Let's enjoy ourselves."

Their pleasure finished, Fay leaned her head on her palm and looked at Pete. "Very nice." She propped herself on an elbow. "Are you interested in telling me a little bit about yourself?"

A hooker who wants to talk instead of rushing out, Pete thought. How novel.

"Sure, I guess, but how about you? What are you all about?"

"We're discouraged from talking about ourselves," she said, "but, hey, you look trustworthy, so I'll take a chance. I'm a student, too."

"At Monty?"

"Nope. Bayfield."

"And is Fay your real name?"

"I can't say."

He stared at her, a stunning young woman who could easily have graced the cover of a fashion magazine. If he'd passed her on the street, he'd never have made her for a prostitute.

"Okay, so maybe Fay, maybe not. How'd you get into this line of work? Can I ask that?"

"Good money," she said, "and I control my hours. I've got my sights set on a high-end escort service after I graduate, you know, paying out $5,000 an hour."

Pete whistled. "Wow. Guys pay five grand?"

"In New York, yes, and more. I'll work a few years, sock the money away, and then open up a design studio."

"I'm impressed. A woman with a plan. In the meantime I guess I got lucky with a high-end date at way-better prices than New York. Well, you are drop-dead gorgeous, and I'm sure glad you're spending time with me."

"Thanks. But you're a nice-looking guy, the kind who'd for sure have a girlfriend, girlfriends, or a wife."

Pete held himself in check. "I guess."

"So, that's off-limits, huh? There's something—I don't know—maybe sorrow, in your eyes. Like they've seen too much of life already, searching for something their owner hasn't found yet."

He offered her a wary smile. "Perceptive. An escort who looks into men's hearts. Are you always like this?"

"Sorry. I didn't mean to give offence."

"No, it's okay. I'm not offended, only curious." She peered into his face for a moment. "I talk too much."

Again Pete assured her she hadn't offended.

With an eagerness in her voice, Fay said, "Would you like me to read your palm?"

Pete's eyebrows rose. "Palm reading? Why not. Any good?"

"Good? Yes, maybe. The only thing is, what I tell people sometimes isn't always flattering."

Pete considered what he heard. "Not to worry. Go ahead."

Escort and customer, still naked yet unmindful of their roles, partially sat up and braced their backs against the headboard.

Fay took Pete's hand, turned it, and studied his palm. A long moment later she said, "These lower lines reveal pain, sadness, torment, a struggle between altruism and selfishness. But mostly they show someone who doesn't quite fit in, who likes to be alone."

She looked at him. "How am I doing so far?"

He gave a small involuntary jerk. "Better than you think. You ever read *Steppenwolf*?"

"The Hermann Hesse novel? Yeah, we studied it in grade twelve."

His eyebrows rose.

"In high school? Boy, you really went to a progressive school, didn't you? Anyway, remember the main character, Harry Hallar?"

"The recluse? Yeah, what about him?"

"I guess you could say I'm a little like him. He identifies with some lone wolf roaming the Steppes. I'm not a recluse. Well, I don't think I am. Okay, maybe somewhat. About the lone wolf thing, I admit I have those tendencies. People, I like them well enough, but I also like my distance. I'm not made for the American dream thing. You know, nice house, wife, two-point-five kids in the 'burbs."

He stopped himself and screwed up his face.

"I don't know why I told you all this."

"Who am I going to tell?" She turned her head and glanced at the digital bedside clock.

"Our time's up. I have to go. Nice to have met you, Pete. I bet you have a real interesting story to tell."

"If you only knew."

"I bet." She slipped on her panties and bra and moved towards a mirror over a chest of drawers. "If you ever want to meet again," she said to his image in the mirror while she applied lipstick, "call me."

"You know, I might take you up on the offer," he said as he

climbed back into his underwear. "Before you rush off to New York and out of my price range." He hurried into a bathrobe and removed another $100 from his wallet.

"A little gift." He followed it with a smile.

"Why, thank you, kind sir."

Pete walked her to the door, surprised when she turned and kissed him.

"Goodbye. Take care of yourself."

She disappeared.

Heads down, Pete's Stillwell class busied themselves with their workbooks. Pete leaned over one or two, commented, praised, or corrected an exercise.

"Time, ladies," the CO called from the back. "Get your things together, and form straight lines."

Men rose. Two lines formed on the opposite side of the divider. The CO made a head count. He gave a nod and pointed to Pete's class.

"Out! No talking. You know the drill. Keep to the wall on the left."

The class spilled out and against the wall. Nigel's class followed.

Guards counted and recounted noses and checked a sheet to make sure the tallies matched. Convicts, long accustomed to ubiquitous waits, looked bored and endured the ritual. This particular day the wait took longer.

Pete and Nigel found themselves in the corridor before their normal time. Both looked at each other with a nothing-to-be-done-but wait shrug.

A convict from Nigel's class showed Pete his profile. Recognition came to Pete at once. Thinner, a shorter haircut, leaner, yet more muscular than when he'd last seen him. Adrenalin flooded Pete. Dusan Kovačević?

As if aware of Pete's attention, the convict turned and looked behind him. Slate gray eyes met Pete's. The man's eyebrows bunched together. He cocked his head for a moment before he returned his focus to the front of the line.

Pete's hands trembled, and his fingers grew icy cold. To hide his shiver he slid his hands into his pockets.

"Are you okay?" Bexley asked in the prison foyer. "You're white as a sheet."

Pete worked to get moisture back into his mouth.

"Fine, thanks. Probably low blood sugar. I didn't eat today. I'll take care of it when I get home."

"You sure?"

"Yeah. No problem."

Pete had to concentrate to get adequate air into his lungs and stop his muscles from aching. He couldn't wait to get home. Then again, was home still the shelter from the stormy blast?

Dusan Kovačević loomed large in his mind. Maybe the guy he saw wasn't him. He could be overreacting.

Pete paced and brooded in his living room. His stomach remained in turmoil. He should try to sleep, but something nagged at him, wouldn't let him be, and told him he needed more certainty.

To calm his doubts, Pete opened his laptop and searched Kovačevic's name. The search brought him to a website called prison locator. He typed in the name again. In seconds the search engine revealed what he dreaded he'd find. One Dusan Kovačević resided in Stillwell Correctional Facility near Martine Maines, Vermont. The hoodlum now served at the government's pleasure, all sixty years.

Mouth open, Pete gaped at the screen. No mistake, the real deal, Dusan Kovačević. So, it had happened, the thing the Serb had initially worried about, the feds putting him away on charges of racketeering. But here, here in Martine Maines?

Waves of anxiety washed over Pete. Breathe, he ordered himself. Breathe. Take deep breaths. Forty minutes later Pete finally brought his breathing under control.

Sleep proved impossible. His mind would not release him from worry. His eyes stared at the ceiling and often turned to see the time on his digital clock. A song from some pop tune came to him: *but sleep won't come the whole night through*. True for him.

Exhaustion at last claimed him. Pete's body indulged itself in involuntary muscle twitches while he slept. His dreams carried impending menace.

By six o'clock Pete rose, fatigued. In the cold morning light, his earlier fears had somehow lessened. He asked himself a new set of questions and reassessed yesterday's encounter. Maybe whoever he saw only looked like the gangster.

Another wave of anxiety struck Pete. He reminded himself that panic offered no solution. Should he run again? No, he'd stay. For now. See what played out. Why throw everything away and hightail it? If and when something changed, he'd deal with it. But in case things went south, he'd think about looking into a new ID.

Chapter 21

In the dayroom, Squeezebox plopped on the bench beside Gates Tally. He pointed to the TV mounted on the wall.

"Anything interesting?"

Gates moved over a few inches.

"'We shape our tools, and, therefore, our tools shape us.'"

"What? Gates, I know you love language, but use less highfalutin' English. You're not in academia, you know." He paused. "All right, I'll bite. Who are you quoting?"

"Marshall McLuhan," Gates said. "He coined the term 'global village' and gave the world great insights into the coming mass media, particularly television. Are you familiar with the phrase 'the medium is the message'?"

"Yeah, believe it or not, I am."

Gates did a passable imitation of a wince.

"I do believe you. At any rate, here in front of us, we have the ever-present idiot box, a strong symbol of society. And I, law offender extraordinaire, sit transfixed like the idiot I am. Why I'm watching this so-called 'reality' tripe is beyond me. I could be reading a book, playing cards, chess, doing the *Times* crossword puzzle, or indulging in an exchange of ideas with my fellow brethren."

Squeezebox chuckled.

"Exchange of ideas?" He glanced around. "How many Rhodes scholars you see on this range? Damn, Gates, you must have been a riot with your students."

"Kind words, sir. 'Riot'? Hmm. I'm not sure, but I'd like to think the master-student relationship resulted in mutual respect."

Squeezebox shook his head.

"Moving on... Listen, you will never believe what I'm about to tell you. I'm still figuring it out."

"You have my undivided attention. Did you receive a pardon or something?"

"A pardon? If I had a pardon, you'd have heard me long before I planted my feet back in the block. No. Still, what I'm about to tell you is incredible."

"So, share your tidings."

"Okay. You know the guy I told you about, the one who stiffed me for the two mil?"

"Hard to forget. The story still makes the rounds. It's better than an urban legend."

Squeezebox thrust out his chin.

"Focus, Gates. You want to hear this or not?" A slow, disapproving shake of Squeezebox's head followed.

Gates hit his chest with an open palm. "My most grievous fault. Apologies. Tell me."

Squeezebox took in a deep lungful of air.

"As you know, I signed up for an English class after the punch-up."

"Which I fail to understand," Gates said. "The class is remedial, and you, my felonious associate, are long past bettering yourself at that level."

"Thanks, but I took it just for something to do. Anyway, the room's split by a divider. My teach does English, and the other guy does math. Okay, ready? Guess who's teaching math?" He gave Gates no time to reply and said, "Stellan Nieves, that's who, the guy who stiffed me. This is either him or his double."

"No! You're serious?"

"Damn straight. The guy who ripped me off. Hair's a lot longer, different threads, and he's got glasses, but I'd know the face anywhere."

"You really think it's him?"

Squeezebox answered with another nod.

"Pretty sure, but I need to be certain."

"He didn't recognize you, this volunteer, assuming it's your guy?"

Squeezebox shook his head.

"Not in the classroom, but out in the corridor. We made eye contact. I'd swear he looked surprised. And frightened. Damn sure I saw fear in his face."

Gates' eyebrows furrowed.

"What's he doing here? He should be in Bermuda or somewhere. It doesn't add up. But let's say, for the sake of argument, it is him. What do you intend to do next?"

"Good question. I'm still getting my head around it. For the longest time, I thought about what I'd do if I ever met him." He threw a hand in the air. "The money used to matter. Maybe it still does. I'm not so sure anymore. Before I lost Anka and the boys, fucking-A he'd pay, but the revenge thing's not so red hot now. Weird, huh?"

"I suppose. It was...is...a lot of dough, but you said yourself you had more."

"Beside the point. What he took wasn't chump change."

Gates squared an ankle over a knee. "But you're a different man with a different take on life now. Maybe that explains your ambivalence."

Squeezebox lost a good night's sleep. He lay on his steel bunk and stared at the ceiling. Over and over he replayed the brief, unexpected encounter with Stellan Nieves. Could it be? Was it possible? He couldn't be sure, but if it ended up being Nieves...

The following morning Squeezebox asked Gates for a favor.

"Can you get anything on the two volunteers who teach in 11-B on Thursday night, and copies of their photos?"

"I'll see what I can do."

Gates returned with disappointing news.

"I can't get near the files right now. You'll have to wait. When I get the chance, I'll pounce."

"Good enough. Thanks."

Four days later Gates slid photocopies containing vital information on the two volunteers to Squeezebox in the rec room.

"Take them over to the card table, open a newspaper, and

pretend you're reading. And make sure the hack doesn't see you. He does, we're in big trouble. Especially me."

"No problem."

Squeezebox unfolded the two sheets and slid them under a newspaper. He kept a wary eye on the CO, busy in conversation with two cons.

The first sheet showed a fresh-faced, head-and-shoulders picture of a man, Nigel Thorpe, who looked like a senior in high school. Squeezebox slipped it under the second sheet.

Peter Harris stared into the camera. Squeezebox's mouth dry, he stared at Stellan Nieves, or someone who looked like him, who lived in Martine Maines.

A quick upward glance told Squeezebox the guard was still in discussion with the two cons. Good. He again gave his attention to the photocopy. Sure looked like Nieves. Give this Peter Harris a haircut, lose the glasses, put him in a suit, and add a little weight, and he'd be the thief who left with his money. And here he was teaching, in Stillwell of all places.

Squeezebox pulled the sheets under the table and ripped them to small pieces. He rose, moved to the garbage bin, and tossed them. Tomorrow he'd find Tommy Morello. In the yard.

He approached Fat Fingers entertaining a group of men.

Morello stopped his tale, threw his arms wide, smiled, and said, "Danny Balls Up, too bad God never made you a paisan. Ah, what the hell, we can't all be perfect, right?"

Squeezebox went along with the ribbing. He gave Morello his best smile.

"We all have our crosses to bear, Tommy."

They embraced. Morello slapped Squeezebox's back.

"Listen to you, talkin' all fancy now, hangin' with the egghead. Never mind. You're still good people. So, what's up?"

"Can we take a walk around?"

"Yeah, sure. Let's go."

A few seconds into the stroll Squeezebox congratulated Morello on his impending release.

"Thanks," Morello said. "Finished my full time and walkin' outta here with my head high. The feds got nothin' more on me. Fuck 'em."

"Glad for you. The only way out for me is the Back Door Parole."

Both understood the jailhouse jargon for leaving in a pine box.

Hands deep in his pocket, Morello said, "Never know. Word's goin' around even those private prisons are overloaded, and the feds are lookin' to make some room."

Squeezebox made a face. "You mean kicking cons out? I'll believe it when I see it. Anyway, I need a favor."

"Yeah, what?"

Squeezebox told him what he'd discovered.

"I want somebody to go into a guy's place on the street in town. Make it clean so the guy never knows it. Get anything on him that proves he is who he says."

"Why?"

"I think it's that accountant who played me."

"The guy who ripped you off?"

"Yeah. Damn sure it's him. He's here as a volunteer, and I saw him."

"What the fuck! No. Ain't that a bitch? Anyway, Cost ya."

"Expected it to. How much?"

Morello thought for a moment and said, "Five large."

Squeezebox shook his head in disapproval. "Five thou? Wow. I thought I'm 'good people'."

"You are, but hey, business is business. You should know."

Squeezebox let out a breath of air. "Fine. I'll get the dough to you. Through the usual channels?"

"Yeah. Stay in touch, and in the meantime have a sit-down with Joey Lasso. Give him the details of what you need. If you need anythin' else, talk to Joey. He'll be handling things for me."

"Got it. And thanks."

A week and a half later, on an overcast night when the temperature dropped and the air suggested the potential for a first snow, a green panel truck parked two blocks from Court Street.

The driver locked the van, slung his backpack over a shoulder, and walked with purpose to his destination. In his corduroy slacks, padded windbreaker, and athletic shoes he'd draw scant attention if he met anyone.

The street remained quiet. No car or pedestrian appeared. The man crossed the street, bent, and pretended to tie a shoelace while he scanned the houses. Satisfied no prying eyes studied him, he looked closer at number 79. Interior lights were on upstairs and down. It didn't mean anything. Only fools left their homes dark.

He crossed the street and approached the house. An outdoor wall lantern illuminated the area at the front entrance.

The burglar spotted the security camera. Okay, here goes. Head down, his baseball cap hiding his face, he stepped up to the front door and rang the bell. If anyone answered, he'd pretend to ask for his friend, Kenny Bateman. "He doesn't live here? Oh. Wonder if I wrote down the wrong info. Sorry to bother you. Take care, now."

No one came to the door. He tried a second time. Nothing. Not even barking. Good. He stepped back from the door and noted the decorative window grates. Too difficult to get in that way.

The burglar walked to the rear of the house, out of range of the camera. A quick look into a side window suggested no one was home. He unlatched a gate to the backyard and spotted another camera. He'd keep to the dark area of the yard, ready to spring if anyone challenged him.

A quick assessment told him he'd have no luck trying to get in the house through the back. Camera and a sensor light would announce his arrival. If the owner went to all that bother, he'd also have secured the sliding door. Okay, so not through the back. Plan B.

The burglar returned to the street. Time to earn his pay. A familiar adrenalin rush surged through him as he set down his backpack and gave the street another cursory look. Nothing. He took a deep breath. Time to give the front door his undivided attention.

He unzipped his backpack. From inside he retrieved a black, strange-looking electronic gadget, much like a portable CD player, with an antenna. He pointed it at the door and flipped a switch on the side of the device. Red dots flashed; seconds passed, and the dots turned a solid red. The burglar exhaled, pleased he'd suppressed the alarm system. Someday, he thought, manufacturers will figure out they need a whole lot more than two gigabytes for good security systems.

He returned the device to his backpack and focused his attention on the lock. Good quality. Not the cheap shit from China. If people really cared about their homes, they'd only install these kinds of locks.

The burglar pulled a lock pick set from his bag and selected the picks he needed. He crouched in front of the lock, slid the picks into the lock, rotated and lifted them to their desired height for manipulation. Every so often he glanced over his shoulder. The muscles in his legs had begun to ache when at last he heard the first satisfying click. A small smile of victory arrived, yet he continued until he heard the final click.

He allowed himself a final look over his shoulder, returned the picks into his set, and opened the door. Confident he hadn't been seen, he entered the house, grateful for the aid of the indoor house lights. Flashlight beams in a dark house are never a thief's friend. Someone might notice a light dancing around the interior.

The intruder started his reconnaissance on the ground floor. Nice furniture, he thought; tasteful, expensive. A man's house. For sure if a woman lived here, there'd be framed photographs on walls and on prominent flat surfaces. To say nothing of knick-knacks and—what was the buzzword?—objects d' art.

Focus, he told himself. Remember your instructions. Look for anything that tells you who this guy really is.

Starting with the kitchen, he inspected the cupboards, the fridge-freezer, the dishwasher, and looked into two cereal boxes and peanut butter and jam jars. Nothing. People hid things in the most mundane places.

The burglar moved to the top floor. Careful to follow instructions, he checked everywhere—drawers, closets, and a bookcase. He looked under the desk, bed, and mattress. The medicine cabinet and the toilet tank also received his attention. Nothing piqued his interest. He next moved to the laptop. High end. No point powering it up; he'd never get past any password protection.

His inspection finished, he returned to the main floor and moved to the small basement. He reminded himself to be careful with his flashlight. Nothing held his attention. Time to go look in the garage.

He cased the usual places people hid valuables. Nothing. Satisfied he'd done a full search, he returned to the front door and aimed his device at the wall-mounted security system. Once more the red lights blinked before they grew steady. He'd rearmed the system. Better get going. With caution, he opened the door, glanced at the empty street, and with little sound shut the door behind him.

Close to his van he met a man walking his dog.

"Evening," the dog walker said and nodded.

The burglar returned the nod. "Yes, good evening. Looks like we could get some snow."

"Let's hope not," the other man answered. "Too early for my liking."

Three days later Squeezebox had his report.

A con in the yard slipped him the folded, one-page write-up. Using the busy, general activity for a shield from any prying guard, Squeezebox read the report twice and memorized it. He tore the paper to shreds and dropped it in a bin.

Later in the evening, he shared the findings of the report with Gates.

"Interesting," his friend said, and stared out onto the walkway. "I'm not trying to rain on your parade, but this doesn't confirm anything."

"Are you inferring I don't know?"

"No. I'm *implying* you don't know for sure...yet."

"Okay, okay, but it's not like this is a court of law. So, the guy didn't find anything with Nieves' name on it. A couple of things are curious. Wanna...? Sorry. Want to know?"

"Sure, go ahead."

"All right. Maybe by themselves they're not much, but you put them together, and you might have something. For starters, this guy's place is super secure. He's got window grates on the ground floor, bars and locks on the sliding door. It's supposed to be in a nice, safe neighborhood in small town Martine Maines. So, why go to all the bother?"

"Maybe he likes to be extra safe. What else?"

Squeezebox gave Gates a long look.

"His computer. The guy who broke in says he couldn't waste time trying to crack it. So, nothing there, but..." He broke off. "Harris is teaching math." Squeezebox let the words hang.

"Think about it. Stellan Nieves was my accountant. Who better to teach math than an accountant?"

"A math teacher, I suppose."

Squeezebox waved an impatient hand.

"You listening or having a bout of being ornery? I'm trying to tell you something."

Gates lightly tapped his left chest. "Mea culpa, mea culpa. Go on."

"Fine, so I'll give you he could be a math teacher. Could be, but unless the state of Vermont pays its math teachers really good salaries, or his parents left this guy a nice chunk of change in their will, he hasn't got the means to live where he's living. You see where I'm going with this?"

"Yes, you believe you've made a compelling argument. But..." Gates drew in a breath. "I know we discussed this before. What are the odds of him being here? You must admit, it stretches the imagination."

"I have no trouble admitting it. At the moment, I don't much care how or why this has come about. All I'm pretty sure of is this Peter Harris used to be Stellan Nieves."

"Let me ask another question," Gates said.

"Another one? Okay, go ahead."

"Two questions, actually. What if it's not him, and what will you do if it is?"

"They're not hard to answer. "If it isn't him, what have I lost? Time and some money, that's all. And time is all I have. If it is him, I'll have something new to fill my days, won't I?"

Gates bobbed his head.

"And then what—find some way to take your proverbial pound of flesh?"

"Ahh. 'The pound of flesh which I demand of him is dearly bought. 'Tis mine, and I will have it.'" Squeezebox grinned at Gates. "Shylock."

The corners of Gates' eyes crinkled.

"Nicely put, Mr. Kovačević."

Squeezebox returned the smile and gave an exaggerated bow.

"Kind of you to say, Mr. Tally. There's always room for Shakespeare, right? If it is Nieves, he'll pay. I'll come up with something. In the meantime, I have to figure out how to meet with him."

Setting up a potential face-to-face with Nieves-Harris proved more difficult than Squeezebox imagined. First, he had to switch classes from English to math. To do so required the permission of Ron Berryman, the assistant manager of ACE, adult continuing education.

Berryman did not fit the stereotype of a jolly fat man. His

personality lent itself to being sullen and suspicious.

"No," he said from across his desk to the inmate. He gaze moved down to the file on his desk. "You're in English, and you'll stay there."

He stopped and peered at Squeezebox.

"Wait a minute, wait a minute. You suddenly want out of English and to join the math class. Why are you wanting to go there? What con are you pulling?"

"None sir, honest. I need math if I want to take the computers class. I heard some of the other cons talking about how much they're getting from the math class. I could stand to improve my math, so…"

"Well, too bad, and the answer is still no. You're in English, and you'll stay there. I'm not having cons jumping around at every whim. This is prison, Kovačevic, not some goddamn community college. Or did you forget?"

He rubbed his stomach. No one had ever seen Berryman's belt, hidden under his mound of fat. The cons called him Diabeetus. Bets were placed on the date of his first stroke or heart attack.

Squeezebox held back his annoyance and listened to the heavy, laborious breathing of the corporal.

Jesus, Diabeetus, pity you're not in charge of the PERT team! We'd start a riot just to see you leading it. It's a wonder diabetes hasn't taken an arm or a leg yet or knocked you on your fat ass. Go scarf down a box of donuts. Bound to improve your disposition.

"Come on, sir. I'm thinking of maybe getting a degree in computers. I need math for it."

Berryman let loose an undignified snort. "A career in 'computers'? Back to earth, Kovačevic. You keep forgetting where you are—Stillwell."

"I know, sir, but they're talking about getting new computers and volunteers to teach us. I'd like to get in on it."

"Where'd you hear this? I didn't hear it."

Squeezebox hadn't heard it, either. He made it up. Rumors were the bread and butter of prison life; one followed the other. Few ever bothered to trace them to their source. And prison guards weren't immune from circulating rumors, either.

"Don't know, sir. Something going 'round. You know this place." Berryman nodded.

"That's a fact. What happened to the austerity kick the Bureau's been yapping about over the last few months? Where they getting the money for this?" He looked at Squeezebox. "Never mind."

He indulged in an exaggerated sigh.

"All right, fine, Kovačevic. I'll let you make the switch this time, but don't bother me with anything else."

With drama he pulled a carbonless copy paper from his drawer, wrote a directive on it, tore off the sheet beneath, and shoved it at Squeezebox.

"Give this to the instructor. And turn in your textbook. Oh, and any textbook or workbooks for this class comes out of your pocket, understand?" He delivered another dramatic sigh. "We're done here. On your way."

"All right, and thank you." Squeezebox held back his smile. He'd conned Berryman. Now to set up the next phase of his plan.

Chapter 22

Pete had returned to his old self. Mostly. He'd caught another glimpse of the convict, Kovačević. To his surprise it hadn't resulted in the same emotional collapse. He remained wary but reminded himself the Serb, not he, sat behind bars. The coincidence did, however, cause him to wonder about the universe. *Of all the places I pick to hide out in, a sleepy little college town where nothing much happens, who do I meet? Unbelievable!*

At home, Pete worked on an essay. Something nettled at him, something other than Kovačević. Long minutes passed before it came to Pete. Small telltale signs told him someone had been in his house.

His gaze settled on his bookshelves. A few of the books were no longer in a straight line. He stared at his shelves for a few minutes before he rose and inspected each room, checked every place someone might be hiding. He checked the windows and doors. No visible sign of a break-in.

When he finished his general inspection, Pete turned his attention to anything that might validate his suspicion. He began with the garage and noted his paint cans weren't quite the same way he last saw them. He moved to the basement and noted the light switch in the down, not up position. Food in his freezer had been disturbed.

In the kitchen Pete stood still and examined the evidence. Someone's been in his house. Without a doubt. A pro. Everything said the thief had entered his house and come in through the front door. Worse, he'd entered and managed to override the security system. How, Pete didn't know, but it troubled him, but not as much as the why. The burglar hadn't taken a thing. Who breaks into a house and leaves empty-handed?

Pete reached an inescapable conclusion: this break-in was linked to Kovačević in Stillwell. His heart raced again. If someone broke into his house once, what's to stop him from doing it a second time and returning with a gun? He doubted the Serb would let bygones be bygones. Especially when it involved over two million dollars.

He took deep breaths. Maybe he should run. He could. His assets were liquid and for the most part offshore. If he ran, he could lock up his house and arrange for Linzie to sell it, contents and all. He'd find a way for her to transfer the funds to him. She might think his sudden departure strange. Who cared? He supposed it might fit some kind of narrative she had of him anyway. Tonight, maybe he should get a room in a hotel. In the morning he'd pack, take care of some necessary things, and vanish. Later he'd get a new identity.

Pete returned to his desk and pondered his situation. So, Kovačević had found him. If he'd wanted him dead, why wait? Maybe the break-in had a different purpose.

Another question arose: did he want to leave Martine Maines? He liked the college town and what it offered, liked it more than anywhere else he'd been. Why do a jack rabbit only to start over again somewhere else? It made more sense to wait and see what Kovačević intended. Blackmail? How? Kovačević couldn't exactly go to the cops. No, Kovačević had something else up his sleeve. Pete had no idea what it might be. Only thing to do would be to wait and see.

Satisfied with his beginning strategy, Pete explored the house a second time. He found no further evidence of anything being disturbed.

He returned to his laptop and searched for a locksmith. He found a local operation that advertised a 24-hour service. It took two hours before a tradesman pulled into his driveway. Pete had used the time to investigate home security systems.

The locksmith removed Pete's old lock from the front door and installed a new one with a steel pocket behind the strike plate of the doorjamb, and a new, quality deadbolt lock.

By the time the tradesman said goodbye, Pete had contacted a salesman from a new security firm. A long conversation convinced him to install a combined motion and vibration sensor system. It would maintain lights at front and back of the house but would also be sensitive to any exterior vibrations.

Satisfied he'd done all he could, Pete went to bed. He didn't know what kind of sleep he'd get, but he quickly fell into a deep, dreamless sleep.

Pete and Nigel entered their shared classroom, ready for another evening. He fished the textbook from his backpack and heard the corridor grate open followed by the sound of shuffling feet. Any second now they'd appear. He'd quieted most but not all of his anxiety.

Inmates drifted into the classroom, heading to either side of the divider. Pete stood behind his desk. His eyes widened at an unexpected sight, and his blood ran cold. For a moment he doubted his legs would support him. Dusan Kovačević veered into Pete's class, a proffered paper in his hand, and his gaze locked on Pete.

"I'm supposed to give this to you, Mr. *Harris*." He placed emphasis on Pete's surname. "I've joined the class."

Pete took the sheet, his mouth dry. He mangled a thank you and told Squeezebox to sit at one of the desks.

Without a word, Kovačević nodded, turned, and took a desk at the back.

It took a few seconds for Pete to bring himself under more manageable control. He worked to get moisture back into his mouth and commenced with his lesson plan. He gave himself over to his task.

The new student listened along with the others while Pete lectured on how to simplify fractions and convert percentages.

Somehow Pete managed to get through the two hours, grateful when at last the CO at the back called out, "Time to close it. Five minutes."

The cons knew the drill. All closed their workbooks, rose, and formed a straight line.

The CO did his count and opened the back door. "Single file.

Keep straight out into the corridor. English class goes first. Keep to the left wall."

Most of Pete's class offered him an obligatory "Good night, sir" before they left. Kovačević lingered for a moment, spun about, approached Pete, and handed him a folded note. "Something to think about for next week...sir."

He hurried to join the line out the door.

Until then Pete had brought his panic under control. The note undid everything. His stomach churned, and waves of anxiety raced through him. He guessed at the note's content, certain it would mention his theft.

At home he opened the note. He admired the penmanship with its concave arcs. Kovačević's? Whoever wrote it had a steady hand.

He read it.

How are you doing, Stellan Nieves? Odd, isn't it, both of us here on opposite sides? You need to visit me. I checked. You can get around the fraternization thing by saying you're giving me some one-on-one extra tutorials. Clear it with admin first, and make sure you bring a workbook and some writing materials. I'm looking forward to seeing you on Saturday morning.

Pete flopped onto his couch, read and reread the note. Could Kovačević have written this? No matter. What should he do?

Go see what he's got to say, an inner voice urged. Talk to the Serb. See what he wants before you split town.

The dreaded meeting arrived. Pete had never been at the institution during daylight hours. Anxious and tense, he, along with other visitors, endured a compulsory search, a long wait, and a check and recheck for anything of a contraband nature. Visitors all waited in a large, empty room. At last a door to the visiting room opened. People hurried in, scattered about, and claimed empty tables.

Pete chose a small one next to a wall. The COs stood vigilant on the four corners of the room. Two patrolled among the tables.

A different door opened, and inmates filed in and searched for familiar faces. The room gave way to a cacophony of tears, anger, and expressions of joy. Inmates and visitors embraced, kissed each other, and slapped backs. Here and there a disquieting voice rose, brought under control by sullen stares and warnings from a CO.

Pete busied himself for a moment with pulling a textbook, workbook, and pencils from his backpack. He didn't notice a shorter, stouter man, sleeves rolled up to show off biceps, stop in front of him. The man made a show of clearing his throat.

Startled, Pete looked up.

"*Mr.* Harris," Squeezebox said, with a strong emphasis on the first word. He took a seat on the opposite side of the table.

Pete swallowed and tried to say something. Should he stand? What did protocol demand here? It didn't matter. Best not to say anything.

Kovačević sat and glanced around the room before he settled his gaze on Pete.

"Busy. Lots of noise. Good." He studied Pete. "You've changed."

"Same for you," Pete said, his mouth dry, afraid the catch in his voice betrayed his true inner state. "Last time I saw you, you had longer hair. Now it's almost a brush cut with bits of gray."

Kovačević tossed a shoulder in nonchalance. "What're you going to do? It's the joint. They invented stress." His eyes steady and unblinking, he said, "But you, you were always in lame suits and had a big stick up your ass." He broke off. "No offence meant."

"None taken. Can't argue with you." He picked up a pencil, opened his textbook and looked at it. He pointed to the other pencil. "Better pick it up and open the workbook. As you said, let's make the visit look believable. Every so often look down at the workbook."

Kovačević looked down at the workbook and then up at Pete. He waved a finger up and down Pete. "And now you've got a whole new thing going. Including the glasses. Are they real or just for show?"

"Real."

"I've got to admit you look way different than the last time I saw you, more chill. See, we're both different. And how about this? Kismet. You and me here together in the same room."

Pete studied Kovačević. Kismet? When they first met, he doubted the Serb could handle most two-syllable words. Now he tossed out the Islamic word for destiny. And, he realized, no bad breath.

Something else about Kovačević caught his attention. The last time they met, the man had trouble sitting still, and his speech was more of the staccato type. This new Kovačević spoke with a quiet assurance, his movements settled.

He'd aged, as well, faster than Pete might have expected. Pete recalled an article he'd read in a popular science magazine. Rapid cellular aging happened to people under stress. Kovačević did say prisons invented stress. Maybe that explained all this. He saw something else in the Serb—a sadness around the eyes that suggested some unfathomable pain.

Kovačević's voice broke into his thoughts.

"You in this room?"

"Huh?"

"Here," Kovačević said. "You here or off somewhere else?"

"Uh, oh, yeah. Sorry. My mind did wander. Okay, let's get to it, shall we? We both know you didn't demand this meet-up to scratch some social itch."

Kovačević looked down at his workbook and back at Pete. "Good one." He leaned across the table and lowered his voice. "Let's start with the why."

"Yeah, about that. What made me take the money, you mean?"

"That's the one. I was always—still am—curious to know."

Pete pressed his lips together in thought for a moment and then said, "A character flaw, that's all. Kind of like Willie Sutton. Ever hear of him?"

"The '30s bank robber?"

"Him, yep. When they caught Willie, they asked why he robbed banks. He's supposed to have said, 'That's where the money is.' Somewhat the same for me, only it wasn't a bank. I guess you could call me a misguided thief. I thought the money would seriously improve my life, and…" He followed the statement with a half-shrug.

"So, that's your handle for yourself, 'misguided'? I could think of better words for it."

Pete felt himself redden at the chastisement. Chin out, he whispered, "I get it. I stole your money, and you don't give a shit about my motives. All I was trying to do was tell you that the money didn't bring what I thought it would. Now, can we get to the punishment part?"

"Bracing for the bad medicine, are you?" Kovačević said. "I'll get to that in a minute. In the meantime I, for damn sure, deserve the right to know how it played out, how you got away with it. So, the dough was there, and you helped yourself. Had to require a fair bit of planning."

Pete tossed a what're-you-gonna-do hand in the air answer. "All right, I stumbled onto your secretary...um, I can't remember her name. Karen?"

"Helen."

"Oh, right, Helen. I caught her standing over the floorboards. It awakened my curiosity, what she was doing. When she went home, I removed the boards, and the rest you know. But let's also talk about what's on both our minds, you wanting your money back, with, I'm sure, some kind of interest?"

"Maybe."

Pete's head shot up at the response. *Maybe?* He waited for more. It came fast enough.

"You're lucky I didn't catch you at the time," Kovačević said. "I'd have ripped your throat out. Different time and place now. I'll just say since I got tossed in this shithole, I've learned to take a broader view of life. It's funny how being in the joint teaches you things you never thought about out in the street."

He paused for a moment. "Back to what we were talking about. I might let you skate, but it's going to cost you something."

Pete did his best to compose his face into one of nonchalance. His insides prickled with nervous, positive agitation at the idea Kovačević might forgive the debt.

"Okay, and what will this something be?"

Kovačević leaned forward.

"This, Mr. Peter Harris... By the way, how'd you decide on your new name?"

"Innocuous," Pete said. "Doesn't stand out like Stellan."

Kovačević replied with a slow, lengthy nod. "Got a point. How'd your parents come up with Stellan?"

"My mother. Has a flair for the pretentious."

Kovačević met the comment with a deadpan expression.

"All right, back to your earlier question of the cost of your theft." Kovačević drummed the table with his forefinger. "I don't have any visitors. I used to. My wife and kids died on the freeway coming here..."

The moment Kovačević mentioned the death, Pete failed to hear the rest of the message. His mind dashed off in a different direction. He understood. It made sense, what he'd spotted earlier—the sadness in the eyes. Kovačević had suffered the worst loss, his family.

As a general rule, Pete didn't spend time thinking of others' feelings. Yet in the moment he conjured up sympathy for the Serb, he couldn't give voice to it.

Kovačević waved a hand in front of Pete's face.

"Earth to Harris. You're off somewhere else again."

Pete shook his head to rid himself of his thoughts and looked at the other man.

"You do it a lot—daydream?" Kovačević said.

"Yeah, I seem to. Um, sorry about your loss."

"Right. Thanks. Anyway, outside visits are like lifelines here. Calling a prison a shithole is being kind to vile places. The dregs of humanity live here. Including me. We're with each other 24/7. Life, if you can call it that, is no life. Cons have three ways to leave other than going over the wall. One, they finish their time. Of those, two-thirds come back. They're here so long, this is all they know. Two, they die here. Three, they hit the lottery jackpot in an appeal. Almost never happens."

Where's this going, Pete asked himself.

Kovačević answered soon enough.

"What little humanity exists gets crushed here." He removed his elbows from the table, leaned back, and gazed around the room. "Get what I'm trying to tell you?"

Pete shook his head. "No."

"Okay, my fault. Try this. The more time you do, the more you come to believe you've split from the real world. Split in the worst way possible. Sure, we watch TV, get weekly movies, read newspapers and mags. Those are our only small connections to the outside world. But they're not the real outside world. The closest real connections are visits."

He drew in a long breath and let it out. "Here's where you come in. I don't get visitors. You, you don't have to like me, but I want you to visit, maybe every couple of weeks. I want to hear about the outside world, to see it through the eyes of somebody who lives there. A couple of hours, maybe on weekends, won't kill you."

"Fair enough," an excited Pete said. "I can manage it."

Kovačević looked at the clock on the wall. "Time's almost up. Before I go, how about we use each other's first name?"

"Sure. Why not?"

"Good. I've been thinking about something else, *Pete*, a real change in my circumstances. Something you said jacked me, and maybe it'll spring me from this shit pit. There might be one other way to leave, different from those three I mentioned. I'm going to try to leave by the front door and take my celly with me. If I can pull it off, it'll be legal-like, and you might be my ticket."

"Me? How?"

"Haven't got clue one. Yet. But I'll work on it. My gut tells me the answer is with someone or something local."

A small scowl formed on Pete's face. "Let me understand this. You don't have a plan to escape, but you will, and when one comes, it'll involve me?"

"Right."

Pete massaged the back of his neck.

"Okay, say you put something together, what if it goes belly up? Will it end up with me being in here?"

Dusan jutted out his chin.

"Relax, will you? I'll figure out some angle. And you, they can't toss you into the can for a crime you haven't committed. You know the saying, 'A chain is only as strong as the weakest link'?"

"Yes."

"I'll find the link and take advantage of it."

Pete wanted to jump to his feet and pump the air with his fists. Dusan intended to forgive the theft and not murder him. Instead, he kept his emotions down and said, "I'm interested to see how you plan this."

"Me, too. I'm going to use your eyes, ears, and intellect to help me."

Pete used his thumb and forefinger to massage his jaw.

"Better than the alternatives I worried about coming here. Say, you mind if I ask you a personal question…Dusan?"

"Yeah, why not?"

"You won't take offence?"

"No. Ask."

"Fair enough. You obviously had more than your share of street smarts to have acquired so much money. But I've got to admit when we first met, I didn't think you were the sharpest knife in the drawer." He held up his hands. "Not meaning to insult."

"Didn't take it as such," Dusan said. "Go on."

"It's, well..." Pete stopped, waited a beat, and blurted out, "Everything's different with you. What happened?"

Dusan rested his chin in a palm and considered the question.

"Good question. Life. Not the one I expected or ever got used to in here." He slowly shook his head. "I look back and wish I'd have been a better man, husband, and father. Other than taking what I wanted, I had no idea how to deal with things. Then I get tossed in here and fast enough lost my family and a real good friend. A couple of good people and a pastor saved me from myself."

Dusan stared over Pete's shoulder for a moment. He returned his attention to his visitor.

"I have a great celly. Couldn't have asked for better. Got me interested in the world and helped get me reassigned to the library. Nothing like the libraries on the street, but I didn't waste time. I read everything, took courses, and my celly's an intellectual..."

"I'm impressed."

"Really? Okay. I'll tell him, and I'll tell you, I'd trade everything to have my wife and kids back. When I get out, I'll going to try and live a better life in memory of them. I..." He waited, blinked, filled his lungs, and said, "From what I know, Martine Maines looks like a nice small town."

"You've been to it?"

Dusan raised a shoulder. "Sort of, if you call being on the prison bus, shackled, seeing the town through grated windows. I think it might suit me. There's nothing for me in Chicago."

The two men looked at each other for a moment.

Dusan drummed his middle finger on the table for a moment.

"So, listen, I'll still go to the math classes. My math skills could stand improving. Besides, it'll be holy hell if I drop the course. I'll be like any of the other cons there." He allowed himself another quick look at the clock.

"So, you okay about meeting two weeks from now?"

Pete answered with a quick bark, followed by, "Sorry." He

lowered his voice and leaned forward.

"After all I've done to you, and you ask me if it's okay to visit every two weeks. It's okay. It's very okay. More, if you want." He made a second conciliatory gesture. "Can I bring you anything to make your life more bearable in here?"

Dusan didn't hesitate to answer.

"Yeah. You sure can. Glad you asked. Books. But rules here say they have to come from the publisher. How about starting with *The Autobiography of Malcolm X*, Eldridge Cleaver's *Soul on Ice*, anything by Aleksandr Solzhenitsyn, and books on critical thinking."

"Wow. Quite a list. No escape-reading for you, if you'll pardon the pun."

Dusan rewarded the joke with a deadpan expression.

Pete felt himself redden and retrieved a ballpoint pen. "Okay, I'll write it down. Go slow, and tell them to me again."

Their time up, Dusan said, "Keep bringing your text, and I'll see you soon." He extended his hand. Pete accepted it. They shook.

"Feels weird, doesn't it? Dusan said.

"Yeah, to tell you the truth, but good weird."

Pete stepped out of the prison full of mixed feelings. *Over two million bucks and Dusan sloughs it off. How was that possible? If the shoe was on the other foot, could I do it?*

No choice but to take Dusan at his word, Pete turned his attention to the talk of escaping from Stillwell. What if some cockamamie scheme of Dusan's went awry and landed him in front of a judge?

He forced himself to shake off the thought. Nothing for it but to wait and see. Maybe Dusan would abandon the idea. "I can only hope," he muttered to himself.

Chapter 23

Pete looked forward to his Saturday mornings with Dusan. He visited his old adversary with regularity and found him to be both a good listener and conversationalist, full of interesting and funny anecdotes. When he didn't ask about Pete's current life, how he filled his days, Dusan delved into politics, society, books, women, sports, religion, and life's meaning. But for the surroundings and circumstances, the two men could well have been any two talking about life and all its vagaries.

Pete often thought about the unusual conditions that led to their meeting. Strange. He'd heisted over two million dollars of Dusan's money and suffered no consequences. The Serb could well have exacted his revenge, even from behind prison walls. Yet he hadn't.

Pete still couldn't believe his good luck. On the other hand, if money ceased to matter, how much more had Dusan squirreled away somewhere? Pete chided himself for thinking it. *Stop it! Don't be ungrateful and second-guess his motives. He's befriended you. Enjoy that and everything that comes with it.*

When examining his life, Pete found it easy to pinpoint the last time he had anything approaching a meaningful friend—Tom Vlahos. Pete couldn't have done better than Tom. Growing up, the two were inseparable.

Tom's mother, Irena, held a soft spot for Pete. "Eat, eat," she'd say when he sat with a heaping plate of moussaka or a thick bowl of bean soup. "A boy like you, you need more meat on those bones."

In Pete's adolescence, Mr. Vlahos moved his family to the suburbs. Pete never saw Tom again. Years later he heard Tom worked as a detective with the Chicago police.

At college Pete had chummed with a few 'buddies.' After graduation everyone drifted off in different directions. At Stringent, billable hours never allowed the building of relationships. With Nina, her family became Pete's by default. He socialized with her brothers and male cousins. He drank beer at get-togethers, talked sports, and told ribald jokes. That was all.

One day Dusan said, "Listen, I'm curious. There's something I want to ask."

Pete tensed. *Uh-oh.* He half-expected Dusan to broach the subject of escape. Dusan surprised him. "Your wife, kids—it ever bother you walking out on them?"

The question somehow rankled Pete. *What, I'm criticized by a mobster Al Capone might have palled with?* He forced the thought down. *Easy. Count to three. It's only a question.*

He drew in a breath and said, "It's complicated."

"Bet it is. Most of the cons in here are defined by a few moments in their lives—a mugging, a stabbing, a shooting, knocking over a bodega or a gas bar, and *wham*, they're doing long stretches or never getting out. Most have narratives that spring from a few short moments."

Pete blinked several times.

"You've become quite the philosopher. All right, to what you were asking, you could say a lot of things led up to a few moments. I should have taken responsibility for them but didn't. Probably never will."

He shot Dusan an uncomfortable smile, still not eager to share. Then again, that wasn't fair. He forced himself to push on.

"I walked out on my family, took your money, and found myself footloose and fancy free."

He ran a hand over his face. "You ever think about those family photos, you know, where everyone's staring into the camera, all smiling like their lives depended on it?"

"Yeah, I guess. Why?"

Pete scratched a cheek. "If you're like everyone else, you've got a whole bunch of those photos stored somewhere. We did, my family. They were mostly lies, us posing and smiling. The wife—see how I've now objectified my ex?—and my kids might have a different take, but there it is."

"In the last couple of years I'd developed a gambling habit, which did nothing for my marriage. I found myself in a kind of high-strung despair. Then you came along."

He licked his lips. "Call it a character flaw, but I'm not one for warm fuzzies, you know, those nice, warm feelings people are supposed to have. As for Nina, my ex, well, she's a survivor. She'll be all right. Knowing her, she'll reel in some other sucker. If she hasn't already."

Dusan didn't react but remained quiet. Pete tapped his pencil on the desk and said, "I have two kids and they, for sure, take after their mother. They're the kind who'd boot me into a senior's home and never visit. But not before they emptied everything out of my bank account."

He broke off and glanced at the guards. "I can't add anything more to this, so let's change the subject." He lowered his voice and leaned over the table. "About the money, I'm still pinching myself about you letting the debt slide. We're not talking about ten thousand dollars..."

Dusan replied with a nonchalant shrug.

"Believe it or not, there's a kind of symmetry in you stealing from me. Wouldn't take an Einstein to figure out all my dough came from ill-gotten gains. Every single dime. I've still got more than enough. Once I get out of here, I'll make it legit and maybe do some good with it."

Pete left the prison and stepped into his truck, the conversation still on his mind. Dusan still spoke with conviction of being freed. Almost with the zeal of a believer. Well, good for him, but Pete didn't share his confidence. *Who am I to burst his bubble? If he wants to hold onto that fantasy, fine.*

A few weeks later, in the midst of a light conversation, Dusan's eyebrows rose at something Pete said. He held up his palm. "Wait, wait, wait. Go back and tell me again about this Lizzy chick."

"Linzie. Yeah, what about her?"

"Something you said. She's a Hayden, this chick you were sticking?"

"Not the most elegant way of putting it, but okay."

Dusan repaid the comment with a lopsided grin.

"Hey, I'm a product of my environment. This is the joint, not some church social. Back to Hayden. The woman's hubby, he's on the prison release board?"

"No," Pete corrected. "His brother is."

"Oh, right." Dusan fell silent and then said, "Interesting."

Pete gave Dusan a hard stare. "I don't know what that means. Where're you going with this?"

"Not sure yet, but I need to know a little more. Maybe I've found something. Anyhow, Linzie's hubby and brother-in-law—you said they were switch hitters?"

"According to her, yeah, and the term is bisexual."

Dusan replied with a mocking laugh. "Not in here it ain't. Tell me this again what she said about her brother-in-law."

"Why?"

"C'mon, just humor me."

Pete lifted his shoulder in a half-shrug. "This is what I heard. According to Linzie both brothers like men, but her husband leans more to chasing skirt. No idea what you're going to do with this, but remember, I'm giving you all this secondhand."

"Hear ya. You know his name, this brother?"

Pete tilted his head in thought. "Something regal. I can't remember."

"S'okay. I'll find it."

"And if it amounts to anything," Pete said, "with what you're already trying to cook up, will you let me know?"

Dusan arched his brows. "I've got to think about this some more. Right now I have the beginning sketch of something. If I think it'll work, I'll do all the heavy lifting. You shouldn't get pulled into anything."

Pete considered the answer. "Glad to hear it, and hope you're right."

Dusan discovered the name. Brice Hayden. The first step, but he needed some solid intel. That meant spending more money.

In the yard he found Joey "Lasso" La Scatto, leaning against a wall, delighting friends with an anecdote.

"Hey, Joey," he said to the heavily muscled man. "How ya doin'?"

"Danny Balls Up!" La Scotto said with all the congenial enthusiasm of meeting a long-time friend. "Livin' the dream, ya crazy Slav." He exhaled cigarette smoke. With dramatic flair, he gestured at the yard. "Another day in paradise. What more could a man want?"

His friends laughed. When it died down, Dusan said, "Can I talk to you for a sec? Something personal."

"Yeah, sure." La Scotto turned and said to the others, "Excuse us, gentlemen. I'll return to this board meeting when the chick with the big tits brings the lattes."

The comment won more laughter. La Scotto directed his attention to Dusan and took his arm. "Step into my office."

The two men walked.

"What's happening?"

"Um, I need a service. Tommy Fingers said to come to you. Here I am." Dusan explained what he knew and what he hoped to find. Negotiations began, and the two men settled on a price.

La Scatto flicked his filtered cigarette onto the pavement. "'Course you know the price is subject to change, depending on time and requirements."

"Has to be."

"Leave it with me, then," La Scatto said. "I'll get back to ya in a day or so."

"Thanks, Joey, and say hi to Tommy for me."

"Will do."

Pleased with himself, Dusan walked away. He made up his mind to keep everything under wraps for now. No point in telling Gates and getting his hopes up.

Prominent Adam's apple and bony aquiline nose were features of the male Haydens. Beyond that, Brice looked nothing like his brother. Where the elder Hayden fought a losing battle with a receding hairline, Brice showed off a luxurious and tangled mane of premature gray. Griffith had gone to seed; Brice took care of himself and had a posture sure to impress a drill sergeant.

Physical differences aside, the brothers had a common psychological resemblance. Both gave off an aura of narcissistic entitlement and self-absorption. Evie Hayden, Brice's wife, once commented to Linzie, "You put a Hayden in a room, and he expects all attention should focus on him, even if he hasn't done anything worthy or said anything worth hearing."

Linzie had chuckled and replied with, "I know what you mean. It always gets interesting when the two find themselves in the same room. As you well know. They're the human equivalent of Siamese fighting fish."

"Good analogy, Linzie. How those two ever get anything done when they're together is one of life's great mysteries."

Brice Hayden did share his brother's proclivity for stepping out on his wife. Evie Hayden knew it but looked the other way. She retaliated by indulging in and enjoying the finer and more expensive things in life.

In adolescence at the private boarding school Brice discovered he enjoyed a broad sexual appetite. Gossip spread among the school. The other boys nicknamed him the backdoor bandit.

Brice's expensive British sedan pulled onto a leafy street in Burlington and stopped in front of an attractive brownstone. Keys in his pocket, he hurried up the four steps to the door. A young, lean, attractive man with decidedly feminine manners smiled and stepped aside for Brice.

The door closed. Neither man noticed a green subcompact

vehicle several car lengths down the street. For a few days the driver watched number 1311 Bicknell Street and noted the pattern of its occupant. Every morning the younger man left at nine and returned before noon.

Tuesday morning a white panel truck advertising Modern Security backed into the driveway and close to the house. The truck would shield the driver from casual observation. With a name tag sewn on the flap of his blue work shirt, he opened the two side doors of the van, confident they blocked the view of any nearby neighbors. If they took interest and approached, he'd spin them his ready-made story.

He rang the bell. No one answered. His eyes moved downward and inspected the door lock. Cheap. Piece of cake getting in. Why do people buy cheap locks for expensive doors? Two minutes later he'd picked the lock.

Inside the house he allowed himself a quick tour. Nice, expensive decor. The intruder found the bedroom. Lots of places to hide the mini camera. Time to get to work.

The intruder stepped out to the truck. To maintain his charade for any snoopy neighbor, he whistled a tune and pretended to search the truck for what he needed.

Good at his job, the man installed two mini cameras in short time. He returned to the street and shut the door behind himself. As a final gesture, he made a show of double-checking he'd locked it. With calm deliberation he climbed behind the wheel and backed the truck onto the street. Fast job. Easy money.

The cameras worked to perfection and caught the lovers in flagrante.

A few days later Brice sipped his morning Caffee Misto and worked his way through a prominent, conservative New York newspaper. From his peripheral vision he caught a bullnecked man in a dark green velour tracksuit approach. The stranger stopped at Brice's table and took a seat opposite him.

"So, h'ya doin' there? Brice, is it?"

Brice set down his paper. Annoyance crept into his voice. He stiffened. "Do I know you, and more importantly, did I give you permission to join me?" He started to wave to the barista, but the other man reached out and grabbed his arm.

"Nah, wouldn't advise it." He twirled a flat chain bracelet on his wrist. "This'll only take a minute, and I'll be gone. Got somethin' you're gonna be interested in. Like I said, a minute or so."

His curiosity piqued, Brice pushed aside his annoyance. "And what would you have to interest me?"

"This." The stranger reached for a hip pocket and produced a cell phone. He tapped the Internet browser and set the phone on the table. Both watched while a naked Brice pressed himself between the buttocks of a younger man.

A feeling of overwhelming panic seized Brice. For a moment he thought he'd have a heart attack. He found it difficult to pull air into his lungs. His eyes moved from the video to the other man. He found his voice.

"What the...? How did you...?" Brice whipped his head around to see if anyone noticed the video.

A small smile of pleasure appeared on the other man's face.

"Me to know, Brice-y." He ended the video. "Thing is, you don't want this getting out, you and your pillow-biting twink there, know what I'm sayin', what with you running for office? Folks don't like to see this kind of stuff from the family values party."

Brice felt his bowels loosen, yet remained determined to show some stamina. He licked his dry lips. "And now you're, what, about to blackmail me?"

The corners of the other man's mouth lifted to suggest the beginnings of a smirk.

"Catch on fast. Guess an expensive education pays off. 'Course I'm blackmailing you, but I also got good news. I'm not needin' money. What I want is two favors. You deliver and you never see me again. But you gotta move fast." He shot Brice another wicked smile. "Simple, huh?"

"Depends on what you're after," an unconvinced Brice said.

"Okay, you're listening. Atta boy. You play nice, you get nice. Now, word is the Justice Department's 'bout to do another early prison release. I gotta couple names for ya. Two. You make sure they get on the list for release. They walk out and you're done with me for good. Like I said, you gotta move fast."

Brice had to hold himself in check.

"Get them on the list? Are you mad?" The words came out in almost a hiss. "You don't know what you're asking."

"Calm down, willya?" his blackmailer said. "'Course I know what I'm asking. Is why I'm askin'. Sheesh! And I know you got pull. So, use it and call in your markers or whatever. Get somebody in the know at Stillwell to play around with the charges. You got dough, lots of it. Everybody knows that. Grease some palms. Afterwards, you get the names in front of a judge. The whatchamacallit, circles you move in, the local big shots, gotta be some judges there. Find one, and have him cut their sentences, and hand out long-term probation. Simple as that."

The other man's gaze remained on Brice.

"I can see wheels turning. I'm real good at reading minds. Real good. Word of advice—don't. You thinkin' 'bout saying no. Trust me, sayin' no lands you inna world of shit. Not worth it."

Brice lifted his now cold coffee and drank to put moisture in his mouth. No sooner had he done it than he saw his hand tremble. He lowered the cup.

"And if I do what you ask, assuming I can, what's to stop you from blackmailing me again?"

"Not a thing, but listen, I couldn't care less about you and your twink. Perverted, you ask me, but hey, whatever floats your boat, I guess." He stopped and again held Brice's gaze. "Do this, I delete the video, and you never see me again."

Brice's shoulders slumped. "I suppose I have no choice."

The stranger answered with a fast, indifferent shrug. "Some, but I'm doubtin' you'd like the outcome."

Brice rubbed his forehead.

"All right." He squeezed his eyes shut, opened them, reached for a pen and paper inside his jacket, and said, "Give me the names. I'll see what I can do."

"Ya gotta do more than see what you can do."

It proved no simple undertaking for Brice, getting the prisoners released. Each step along the way he encountered difficulties, especially at the judicial end. He lost track of the times he thought he might abandon the whole project. The specter of his name, the family name, blasted all over the news media, pushed him on.

At long last he succeeded but regretted the thousands of dollars, to say nothing of countless sleepless nights, it cost him.

Federal Judge Marian Penobscot initially resisted Brice's attempt at bribery. She expressed her moral outrage and threatened to report him. Brice's calm demeanor, plus a sizable cash payment, a lifetime of free leases from his German car dealership, and a promise to hire her analyst son at Sperling Data brought her around.

"This is it, right, Brice?" she said over a luncheon meeting at The Cat and Fiddle bistro. "No more after this. Ever. I don't know how I let you talk me into this."

Brice held up an open palm.

"Calm yourself, Marian. I have a stake in this. If this got out, we'd both be in enormous trouble. No one will find out. You have my word."

She leaned across the small table.

"Good." She picked up her glass of water, sipped, set it down, and fixed her gaze back on Brice. "How in heaven's name did it come to this for you?"

Brice slowly shook his head in answer.

"I wish I could tell you, but best you don't know." He studied the menu. "The tilapia looks good. What do you say we try it, along with a nice Sauvignon?"

On a cool autumn afternoon, Brice took a seat in the back pew of courtroom 19 and listened to case numbers 211 and 212, Dusan Stephen Kovačević and Gates Merit Tally.

Both men stood in civilian garb in front of Her Honor, Judge Marian Penobscot. Brice studied them, one muscular, probably a bruiser; the other thin, a man who looked more like a teacher than a convict in his tweed jacket.

Which man, Brice asked himself, set these wheels in motion? He guessed the shorter one and returned his attention to Penobscot. She looked from documents to the men and in a clear voice said, "The Court has studied the two pre-sentence reports on Misters Gates Tally and Dusan Kovačević. On the basis of the recommendations in front of the Court, it commutes the prison sentences of both men. They will henceforth be released to the community, under supervision of probation officers."

The order proclaimed, Penobscot banged her gavel and turned her attention to her next case. Not once did she make eye contact with the man at the back who silently slunk out of her courtroom. He left the courthouse, drove his luxury vehicle to an upscale bistro, and ordered a double of their finest malt whisky. He settled back into the comfy padded chair and sipped. He needed this. Hell of a roller coaster ride, he told himself. Anyway, thank God it was all behind him now. He took another sip and mulled over whether his blackmailer would hold up his end of the Faustian contract.

Something told him he would.

Chapter 24

With a wide grin, Dusan threw himself onto the chair across from Pete in the visitor's room. He pulled his chair closer to the table. In a conspiratorial voice he whispered, "We did it, man! I can't believe it. I can...not believe it."

"Believe what?" Pete said. "What are you talking about?"

"Oh, forgot you don't know. I didn't tell anyone, not even my celly, Gates, until a couple days ago. We're walking out the front door."

Pete's eyebrows shot up.

"What! Incredible. Really? What happened?"

"What happened is..." Dusan detailed the events that led to his upcoming release. When he finished, he exhaled. "I better calm down. Don't want any extra attention." Yet his grin remained.

"Something told me I'd find a way, but to tell the truth, my inner confidence didn't always match my words. There were so many ways for this to go sideways."

"Wow," Pete said. "What a surprise. You pulled this off by yourself."

"Don't be modest. Without you I might not have figured this out at all."

Pete tossed a shrug. "Doesn't matter. Are you and, um, Gates, getting released to the same place?"

"Nah. He's heading for Hawaii to a halfway house. He wants to be far away from his ex's family. Thinks he can work his way back into the academic world. I'm going to miss him. Taught me a lot. We're not allowed to stay in touch." A lopsided lip curl arrived. "Yeah, good luck with that."

"And you," Pete said, "still planning on coming to Martine Maines?"

"Haven't changed my mind. They got me in a halfway house on Franklin, Condonation House. Ever hear of it?"

Pete shook his head. "No. Why would I? Don't even know what

it means."

"Forgiveness, I think. I have to stay eight months to a year, depending on reports submitted on me. Curfew, no drugs or booze, pee in a cup, keep a job, stay out of trouble, don't hang around with undesirables. If everything goes well, I can apply to get my own pad. I'll wait five years, hire a lawyer, and apply for my probation to be reduced or cancelled."

Pete turned his head to see where the COs were.

"Sounds like a plan. I need to ask you something." Aware of the sensitivity of the topic, he dropped his own voice. "Aren't you worried the feds will come after any money they see you with once you're out?"

Dusan brushed aside the worry. "Got it covered. They can't seize what they can't find. On top of that, had an insurance policy on my family. For a lot of dough. Never really expected to cash it in."

A hitch in his voice, Dusan blinked several times and gazed at a wall. He released a long breath. "Trade everything if I could get them back, but I can't." He fell silent and looked at Pete. "I'm going to set up a small business. When it's up and running, I'll slowly bring my other bread back."

Pete waited, sure Dusan would add more.

His friend didn't disappoint. "What was I saying? Oh, yeah, I'm thinking about buying one of those East Coast bakery-café franchises. You think Martine Maines can handle one?"

"I'm sure of it, especially with the college here."

"Cool. And if I find any dependable cons at the halfway house, they can come and work for me." He laughed. "I could hire you to check my books. On second thought, nah, better not."

Pete joined in the humor. "Exactly. Once bitten..."

Another long moment of silence passed. Dusan broke it. "I still can't believe I'm leaving this shithole."

"When?"

Dusan tossed a shoulder. "Not sure. With luck maybe

somewhere around a month."

"Really? How come so long?"

"Paperwork, I heard. Listen, are you okay with me contacting you once I'm in town? We don't have to hang out or anything, but maybe meet for coffee or something to eat?"

Pete didn't mind at all.

"Yeah, sounds good. I mean, how many other people know me like you? We'll work out something. And when we go out to eat, I'm buying. I can afford it."

The last sentence hung there for a moment. Pete wondered if he'd said the wrong thing until Dusan threw back his head and laughed, loud and hard. The reaction won him glances from those nearby and a stern look from a patrolling CO.

Dusan held up his hands and mouthed, "Sorry." He looked at Pete. "Just struck me funny, is all."

The two men returned to their conversation. "Something I want to ask you," Pete said.

"Uh-oh." Dusan pointed. "I know that look."

"No, seriously."

"In that case, go ahead."

"Are you done with the whole life-of-crime shtick?"

Dusan nodded. "Not saying I'll be goody-two-shoes, but I made a promise to Anka that I wouldn't pick up where I left off. Like I told you, from a financial point of view I've got no problems."

Pete met the comment with a nod. "Glad to hear it. So, you'll be out soon. The next time we see each other will be on the street. I can't believe it."

"Me, neither. Going to pinch myself for a while yet."

"Do you need a ride into town?"

"Nah. Don't worry about it. I'll find my way."

"Are you sure? I don't mind."

Dusan shook his head. "Looking forward to doing things by myself again. The joint controls your life. Pretty well everything is decided for you. And then, just like that, you find yourself out on the street again. You ever hear of something called reverse culture shock?"

"Can't say I have."

"It's what psychologists say happens when someone goes back into an environment they were yanked out of. Like me. So, this is the beginning of me learning to adjust again."

Friday afternoon Pete sat at a long table in the study hall of the Autry Library and proofread his essay on Silas Marner. Had he hit enough of the main ideas to get a decent grade? He leaned back, rolled his shoulders, and guessed he might get a B minus, maybe a B. He didn't need a better mark, but the essay wouldn't offend his work ethic.

Ready to rise and return to the stacks, a female voice whispered, "Hi, Pete. Want some company? I promise I won't talk and interfere with you studying."

Pete turned to see Bexley Stryker lean over and give him a grin. He smiled back at her. "Hi, Bexley. No, happy to have you." He wouldn't object at all. She could talk all she wanted. He liked listening to her sultry voice. If law practice didn't claim her, she could always get a career doing voice-over commercials.

He fought the impulse to ask why she'd arrived alone. Whenever he caught sight of her, some guy always hovered nearby.

"Sit, sit," he said, and gestured to an empty chair next to him. "I'm heading off to look at some books for a paper. Would you mind keeping an eye on my stuff? I'll be back in a bit."

She pushed a strand of hair behind an ear and pulled out a chair. "Sure, go." She undid the knot in her beige trench coat. "See you when you get back."

An hour later, Pete glanced out a window. Soft, red, and fading streaks of sunlight bathed clouds over the western sky. He rolled his shoulders again and turned to Bexley. "Everyone's gone. It'll be dusk soon. I think I'll head out, too." He powered off his laptop.

Bexley nodded. "Me, too." She gathered up her material and stuffed them into her backpack. "Satisfied with what you got from the stacks?"

"Pretty well," Pete said, rose, slipped on his bomber jacket, and placed his laptop into his backpack. "I'll go over the essay a final time at home."

Outside they glanced around the green.

"You ever notice," Bexley asked, "how by midafternoons on Fridays you could fire a cannon and not hit a soul?"

"I have. Everybody disappears."

Should he say goodbye now? Pete asked himself Maybe not. Invite her to join him for a beer and something to eat. Why not? If she declined, he'd go home. "Hey, listen, you rushing off somewhere, or interested in getting a beer and some food? We could talk and get to know each other a little bit better."

Bexley gave the question some thought. It unnerved him. How much consideration did it require? He hadn't held out a proposal of marriage. She spoke. "Sounds good. What have you got in mind?"

They ended up in The Legends of Cause, a popular pub with the campus crowd. "I never understood the name of this place," Bexley said while they studied their menus.

"Me, neither, though it is intriguing. We should ask the server."

They indulged in light conversation while drinking beer and waiting for their burgers. Pete thought it odd sitting with this attractive woman he'd only ever shared a few polite words with. Had she ever shown any interest in him? He searched for clues and came up empty.

Their food arrived. Bexley bit into her burger, chewed, wiped the corner of her mouth with a napkin, and said, "Um, Stillwell…are you still liking it?"

"I am. You?"

She affirmed she did.

Pete took a fry from his plate. "One of my students is set to be released. He's coming to Martine Maines."

"No."

Pete nodded. "Yep. Made up his mind the town would suit him, even though he's never been here. He's going to a halfway house. I like him. Once he gets settled, we'll meet for coffee, lunch, a beer, whatever."

"Is it allowed, him coming here, I mean, so close to Stillwell?"

"I asked him. He said there's no rule against it. His name is Dusan Kovačević."

She echoed the name. "Don't know it. It should be interesting to see how he adjusts."

They moved on to other topics. Pete discovered Bexley hailed from Albany, New York. Her father owned several pharmacies, and her mother taught at middle school. She was the youngest of three siblings and had two older brothers—one, a physician working in Saudi Arabia, and the other, a detective. She lived with three other women in a house off-campus.

She told Pete she'd already applied to several law schools but had her sights set on the Vermont Law School in South Royalton. "I'm interested in Environmental Law and think I have a good chance of getting in next year. If not, my second and third choices are Northwestern and Fordham."

She waved a hand in front of his face. "Were you listening? You looked like you were somewhere else."

He chuckled. "Dusan says the same thing to me, and yes, I did hear you."

"So, what about you? You've heard about me. What's your story?"

Pete knew like spring followed winter the question would arrive. He dusted off the new-and-improved story he'd once told Linzie and replaced institutional care with private care.

"That's about it, and I haven't taken the meds in quite some time now."

His narrative turned out more difficult than he had imagined. Bexley asked questions, lots of them. What happened to his parents? Why wouldn't his mother have kept him? Did he have other family? Who decided he could live on his own? Her questions didn't come in an interrogative style, but he flinched under them anyway.

The more questions Bexley asked, the less Pete felt in control. On several occasions her forehead furrowed at an answer. In turn, Pete squirmed inside, afraid she'd somehow unmasked him. He didn't like feeling vulnerable. Hated it, but pushed on.

"Phew, I've never had to work so hard at explaining my history to someone. I can see why you want to be a lawyer."

She responded to his glibness with a straight-faced look. Pete flushed. A quote came to him from Nietzsche: *I'm not upset you lied. I'm upset that from now on I can no longer believe you*. Maybe he should cut his losses and leave? They weren't on a date, only two people hanging out on a particular night. For sure, he'd better work on his story more; his telling had to sound convincing.

He made a show of looking at his watch. "Hey, listen, it's getting on, and I'm sure you've got other places to be and people to see."

She tilted her head. "You look upset. Did I do something? If I did, I didn't mean to. It's a sad story, yours. I was only trying to understand it."

The response endeared her to him. He'd misinterpreted her body language. She felt touched by his tale.

Careful to keep his voice even, he said, "Not at all. Sorry if I gave you that impression."

"Not to worry. Do you have somewhere to be?"

"I'm good," he said. Afraid conversation might edge back to him and his life history, he did his best to keep conversation off himself. He told his best amusing anecdotes.

They ordered more beer. By nine the evening crowd arrived, and the pair readied to leave. Outside, Pete asked her where she lived.

"Not far," Bexley said. "About an eight-minute walk."

"Well, if you don't mind, I'll walk you home."

"All right, if you like."

"I have to get my bike first."

"Lead on."

They talked about the weather. "This might be the last day I use my bike for the season," Pete said. "It's getting too cold to ride."

"But you live close by, right?"

"I do, but still…"

She pointed and stopped. "This is where I live." Pete liked her and toyed with the idea of asking her out.

"I had a great night, Bexley. Do you think you're up for another night out sometime?"

"Yes, sure. Do you have one of those smartphones?"

"Yep." He reached for and unzipped his backpack. "Okay, give me your number." He took her number. "Great. I'll call you, and we can set something up."

"I'll look forward to it."

Pete swung his leg over his bike and pedaled home. What a day. He liked her. Would things go anywhere with her? Slow down, cowboy, his inner voice said. See how things play out.

He found himself at his house before he realized it. How much more should he tell her? Other than Dusan, he couldn't show his real self to anyone. If anything came of a relationship with Bexley, he'd have to be extra careful about what he disclosed. He needed an airtight narrative able to withstand the closest inspection. He'd work on it tonight and examine it more for possible flaws. No slip-ups.

Chapter 25

The nation geared up for the upcoming annual Thanksgiving mania. Airport, rail, and bus terminals swelled with passengers heading home for the holidays. City traffic arteries gave evidence of drivers' urges to be somewhere fast; bumper-to-bumper traffic set nerves on edge. Billboards, newspapers, television, and the Internet announced the glories of upcoming Black Friday sales.

Thanksgiving Day at Stillwell, however, only meant a day free from work and studies. For supper, prisoners received pressed turkey with cranberries. Dusan, Gates, and three others enjoyed a different experience. They held onto their few personal items and waited by a grate to leave their block. All knew the drill. They'd seen other cons finish their time.

A genial CO escorted the five down to the Release Center. He opened the grate to an empty cellblock. "Pick any one, boys," he said, and let them pass through.

The releasees in, he locked the grate. Full of excitement and nervous energy, the five joked and speculated what they would do the following day with their freedom.

"Gonna get laid, is the first thing I'm doin'," broad-shouldered Wally Yannick, with jailhouse art from knuckles to chin, said. He threw his arm around Dusan, who offered his former enemy a tight smile.

Dusan recalled his first run-in with Yannick, who tried to muscle him for his radio. The Serb refused. Yannick sucker-punched him. Dusan fought back. When guards separated the two and led them down to the hole, Dusan sported a swollen lip, a bruised rib, and cut knuckles. Yannick suffered a broken nose and a groin injury. He stayed clear of Dusan after that.

Now Yannick, perhaps exuberant because of his impending freedom, gave Dusan an extra squeeze, kissed his cheek, and said, "No hard feelings, eh, Kovačević? It's the joint. You know how it is."

"Yeah. No sweat."

"Lock-up," their guard called, and entered the block. Gates pulled Dusan aside. His voice low and husky, he said, "Before he locks us up, I want to tell you, Dusan, I owe you a lot. To my dying day I'll marvel at how you pulled this rabbit out of the hat. Actually, two rabbits." He chuckled. "If you ever need anything, anything at all, you contact me and let me know."

"Count on it, Gates. You've been the best kind of homie a guy could want. You and West Wind, both quality men. I don't know how I could have made it without you. And Pastor Lister. When I get settled, I'm going to make an anonymous donation to her church."

"Cool. Do you think you'll ever come and see me?"

"No worries there, my man. Always wanted to see Hawaii anyway. Now I have an extra reason to visit." Dusan lightly punched Gates' arm. "What time are you heading out to the airport?" He knew the answer but sensed Gates was on the verge of tearing up. Best to distract him.

"I take an early bus to the Burlington airport tomorrow," Gates said. "A shuttle to O'Hare, and then my flight to Hawaii leaves at ten. If all goes well, I should be gone from here before you wake up."

"C'mon, fellas," the guard called. "Into your cells."

An empty ache settled on Dusan in the morning, with the absence of Gates. He swallowed hard several times and joined the other three in their march to the dining hall. Directed to a separate bench away from the rest of the prison population, they ate in silence. Each man searched for familiar faces and gave small waves to old pals.

Breakfast done, the four waited for someone to fetch them. A female CO arrived. They followed her to the Receiving Room. Four separate bundles of civilian clothing awaited the men on a countertop.

Dusan blinked several times and said a silent prayer to his wife.

I did it, Anka. I don't know if you're proud of how I managed it, but I'm free. I'll try and do better with my life. Pray for me, and tell the kids I love and miss them.

A CO behind the waist-high counter beckoned the men. He swept his arm over the counter. "Your earthly treasures, gentlemen, from when you arrived. Everything's been catalogued on the sheet, including watches, wallets, rings, money, whatever. If you agree these are the items you surrendered, sign off on the sheet provided."

Dusan recalled arriving in an expensive, tailor-made suit, button-down linen shirt with French cuffs, and high-end Italian loafers. He'd surrendered over fifteen hundred dollars cash, a gold watch, and expensive designer bracelets.

He slipped into his monogrammed Oxford shirt and inserted his onyx cuff links, aware of eyes on him. Done, he checked his Windsor knot in the mounted piece of sheet metal that substituted for a mirror. Soon, he told himself, he'd be out in the world again, where they had real mirrors.

His wallet and money clip tucked into his pockets, his watch on his wrist, Dusan put the gold chain bracelet in his suit pocket. Bling-bling. He'd outgrown it. He climbed into his cashmere overcoat and slipped the scarf over his head. Nice to be back in comfortable civilian clothes, free of the demeaning clown suits of the prison.

A new awareness arrived: maybe the clothes no longer fit his persona. He'd changed his interior; why not change the exterior? Made sense. He'd get a new look, something casual, small-town New England and less mobster chic. Yeah, he'd get good quality slacks, shirts, and even a couple of tasteful sports jackets. Anka would approve.

He sat.

The CO called him back. "Some paperwork to finish," he said when Dusan reached the counter. He stabbed at a manila envelope with his finger.

"Your release papers are in here. Read everything, and make sure you understand. When you're done, come back to the desk, and put your John Hancock on this sheet to say you received it." He pointed to a separate sheet.

Dusan sat and read through his release papers. Finished, he rose, returned to the desk, and signed the sheet. The CO placed a copy of the signed sheet in the envelope and handed it back. "You're set, then." His gaze rose to the others. "Everybody ready?"

The releasees assured him they were.

The CO called out to another guard. "Show them out, Alex."

The four men followed the CO through several heavy, swing-clear doors out into a wide, open-spaced yard with walls on three sides and a thick steel gate on the fourth. The CO nodded to another guard, who opened a mesh security fence in the gate. The releasees stepped through without acknowledging either of their captors. All breathed deeply as they sucked in the air of freedom. New snow, maybe two inches, covered the landscape. Trustees had shoveled the road to the highway.

Grins in full evidence, the men shook hands and offered each other best wishes. The other three walked toward vehicles waiting to take them somewhere.

Dusan turned and faced the prison. "Can I get somebody to call me a cab?" he called out to the CO in the prison yard. "Need a ride into town."

The guard gave him a thumbs-up and shouted, "I'll phone now. Shouldn't take too long."

Dusan turned and studied the structure that held him for so long. *Damn! I'm standing in front of the very place I thought would hold me until I died. The word strange doesn't come close to how I feel.*

He turned and faced the road again. The air was nippy, but he didn't care. He'd rather be out here freezing than back in there, warm. He inhaled several deep breaths. The cold from the asphalt seeped up through the paper-thin soles of his Italian loafers. He looked down. "Good for walking around Naples, not much else," he muttered to himself.

A cab arrived fifteen minutes later. Dusan climbed into the back.

The driver craned his neck and said, "Where to, bud?"

Dusan almost blurted the address of his probation office but changed his mind. He had until 4:00 to show up and 6:00 to be at the halfway house. Until then, he could do as he pleased. But why not go to the cop shop and register first? Get it out of the way now.

"The police station. You know how to get there?"

"In Martine Maines? You kidding? The stories I could tell you about taking fares there."

The cab moved off. Trustees stopped and watched it drive by. A few waved. Dusan waved back in a half-hearted manner, his mind elsewhere. Should he get a beer? Be nice, real nice to taste a cold one. No, better not. For sure, his probation officer would ask him what he'd been up to since he stepped out of Stillwell. Or insist on a urine drug test. No point starting off on the wrong foot. And the halfway house would probably do the same. He'd stick with coffee and a good meal.

The police station sat in the middle of town. Dusan approached the front desk and spoke through a Plexiglas window.

"Just released from Stillwell," he said to a dour-looking uniformed woman. "Supposed to report."

"Okay. Have a seat. Somebody will be with you shortly."

Twenty minutes later, fingerprinted and his photo taken, Dusan left the station and found a diner. He ordered a double serving of bacon and had two coffees. So good, all of it, especially the coffee, not like that swamp water in the joint.

A pretty, dusty-blonde teenage server hovered over him and interrupted his daydreams. She stepped closer. "Business or pleasure?"

Dusan looked up. He hadn't been this close to an attractive female in a long time, especially one with a tight uniform. The nearness of her aroused him. *Easy, easy. She's making conversation, nothing more.*

He shot her a smile. "It shows I'm a stranger?"

"Not always," the teenager said and smiled. "But a lot of the time."

Dusan nodded. "Hmm." He glanced at her name tag. "Listen, Ashley, is there some kind of a department store nearby or maybe a men's clothing store?"

"There's Gormon's three blocks down." She pointed. "You can also go to the mall outside of town. They've got a Kohl's and a Penney's."

"Gorman's will be fine. So, three blocks this way?"

"Right."

"Okay, good. Thanks."

An hour and a half later, his suit and shoes in a new wheeled duffel bag, Dusan stepped out of Gormon's in corduroy slacks, a pea coat, and a knitted cap. What next? Why not walk around town, explore some more?

He enjoyed the walk and luxuriated in his freedom. No imposed restraints. He could walk anywhere without needing anyone's permission. How he'd taken this for granted and later missed. He meandered around the town without purpose, impressed with the town's layout, its cleanliness, the natural beauty of the nearby mountains. It probably had a cool college vibe, Dusan told himself. The bevy of cute coeds wasn't hard to take, either. Yes, he'd like living here. Maybe he'd take some classes. Why not? Pete did.

He kept an eye out for Pete, even though he knew he hadn't the slightest chance of running into him. Would Pete really contact him? At first, Dusan never doubted it, but later uncertainty settled in. Maybe he wouldn't. Dusan had no hold on him. Stop thinking like that, he warned himself. Wait and see. He thought of the old Doris Day song Anka liked to play, *Que Sera Sera*. Good advice.

Dusan couldn't help but notice Christmas and holiday shopping had shifted into high gear in the business district. Decorated store windows offered an array of temptations to passersby. Street holiday lights would come on soon. Loudspeakers pumped out cloying Andy

Williams and Burl Ives songs. So different from the joint.

He found the Federal Probation and Supervised Release office over an appliance store on Main Street. He took the stairs and noted the elevator of the two-story building. Probably for people with mobility problems, he imagined. He opened the door to the office and stepped over to a reception desk. A miniature artificial Christmas tree sat at a table in a small waiting area to the right.

A middle-aged receptionist raised her head to study him.

"May I help you?"

"Yes, I'm here to see a Mrs. Angie Lloyd."

"It's Ms. Lloyd," she corrected him. "And your name?"

Dusan sounded it out slowly.

She answered with a nod and picked up a phone. "Your four o'clock appointment is here." She hung up and looked at Dusan. "Have a seat. She'll be with you soon."

Two other men and a woman sat in the small waiting area. Dusan joined them. All worked hard to ignore each other. Lost in his private thoughts, Dusan didn't hear a female voice call him the first time.

"Dusan."

His head shot up. A diminutive woman, maybe pushing sixty, with snowy-white hair in a bun, with wire-framed glasses and a warm smile approached. He guessed she couldn't be more than 110 pounds wet. She wore black wool trousers, a blue silk shirt, and no adornments. Not even lipstick. Time had yellowed her teeth but took nothing away from the warmth of her smile.

He stood up.

"Yes."

"Would you come with me, please?" She half-turned and waited for him. Without a word, Dusan retrieved his wheeled duffel bag and followed her, she in comfortable flats, he in desert boots.

Other staff passed them, nodded to her, and gave him a blank look. All carried holstered pistols on their waists.

They entered her small, cubbyhole office, replete with plants and tasteful classical prints on two walls. Lloyd sat at her desk and gestured for Dusan to take the chair next to the desk. Seated, she pulled herself closer to her desk, swiveled in her chair, and faced him.

"I'm Angie Lloyd. I answer to either. How about you? Do you prefer Mr. Kovačević or Dusan?"

"First name's fine, and by the way, I'm really impressed you know how to pronounce my name. Doesn't happen often."

"Thank you," she said, but offered no further explanation.

He returned to his thoughts and couldn't imagine referring to this woman, who could be somebody's granny, by her first name. He had trouble thinking of her as a probation officer, as well. She reminded him of **Pastor Lister. Not physically, but in her demeanor.**

The object of his scrutiny pulled open the bottom drawer of a small filing cabinet. His gaze caught the gun and holster on the bottom of the drawer. Wow! A pistol-packing granny.

Angie Lloyd paid no heed to the gun and let her fingers scrabble through vertical files. She pulled one, looked at Dusan, and said, "Give me a minute, please, to study this. It only came the other day."

A few minutes later she closed the file and set it on her desk. "Welcome back to your life, Dusan."

"Thanks."

"So, now we need to talk about what's ahead," she said. "I'll start with the conditions of your probation."

She used her fingers to itemize her points. Dusan felt certain she recited from memory while she warned against unlawful controlled substances and association with felons, "except those you'll be living with at Condonation House."

She stopped and asked him if he had any questions so far.

"No, I'm good."

Lloyd informed him he also had to "provide either me or the Condonation House a urine sample anytime and on demand." She made it clear he had to meet with her at regularly scheduled times, couldn't hold or own a firearm ever, and had to receive written permission to leave town.

Dusan nodded.

Lloyd finished with, "You must truthfully answer all questions I ask and abide by the curfew set by Condonation House. And last, you're required to find meaningful work."

The two looked at each other. Lloyd licked her lips and said, "A long list, I know, but not so difficult to follow. Any deviation will result in your returning to Stillwell. But you can do it, you'll see." She stopped. "I'll repeat myself. Do you have any questions?"

"Um, about the work part, I'm planning on opening a business, a café, one of those chain things, but I need a business plan first."

Lloyd showed immediate enthusiasm for the idea. "Great. Do you have the resources to buy into one?"

Dusan swallowed and whispered his answer. "Yeah. It's an insurance payout from the death of my family."

"I see. I did notice a mention of it in your file. I'm sorry for your loss. And worse, how awful for you to hear about it while in prison."

"Thanks."

Something about the delivery of her response touched him. He hadn't known what to expect from her. Would she be like the female guards, eager to prove herself to male counterparts as a ball buster? No, he guessed they broke the mold when they created her. He made up his mind he could get along with this authority figure, given he had no choice.

Neither spoke yet maintained eye contact. Lloyd broke the silence.

"Well, good, then, about starting a business. This may change some things, but for the better, I think. We'll see. I'd like to be kept in the loop when you put together your business plan."

"Yeah, sure. No problem. Um, the curfew—is it set in stone?"

"Nothing is set in stone. If you get good conduct reports from the Condonation House, it can be amended...by them."

"A couple more things," Dusan said.

"Yes?"

She waited for him to speak.

"Can I drink? Nothing big, a beer here and there."

She reached for his file and looked through it. "I don't see anything to say you've had problems with alcohol abuse. I think we can make allowances for moderate drinking, but you have to inform the Condonation House. They can check with me if they like."

Pleased with what he heard, Dusan asked if he had to remain at the halfway house for the full six months.

"No, but let's see how you do first. If you do well, who knows? And Dusan?"

"Yes?"

"Don't fail me, because if you do, you fail yourself. Behave and prove you've changed."

"I'll do my best."

"I have every confidence in you."

Dusan tucked her business card into his pocket and set out in search of a cab. His meeting with Condonation House staff went well.

A three-story refurbished Edwardian house with narrow windows and a porch portico, the halfway house sat on a quiet street at the west end of town.

A day shift supervisor, Sanne Mathers, whose resting facial expression was sour and contradicted her true inner state, gave him a tour of the dining room, kitchen, living room, and laundry room. She explained how everyone pitched in with chores, which included the preparation of meals and the washing of dishes.

"Any questions?" she asked.

Dusan shook his head. "None. It's all pretty clear. Thanks."

"Good. Now I'll take you upstairs to where you'll sleep."

He followed her and waited while she opened a door. Both stepped into the bedroom. "Your roommate, Dwayne," Mathers said, "will be home soon. You'll meet him and the others."

Dusan liked the large room with its hardwood floor and original wainscoting. The furniture, a mishmash of old, scratched, and Ikea-like pieces, included chests of drawers, a desk, and a pair of four-poster beds.

Mathers pointed to plywood foot lockers. "I'll get you a lock and key, and you can store your things in there."

She brought him into the office and went over the rules and regulations.

By 7:00 the residents sat down for supper, Dusan with them. Quick introductions were made. Dusan recognized two men from Stillwell. From what he could tell, everyone got along.

Dishes done, the residents watched a football game between the Cowboys and Jaguars. A night shift supervisor entered and pointed to Dusan.

"Phone call for you."

Dusan pointed to himself. "Me?"

"Yep."

Dusan rose, entered the office, and picked up the phone, unsure of what to expect.

"Hello?"

He heard a familiar welcoming voice. "How's it feel to be back in freedom, dude?"

Chapter 26

Pete's green pickup sat outside 211 Glostner, its engine running. He watched the front door of the Edwardian house open as a man in a pea coat and knitted cap stepped out into the cold.

Pete honked his horn.

Dusan spotted the pickup and shot Pete a short, self-conscious wave. Seconds later he climbed into the warm cab. Both men grinned at each other.

"Look at you in your new duds," Pete said. "At least I think they're new. Are they?"

"Yep. Chicago mob chic was no longer working for me. But hey, speaking of look, how about this?" He waved his arm at the interior of the truck. "A fucking *pickup*? An accountant in a pickup? What's the world coming to?"

Pete chuckled. "A *former* accountant, thank you very much. You hear the joke about the interesting accountant?"

Dusan shook his head no and waited.

Pete supplied the punchline. "Me, neither."

A full second passed before Dusan caught the joke. He threw his head back and let out a full-throated laugh. Pete joined him. When the laughter died, he tapped Dusan's arm with his fist. "You're out on the street. Unbelievable. The only thing I still haven't fully adjusted myself to is you letting me keep the money."

Dusan groaned.

"You going to start that shit again? Listen, without you, I wouldn't be sitting in this pickup, so money well spent. I'm here, you're here. We're sitting in your truck. I never imagined I'd see something like this." He took a breath. "Everything's ancient history. Now, you got somewhere in mind for us to go?"

"I do. There's a tavern on the outskirts of town called The Melody Hut. Great music, if you like blues. It's…"

Dusan reached out to stop Pete. "You kidding me? We're from Chicago. We've got blues running in our veins. Only thing is I have to be back by curfew."

"Which is when?"

"Ten."

"Then, we better get going," Pete said. "Good music, good burgers, beer on tap. And the babes, ohmigod."

"I've eaten," Dusan said, "but it wasn't as tempting as what you're telling me. I'll make room. Looking forward to being surrounded by a roomful of good-looking chicks." He gave up a cocky wink. "Especially after where I've been."

"Hear you."

Pete put the truck in drive and pulled away. "What's with the truck?" Dusan asked.

"This? It somewhat connects to you," Pete gave up the story and finished with, "Now I've got used to driving it and kind of like it."

"Cool. Aren't we a pair of lawbreakers?"

"But reformed ones, right?"

"Yeah, right."

"Say it with conviction."

"Yes. Right!"

The men waited for a hostess to seat them. An attractive server in a denim miniskirt arrived and led them to a booth. She handed them menus and took their order for beer.

"Easy to take," Dusan said when she walked away. "And you're right. A lot of eye candy here. Good choice, this place."

The server came back with their beer. "Do you know what you want?" She almost had to shout to compete with the band, and pointed to the posted chalkboard menus.

Pete and Dusan considered the offering. Both ordered the bar's Killer Burgers and zesty fries. She left. The two men clinked their beer steins.

"Happy times," Dusan said in a loud voice.

"I'll drink to that."

They made idle talk for a few minutes until their food arrived. "If

I had a set of wheels, I'd come here a lot," Dusan said. He popped a fry into his mouth. "You?"

Pete shook his head and matched Dusan's voice. "Can't. Good comfort food, but too much of it and I'd be big as a house. I mostly come for the bands. So, do you mind saying—you have any conditions that come with your release?"

Dusan chewed, swallowed, and said, "Yeah, but it's not something hard to take. After the joint, this is a cakewalk."

"Good attitude. Uh, moving along, I've got to ask you how...how'd you manage to get someone to break into my house?"

Dusan grinned. "Wondered if you'd notice. Guess you did. When I paid for the, uh, service, I told my contact person that the guy who did the job shouldn't do anything to make you suspicious." He offered up a thin smile. "Good help's hard to get these days. You can still buy things in the joint. It's not easy but not impossible, either. Paying for a B and E on the street means you have no control and hope it works out okay. It mostly did. Cost me a bundle."

He told Pete how it happened. When he finished, Pete said, "Maybe another man might not have noticed, but I'm an accountant. We pay attention to details. It scared the shit out of me when I discovered somebody had been in my house. I changed the lock, the security system, and turned my house into a mini fortress. Now it's all good and, I suppose, even funny in its own freaky way. Too bad we'll never be able to tell anyone about it."

Their server returned. Did they want anything else?

Both said no.

She left. Dusan's lustful gaze tracked her until she disappeared into the kitchen. "Man, check out those legs. Spend a night or two with her is what I want." His gaze returned to Pete. A malicious grin arrived. "You getting any?"

Pete had half-expected the question. Why wouldn't sex be on Dusan's mind? He twirled his glass.

"I've started seeing a coed. Bexley. I'm not at the 'getting any' stage and not rushing it, either." He hesitated, drank from his glass, and said, "And while we're on the subject of getting some, I should tell you about an escort service I've used. They're discreet, and the girls are knockouts, too. If you want, I can help you set something up. Even get you a motel room, seeing you can't leave town without permission."

"Yeah, great," Dusan said. "Sooner the better." He fell silent for a moment. "Tell me if I'm out of line, but what's a guy like you doing with an escort service?"

Pete's mind flashed back to the day in Stillwell when Dusan asked him if it ever troubled him walking out on his family. That question rankled as much as this one.

Jesus, Dusan, you know anything about personal boundaries? Why not say the first thing that pops into your head? He pushed his annoyance aside. Stop being so sensitive.

Aware of his body language, Pete forced his shoulders back and told himself to relax. He shot Dusan a half-smile and a shrug.

"Interesting question. Penetrating one, too. They seem to come easy to you."

"A bad thing?"

"I guess not," Pete said, and broke off. "Maybe we should have another beer." He signaled for their server. When she arrived, he wagged his finger at the empty glasses. "Two more, please."

She brought their drinks. Pete drained the foam from his new glass and set it down. "There's this joke that goes something like this—the difference between kinky and perverted is, kinky is using a feather, and perverted is using the whole chicken."

Dusan chortled.

Pete continued. "Sometimes I think the chicken part interests me more. I don't know, well, no, not really." He drew a long breath. "I have trouble explaining it to myself let alone to anyone else. Thing is, I do worry about my sex life."

Dusan blew out his cheeks. "Look, man, you don't have to go on."

"Too late. Probably good for me to talk to somebody about it anyway."

Pete looked away for a moment.

"When my ex and I were first married, she was hot stuff, and I was a real horn dog. Looking back, not exactly the best building blocks for a sound marriage. Once the wife got pregnant, she lost interest in sex and turned into her mother—a nagging bad-tempered woman.

"I remember thinking we needed to do some things to spice up our marriage. I bought some toys and lingerie. The wife looked at everything, laughed in my face, and called me a perv. I learned my lesson and never went there again."

Pete leaned back. "If ever there was a woman who made you feel weak and unmanly, it was my ex. I turned to gambling either out of frustration, anger, or both—take your pick—and worsened my situation."

"If it's of any comfort," Dusan said, "the two goons I sent to your house said your ex was a grade-A bitch and wouldn't fuck her if she paid them."

Something about the comment and its delivery created an image in Pete's mind. He envisaged Muscle and his partner being propositioned by Nina. It brought a smile, then a chortle, and finally a full belly laugh.

Dusan looked puzzled at first but perhaps getting caught up in the moment, joined in. The laughter grew. The two men slapped the table and caused nearby customers to stare at them.

When Pete brought himself under a bit of control, he said, "Leave it…to…guys…to…get things down to the…lowest common denominator." He wiped at his eyes. "Yeah, she was a bitch." He took another swig of his beer, set in down, and continued.

"One other time I did have some extra dough she didn't know about. Found a classy call girl. Best sex in a long time." He stopped, raised his eyebrows in a what're-you-gonna-do look, took another pull of his beer, and said, "After my windfall, at your expense, I got it on with Linzie. She didn't have—doesn't have—sexual restraints. Things went south because of me. I then found my way to this escort service. You can ask for anything and not worry about seeing the girls again."

He blew out his cheeks. "So, there you are. Now you know."

Dusan ran a palm over his chin. "So, to the sex life thing you just described, I didn't hear anything about pedophilia, rape, animal perversion, or creepy voyeurism. I gotta tell you, what you're laying out is tame. Not much surprises me anymore. I've just left an institution with a lot of nasty, fucked-up guys doing serious time for sick stuff. What you said doesn't even come close. Ever."

Pete shook his head. "No, my tastes aren't perverted like that unless you ask someone who lives in Alabama."

The comment brought quick, soft laughter from both men.

Dusan spoke. "So, if your tastes don't run to that, what's the problem?"

Pete exhaled loudly.

"Okay, I'm not doing a good enough job of explaining myself." He raised a hand and let it drop. "Linzie, like I said, she was unrestrained and liked the same things I did, and a few more. Never met anyone like her. But that's done, and there's nothing I can do to get her back. The call girls? For me, it comes down to pleasure—mine—and then it's all settled with a satisfactory business transaction. They make no demands, take my money, accommodate me, and leave. When I'm with them, I've had no trouble delivering the mail, if you get my meaning."

Dusan replied with a mirthless laugh.

"'Delivering the mail'? Code for keeping it up." He leaned back from the table. "C'mon, man, you're what, in your late twenties? You should have no problems there. Sounds like you didn't with this Linzie. And if you do, why not take one of those, uh, little blue pills?"

The intimate conversation surprised Pete. Why had he shared so much? He'd never done this with anyone, least of all Nina. Should he push on or change the subject? Something told him to stay with the conversation a bit longer.

"It's more than a little blue pill, and maybe I'm worrying for nothing. Linzie has a dirty mind to match mine. The call girls, well, I've already told you. This Bexley, she's one of those, you know, wholesome, Suzie Creamcheese types. I'll admit I do worry a bit about performing with her. It's bound to happen—I mean, us having sex."

Dusan shook his head with slow deliberation. "I think I'm starting to understand. What if she's open to the same interests as this Linzie chick?"

Pete snorted. "A Suzie Creamcheese? I doubt it."

Dusan ran a fingertip along the edge of the table.

"Never know until you get there. Besides, maybe there's something deeper going on here, like keeping Stellan Nieves under tight wraps. It's got to be stressful, this double life, always wondering if you'll slip up."

"Zank yoo, Herr Doktor Freud, for geevink to me sometink, a new voorry, ja."

Dusan held up his hands in surrender.

"Good imitation, and sorry. Trying to get you to see the bigger picture. Go day by day. See what each one brings."

"Maybe. I'll have to think on it some more. Anyway, do you want me to set up something with the escort service or not?"

Dusan nodded. "Yeah. For sure. How do you pay?"

"Don't worry. I'll take care of it."

"Thanks, man."

"Least I can do."

Pete dropped Dusan off and drove home. He'd given Dusan his cell phone number. They'd set up something soon. He might even introduce Dusan to Bexley socially.

Condonation House held its annual Christmas party/open

house. Residents were allowed to bring two guests. Dusan invited Pete, who in turn brought Bexley and introduced her.

She took Dusan's hand when he extended it. "Hello, Dusan. I've heard nothing but nice things about you from Pete. I volunteer with Pete at Stillwell."

"Oh, do you?" He released her hand. "Too bad I didn't take your classes. I bet they're well-attended."

Bexley answered with a forced smile. "Thank you." She waved a hand at the surroundings. "How are you liking it here?"

"I like it. A good bunch of guys, and the staff...you couldn't ask better. Now, let me take your coats."

Pete and Bexley shed their coats and handed them to him. Dusan pointed to the other side of a crowded room. "Nibblies and non-alcoholic refreshments across there. I'll see you in a minute." He returned to find his guests in conversation with a staff member.

Dusan joined them and gently tapped Pete's arm. "I wouldn't worry about her," he whispered. "She's nice. Be good to her."

"I intend to."

"Glad to hear it, and if you ever cut her loose or she throws you to the curb, let me know."

Pete made a wry face. "Droll."

The two turned back to Bexley, who finished her conversation with the staffer. She looked at Dusan and said, "Got any good New Year's resolutions?" A natural conversationalist, she drew Dusan out with ease. He told her about his new business venture. "If I can make a go of it, that would be the best."

"Something tells me you will."

"Nice of you to say."

An older woman in a gray, two-button pant suit walked by. Dusan tugged at her sleeve. She turned.

"Angie, got a second? I want you to meet two nice people." He made the introductions. Within minutes the foursome found themselves in easy conversation.

"You're a probation officer?" Bexley said to the older woman. "Sorry, but you don't look the part."

Dusan agreed. "Same thing I thought when I first saw her. But she is, and very nice. I now feel comfortable using her first name."

Angie arched her eyebrows.

"I suppose it's good to keep people on their toes." She freed a finger from her glass and wagged it between Pete and Bexley. "How do you two know Dusan?"

"We both volunteer at Stillwell," Pete said. "Dusan took my math class. I got to know him a little bit better, and…"

A tingling, indefinable suspicion descended on Pete a few days later: someone had him under observation. He scanned his surroundings while he waited for his prescription to be filled. Nothing. No one had him under observation.

The feeling wouldn't leave. Your imagination's getting the best of you, he told himself. Why would anyone follow you? Shake it off.

Darkness had already descended when Pete left by the back door of the pharmacy and walked to his truck. He scanned the municipal lot. Nothing to cause him worry. Time to pick up Dusan at his renovated store.

A large man in a bomber jacket, a knit cap pulled over his ears, approached. Pete at once sensed danger. Was he about to be mugged? He couldn't imagine it. That kind of thing didn't happen here. New York, Chicago, the big cities, sure, but not this small college town. Yet the stranger continued to advance.

Pete searched for an escape route as the man drew closer. In a flash recognition came to Pete—Muscle, from Chicago.

Aroused levels of anger and fear swelled in Pete. His stomach muscles tightened. He found it hard to catch his breath as the thug stepped in front of him.

"Hey, how're ya doin' there, Stellan?" the croaky voice said, moving from foot to foot while tugging at his gloves.

Pete pulled air into his lungs. He'd give anything to know how

Muscle had found him. Had his cover been blown for good? His mind raced for an appropriate response to the greeting. He couldn't think of anything and made a motion to sidestep Muscle.

The thug again blocked his way, splayed his fingers, and said, "C'mon, sport. You gotta talk to me. Talkin's good. I need you to do something. Make this right and I go away." He glanced around at the parking lot.

Pete backed away and tried to get moisture in his mouth. He pulled air into his lungs and in a wavering voice said, "Listen, I don't know who you think I am, but you're mistaking me for someone, and you're blocking my way. Not cool, and you don't want to come to the attention of our town's finest."

Muscle didn't move.

A young couple walked to their car. Pete's first instinct was to run and join them, yet his legs wouldn't move.

The couple gave Pete and Muscle a curious look, entered their vehicle, and drove off.

The two men returned their attention to each other. Muscle exhaled. An overhead light caught the frosted air plume. "Not diggin' bein' out here in the cold, so let's finish this. Stellan Nieves. You fucked off with over two mil of my boss' dough. You're lucky it's me who found you and not him. He gets his hands on you, you'll be floating in the river over there." He pointed eastward. "But not before he's had his fun with you."

Muscle's boasting gave Pete his first ray of optimism. So, loud-mouth didn't know Dusan was out of prison.

"I'll say it again. I'm not who you think I am."

"And I'll say I ain't got time for this shit. You're Nieves, and you need to listen to me."

Pete pretended frustration.

"All right, for the sake of discussion, let's say I'm this, um, Stellan whoever."

"Wrongo, sport. You *are* Stellan."

"Yeah, sure, whatever. Anyway, if I'm hearing this right, this Stellan stole money from your boss, and now you're what—hoping to blackmail Stellan, me, for it?"

"Bingo. You got it."

"Say I give you this money," Pete said. "Here's the thing. What's to stop your boss, whatshisname...?"

"Dusan, like you didn't know."

"But you're the one who's blackmailing me. You. I'm guessing, then, you're going rogue."

"Speak English. I don't know what the hell that means."

Pete pressed his lips together.

"It means you're doing it behind your boss' back. What's to stop this Dusan from finding out and coming after you for double-dealing?"

"My worry, not yours."

Pete tossed his shoulders. "Easy for you to say."

"Listen, asshole, do yourself a favor. Get me the dough, and don't fuck around."

Feeling emboldened, Pete continued.

"Sorry. I can't give you what I haven't got. I'm not who you think I am."

The defiance hardened the other man's facial muscles. He puffed up his chest and stepped closer to Pete.

"Careful," Pete warned. "More people are coming into the parking lot. You don't want attention."

Muscle stopped. "Okay, smartass. I guess I go tell the boss where you are."

Pete gave his best I-couldn't-care-less shrug.

"Fine, and I'll tell him about this little conversation. But for the sake of discussion—only asking—how much are you wanting?"

"All of it, and you get to keep your life."

Pete replied with a contemptuous laugh.

"You're not greedy, are you? I thought maybe you'd ask for a big payout, but you want it all. Well, I guess why not go for the gusto? And then when I give you this supposed money, what's to stop you from coming back and hitting me up again?"

Muscle shook his head. "Not too bright, are you? Why would I? I've got all the dough. Like I said, gimme the money and I'm gone for good."

Neither man spoke. Muscle studied Pete for a long moment. "Tell you what I'm gonna do. I'll give you 'til tomorrow to get the dough together. I'm not hanging around this nothing town longer, got it?" He reached into his jacket, pulled out a scrap of paper and a pen. He scribbled something on the paper and handed it to Pete.

"My cell. You call me. I better be hearing from you."

Pete gave him a slow shake of his head.

"You're still not getting this. I'm not this Stellan guy. Suppose I was. Do you think I'd be dumb enough to hide all that money in big garbage bags under my bed? It'd be dispersed."

"What's that mean?"

"Broken up," Pete said, and wanted to add "dumb ass" but held back. "If I went to all the bother of stealing a lot of money, I'd invest it, buy property, bit coins, stocks, whatever."

"Then we got a different problem," Muscle said. "Meet me tomorrow with some of it as a sign of good faith, and we'll talk some more about how to get the rest of it to me." Muscle turned and walked away. "Tomorrow," he said aloud.

Pete watched him round a corner. Amusement and defiance nudged out earlier feelings of fear. The guy clearly didn't know Dusan's status. The easiest thing would be to tell Dusan. Should he? He didn't know, couldn't guess how his friend might react. Would he take it upon himself to handle the problem? If he did, it might land him back in Stillwell. Pete didn't want that on his conscience.

One thing, the only thing for sure, Muscle wasn't going to go away empty-handed. Maybe some kind of other strategy would come to mind before the evening finished.

Chapter 27

Hands deep in his pea coat, Dusan stood in the small recess of his store and watched the road for a green pickup. Interior lights were on against the darkness, and vehicles passed by while he thought back to his recent progress with his new bakery-café.

A month ago he'd slipped into his extra-starched white shirt, knotted his tie, and readied to meet the team from bakery-café corporate office. He felt like a bundle of nerves while he waited. Everything had to be work. It was all new territory for him, this schmoozing and winning others over.

The three arrived. Dusan remembered Gates' advice about getting one chance to make a good first impression. He rose and greeted the two men and one woman in the upscale restaurant with its reminiscent art nouveau design.

Introductions made, Dusan kept his voice calm and slowed his words so the team could follow everything. He had a mental list of prepared safe topics and appropriate jokes.

If the team sensed any nervousness, Dusan couldn't tell. They laughed at his jokes and listened while he explained his vision for the café. They assured him his plans were well thought-out and followed the comment with rapid and assuring nods. Two hours later they shook his hand and left.

A week and a half later a thick USPS Priority package arrived at the halfway house along with a letter advising him that he'd been approved in principle as a franchisee.

"Unbelievable," an excited Dusan said to his roommate, Daryl Lyle. He waved the letter and waved the document. "From what I heard, it mostly takes a couple of months."

"S'good, right?"

"Good? It's great. And you, you crazy drug pusher, you got a job if you want one. I'm going to need bakers. Cooks, too. Steady work and good pay."

The large, tattooed man grinned at Dusan. "Baker, me? Cool.

Thanks, man, but you know I can't bake for shit?"

Dusan laughed, "Don't worry about it. We'll train you."

Dusan shifted his weight and continued to watch for the pickup while he thought about the last few days. He'd spent a great deal of time reading the company's manual. So much so, he thought his head would explode. Still, he managed to absorb everything and developed a good grasp of the contract, including the section on franchise fees. He'd have to get a business lawyer to go over the details.

He'd also discovered he'd have to attend an upcoming mandatory training session in Chicago. New owners would learn everything from A to Z in running their new business. The course would take a month and a half.

Chicago. Life was interesting. They could have picked New York, Philly, L.A., even Montpelier, but no, they picked the one place that didn't interest him. All right, he told himself; he'd make the most of it, following permission from Angie, of course. He doubted she'd object but would want to know about his living arrangements while away. Maybe she'd have him report to a Chicago probation office.

Angie did object. She heard his request without comment and opened his case file. A minute passed before she looked up.

"No, I don't think so. Chicago? You're asking us to send you back to the wolf's lair. There's far too much temptation and possible trouble awaiting you there."

Dusan felt himself flush. What the hell! Where did she get off saying no? He had a legitimate reason to attend the training session. If he didn't go, where would they hold the next one? And more importantly, when?

He forced himself to stay calm. It wasn't the end of the world. Several long, deep, silent breaths accompanied by considerable blinking occurred before he trusted himself to answer. A quote from Son of the West Wind came to him.

"All right, I get it. Your job is to protect me from society and from myself, but you know the saying 'No man steps into the same river twice'? Well, it sums me up."

"It's the river I worry about, Dusan, and what you might do on it."

They discussed the matter in detail. Dusan argued the facts: time, money, his commitment to be and do better.

It took some time, but he brought Angie around in the end. "You've made a convincing case," she said, "so I'll take the chance and let you go. Give me time to set you up with a visit to one of our Chicago offices. Come back and see me before you leave, and I'll go over everything with you."

Dusan left the office, pleased with how well he maintained his composure. "You listening, West Wind?" he whispered under his breath. "You must have been."

Dusan arranged a meeting with his new lawyer and took along a certified check.

"Everything looks good, Mr. Kovačević," Tracy Weeden, the heavyset friendly woman who shunned makeup, said. She followed with a nod. "All I need now is your signature on the FDDs (financial disclosure documents), and I'll send everything off on your behalf."

Dusan complied. He thanked her and shook her hand.

"Nice to do business with you. You'll see me again."

"Thank you. How did you find your way to my practice anyway?"

"I asked around."

"Ah. Word of mouth. Well, good luck with your new business. I'll be pulling for you."

Dusan next searched for a suitable location to live. By luck, he found one through a realtor, close to the college.

Now outside, Dusan stamped his feet and saw the green truck approach. He waved and stepped onto the sidewalk.

"Damn. Glad to get out of the cold," Dusan said when he climbed into the cab of the truck. He tugged at the seat belt harness. "How're you doing, my man?"

"Fine, fine," Pete said. "You?"

"Great. I'm hungry. Let's go eat."

They drove in silence. Dusan never made Pete out to be a chatterbox, but thought him withdrawn. Maybe not, he told himself; maybe he only imagined it. He'd give the guy a chance.

Inside the tavern they found an empty booth and slid in. A server in jeans too snug for her generous shape took their orders for beer and burgers.

They watched her walk away. Pete tossed his head in her direction and smirked. "Could stand to lose a few pounds. I'm surprised they hired her."

"No kidding. Guess she never heard tight jeans look best on skinny broads. Ah, well. Put her in the joint, and there'd be a massive lineup."

Pete grinned.

Their beer arrived. Both raised their glasses and chugged.

Dusan set his glass down first. "You got that same zoned-out look you had when I first saw you in the joint. Something bothering you?"

"What do you mean?"

"Mean about what—the zoned-out part or something else?"

"Both, I guess."

Dusan picked up his beer again. "Everything okay with Bexley?"

"Yeah," Pete said. "I'm pretty sure I'm heading for a meet-the-family soon."

Dusan tilted his head and looked at Pete.

"You make it sound like a death sentence." He waved the remark off. "Okay, what's really bothering you? Something is."

Pete answered with furrowed brows and looked like a man in worried contemplation.

"I wasn't going to say anything, but..." He leaned forward. "You know the guy who used to work for you, the big muscled guy? I never got his name."

Dusan's smile slipped. His eyes narrowed. "Boban Rakitić."

"I guess."

"What about him?"

"I met him today. He's trying to shake me down. I'm not sure yet what I'll do."

Dusan didn't hear the last sentence. He leaned forward.

"*My* old employee, you talked to him here, today, putting the squeeze on you?"

"Uh-huh, and it doesn't take a Sherlock Holmes to figure out this guy's on your shit list. He the one you talked about before, the one who ratted you out to the feds?"

"The main one," Dusan said. "He's here?" Dusan stabbed downward with his index finger.

"Yeah. You already asked me that."

"Excuse *me*, Miss Manners. I forgot myself. I guess my brain couldn't quite register what I just heard."

Pete held up his hands in surrender.

"C'mon, dude, sorry. It came out wrong, I didn't mean to annoy you. I guess I got more wound up about this than I thought. I shouldn't have said anything to you about this Boban."

"I'd have been really pissed off if I'd found out he'd slunk in and out of town like the rat he is, and you didn't tell me. I want to know. And about the other thing, forget it." He waved a hand as if to swat a fly away. "No hard feelings."

Their burgers arrived. Both retreated into silence while their server set the plates down. "Enjoy, guys. Anything else?"

"We're fine," Dusan said.

The server left. Dusan glanced at his food but left it. Pete ate a few of his curly fries.

Dusan took another swallow of his beer and set the glass down again. "So, talk," Dusan said. "Tell me about your run-in with him."

Pete slowly blew out his lips and moved into the story. "So, I'm in the parking lot, you know, the one behind the drug store. He came out of nowhere. Next thing I know he's shaking me down for the money."

"What else did he say? You leave anything out?"

"It's all I got, man."

Both men again stopped talking. Their server returned, stared at their food, and said, "Is something wrong with your meals?"

Pete answered.

"No. We got carried away with our discussion."

She gave him a polite smile. "It's probably cold now. Do you want it reheated?"

They shook their heads.

"Maybe doggy bags," Dusan said, and looked at Pete. "You okay taking it to go?"

"Sure, yeah," Pete said. "Good idea."

She took their plates. Dusan turned his attention back to Pete.

"So, you've got until tomorrow to answer Boban. Okay, listen. Here's what I'm thinking. Call the fucker and say you'll meet him at 6:00 at the same place. Tell him you need more time to get cash together. Okay?"

"Six? Yeah, I guess."

Dusan drained the last of his beer, when the server returned with their food in boxes.

"Would you like more beer?"

Dusan looked at Pete, who shook his head. "No, we're done. The bill, please."

She wrote it up. Pete took it, studied it, and reached for his wallet. He retrieved several bills and handed them to her. "Your tip's in there."

She did a fast count, looked up, and shot him a final smile. "Thank you, and please come again."

They assured her they would and watched her leave.

Dusan returned his attention to Pete. "When you call Boban, let him know you want to meet at the far end of the parking lot, near the trees. You'll drive your car there and park so no one can see you." A grunt followed, and Dusan finished with, "I'll take care of the rest."

Worry clouded Pete's face. "I don't know... I guess this is why I didn't want to say anything."

His voice forceful yet controlled, Dusan said, "Listen, man, you owe me. Have I even once asked for my money?"

"No."

"Have I put any plan into action that endangered you?"

"No, but..."

Dusan held up his hand. "Save it! I don't want to hear buts. My own doing, getting tossed into the slammer. I've got nobody else to blame. But Boban, the rat, I treated him well, like a brother, and look..." He clenched and unclenched his jaw. "I might have beat the rap against me if not for him." His voice trailed off. He squeezed his eyes shut and reopened them. "I never gave up settling with him."

A numbing silence settled over their booth in spite of the raucous band.

"Life's funny," Dusan said. "Couldn't go to Chicago without a good reason and permission from Angie. And guess what? Rakitić comes *here*."

A vein throbbed in his neck while he stared off into the distance. At last he returned his gaze to Pete. He pressed his lips together. "I've got to do this, and I need your help. I won't ask you for anything again."

Pete wouldn't look away from Dusan's fixed stare. He remained quiet for a moment, and at last spoke. "All right. I do owe you. So, let's plan this out so there are no loose ends anywhere. Agreed?"

"You got it."

"Good. I don't want either of us in jail cells. Let's start with, won't he get suspicious if I ask to meet him at the far end?"

The server walked by. Pete called her over.

"We changed our minds. Another round of what we had before,

please."

"Coming up."

The two conspirators sat and schemed the ruin of one Boban Rakitić. The plan at last in place, Pete called Rakitić. He did his best to sound wary and nervous. He got off his cell phone, looked at Dusan, and said, "You heard."

His friend awarded him with a fast nod. "Sounded convincing. Let's hope he shows up."

"Yeah, let's."

A light layer of snow had just fallen. With his pea coat collar turned up, Dusan tucked himself into the trees at the edge of the parking lot. He sniffed the air and studied his faint footprints in the snow. The falling snow would soon blot them out.

He shifted from foot to foot and glanced at the serrated steak knife he'd boosted from an upscale restaurant. Not his first choice, but it would do. He'd found it awkward to walk with it in his pea coat and moved it against his inner wrist.

Dusan sniffled in the safety of the trees. *It's not too late*, an inner voice urged. *You could just let it go. Anka would have wanted you to.*

He dismissed the voice. No! This had to be done. He reviewed everything: keep a firm grip on the knife; don't let it slip; make sure to keep his torso away from Rakitić.

Movement caught his eye. A man in a knit cap and bomber jacket was walking toward him. Dusan recognized Rakitić. Yes! His heart raced, and his senses heightened. He backed into the trees. He needed to surprise him. Of the two, Rakitić outweighed Dusan and could easily fend off a frontal attack.

Rakitić stopped at the edge of the trees. His body language told Dusan the enforcer suffered the effects of the cold.

Snow continued to fall. Rakitić stamped his feet and hunched his shoulders. "C'mon, c'mon," he said loud enough for Dusan to hear. "Get here. Fuckin' freezin'. It ain't like I got alla time in the world."

Something made Rakitić turn and stare into the trees.

Dusan held his breath. Had Rakitić seen him? The enforcer at last turned again and faced the parking lot. Dusan exhaled through his mouth.

A car started. Rakitić backed closer into the cover of the trees. The car turned, its headlights headed away from Rakitić.

Dusan sprang. Aided by a surge of adrenalin, he wrapped a forearm around Rakitić's neck and pulled the surprised enforcer into the trees. Rakitić flailed.

The force of Dusan's knife sliced through Rakitić's clothing and into his body. He gave a high-pitched grunt. His former employer knew the knife had found its mark, a kidney.

Dusan kept his legs apart and maintained a vise-like grip on Rakitić's neck. "You better hope I only nicked you, you fucking two-faced rat," he whispered into Rakitić's ear. "You probably won't bleed out if you leave the knife where it is until they get you to a hospital. Remember this special moment. If you ever come back here again, I'll finish the job but not before I give you more pain on your way to the next life."

His message delivered, Dusan lowered his victim to the ground.

"Help me, please, Dusan," Rakitić implored, his eyes wide with fright.

An indifferent Dusan answered with scorn.

"You mean like you helped me? Nah. Not going to happen." His eyes scanned the parking lot. No one. He reached for Rakitić's back pocket, found the wallet, and removed the bills. A couple hundred bucks by the look of it. The money disappeared into Dusan's coat. The wallet fell next to Rakitić.

"Remember what I told you about the knife."

Dusan turned, walked across the parking lot, and made his way out onto the street. He stopped at a pay phone and called the hospital. When the switchboard answered, he told the woman a man was lying bleeding near the municipal lot in some trees. "Please get an ambulance there fast."

"Well, sir, you should call the..."

Dusan hung up, pleased no one had a recording of his voice, like with 9-1-1.

A few short minutes later he stepped into a donut shop and ordered coffee. Beverage in hand, he sat at a Formica table and examined the front of his coat. Nothing. He looked closer. A bit of blood on the right sleeve. Easily taken care of. He set his coffee on a table and moved to the restroom. He rinsed off the blood. Finished, he returned to his coffee.

Three days before Christmas Dusan received a phone call from his probation officer. She told him to come in for an interview. At once.

He knew why she'd summoned him. Rakitić. All the same, it caused his heartbeat to race. *Hang onto your cool*, he ordered himself. He'd been in tighter situations than this and had his strategy ready — play dumb.

The receptionist phoned Angie to announce him. She arrived, nodded, and escorted him from the reception area. Nothing in her eyes or voice invited comfort as she led him into her office. Two men in ill-fitting suits waited.

Her hand out toward the two, Angie said, "Dusan, these are Detectives Welthram and Pentti. They want to talk to you about an incident."

"Ask me about what incident?"

The balding Welthram stepped closer. "Take a seat." He gestured to a chair.

Okay, Dusan thought, *so he's playing the alpha dog, the lead-off.* "No thanks, I'm good standing. I don't know why I'm here or what this is about."

"It's not an invitation," the other cop, Pentti, said and pointed to the chair.

Dusan still wouldn't cooperate. Sitting gave the cops a psychological advantage. "Nope. Nothing in my probation order says I have to sit because somebody tells me to. In the joint, yes. Here, I have some rights."

Angie intervened.

"How about if we all sit? I'll bring a few extra chairs."

"Sure, okay," Dusan said.

All seated, Welthram started again.

"We're here to ask you some questions about a Boban Rakitic." He mispronounced the name and indicated the date of the assault. "This man says you tried to kill him and that you know each other."

Stay close to the truth, Dusan warned himself.

"I do know a Boban Rakitić." He corrected the pronunciation and waited a moment. "I haven't seen him since I went up river. He lives in Chicago. I live here. How am I supposed to kill him?"

Welthram ignored the question. "At the moment Rakitić's here in ICU. He's given a detailed account of how you stabbed him."

Eyes trained on Dusan, the other three waited for him to answer. Thanks to Gates, he'd become a voracious reader. He recalled an article on the psychology of lying and how cops were trained to spot a liar. The writer, a presenter to police academies, noted that when lying, people tended to look up and to the right.

His eyes moved to the upper left corner of the room, then returned their focus to Welthram. "Well, if this is the same Boban, news to me he was even in town. Can't figure out why he'd finger me for something I didn't do."

Welthram looked like a man ready to roll his eyes.

"Care to account for your movements at the time of the stabbing?"

"I guess. What time are we talking about?"

The bull-necked Pentti answered. "Six PM."

"'Course," Dusan said. "I was at my café, working on getting it ready. So much to do."

Pentti's deadpan expression never changed. "Anyone verify?"

"Uh, yes...no, I guess. Wait. I took a coffee break at Donut Land around then. A girl there should remember me. A pretty redhead. Stacey. I remember her name tag."

Welthram pulled a small notebook and a ballpoint pen from his jacket, flipped it open, and wrote something in it. "So, she'll back your story?"

Dusan replied with a shrug. Careful to pronounce every word, he said, "Have to ask her."

Both cops maintained their stare. Dusan ordered himself not to squirm. *Stay cool. Keep your hands from fidgeting. Let them show what they've got.*

Pentti resumed his questioning.

"You don't think it's a reach that this Rakitić, who used to work for you, is here in town, almost murdered, and guess who he points the finger at?"

Comforted knowing the cops were fishing, Dusan's eyes moved among the three before he settled on the questioner.

"In your police training, Detective Pentti, a hypothesis gets formed. The next step would be what, getting results? A man is stabbed, I know the man, and so I'm the stabber. Let me say conjectures aren't evidence and are often seen through biased prisms."

He intended to say more, but the detective spoke over him to his colleague.

"See what happens, Gord, when convicts get a little education?"

Dusan felt his cheeks turn crimson. He wanted to retaliate with a smart rebuttal but held back.

Angie spoke up.

"There's no cause for that, Detective Pentti. You're an officer of the Court. So am I. We follow the law, and we treat everyone with civility."

Welthram jumped in. He pointed to Dusan. "You're taking his

side?"

"I'm taking no one's side, Detective. You're questioning one of my probationers. He's being investigated for a stabbing, but let's do this with the highest degree of professionalism. How about we stick to the facts and nothing else?"

Dusan could have sworn he saw both men squirm at the takedown. Neither looked Angie in the eye.

Pentti turned and fixed his gaze on Dusan again.

"Can you think of any reason why a former employee would arrive in town, be attacked, and say it was you?"

Dusan shook his head. "If this is the Boban Rakitić I know—and how many can there be?—I've no idea what motivated him to come to Martine Maines and say I tried to kill him. Yes, he once worked for me. That was then. This is now."

The room again settled into silence.

Welthram stood up and approached Dusan. "Hold out your hands."

Dusan obeyed.

Both cops examined his palms and the backs of his hands. Welthram pointed to Dusan's pea coat. "This the coat you wore last night?"

"Yep."

"The only one you've got?"

"No, I have a cashmere overcoat I never wear unless it's for something special."

Neither man asked to see it. "Take off your coat," Welthram said.

Dusan complied and handed it over. Everything he'd seen and heard so far said they had nothing on him.

The cops studied the front of the coat. Pentti sniffed it and returned it to Dusan. He rose. "All right. That's all for now, but the investigation is ongoing."

Welthram added, "And you're a person of interest."

It took everything for Dusan not to chuckle. A person of interest?

They had nothing stronger.

"Don't leave town," Pentti said.

"Can't help you there. I have to go to Chicago after Christmas for a training course. I've already cleared it with Ms. Lloyd." He looked to Angie for confirmation.

She gave it. "Yes, it's all been arranged."

Welthram brushed off the comment and turned to Dusan. "We'll contact you if we need to."

The men left. Dusan and Angie contemplated each other for a moment. She tilted her head and studied him.

"I don't know if you're responsible for this, Dusan, and I won't ask you to incriminate yourself. I'm not always the best judge of character, but I saw something good in you. Don't disappoint me." Inquisitive eyes studied him.

Dusan had been able to withstand the intense scrutiny of the two cops, but Angie made him uncomfortable. He smothered an urge to squirm. Lying had always come second nature to him. He grew up thieving on Chicago's mean streets. Everyone he hung out with lied. You erred on the side of the truth only when it suited you. If you told Big Anthony you wasted some guy he wanted dead, you'd better not be lying. Otherwise, from morning to night you and everyone in your circle lied.

In the joint, from the moment cons stepped off the prison bus to the time they left, they lied. Even when they didn't have to.

Son of the West Wind and Gates proved the exception.

Anka had loved Dusan. He knew she knew he often lied to her. Her big heart always forgave him.

In front of Angie he'd lied to the detectives, something he had to do. A measure of guilt nagged at him when he spoke.

"Believe what you want, Angie, but there's zero gain in me lying about Rakitić. If it's him, I didn't know he was in town. I never met him here. I never saw him. Did he say what he was doing in town?"

"He claims he was about to meet a friend but didn't give the police anything more." She threw her hands in the air. "We'll have to leave it there, I guess. We may never get to the truth."

"And he's in ICU, Rakitić?"

Angie didn't answer for a short moment.

"I guess. They stopped the bleeding, and they're transferring him to a Chicago hospital. I imagine they'll assess what, if anything else, needs to be done to his kidney."

"It's good, then, that he's alive," Dusan said. He meant it. Far better for Rakitić to stay alive and suffer. So far everything had gone according to plan.

Chapter 28

Pete and Dusan left town before dawn. They wanted to make good time and agreed the 15-hour trip would best be broken up with an overnight en route. Pete kept to the speed limit on I-90. The stereo on, neither man said much.

"Decent of you to drive me," Dusan said.

"Pleasure," Pete replied. "I wanted to go see my father's grave anyway."

A few miles later Pete said, "The thing with Boban, you didn't give me any details."

"You really want them?"

"Yes and no, but I wanted to ask you about your probation officer. No lingering suspicions after the cops left?"

Dusan shook his head. "Nah, I don't think so. Maybe just a little iffy after those two Keystone Kops left, but I think she believed me."

Pete kept his eyes on the road. "And the stabbing, what did you feel about that, during and after?"

"Feel? Nothing at the time, just full of adrenaline, and then everything happened so fast. And afterwards, when I thought about it, I was amazed I managed to pull it off. You've seen Rakitić. Big fucker. So, it's done, and I'm pretty sure I got away with it. Not proud of it. Hope I never do anything like that again, but I don't have regrets." He finished and looked at Pete. "Okay, we done with this?"

"We are."

"Then, let's move on. How are things with Bexley?"

"Not much to tell," Pete said. "It's all good."

Something in the answer told Dusan his friend wouldn't give him more. Fine. He'd leave the subject alone, though he felt tempted to ask why Bexley hadn't come along.

They stopped for breakfast. Neither man was in the mood for conversation, so they focused on their food. Back on the highway Pete said, "Strange, huh, the two of us driving to Chicago together, our home town? When we left, I was on the run, and you were in handcuffs. Now look at us."

Dusan stared sightlessly at the road before he answered. "Does make you wonder how things unfold in this universe of ours. Like why my course will be held there and not somewhere else."

Neither added anything more, and the subject died.

"You think you'll check out your old stomping grounds?" Pete asked.

Dusan flicked a hand. "Probably not. No real need. I've been thinking about bringing my wife and kids' remains to Martine Maines. Somebody at the cemetery might help get me started with that."

"You're a good man for doing that."

"I guess. And you, staying extra-long and maybe swing down memory lane?"

"Uh-uh. Definitely not. Stellan Nieves fell off the face of the earth, remember? I intend to make sure it stays that way."

At dusk Pete pulled into a hotel chain. They ate in the restaurant, had a couple of beers, and stared at an overhead TV screen.

"You into b-ball?" Dusan asked.

"Not much until it gets playoff time."

"Yeah, me, too."

The two fatigued travelers wished each other a good night. They met for breakfast at 6:00. Four hours later the pickup approached Dead Man's Curve, and they saw the sign cautioning drivers to slow down.

Dusan had prepared himself for this moment. He knew from reports this was where Anka and the boys had met their deaths. He felt his eyes glisten and heard himself sniffle. The noise caused Pete to turn and glance at him.

Dusan berated himself. The very thing he didn't want, a goddamn tear fest. He swallowed hard several times and refused to meet Pete's gaze. A minute later he pointed ahead and in a wet voice said, "Pull over anywhere here, will you? I want to stop."

"It's a corner," Pete said. "A sharp corner."

"Yeah, I know, but I need to get out. Just be careful."

Pete answered with a fast nod, checked his side mirror, slowed down, pulled away from traffic as far as he could, and stopped.

Dusan asked for the key to unlock the deadbolt of the truck bed. Pete handed it to him. Dusan stepped out and unlocked it. He reached in and pulled out his rolled duffel bag and placed it on the ground. With a whisk of the sturdy zipper, he reached a hand into the bag and removed a small Serbian flag, a five-inch Serbian cross, and red silk roses. With care he arranged everything against a concrete divider and examined his work while he swiped at his eyes.

"Anka, boys," he whispered while vehicles whizzed past, "this is nothing, I know, but it's the only thing I can do right now to honor you." His shoulders slumped forward. "I'm a bad man. I was a bad husband, a bad father, and you paid the price. For that I will forever be sorry."

A moment later Dusan turned, ready to climb into the pickup, when a Trans Am sped by. The driver honked and caused a startled Dusan to jump. Incensed at what he considered deliberate disrespect, he shot the passing car a stiff middle finger salute.

The Trans Am's brake lights came on. For an instant the car fishtailed before it pulled over to the side of the road. Reverse lights came on. Tires squealed, and the Trans Am raced toward the pickup.

Dusan understood the intent. A graduate of one of the most violent federal prisons, he balled up his fists and moved to engage the driver.

The driver side of the car opened. A beefy man in his late twenties with a belly over his belt stepped out. He carried an 11-inch, Pee Wee baseball bat. In a deep, gravelly, rumbling voice, he shouted, "You got something to say to me, asshole?"

Full of rage, Dusan rushed in and closed the gap before the other man could set his feet and swing the bat. He hit the man with a rabbit punch and followed up with another to the throat. His opponent dropped the bat. Eyes widened in horror, his hands flew to his throat. He gasped for precious air. A moment later, he dropped to his knees. Dusan shifted his weight, ready to deliver a kick, when Pete slammed into him. The Serb tumbled next to the driver.

Pete reached down and yanked Dusan to his feet.

"Are you fucking nuts?" he yelled against the noise of the traffic. "You're an ex-con on probation. In a hurry to get back in the slammer?" He pointed to the other man struggling to get air into his lungs. "You better hope you didn't break his trachea. If you have, he'll die."

Pete helped the gagging man to his feet and kicked the bat away. He watched the man work to get well-needed air into his lungs.

"I guess you'll recover," Pete said. "Look at the unwanted attention you brought." Passing motorists and gawkers had slowed to watch the drama unfold. A minor rear-ender ahead had caused two other cars to pull over.

Pete slowly shook his head. "Too late to leave now. You started this, pal. You had the bat in your hand. If the cops come, you're in a mess of trouble. Clear out before anyone gets here."

A siren wailed. Pete saw a gray police car approach, its light bar on. "Too late now. Here we go." He looked at Dusan. "Keep it together, and let me do the talking."

A lean state trooper, his knit cap down over his ears, stepped out of his cruiser and approached the three men.

"Who's going to tell me what's going on?" Two additional trooper vehicles pulled up behind the first cruiser.

An hour passed before the police had everything sorted out. Pete, in his calmest voice, had recounted the events to the trooper.

"Okay, maybe not the brightest thing for my buddy to shoot this guy the bird." He pointed to the makeshift memorial. "He's lost his wife and kids here." He tossed his head in the direction of the police cruiser, the Trans Am driver in the back. "Rambo there decides to get out with his baseball bat."

The trooper looked at Dusan. "It was your wife and kids who were killed here?"

"Yes," Dusan said softly.

"Aw, sorry, sir," the cop said. "I was one of the first responders. Terrible." He took in a breath of air. "I can understand the need for your memorial, but those aren't safe, you understand? Especially here at what everyone calls Dead Man's Curve if they blow or find their way out onto the road."

He gestured to the man in his cruiser. "The fact he exited his vehicle with the baseball bat is a chargeable offense. It's dangerous to the public, disrupts peace. You defended yourself. Although I wouldn't recommend hitting anyone in the throat again."

"Same advice I gave him," Pete said.

The trooper closed his notebook.

"I've got all your information, both of you. You may be summoned, but I doubt it." Once more he pointed to the police vehicle. "He looks defeated. Good chance he'll get a lawyer and plead the charge down." He returned his gaze to Dusan. "So, we're done here. You're free to go. Stay safe and no more altercations. And be careful when you pull back out into traffic."

The two friends drove for forty minutes before Dusan recovered.

Pete spoke. "Sorry for knocking you down."

Dusan waved the apology aside. "S'okay. And you were right, it could have gotten out of control."

"Well, we dodged the bullet, for sure. You good?"

"Shoulder's a bit sore, but that's all."

"You run into this kind of thing in Stillwell?"

"What kind of 'thing'?"

"Baseball bats."

"Bats, no. Imagine what the joint would have looked like if we'd got hold of them. Shivs were the weapons of choice. Shivs and fists. Back in Chicago, different thing."

"So, what do you think happened to you back there?"

Dusan took a deep breath.

"What happened? I got caught up in my own misery, what I did to my family, and this dipshit spoils my...my devotion or whatever you want to call what he did. It was like mocking, defiling something important. If he hadn't braked and come back, we wouldn't have gotten into it. When he did that, everything bubbled to the surface."

A long pause. Dusan glanced at the landscape for a moment. "My pastor in Stillwell always said shame and runaway anger were two sides of the same coin. Both speak to inadequacy."

"Inadequacy? Deep. Never would have put those two things together."

"Me, neither. So, back there, I think I wanted, I needed, to feel bad. Something tells me I'm always going to feel that in one way or another. Maybe it's the only way I can ever atone."

Pete kept his attention on the road ahead. A few minutes later he said, "This, um, what did you call it, need to feel bad? Maybe you should be kinder to yourself."

Dusan let the comment pass. *You should talk.*

Neither spoke. Miles down the highway Dusan broke the silence.

"I've done some bad things, and I know I'll be judged, but you know, none bother me like how I treated Anka and the kids. When I think back, there's almost nothing I wasn't selfish about. I was so busy building my empire and chasing every pleasure that came my way. It's a wonder I didn't get a sexual disease, become a coke addict or an alcoholic."

Pete had nothing to add.

They retreated into their private thoughts until Dusan said, "You know Lucille?"

"Lucille?"

"Yeah, the escort girl."

Pete shook his head. "No. Haven't had the pleasure. What about her?"

"Really cute. But she's got a mind, Lucille. She's studying forensic toxicology."

"No idea what that is, but who'd have guessed? Those girls have interesting sidelines and career ambitions. Or it's probably more accurate to say the escort service is the real sideline. In any case, I can't say I've had too many in-depth conversations with them."

Dusan kneaded his shoulder with his fingers. "Funny how it came about."

"How *what* came about?"

"A conversation I had with Lucille. A sort of a heart-to-heart thing. Anyway, she took a risk and told me I'm a wham, bam, thank you ma'am kind of lover. Took guts."

"No kidding?"

"Yeah. She's right. I was a lousy lover with Anka and all the other women." He shook his head at the memory of it. "A lot of screw-ups. And then there were my kids. You remember the *Cat's in the Cradle* song?"

"Uh-huh."

"Me times ten. But people can change. I'm hoping I can and maybe put some of my guilt to rest. I do have some good things ahead for me—the café, and, believe it or not, Lucille's agreed to go out on a date."

"Why wouldn't I believe it? You're not the Hunchback of Notre Dame."

"Thanks, I think."

Pete turned and looked at his friend. "Sorry. Didn't mean to give offense."

"No problem. Anyway, Lucille's graduating in the spring. Already got a job lined up. Owns her own condo, too."

"Doesn't surprise me. They make good money, those girls. None of my business, bud, but uh, the way you're talking, is dating a hooker a good idea?"

Dusan replied by giving Pete a long, piercing look. A few minutes later Dusan said, "Funny, you calling them hookers. *You*. For your information, most work for themselves, don't have pimps, and use their money to do other things. So, get off your fucking high horse."

Tense silence followed.

Pete spoke again. "Sorry, I guess that was out of line."

"Forget it. You know, we're both broken in our own ways. I'm working on my demons, and I'm hoping you'll work on yours."

"You think I have demons?"

Dusan let out a harsh breath. "I accept you the way you are, so we'll leave it there, okay?"

Nothing else to say, Pete offered a noncommittal nod.

I-90 brought them into Chicago three hours later. Pete approached their destination, a hotel suite near the Cultural Center.

"Strange, being back in the city," Dusan said. "So many memories. Not all of them good."

"Agreed."

Pete jutted his chin. "Man, this traffic. I'm not used to it anymore. The rush hour in Martine Maines lasts, what, fifteen minutes?"

"Or maybe less, depending on the day."

"Guess we're becoming small-town boys."

Pete pulled up to the front doors of the hotel and unlocked the truck bed. Dusan extracted his duffel bag. "Sorry I can't go back with you."

"No problem. Good luck with everything, and see you back home."

They gave each other a fast embrace and back thump, then pulled apart.

"Thanks again for stepping in back there," Dusan said.

"Welcome. Stay cool."

Pete drove off. Dusan watched until the pickup turned a corner. He entered the hotel. At the reception desk he announced himself. "You have a reservation for me? I'm here for the training course, Olde World Café."

"Oh, yes, Mr. Kovacevic," the pleasant young man with a decided Jamaican accent said. He stared at his monitor. "We have you booked in room 612. There's a reception desk behind you, and they will give you all the information you no doubt need."

Chapter 29

Pete pondered where he should stay. Chicago in the dead of winter and Christmas gone, he'd have no trouble scoring a room. Belsano Arms, near the cemetery where his father was buried, came to mind. He drove to it. The five-story family-owned hotel still occupied its familiar place on the busy intersection. A throwback to another time, it thumbed its nose at modern, antiseptic hotels.

Pete drove around the parking lot twice before he found a spot. The front desk let him know they'd be happy to have him as a guest.

"Here's the key card to your room, Mr. Harris," the bookish-looking young woman at the counter said when she returned his credit card. "Room 411. Will you be staying long with us?"

Good question. "Two days for now."

"Yes, of course."

Pete liked the European ambiance of the hotel, the oak paneling, and the polished brass. Not much had changed other than the carpeting. He and Nina had eaten in the restaurant once. So long ago. Another life. The world moved on. Nina lived miles away in the suburbs, and he'd become Pete Harris.

He dismissed his old memories and admired the small but cozy room. A glance at his watch — 3:30. He could visit the cemetery, but why not wait until tomorrow? He'd go to the lounge for a drink.

Ten minutes later Pete sipped his Classic Manhattan and let his thoughts shift to Bexley. He'd told her he planned to take Dusan to Chicago and had a "few things to do."

"Like what?" she'd asked.

Oh, he had to see his accountant to discuss his taxes and IRA contributions. And he'd visit a few people.

What about his school work?

No problem, he'd said. He could catch up.

She didn't answer for a moment. "Would you like me to come with you? It might be fun spending a couple of days there."

The comment both excited and intimidated him. On the one

hand, her coming and sharing a room suggested a new intimacy. But she'd ask probing questions and search for clarity; he favored vagueness.

"No, it's a guy thing," he told her. "We'll have some yaks in the truck, and besides, I'm task-oriented. Get to do things I want to do on my time. You understand?"

Her face said she hadn't. She'd looked hurt. He'd pulled her to him. "But it would be nice to have you in a hotel room for a couple of nights."

She'd given him no clear indication the offer placated her. Instead she said, "We'll see," and followed with a tight smile. "But you will call me when you get there, right?"

Pete promised he would. What was it with women, always making demands? Maybe Dusan had it right. Be up front with everything. It made sense and would remove a lot of unnecessary hassle. *Oh, what web we weave when first we learn to deceive.*

He took another sip of his cocktail. The drink centered him and helped chase away his nagging worries. He reached for his cell phone and phoned Bexley. He'd promised he would.

He dialed. She picked up, glad to hear from him. Nothing in her voice gave him cause to be defensive. She asked how the trip went. Uneventful, he replied. She chatted about her day, school assignments, and her friends.

"When do you think you'll be back?"

"Well, the earliest might be Sunday, but it would mean a lot of hard driving alone. So, I'm guessing Monday. If it's longer, I'll call you."

"All right. Stay safe and see you soon. I miss you."

"I miss you, too. Bye."

He hung up, grateful the conversation hadn't brought on another interrogation. His inner voice kicked in. She wouldn't call it an interrogation. Probably no rational person would. Questions are what couples use when they're involved in each other's lives.

Pete knew being open and honest would usher in more than a measure of discomfort. True, but it also produced more personal intimacy. A final swallow of his drink and Pete rose. In the mood for a stroll, he returned to his room for coat, gloves, and cap.

The walk invigorated him. His stomach growled. He stumbled onto a trattoria that looked interesting and stopped to read the posted menu. The osso buco parmigiana appealed. Hmm. That might be nice with a Zinfandel if they had it. If not, some other red. He peeked into the restaurant and liked the look of the small, homey-style interior.

He entered. Close to an hour later he lingered over coffee and dessert and let his mind return to the earlier conversation with Dusan, in particular the comment about demons. Was Dusan just spouting off, or did he really think Pete had inner demons?

Come on, Pete, his inner voice said, *who you kidding? You know you're not in good working order.*

Had he been asked, Pete might have used adjectives like dark or evil to describe those inflicted with demons: psychos like murderers, kiddie molesters, wife-batterers, druggies, alcoholics. He didn't belong to those groups. Dusan's charge had to be something of an exaggeration.

He took another sip of his coffee. If Dusan's claim held some truth, was demon the right word anyway? Well, what better word could he have offered? he asked himself. How about broken? Yeah, more fitting.

His inner voice scoffed. *Demon? Broken? Potato, potatto. Does it really matter? Call it what you want, but it doesn't change the fact you've got personal struggles you can't overcome.*

Pete examined the trajectory of his life. In truth, from his mother on he'd had poor or unsatisfactory relationships with females. In some ways he'd always been defensive, secretive.

Nina had her own neuroses to counterbalance his. Probably, neither of them noticed and only reacted to outcomes.

The weight of an inescapable truth settled on Pete: *Goddamn it, I'm destined to make any woman unhappy. My fate's sealed like some Greek tragedy.*

He sat at his table, mouth ajar and stared out the front window. A sadness enveloped him, and his eyes began tearing up. With rapid movements he blinked the moisture away.

A waitress came to his table and looked down at him. "Everything all right, sir?"

Pete hoped his voice wouldn't give him away. He didn't look up, cleared his throat, and said, "Fine, thanks. Just the bill, please."

"Very well, sir."

She brought the bill. He paid and made his way back to the hotel. A cocktail lounge caught his eye. He didn't know why but stopped and peered through the frost-covered window. He liked the look of the marble bar and the subdued light behind the display of bottles on the shelf. Two barkeeps, one male, one female, worked behind the counter, both dressed in matching white shirts, black ties, slacks, and gray vests.

On impulse Pete pulled open the door, entered, and took in the red leather barstools alongside the bar and the round wooden tables, the tops done in marble. Comfy swivel chairs surrounded the tables. A plush burgundy carpeting and soft lighting gave the room an intimate feel. Patrons sat at a few of the tables.

He made up his mind to stay. Where should he sit? He gave the bar a second look. No, he didn't want to rub shoulders with anyone, so he chose a seat at one of the empty tables.

Pete tossed his coat on a nearby chair, then sat and ran a hand over the tabletop. Marble? He doubted it. He waited for service. A wheat blonde with shoulder-length hair came out from behind the bar and stood alongside of him.

"Hi. You look like you lost your last friend," she said in a breathy voice.

Pete gaped at the beauty. Why was she slinging drinks when she could have been on the cover of a fashion magazine? He shook the thought from his mind.

"Bad day, is all. I'd like a Gibson. Do you make a good one?"

She smiled and showed perfect large, white teeth. "The best."

"So, no gimmicks or shortcuts?"

"None. You'll like what I put in front of you."

"I'll hold you to your word."

A short bob of her head and she was gone. Long minutes later she returned with a small bowl of nuts, leaned forward, and set it down. "Your drink's coming."

Pete followed her with his eyes. So did two men at another table. He admired how her slacks followed the contours of her hips. For sure, her employers hadn't customized those slacks for her.

The barkeep returned. She set his drink down in a demure manner, straightened, and said, "Try it."

He sipped and looked up. "You delivered."

"Glad you like." She shot him a Colgate smile, wheeled about, and left.

Pete hoped the Gibson might alter his mood. It didn't. He didn't know what it would take to shake himself out of his funk. *Damn, soon as I finish this, I'm going to bed. Maybe tomorrow I'll feel better.*

The woman cleared and wiped the table next to him and looked over at Pete. She approached. "Another?" She pointed at his drink.

"No, I better not."

"You driving?"

"Uh-uh. Walking."

"You look like you can hold your liquor."

"Thanks," he said. "I can, but... Ah, never mind. Okay, one more."

"Coming up."

She returned with his second drink, watched while he sipped, and then looked around the almost empty lounge. "Happy hour's underway. It'll get busy soon. Real busy. Um, do you mind if I make a comment?"

Pete furrowed his eyebrows, unsure of what came next. "I guess not."

The blonde studied him for a long moment. "Something about you says sad. Am I wrong?"

He lifted his eyebrows at the remark. "You could say that."

"Well, then, would some company cheer you?"

Pete did a double take. "Company? You?"

She shook her head.

"No, not me, but I can arrange for someone young and pretty to keep you company."

A light bulb went on in Pete. He lowered his voice and craned his neck.

"Are you a cop?"

"No. Are you?"

He shook his head. "No, but how do you know I'm not lying?"

"I'm a pretty good judge of character."

"Huh. Let's go back to the start of this conversation."

"In which I asked if you'd like some company?" she said.

"Yes, that one. If you're not a cop, are you a pimp?"

She sounded out the word.

"Pimp. So provincial, so twentieth century. The world's changed. Nobody pimps anymore, well, except low-life losers who hustle slum crackhead girls." She glanced around the room. "I'm an entrepreneur running a small service. I provide, you enjoy. Simple as that. Everyone's happy."

Except the cops, Pete thought. "And you're not worried about getting caught?"

She shook her head. "Haven't yet. Been doing this for a couple of years. Like I said, I'm a good judge of character."

"What about your employers? Are they all right with it?"

"They incur benefits. I'll leave it there."

Pete felt the beginnings of excitement in his groin.

"You've sold me. I could use a pleasant diversion. Invite your young friend over. Oh, and one important question: how much of a gift are we talking about so I might be able to show my appreciation for time well spent?"

"Five hundred for an hour. Cash."

Pete made a decision. "Cash? You don't take credit cards?"

"Someday maybe, but not at the present."

"In that case I have to visit an ATM."

The woman bobbed her head. "And while you're gone, I'll reserve this table for you." She pointed to his Gibson. "I'll take this back and make you a new one."

Fifteen minutes later Pete returned. The lounge had filled. The barkeep returned with his drink, bent next to him, and said, "She'll be here in about half an hour."

"Fine. I'm in no hurry. Say, listen, I won't ask how you got into your line of work, other than bartending, whatever it is you do here, but...?"

She gave up another disarming smile.

"The less said the better. You get to meet a lot of interesting people. Like you." She stopped. "Okay, I've got to get back to work. The woman you'll meet, her name's Brittany. You got a name?"

"Yeah. Steve."

He didn't know why he gave her a bogus name. It came out before he'd finished thinking about the question. The financial transaction didn't involve any credit card. Maybe it was the booze.

Pete sipped his cocktail and felt the glow of a buzz. Best not to finish his drink, he thought. He set the glass down and studied the antics of the meat market crowd. Professionals of all sorts, the men trying to impress the women.

His mind wandered back to the blonde. She didn't like the label 'pimp.' A rose by any other name... But then, had they invented other words to describe what she did? None came to mind.

A young woman, her red hair tied in a ponytail, entered the lounge and looked around. She set her sight on Pete and wended her way around the tables. More than a few eyes took in this tall, slender beauty in a scarlet, knee-length, wool coat with a tie belt. A black scarf hung loosely around her neck. Black stiletto heels gave her an equal height to him.

"Steve?"

Pete remembered his phony name.

"Yes." He smiled up at her, pushed his chair back, and came to his feet. He shot the woman a fast smile. "Brittany?"

A bright, lip-glossed mouth revealed a winsome smile, and she held out a slim black-gloved hand.

"Hi, Steve. Nice to meet you."

"You, too," he managed to get out, already in the early throes of excitement. "Let me put on my coat, and we can go."

"Take your time," she said and adjusted the strap to her over-the-shoulder purse.

Brittany gave Pete his money's worth. He found her to be an enthusiastic partner and not mechanical like some of the escorts. She also proved herself to be an exceptional conversationalist.

Time in his room passed before Pete knew it. Brittany fixed her makeup, dressed, moved closer, kissed his cheek, and said, "Gotta run. I enjoyed our time."

He walked her to the door.

"I liked it, too. If I'm ever back this way, I'll know how to ask for you again."

"Oh, how very nice." A final buss on his cheek and she slid out the door.

Pete locked the door. What should he do now? No point getting dressed again. He'd already eaten, so maybe TV and then get an early night.

Propped against the bed's headboard, he used the remote to scroll through the dozens of stations. Nothing caught his eye. He settled on a black-and-white movie with subtitles, *La Grande Illusion*. He'd missed the opening three minutes.

To his surprise, he found the movie engaging. He liked the interwoven themes of loyalty and decency. In turn, it led him to think about his own situation. On the face of it he had everything he could want: money, a good friend, an attractive and bright girlfriend. Then what explained his defensive shift with Dusan? And this cheating on Bexley?

He could learn a lot from these movie characters, he told himself, yet he dealt with things through denial, drink, and disloyalty.

The recent enjoyment with Brittany faded, replaced again by the emptiness he'd experienced in the trattoria.

He turned off the TV and stepped into the bathroom to brush his teeth. Done, he climbed into bed, pulled the blanket up, and closed his eyes. Why did he have to make life so hard for himself? It should be, could be, much easier. Maybe it was time to talk to a counselor. It couldn't hurt.

Pete lay awake for the better part of an hour, running themes of shame and inadequacy over and over in his mind. Before he slipped into sleep, he promised himself he'd develop greater discipline and make real, lasting changes.

The guest in room 411 tossed and turned and ground his teeth through much of the night.

Chapter 30

Pete woke at 6:00, tired and with a headache. He rolled his shoulders. He'd take some aspirin with breakfast. He allowed himself a long, leisurely shower and reassessed the cause for yesterday's blues. True, he had flaws, but who didn't? And no one would nominate him for canonization. If he could stay honest with Bexley and not get lured to other distractions, things might be fine.

Easier said than done, he admitted, but he'd find a way.

Cheered some by his new resolve, Pete dressed and went out in search of breakfast. Aware the cemetery gates didn't open until 10:00, he stopped at a diner. Halfway through the *Sun-Times News* and his second coffee he glanced at his watch. The cemetery would open in forty minutes. He guessed the walk over would take eight minutes.

Breakfast finished, Pete paid his bill and arrived at the front gate a few minutes before the custodian swung it open.

"Need help, sir?" the man called out to him.

Pete waved. "I'm good, thanks. Thought I'd get a little morning exercise walking." He knew the way. He'd been to his father's gravesite often. Lot L, number 184.

A recent storm had dumped two inches of powdery snow. The roads hadn't been cleared yet, but Pete didn't mind. He'd come prepared for anything. His insulated waterproof boots took care of snow, slush, and the cold. His thick hooded jacket, knit cap, and gloves kept him warm.

He walked past a large memorial dedicated to the memory of one Ezekiel Harmsworth. Pete looked at the date. 1917. *Long time dead, Ezekiel.*

Pete spied his father's black marble two-foot headstone and stopped in front of it. Someone had been there and left flowers, now wilted. Who…and when? The roses were frozen and wouldn't give up their secret. Who might have stopped to visit? His Aunt Freda? Or maybe even Ashlynn.

He told himself it didn't matter. He'd pay his respects and leave.

He studied the headstone.

Joseph Nieves, loving father to Stellan and Ashlynn, devoted husband, and fond brother to Freda McKay. Loved and missed by all. Rest in Peace.

Pete's eyes moved down to his father's dates of birth and death. Young, in the relative scheme of things. Joe Nieves should have lived much longer, so much longer. A simple, everyday occurrence, an innocent ride through an intersection, and his life ended without warning.

They'd argued, Pete and Ashlynn, on what to inscribe on the headstone. Ashlynn had been more forgiving and wanted to include their mother's name. Pete wouldn't allow it. The argument replayed itself in his mind. "Our mother made her choice, Ash," he'd said. "She stopped being a Nieves the minute she spread her legs to Vincze. She's not getting any mention on Dad's headstone if I have anything to say about it."

"Don't be vulgar," Ashlynn had shot back. "Like it or not, she's still your mother."

Pete had brushed aside her response and pointed to the pamphlet from the monument company. "She's only my mother by birth and nothing else. I'm under no obligation to be kind or anything else."

"You're hard-hearted, Stellan. It's going to hurt you in life."

"Coming from you... Ah, never mind. All I know is I don't want her name on the headstone."

Pete pushed the memory away and tugged at the collar of his jacket. Did he imagine it, or had the temperature dropped? He snuffled and stared at the headstone.

He allowed himself another quick look around to ensure no one could hear him.

"Hi, Dad. Long time since I've been here, huh? I would have brought flowers, but in this weather, they'd freeze within the hour. In any case, I'm sorry I haven't visited. I've been busy and living a lot of miles from here. As if you couldn't tell."

Pete knew his father wasn't there. Still, he drew comfort from being connected to the man he and his sister loved. He felt himself tear up.

"Guess I'll go, Dad. Please remember I haven't forgotten you. Never will. Until I see you the next time, bye, Dad."

He started to turn when he heard a car come up the road and slow, a small one by the sound of its engine. He grew uneasy. Why's it slowing? *Stop being paranoid*, he ordered himself. *It could be anything.*

The self-talk did nothing to calm him. *Move along, move along*, he silently willed the driver. *Don't stop.*

The silent command failed to reach the driver. The car stopped, and the driver cut the engine. With full certainty Pete knew the driver intended to visit his father's gravesite. *Go, go, go*, he ordered himself. Hands deep in his jacket, he did his best imitation of someone with a casual lack of concern and stepped past Joe Nieves' marker. Which way should he head? It didn't matter. Away from whoever had stopped. He'd get on the road and keep his head down. If he encountered any car or truck, they wouldn't see his face.

A female voice, one he'd recognize anywhere, stopped him in his tracks.

"Stellan! Stellan, stop. Where you going?"

Ashlynn. How? *Keep walking*, Pete ordered himself. *She's guessing it's you. Don't look back.* Yet something made him spin about and face his sister in her long, bluish-green checkered wool coat and fashionable, thigh-high boots. If he'd had time to think about what his eyes took in, he might have thought she'd become a different woman.

Mouth ajar, her eyes wide, the object of his attention hurried toward him and threw her arms around him. "Ohmigawd, Stellan, it's you. Ohmigawd, ohmigawd, ohmigawd! We all thought... Everyone thought you were dead, or the earth had swallowed you."

Pete placed his arms around his sister for a moment before he disengaged. He held her at arm's length, shot her a lips-over-the-teeth smile, and said, "How'd you know it was me?"

Ashlynn waved away the question.

"I'd know you anywhere. Anyway, who cares?" She pointed to him. "Look at you. My god, so different. Your hair's longer, and your beard... No suit. Stellan Nieves *not* in a suit. Are we in the End Times?" She stopped, looked at him, and said, "You're not in some witness protection program, are you?"

She didn't wait for an answer. "No matter. Look at you! You're here. Flesh and blood. I couldn't have imagined this if I tried. How are you?" She didn't wait for an answer. "You know, I wasn't going to come until tomorrow, but I had some free time and thought, ah, I'm in the neighborhood, so..."

Speechless, Pete inspected his sister. She'd lost a lot of weight. When he last saw her, she'd carried at least fifty extra pounds. This Ashlynn's face looked more angular, softer. Nose and eyebrow piercings she'd shown to the world as symbols of defiance were gone. So, too, were the black Goth lipstick, replaced by a bright red. And her hair, no more neon rainbow colors. She'd returned to her natural copper-red, cut in an above-the-shoulders stylish look. His gaze shifted to her neck. The small tattoo, the Celtic cross. Did he imagine it, or was it gone?

He thought back to his memories of Ashlynn. She'd been pretty and never wanted for attention but fell in with a crowd of losers in junior high. To fit in, Ashlynn had abandoned dresses, skirts, and traditional makeup. In their place she chose black or deep purple clothing, dark makeup, leather chokers and bracelets, torn jeans, and must-have Doc Martens.

Her grades fell. She became surly and rebellious. Drugs came next. A few months later, Pete entered college.

Ashlynn waved a soft-gloved hand in front of his face.

"Hell-ooo, Stellan. Back to earth. You tripping?"

Pete recovered. He hadn't expected what came next, a

debilitating wave of shame over abandoning Ashlynn, his sister. A panic attack followed. Pete found himself gulping air.

Ashlynn stepped closer. "You okay? What's going on? Tell me. The color's left your face." She looked around. "I don't see another car. It's cold. You want to come and sit in mine to warm up?"

Pete made a show of shaking his head. "I'll be fine. Something I ate."

Ashlynn replied with a slow, deliberate look around the cemetery.

"I take it, then, you walked in. I'll drive you somewhere, anywhere. Do you want a couple more minutes with Dad? We can go for coffee later. If you'd like."

He wanted to very much, but wouldn't that violate his former pledge to be forever removed from anyone connected to Stellan Nieves? Still, he hadn't sought out Ash. By luck she'd found him. Why not go? To do so might lessen the intense guilt of leaving her high and dry. He'd have to dipsy-doodle through any intrusive questions she'd fire at him.

"A coffee? Sure. Why not? But I can't stay too long. I have to meet a friend a few blocks from here later."

His sister lit up at the reply. Her head bobbed up and down. "Great! You're being a little mysterious, but okay. Let's visit with Dad, and then we'll go."

They moved back to the headstone. Pete pointed to the flowers. "Are those from you?"

"Mm-hmm. They don't last long in this weather, but it's something I needed to do. I didn't bring any today. I should have."

The comment touched Pete and brought him back to an Ashlynn from his past, long before adolescence. "Better than I did."

Ashlynn brushed aside the comment with a wave. "I'm betting Dad's really happy to have both of us visit."

Pete heard the tenderness in her voice. "Agreed."

They stood in silent reverence for a few moments before Ashlynn snuffled. "Cold. We should go."

"Okay." Pete stepped closer to the headstone. "Bye, Dad. I'll come again, but I can't say when right now."

"Bye, Daddy," Ashlynn echoed.

They climbed into Ashlynn's blue-lilac Accord. Pete enjoyed the new car smell. "Nice. New?"

"Four months old, so, yep, new. Where would you like to go?"

"Anywhere around here's fine."

She started the engine. "I can't believe how much you've changed. At least outwardly."

Pete nodded. "Change comes to all of us sooner or later." A fluff answer, but he hoped it would do.

Ashlynn pulled onto a small street with upscale clothing boutiques, jewelry stores, bistros, coffee houses, and a bookstore. She climbed out and put money into a meter. "We're good for a couple of hours." She studied the street. "Anything here grab you?"

"I'm easy."

She pointed. "What about there, the Café Locale?"

"Perfect."

They entered and inhaled the delicious smells of the baked goods while they searched for a place to sit. *Gorgeous*, Pete thought. *Why had I never been here?* The answer came fast enough. Chicago. A big city.

A young woman behind the refrigerated baking display called out to them. "Please, sit anywhere you like."

They moved farther into the café and took in the polished wooden floor, the dark paneling, the wooden tables, black lacquered chairs with red vinyl seats. A few customers were sprinkled throughout the café. Ashlynn led Pete to a table near a far window, where both shed their coats.

The server arrived. "What can I get you?"

Pete looked up. "Coffee for me."

Ashlynn answered with a fast nod. "Same."

The server left. Pete watched his sister. "No dessert? You love desserts."

"Yeah," Ashlynn said. "And I became a butterball. I don't do desserts anymore. And a lot of other things, too."

The message hit home when Pete took in Ashlynn's coal-black pullover blouse. The sheer fabric on the sleeves allowed him to see her arms. Tattoos gone. He gaped and pointed. "Ash, your tats. Are they gone?"

She grinned and followed his gaze.

"You noticed, huh? Cost me a pretty penny. They told me being light-skinned was an advantage in clearing the ink. And I also didn't have any solid, heavy colors."

Their coffee arrived. The server set them down and left.

Pete reached for the cream. "Am I allowed to say congratulations on the new you?"

Ashlynn took her first sip and set the coffee down. "Of course, and thank you."

By her second sip, Ashlynn moved on to the other changes in her life. A natural with computers and technology, she'd applied for a job with a high-tech startup company. They realized what a gem they had and soon promoted her.

"I hit a different kind of glass ceiling. My bosses told me I wouldn't go any further unless I changed my appearance." She gave a small laugh. "See? We've both changed." She took another sip of coffee and glanced around the room.

"It was kind of a domino effect for me. I bought new threads and started using makeup. Sensible stuff, this time." She smiled at her remark. "My then-partner, Shannon, and I got into more than a few doozies. She accused me of selling out.

"We split. I found my own place, got laser done on my tattoos, and took a Dale Carnegie course. It helped me get promoted again. I'm now assistant marketing manager. The rumor mill has it my boss is leaving. If he goes, a fair chance...wait, no...a great chance I'm in line for his job. And salary, I hope. He likes me, and I think he'll talk me up." The corners of her eyes crinkled when she smiled. "Not bad for a gal with only a junior college education, huh?"

"Not bad at all," Pete agreed. "I'm impressed. What about, um—how do I say this delicately—your sexual orientation?"

"Oh, yeah, that. It's okay if you ask." She let her finger trace a sewn pattern on the tablecloth. "Sexuality's complicated because people are complicated. Attraction is attraction. You don't get to choose who you're attracted to. I liked Shannon. Then. Now I'm living with a guy, Kevin. He's kind, funny, whip-smart, and in some ways he reminds me of Dad. You'd like him. And the rest, well, what's the saying about life not being lived by looking through the rearview mirror?"

The server came over. "Can I get you anything else?"

"Yes," Pete said. "More coffee, please."

"For both of you?"

Pete looked at Ashlynn. "All right," she said. "Why not?"

They watched the server walk away. Pete started the conversation again.

"So, tell me, what's happening with Mom?"

"Ah, our mother. Still trying to be queen of the ball, putting on airs. Sometimes I think she spends Vincze's money faster than he can earn it. She always asks me about you." Ashlynn made a face. "Like I knew something. She wanted your approval, your blessing. She knows you blame her for what happened to Dad."

"And you?"

"Blame her? I've forgiven her for being imperfect. We're not close, but I do go see her and Vincze." Her eyebrows shot up. "You know, she played with the idea of hiring someone to track you down. Once Vincze saw the cost, he said no."

Nothing else to add, Ashlynn drank some of her coffee.

Conversation with his sister had gone better than Pete thought possible. He struggled to recall the last time the two of them had had anything close to a civil exchange. Some unspecified thought sat on the edge of his consciousness. It wouldn't come forward or go away. At last it revealed itself. He sensed his sister had worked hard to avoid any mention of Nina and the kids. No one would accuse Ashlynn of being a wallflower. If she had something to say, she said it. Yet she'd held back. Out of respect for his privacy? Or perhaps she didn't want to venture into new, unknown territory. Nor did he want her to.

Ashlynn finished her story. "So, what do you think?"

"Think? Uh, uh..."

"You haven't been listening, have you?"

Pete felt himself flush. "Caught. I get accused of that a lot." He released a slow breath and said, "Um, listen, Ash, haven't you been curious why I didn't ask about Nina or why I disappeared?"

She wet her lips. "You have your reasons. If you thought it important enough, you'd tell me. I'm not as intrusive as I used to be."

"I can tell."

"Really? Good." She took a final swallow of her coffee and wiped her mouth with a napkin. "I know we have our history, but right now I'm here, you're here. What happens after this, who knows? All I can say is in this space and time, I want to try and be a better sister." She reached a hand and squeezed his arm.

The gesture provoked a tenderness in him. He felt a need to offer some explanation.

"Funny you should say that...about being a better sister. Me, I've let you down as a brother. Okay, look, it's not the best-kept secret Nina and I weren't much at the end." He squeezed his eyes shut, opened them and said, "I can't justify my actions, and I won't. Before I split, I knew I'd end up being just another one of those noncustodial dads with visits every other weekend. I'd have been cut out of any real parental decisions unless I fought for them, which I didn't want, mainly because the kids turned into little Ninas."

Brother and sister offered each other quick fake smiles. Pete broke off eye contact and stared into his empty cup. Should he say more? If so, what? He would, but he'd be careful. He raised his head.

"Something happened. I caught a break. I can't, won't, go into it, but I seized on the chance and split. Dad had been gone for a long time. Mom, well.... And the two of us didn't have much in common then, did we?"

Ashlynn turned her head and waved to the server. "Looks like we'll be here a while yet, Stellan. Want another coffee?"

He hadn't planned to stay as long as he had and wanted to say he'd already been over-caffeinated. To do so might break this intimate brother-sister bonding time. He gave her a warmer smile. "Why not? I may be like a Mexican jumping bean the rest of the day, but it'll be worth it."

"Glad you think so."

The server brought coffee with a small plate of cookies Ashlynn had ordered. "Something to nibble on," she told her brother.

Each took a cookie, and Ashlynn stirred her coffee.

She spoke. "Before we leave the subject of the lovely Nina, I did want to say something about the kids. Well, Mia anyway."

"Yeah? Go ahead."

Ashlynn scratched her nose with a manicured finger. "In many ways the girls are their mother, but you have to look a bit deeper with Mia."

Pete waited to hear more.

"Mia's already different," Ashlynn said. "Of course, both talked about you when you disappeared. Joanna now totes the Nina line and doesn't mention you unless it's in anger. Mia, she still asks me about you, wonders where you are and how you're doing."

"No kidding? Not angry and everything? You know, runaway, deadbeat dad?"

His sister offered a fast shake of her head. "No. She's made of different stuff. I think she has a lot of our Dad in her, and you'd be impressed."

Pete allowed himself to think back on the girls. He recalled a childhood incident when Mia had given Joanna her balloon when her sister's had escaped.

He returned to the conversation. "Like Dad. Wow."

"And she calls," Ashlynn said. "I take her for hot chocolate every couple of weeks. Joanna doesn't much care about her Aunt Ash. As for Mia, she and I have had some interesting conversations. She'll very much be her own person."

Pete bowed his head and stared at the table. In an almost whisper he said, "Boy, I got her wrong. Guess it's too late now."

"Who knows, Stellan? Never say never." Ashlynn reached across the table and patted his hand. "So, this—what did you call it?—catching a break thing. Can I ask, was it legal? I mean, you didn't diddle a client's account or anything like that, did you?"

Pete chuckled. "Good to see a bit of the old Ash come back." If she only knew. He did much more than diddle a client's account. "No. Nothing the law or my old firm would come after me for. I did come into some money, but I can't expand on it."

"Hmm. Intriguing. Okay, so can you tell me where you're living now, or will you keep that info on a need-to-know basis?"

"I have to keep it on a need-to-know basis. Can't be helped. I need to protect my anonymity. Part of it is my new life and lifestyle." He glanced down at his clothes and waved a hand in front of himself. "As you can see...sort of."

"I'll say. When did you last wear jeans? Anyway, it's a good look, and I like it. Mom would freak out if she saw you."

"And Nina?"

"She'd lose it no matter how you arrived."

"True, true. Do you go over there much?"

A quick side-to-side movement of her head gave Pete his answer.

"I never got along with Nina. You know that. Now when she sees me, she thinks of you. It doesn't help. I only go over to pick up Mia. I sit at the curb. She comes out and we drive away. And an electrician moved in with Nina. I guess he's good to the kids, from what they say, and they get along with him okay."

Ashlynn finished and studied her brother. "Hope what I said doesn't upset you?"

"No," Pete assured her. The news brought a small measure of relief. Life had moved on for the family.

Ashlynn straightened in her chair.

"Oh, and before I forget, Nina's filled out an affidavit declaring you missing. When the judge signs off, you'll no longer be married. She thinks it'll be done in a couple of months. Then she has to put some kind of notice in the newspaper."

"Good, the not spending a lot of dough to unload me. The world keeps turning. You're doing all right. Mom's mom, and Nina and the kids have a new chapter in front of them."

"What about you, Stellan? Are you happy?"

Pete repeated her question. "Am I happy? You know me. Have I ever been happy, I mean, in any popular sense? No, not really, especially after Dad died." He exhaled. "As I see it, happiness is subjective. I have had periods, and still do, where I know contentment. It's a different word, but a lot of people don't have that, either."

He stopped and broke off a piece of cookie. "Anyway, I'm not grim or gloomy, but I can't say I'm perpetually full of joy and pleasure, either. I guess I'm in a satisfactory state. But you, Ash, you look happy."

"I would say yes, I am happy."

They retreated into silence. Pete used the opportunity to look at his watch.

"Listen, I have to go. I do have to meet someone."

"Can I drive you there?"

"Thanks," Pete said and stared at his cup, "but it's not necessary. It's only a short walk." He raised his eyes and took in his sister. "It was wonderful seeing you, and a delightful surprise."

She blinked twice, placed a palm over her heart, and said, "Same for me, Stellan. The very same for me. I was going to stop at my pharmacy to get my prescription refilled. Good chance I would have missed you if I'd done it. Have you come before this?"

He slowly shook his head. "No. This is the first time since I left."

Ashlynn bobbed her head in understanding.

"Will I see you again?"

Pete crossed his arms. "I have to leave things the way they are for now. Who knows? It could change, but I need to stay under the radar."

Disappointment etched itself on his sister's face. Her chin dipped; her eyes misted. She pulled a tissue out of her purse and dabbed at them.

"I understand, I guess. We've missed so much, you and me. And now you'll be gone again. Is there no way I can at least stay in touch with you on some kind of a needs basis?"

Pete rolled the request over in his mind. He, too, had enjoyed this visit with Ashlynn, however short. Should he take a chance and allow her to contact him? He arrived at a decision.

"I've got an idea. I'll give you a snail mail address. I don't go or live anywhere near the address, but it's a safe way to reach me." He stopped and drew in a breath. "And there's another, faster way via computer. It'll allow us to stay in touch faster. Give me an email address, and I'll send you something. Have you got a business card?"

"Yeah. Hang on." Ashlynn opened her purse, pulled out a business card and pen. She wrote on the back and handed it to her brother.

Pete examined it. "Perfect. When I get home, I'll contact you."

"Are you sure I can't talk you into staying a little longer?" Ashlynn said.

Pete shook his head. He stood up, extracted bills from his wallet, and set them under his saucer.

Ashlynn rose to her feet. She stepped closer.

"So glad to see you, Stellan. Be careful, and I hope you're not in trouble with the law or anything. You're sure you're not?" She searched his face for an answer.

In return he gave her his best beatific smile. "You needn't worry on that account. Honest. No cop anywhere is looking for me. But given everything I've gone through in the last while, I have to keep things as they are. Please don't tell anyone you met me, especially Mom, Nina, or the kids. The less they know, the better."

"Your secret's safe with me."

"I'm glad. I *will* be in touch."

Ashlynn pulled him to her. He found it easier this time to wrap his arms around her. The embrace even brought him to the edge of becoming misty-eyed. Both pulled away, each avoiding eye contact, each sniffling.

Pete took a deep breath and hoped his voice wouldn't let him down. "Bye, sis. Take care, and you'll hear from me soon."

"Bye, Stellan," Ashlynn said.

Stellan? The name still sounded so foreign to Pete. He spun and made for the front door and back to his hotel. Cautious to a fault, he checked over his shoulder for any signs of a blue Accord.

In his room Pete packed and double-checked for anything he might have left behind. He headed to the front desk.

"We hope you had a pleasant stay with us, Mr. Harris," a middle-aged woman said, and gave him her best accommodating smile.

"Yes, fine," he replied while she readied his bill. "Very nice."

Heavy traffic kept Pete from making a faster exit from the city. Once past the suburbs, he allowed himself to relax.

He turned off the radio and brought himself back to his meeting with Ashlynn. What a shock, both meeting up and then visiting with her. If he hadn't run into her, he wouldn't have known about the changes in her life. They'd had a great conversation in their short time together.

His mind wandered over the topics and stopped at Ashlynn's comments about Mia. That came as a small shock. The things his sister had seen in Mia that he'd missed astounded him. Had it been there all along?

Pete scanned his memory for telltale signs of Mia being her own person. She liked many of the same things Joanna did, but she also liked to read and did well in school, dissimilar to her sister.

Pete worked to pull himself out of his thoughtful sadness. "There you go," he said aloud. "See, this is what happens when you get introspective. You end up being morose."

Chapter 31

Bexley leaned against the backboard of the bed and peered into Pete's face.

"You're sure you're okay about coming to Albany with me for a few days over Spring Break?"

Pete answered her question with his own. "Of course. Why would you doubt it?" Judging by the number of times she'd brought up the subject, she'd made it clear she had little confidence in his response. Okay, so maybe he only had himself to blame for that.

"I don't know," she said. "I wanted you to come at Christmas, and you didn't, but..."

Pete cut her off before she finished. "Let's not go down that road again, all right? We've done it more than enough times." He jammed a hand into his pocket. Women. They're always at you about something. Why couldn't she leave it alone? He believed things had gone rather well since his return from Chicago.

Back from Chicago, Pete had braced himself for some kind of grilling. Bexley surprised him by doing the opposite. Other than asking if he'd had a good visit, she stayed clear of the subject.

They settled into their familiar routines around school again. In their free time they attended a few concerts, took in some movies, and socialized with her friends. They also invited Dusan and his girlfriend, Lucille, over to Pete's house for dinner.

Bexley now spent more nights at Pete's than at her own. In late January she floated the idea of bringing him to meet her family. Pete guessed this day would come. It had to be the natural order of things. He shared the news while they sat at a table in Dusan's café. The room filled with the clatter of voices, cutlery on plates, and the rush of servers hurrying back and forth.

"Chill," Dusan said. "It's not such a big deal. You go, put on your best face, do the old glad-handing thing, and you're done. You never know, you might even like it."

"I somehow doubt it. And she has a brother who's a police

detective. Makes me a little nervous."

"What, a cop? Ah, who cares? You haven't broken any laws. Besides, it's not like the guy has X-ray vision and can read your mind."

Pete pressed his lips together. Aware of his hunched shoulders, he straightened and said, "I know what you're saying, but I still wish we could skip this whole thing...without her getting upset."

Dusan scowled. "Get serious, will you? Everybody does the meet-the-folks thing. It's the natural order of things. Or did you forget? Anka and I did it. You probably did it with 'the wife'." He swiveled his head to check on his customers and his wait staff. "Bexley's nice. You should feel lucky to have her, so suck it up, buttercup, and stop bitchin' about it."

Pete made a disapproving face. "Comforting words, Dr. Phil. I could have done better with Dr. Pepper."

Dusan laughed softly. "Pretty good. So, what'd you expect me to say?"

"A little support would have been nice."

Dusan raised the palms of his hands. "I gave it to you. Go, and don't make mountains out of molehills. You'll survive this and come back with some interesting stories."

"It's the 'interesting' part that worries me."

Bexley and Pete left mid-afternoon, encouraged by the weather reports. No storms were on the horizon. "The roads are safe and dry," Bexley said. "We'll make good time and be at my parents' house in a couple of hours. Unless, that is, we stop somewhere along the way." She looked at Pete, his eyes on the road. "This will be fun."

"I'm sure you're right," he said.

"You're *not*?"

A land mine up ahead, Pete told himself. *Careful where you place your foot.* "No, no," he lied. "Just agreeing, is all." *Had she read something in his voice, his tone?* "It'll be good. I'll be fine, you'll see."

The comment won him a gentle squeeze on the arm.

"You'll like everyone, and they'll love you. Cabo would have been more fun, but I wanted you to meet my family. If things go well, we could maybe come again over Easter?"

A fast head bob and a smile satisfied Bexley. Mentally, Pete thought, *Easter? Already? We haven't even got to Albany, and she's planning our next excursion.*

Darkness arrived quickly and denied them further sightseeing pleasures. Hungry, they stopped at a pizza chain.

"Um, your brother, the detective," Pete said while he wiped sauce from the edge of his mouth, "does he specialize in anything?"

"Quinn? He works for the New York State Attorney's Organized Crime Task Force."

The comment did nothing to relieve Pete of his anxiety at meeting her brother. "Sounds intriguing. What does that involve?"

Bexley raised a hand and let it drop onto the table. "Not sure I understand most of it, other than they monitor and investigate organized crime. Things like financial crimes and so on. Why?"

"No reason. Making conversation. You'd have made a good investigator, you know? You ask pertinent questions when you're trying to figure something out. Did your brother teach you?"

"Mmm. Never thought about it. Mom and Dad wanted us all to be critical thinkers. I guess they succeeded."

"I'd say so," Pete said, and thought he'd really have to watch he didn't step on any land mines.

The three-story, red brick Stryker home on Palisades sat among many similar houses on a tree-laden street. Linzie sprang to Pete's mind. This was the kind of street she'd have called leafy if she sold it in the summer. Now stark trunks and bare branches held something of a sad, eerie feeling.

"Turn here," Bexley said, and then pointed to number eighty-seven.

Pete pulled into the double car driveway. He gazed up at the imposing building with its rounded arches over triple glass, vinyl clad windows and door with portico. He stopped the truck. "Impressive. This house looks like it could withstand a siege."

"You may not be far from the truth. It belonged to my maternal grandfather and reflects the times. It even had a servants' entrance, which we bricked up to keep the heat in."

Most of the neighborhood houses dated back to the nineteenth century, she told him. Her mother inherited it, and her father updated it. It required a lot of insulation and a new energy efficient furnace, but in the winter they still closed down parts of the house to save on heating bills.

"So, high maintenance?" Pete asked.

"For sure, but people who live here must think it worth it. The taxes are horrible, of course. Everyone complains about them, but nobody leaves until they can't take care of their house anymore." She pointed. "This one, she's an old lady, our house, needing lots of care, but we love almost everything about her."

Bexley waved her arm down the street. "Most of the houses are in the National Register. Some have been split into separate units. Not all, and for sure not this one." She jutted her chin at the truck. "Let's get our things and go in."

Their luggage in hand, Bexley unlocked and opened the front door and shouted, "We're here!"

A moment later, Pete heard the sound of shuffling feet approaching from the back of the house. A late middle-aged couple appeared, the woman preceding the man.

"Ah, you're here safe and sound," the woman said and pulled Bexley to her. The tall, lanky man rubbed Bexley's shoulder, moved past, smiled at Pete, and stuck out his hand. "Henry Stryker, Bexley's father. Welcome. You are, of course, Pete."

Pete took his hand and smiled back. "We're all going to be in trouble if I'm someone else," he joked.

The joke fell dead, met by a stoic look.

Stryker pulled his hand away. "Nice of you to drive her here. Bexley's told us much about you."

Pete guessed Bexley's father had to be at least six feet tall. He thought the man, with his high forehead and prominent brow ridge, looked like someone who should be typecast in a British spy movie. Bexley didn't get her looks from her father.

Mrs. Stryker, Abagail, detached herself from her daughter and introduced herself. Pete caught the mother-daughter similarities: the cheekbones, blue eyes, and the small jaw. Bexley's mother wore her hair short. He supposed her sandy-brown hair coloring came from a beauty parlor. She'd kept her figure. He imagined her as a younger woman and concluded Henry Stryker likely had serious competition for her hand in their day.

"Let's get you settled," Mrs. Stryker said. "We have your rooms ready, and Bexley can show you the way."

Without a word, Bexley picked up her small soft-sided luggage. "See you down here in a few minutes."

Pete followed her to the wide, oak stairway. His eye caught the skylight. Probably modern. It made sense, adding natural light to a darker interior. His gaze moved to the luxurious, patterned, bronze-red stair runner under his feet. He wouldn't want to be the one keeping it clean.

He caught up to Bexley and whispered, "Something tells me I'm not the only boyfriend whose jaw dropped when you brought him home. You didn't tell me you were filthy rich."

In response Bexley gave him a playful jab with an elbow. "It's all relative. If you were homeless, it might be fair to say we were rich. You aren't and we're not."

She led him down a long hallway with paneled walls to his en suite bedroom. He gave a low whistle after he'd inspected everything.

"I've stayed in five-star hotels. This house makes some of them look like roach motels." His eyes flitted around the room and took in the large platform bed and tasteful bottle-green comforter, two nightstands, and a matching maple dresser.

He set his duffel bag down and grinned at Bexley. "Bed's more than big enough for the two of us," he hinted.

Bexley shook her head. "No can do. This is *your* room. Meet you downstairs. Turn left at the bottom of the stairs, and you're in the living room."

Pete unpacked and stepped out into the hallway. He gawked at everything on his way downstairs. He felt certain this house, and probably this whole street, was on some Charity Home Tour every summer. Everything gave off a grand sense of boldness and importance, from the wide stairway and hallways to the detailed hand-carved, wooden crown molding of the banister and the antique wall sconces. Even the two stained glass windows at the foot of the stairs were impressive.

He found his way to the living room, nothing like most living rooms he'd visited. In keeping with the rest of the house, it showed itself to be grand in scope with an impressive fireplace, two large leather couches in some kind of muted earth tone—smoky gray, he guessed—and three red Queen Anne chairs.

Bexley and her parents took up positions opposite one another. Pete stepped into the room, his smile firmly affixed, and onto a thick Oriental rug. He sat on the couch alongside Bexley.

Mrs. Stryker opened the conversation. "Bexley tells us you've eaten."

Pete bobbed his head up and down. "We have, yes, thank you."

Mr. Stryker seized on the opportunity to suggest drinks. He clapped his hands and said, "We have all manner of things, which I suppose should shame us but doesn't." He grinned at Pete. "So, what will you have?"

Pete brightened at the idea. Booze, the great leveler. It would help him loosen up. "What will I have? Any good at making a Classic Manhattan, Mr. Stryker?"

"I am, and please feel free to call me Henry."

The drinks loosened everyone up, and soon enough the four chatted easily. Past eleven, Pete's eyes grew heavy.

Mrs. Stryker pointed to him. "I think it's getting late. I'm not sure Pete or any of us will make it to the witching hour."

"Or why we would want to," her husband added.

"Precisely."

Pete woke mid-morning, his mouth dry. He looked at his watch and flew out of bed. In the bathroom he gave himself a quick wash, brushed his teeth, and ran his electric shaver over his face. Done, he hurried into a change of clothes.

"Good morning, sleepy-head," Bexley said when he found them in the dining room. "We couldn't wait any longer. There's toast, buns, and cereal laid out on the kitchen table. Hot coffee, too. Join us when you're ready."

To Pete's delight, time at the Strykers raced by. During the day, Henry Stryker went off to work. His wife also left, busy with her volunteer work. Bexley took Pete to the Irish American Museum, the Shaker Settlement, and downtown to shop and meet with a few old high school friends. One evening they attended a rock concert at the Palace Theater, and on another, Henry made reservations for all of them at an exclusive French restaurant.

It didn't take long before Pete grew wary of Henry Stryker asking penetrating questions about his past. Twice Pete caught him posing the same question in different ways. It unsettled him. *Sonofabitch. First Bexley, and now him. Am I somehow giving off untrustworthy vibes? Isn't my story tight enough?*

He couldn't make up his mind which it might be. In order to insulate himself from more prying inquiries, Pete grew less spontaneous and more wooden.

"Are you all right?" Bexley whispered while her parents were in the kitchen after dinner. She sat next to him on the couch.

"Yeah," he said. "Why do you ask?"

"Something's different. Like you've pulled into yourself." She patted his arm lightly. "You'd tell me if something was bothering you, right?"

"'Course."

Their last night, Pete Bexley's brother, Quinn, and his pretty, chatterbox wife, Helen, arrived at the Stryker home. Dinner would soon be underway. Everyone sat in the living room, talking and drinking.

Pete considered the couple. Helen giggled a lot and liked to tuck up against her husband. Her hand caressed, touched, and patted his upper body. He, in turn, paid her little mind. In conversation his eyes moved from his parents to his sister and at times to Pete.

Pete studied Quinn's white complexion and couldn't help but notice something on his nose. Rosacea? His piercing eyes matched Bexley's; his brow ridge, Henry's; and the shape of his face, Abagail's. As for the receding chin and dark hair, Pete couldn't say.

From the moment Quinn gave him a vice-like handshake, Pete took an immediate dislike to the man, his dead, low-and-rough voice and condescending attitude. Why had no one else in the family reacted to it? Perhaps they'd become used to it. Had Quinn worked to cultivate his voice? Maybe his voice and predatory stare made criminal offenders quake.

His antipathy to Quinn did nothing to ease Pete out of his coolness. He answered general questions and supplied the odd comment but little more. He caught a look from Bexley but refused to meet her gaze.

"So, Pete," Quinn said, "Bexley's been telling us about your childhood. Must have been pretty rough."

Pete's eyes moved from Quinn to Bexley. Did he imagine it, or had she turned red? She gave him the slightest head shake, jutted out her chin and spoke to her brother.

"Waaaaaaait a second. I haven't told you much about his childhood. You asked me what I'd heard, and I said it wasn't the usual upbringing."

Brother and sister held a brief staring contest until Quinn looked away. He turned back to Pete and held up his hands in surrender. "She's right. Hope I didn't upset you."

Pete answered with a dismissive wave of his hand. Some sixth sense told him Quinn did intend to upset him. He wanted to be out of this house. *You're almost done here*, he told himself. *One more night, and you'll be on your way.*

An awkward silence hung over the group, broken by Bexley's mother.

"Dinner should be in another ten minutes or so." She rose. "I'll go see if everything's ready to go."

"I'll join you, Mom," Bexley said.

"Me, too," Helen added.

The women disappeared. The men, perhaps sensing the absence of the female gadflies, made minimal eye contact. Pete stood up.

"Going out to the truck," he mumbled. "Back in a few minutes."

Neither of the Strykers commented.

He made his exit. In spite of the cold, he sat in the truck, grateful for the chance to be away from the Strykers. Five minutes later, since he'd left the front door unlocked, he easily reentered the house. Voices loud enough for him to hear came from the kitchen. He heard his name. Intrigued, he listened and closed the door with little sound. He tiptoed close to the kitchen doorway and hoped no one would come out.

"Something hinky about the guy," Quinn said. "And a pickup. Who the fuck drives a pickup?"

"Watch your language," his mother warned.

"Something's not right." After a pause, Quinn spoke again. "You had to know, sis."

Bexley spoke.

"First, Quinn, don't be such a snot. Driving a Lexus doesn't make you a better human being. And the rest, I'll admit the pieces don't fit easily together. I know there are things he's holding back. I'd hoped sooner or later he'd confide in me, and the truth, whatever it is, would come out."

"I'm not sure he's somebody you should be with, darling," her mother said.

Pete felt color rush to his face. He'd heard enough. On tiptoe he made his way to the front door and drew in several long breaths to expel his anger. After a final inhale, he opened and shut the door with drama.

Mrs. Stryker and Bexley came into the dining room with silver trivets for the dishes. A moment later the others joined them.

A fixed smile on his face, Pete said, "Do you need any help?"

Bexley looked up and matched his smile. "I think we've got everything covered."

Her mother fussed over the table, spun about, and reentered the kitchen.

Pete made it through dinner and the inane small talk. *Absolute longest night of my life*, he thought. The rest of the table's occupants worked to draw him into the conversation. After dinner they all adjourned to the living room for drinks and cards. Pete accepted a cocktail but declined the invitation of cards.

Time crept by. When enough time had passed, Pete made a show of looking at his watch, yawning, and announcing he intended to retire. "If you'll excuse me, I think I'll head off to bed." He looked at Quinn and Helen.

"Nice meeting you," he said, and walked toward his room. He felt their eyes bore into his back.

"It's over," he whispered to himself on his way up the stairs. "First thing in the morning, I'm out of here."

With lights out, he'd almost fallen asleep when he heard a soft tap-tap on the door. He ignored it. A moment later her whispered voice called out to him.

"Pete? Are you asleep?"

He didn't answer and kept his eyes closed. She shut the door.

Pete endured breakfast, glad Quinn and his wife hadn't come downstairs. Aware of a stiffness and little eye contact between himself and Bexley, Pete focused on his toast and coffee.

The Strykers made more small talk until Pete turned to Bexley.

"We better get going. It's a long drive. Are you ready?"

"I guess."

Their belongings in the truck, Bexley hugged her parents and said goodbye.

Pete held out his hand to her father. "Thank you for everything. It was a lovely time."

"We hope to see you again, Pete," Henry Stryker said.

Like a bad case of the clap, I bet, Pete thought. He kept the opinion to himself. "Would be nice, yes."

He backed his truck out of the driveway. A sense of relief flooded over him. Free, free of the lot of them. Now he had to deal with Bexley. Would she say anything? If she did, how would it go?

On the highway Bexley opened the discussion. "Do you want to talk about it?"

He shook his head.

"What's upset you?"

Pete let out a rush of air. "You, them, us."

She looked at him. "What does that mean?"

"It means what it means, Bexley. You're not sure about me, and I'm starting to think I'm not a good fit with you."

He sensed her eyes on him while he watched the road. A wetness in her voice, she said, "You heard, didn't you?"

A fast nod confirmed her suspicion. She sniffed and reached into her coat for a tissue.

"So, who gets to dump who first?"

"Does it matter?"

"I suppose not," she said. "You've held a lot back from me. I suppose I could have come to terms with it, whatever it is or was."

She blew her nose and gave out a rueful sigh. "All the little secrets. How many escorts have you been seeing?"

The question caught him off guard, so much so he almost veered into the other lane.

He swerved back into his lane.

"What are you talking about?"

Bexley answered with a slow shake of her head. "Come on, Pete. I'm not stupid."

"How... How do you know?"

In a near whisper, she said, "So, you admit it. Why do you think I insisted you wear protection?"

His voice rose and he said, "I asked you a question."

Her voice thick with conviction, she said, "And I'm not answering it, all right?"

He stared at the road ahead.

"There is so much dysfunctional stuff going on here," she said. "And me, aren't I the biggest chump in the world? I gave you plenty of chances to tell me the truth, but you made up your mind to do the opposite."

They drove most of the way in silence. Close to town, Bexley's voice took on a sense of resignation. "I'll get my things from your place and then take a cab home."

Pete could no longer muster his previous outrage and found it replaced by a sense of melancholy. Every fiber in his body knew he'd lost her. He made a last feeble attempt to bring himself back to grace.

"Listen, Bexley..."

She held up her hand. "No. I don't want to listen or talk about us anymore. We were always fragile. Something like this had to happen eventually. Better now than later. Please. If you respect me, let it be. I won't bad-mouth you to anyone, in case you're worried. When I see you at school, I'll wave and say 'Hi.' Nothing more. We're done."

She collected her few belongings from his house and pulled out her cell phone. "At least let me drive you back to your place," Pete said. "I promise I won't talk you into anything. I'll be quiet."

Bexley peered at him and at last reached a decision. "Fine. I'm ready to go."

He kept his word. She stepped out of his truck, shut the door in her gentle Bexley way, and never looked behind her.

The panic attacks started within an hour after Pete returned home. He worked hard to puzzle out how she'd found out about the escort service. He'd been so careful. There were no records; well, other than debit transactions on his cell phone. But she'd have no way of accessing his phone and didn't know his password.

The more he thought about it, the more he grew convinced the answer rested with his phone. It didn't matter now, did it? He'd prided himself on being so clever, and guess what?

He paced, sat, and composed text messages to Bexley and discarded them all. In his heart he knew he'd lost her. No matter what he did, said, or plotted, nothing would bring her back.

By nine the next morning, unwashed and unshaven, Pete drove to the Olde World Café.

"He isn't here yet," a hostess who recognized Pete said. "Knowing Dusan, he should be here within the next ten minutes. Would you like to wait? I can bring you coffee."

Pete didn't know if his acid-churning stomach could handle coffee, but he didn't want food, either.

"Yeah. Coffee will be fine. Thanks."

As predicted, Dusan arrived a few minutes later. The hostess pointed to Pete. Dusan poured himself coffee and slid into the booth.

"You look like shit."

"Thanks. Hello to you, too."

"Sorry, man. Something happened in Albany, I bet. Tell me."

Pete did. He recounted in detail everything up to driving Bexley home. When he finished, his friend pointed to the coffee. "It's not what you need right now. Let me get you something for your stomach. How about warm milk?"

"I guess."

Even when the morning crowd arrived, Dusan remained with Pete. He let Pete retell all aspects of the story. At last Pete said, "Listen, you've got a business to run. I don't want to drag you and it down. Thanks for listening."

"Happy to do it, man. I'll call you tonight. Take care."

"Thanks."

Pete left.

Pete ached. The ache was made worse when he realized how much he'd cared for Bexley and realized how little he'd valued her.

He continued to compose texts and continued to delete them. "I may have trouble with other aspects of my personality," he said aloud, "but I don't have trouble with reality-testing. She's gone and will stay gone."

Pete dropped out of classes, lost weight, and roamed his house in pajamas.

Dusan and Lucille came over almost daily and hired a housekeeper for him. Lucille even shopped for him and filled his fridge and pantry with "good, healthy food."

"You're great, Lucille," he said on her last trip. "I'd hug you if you'd let me, but I also stink."

She moved forward, embraced him, slapped him on the back several times, and pulled away. "You're right, Pete. You don't smell too good. You, for sure, could have been better with your girlfriend. I don't mean to be unkind, but I get why she was so upset with you."

He gave her a weak nod. "Me, too, and I still miss her."

"And Pete, get back in the saddle again, back to the land of the living, and no more moping about."

"You're right. I know you are absolutely right."

A month had passed since then. Pete climbed out of his pajamas, showered, paid closer attention to his grooming, and made himself a good breakfast. He still ached for Bexley but resolved to live with the loss. He couldn't, wouldn't, go to school for the remainder of the academic year. Seeing her would be too painful. It would also save her from any possible awkward meetings with him. She'd graduate next month anyway. He could always return in the fall. She'd likely start law school by then.

Spring arrived in full force. Pete used the time wisely. He planted a garden in the back, rode his bike around town, and scanned the websites for a puppy. A dog would cheer him up and keep him company. He would train it. He considered his own personality and honed in on the breed—an Australian Shepherd.

Before he made his purchase he invited Dusan and Lucille over for dinner. "I owe both of you a lot and more." After an elaborate dinner and dessert he told them about his desire for a dog. "I'm going to buy an Australian Shepherd pup." He focused on Dusan. "I've been thinking about names. As a favor to me and in honor of your wife, can I call the pup Anka?"

Dusan beamed at the honor and gave his blessings.

Pete loved the black-and-white puppy, and it reciprocated. The kids on the street loved her, too. Owner and dog went everywhere and soon became a common sight. When Pete visited a store, Anka waited outside without being tied up, eyes on the front door, watching for Pete.

Dusan and Lucille married. The best man, Gates Tally, paunchy, with no more than two dozen hairs left on his head, gave an impressive toast. Self-effacing with a quick smile and even quicker wit, he had everyone in the hall roaring with laughter at stories of his former cellmate.

Pete enjoyed several hours of good conversation with Gates and his easygoing girlfriend, who had an infectious smile.

A few of Lucille's bridesmaids showed interest in Pete and asked about him. He didn't reciprocate their attention.

"Gotta get back in the game sooner or later," Dusan said when he, Lucille, and Pete relaxed over a beer.

"I agree," Lucille said. "This might be a good place to start."

Pete glanced over the hall.

"Nice of both of you to help out, but truth is I'm damaged goods. I don't do well in relationships and will probably carry a torch for Bexley for the rest of my days."

Dusan shook his head at Pete's decision. "Man, you can be stubborn."

Pete would not be swayed. He threw his hands up in surrender. "True, but this works better for me. Nobody gets hurt."

Pete ran into Linzie several times, the meetings cordial and fast. He never saw Bexley again and heard she'd left town.

Postscript

Twelve years passed. A letter arrived at his private post box one August day.

Dear Pete,

It's been too long. Way too long. I'd love to be able to have you more active in my life. We're both older and could both benefit from being more close-knit.

Everyone at this end is fine.

I'm still with Kevin. Nina's remarried. Joanna's a cosmetician and Mia's at college, thinking about a career in English. And Mom, she's still Mom, but Vincze died. She's got her line in the water and is trolling to see who else she can reel in. Nothing ever changes with her.

What I'm really writing about is Mia. This may come as a surprise, but she wants to see her father. I told her about you and knew she could handle the truth. I'd never tell airheaded (I guess I shouldn't say that) Joanna. I'll cross my fingers and hope you didn't mind. It might help Mia understand you better. Would you be willing to meet her?

Love,

Your sister

Pete read the letter three times and then a fourth, unable to come to a decision. He looked down at Anka. "What do you think, girl? Do you want to meet your aunt and cousin?"

The dog responded with a fast thump of her tail.

Ten days later a green Subaru pulled into Pete's driveway. Anka barked, and did fast turns in front of the door.

Pete opened it. Anka shot out and charged toward a lean, sparse-haired man who climbed out from behind the steering wheel in khaki shorts, a checkered shirt, and leather sandals. Anka sniffed him. He held out a tentative hand and petted her.

That has to be Kevin, Pete thought, stuck out his hand, and introduced himself. "Kevin, right?"

The other man nodded and took the hand. "It is, yeah, and you're Pete. Pleased to meet you."

Ashlynn hurried over and pulled her brother to her. A long embrace followed before they separated. She smoothed out the front of her denim skirt and said, "So good to see you, Stel... I mean, Pete."

"You too, Ash. You're right. It's been way too long."

Aware of the third passenger, he let his eyes move to his daughter, now fully grown. Taller than her mother yet with the same skin tone. Pete would have recognized her anywhere with her long, dark lashes and full lips. She'd let her hair grow longer and bleached it ash blonde. Her sleeveless yellow sundress and bare legs would have won her attention on any street.

Father and daughter did little more than offer each other curious looks.

Mia spoke first.

"Hi, Daddy."

"Mia," Pete said, and put out a hand. "Is it...?" He found it difficult to carry on with the sentence. For the briefest moment he thought he might tear up. He brought himself under control and cleared his throat. "Is it okay if I give you a hug?"

She answered with an action, not words, and stepped into his arms. Pete threw his arms around his daughter, certain he'd never let go, enjoying her warmth. A flood of memories he didn't think he owned washed over him.

The first tear rolled down the side of his temple. *His* daughter, *his* flesh and blood here, far from his old home. Could he ever have imagined such a thing?

They pulled apart while the other two looked on with pleasure.

Ashlynn's voice broke the spell. "Okay, we came with lots of goodies, so let's unload." She glanced up at the house. "Nice, Pete. You sure you got room for everybody here?"

"Nothing you need to worry about, Ash. I'm always going to make sure I have room."

With the last of the car unloaded, Kevin locked the doors.

Pete swung his arm around his daughter, Mia, and with Anka

running alongside of her, they walked into the house.

Made in the USA
Monee, IL
23 September 2020